CW01082100

About the author

Mark O'Dell was born in Great Yarmouth on the east coast of England. Following military service and education at various universities, he now works as a scientist in a leading science and engineering company. This is his first novel and his choice of the fantasy genre stems from his love of high fantasy and his time as an artist illustrating a fantasy magazine for a well-known role-playing game.

THE SHADE OF HIGHFALL
THE TALE OF SHREW

Mark O'Dell

THE SHADE OF HIGHFALL
THE TALE OF SHREW

Vanguard Press

VANGUARD PAPERBACK

© Copyright 2021
Mark O'Dell

A CIP catalogue record for this title is
available from the British Library.

ISBN 978 1 784659 53 0

Vanguard Press is an imprint of
Pegasus Elliot MacKenzie Publishers Ltd.
www.pegasuspublishers.com

First Published in 2021

Vanguard Press
Sheraton House Castle Park
Cambridge England

Printed & Bound in Great Britain

Dedication

I would like to dedicate this book to Pete, who was also known as Hengist in another time and in another place.

Acknowledgements

I would like to acknowledge Roger Gordon-Cumming and Mark Baggott for their proof-reading of the early drafts.

PROLOGUE

Like a drunken man, Armeris moved erratically, yet with surprising swiftness, through the turbid stream that flowed through the old brick tunnel. He needed neither oil lamp nor wisp-light to show him the way through the stygian darkness; he was one of the fey, and his narrow almond eyes could clearly see the incline and the course of the round winding stone-work.

"Nei'ca!" he screamed, as he almost stumbled, and then with greater urgency he strode forward, sweeping aside the shaggy tendrils of lichen that hung in his path with the short blade in his hand.

The tunnel widened and either side dark holes like gaping mouths appeared in the walls, deep channels that plunged to unseen depths, stealing some of the water of the stream.

"Nei'ca, Tirriel!" Armeris screamed again, but louder, shaking his head violently. His voice echoed and carried in the darkness, travelling far into the vast labyrinth of the Everdark. Then, with great effort, he broke free from his apparent madness and turned his attention to the dagger in his hand.

"Talha'ri cea Tirriel" he growled. His mouth foamed and his eyes shone with pale light, glowing like moonlight seeping through a veil of cirrus.

"Talha'ri cea, Tirriel!" he repeated louder, and hurled the dagger into one of the dark openings within the wall. For a brief moment, blue light glinted off the falling blade and there was a faint sound like a woman's scream. Then it was lost in the consuming darkness.

The Lands of Sillaesia

The Orphan and the Dagger

Sunglow

Year 5121

The City of Highfall

CHAPTER ONE
LIFE IN THE LOW REACH

The black kite soared; its wing-tip feathers flared as it rode the rising air and then it plummeted through a break in the clouds. Far beneath the falling bird was a corrugated ridge of mountains, whose last peak appeared to have collapsed and spread itself in a sprawl down to the valley below — but this was no random rock fall brought about by nature's forces. At the highest point, slender ivory towers rose to pierce the sky, and from this lofty apex to the silver line of the river in the valley below lay a great city of grey stone and timber roofs, veiled in the smoke from a thousand hearth fires. This was the great walled city of Highfall, capital of the Sillaesian continent and home to over two hundred thousand souls.

Highfall was a three-tiered metropolis. From the ancient High Reach and its cloud-wreathed towers and minarets, this fortified city descended down through the tree-lined avenues of the Middle Reach to expand into the vast conurbation known as the Low Reach, which formed the lowest part of the city and housed most of the city's burgeoning population. Here, there were welcome hostelries, bustling markets, neat narrow streets, countless shops and a multitude of churches and temples covering entire pantheons of gods and saints. Here, too, however, were areas where folk lived one day to the next trying to survive and where the less desirable members of Highfall's population plied their wicked trades. Most notorious of these areas lay close to Highfall's far southern wall, which was a bowshot away from the foul-smelling Mucmarsh, an expanse of stagnant pools and marshes into which most of the city's sewage and unwanted flotsam spilled. This area was known to the locals as 'The Duns'.

The rains had stopped and now shafts of golden sunlight pierced the clouds, causing Highfall to become a patchwork of light and shadow.

Somewhere in the Duns a pale beam of sunlight penetrated the gloom of a narrow alleyway and lit the greasy street cobbles and bare foot of a child hunched in the shadows. In an instant, the foot had vanished. The youngster had withdrawn into the shadowy recess of a doorway and now stared fixatedly at the traders setting up their stalls in the street beyond the alley. Slowly, like a cat that had just spotted its prey, the child moved forward, with sharp blue eyes focussed intently on the small pile of tawny apples that the fruit trader had just placed on his table. Crowds were now gathering, eager to barter for the meagre goods that were now being touted by the stallholders. In a swift motion, the child had joined the street, tagging along behind a portly dowager whose attire suggested she was from one of the Low Reach's many pleasure houses. Then, in a manner that bespoke of experience from countless similar escapades, the small figure turned and vaulted on to the grocer's table.

"Shrew!" several voices cried out in alarm and warning. The grocer reached out to protect his wares, but he was too late to save two apples that were scooped up in the small thief's hands.

"Stop her!" The grocer lunged, but the agile young thief had already leapt to an adjoining table and then the next, picking up a small loaf on her way. Shrew was her name and this title seemed aptly bestowed, for as a group of traders and their sympathetic customers converged on her path, she seemed to vanish! Pandemonium ensued; a table overturned, spilling its load of potatoes and turnips on to the wet cobbles of the street, causing several would-be thief-catchers to lose their footing. One fell, dragging down the flimsy awning and drape of a bird-seller's cart, several wicker cages broke open and a flock of frightened chickens, ducks and guinea fowl added to the confusion.

Back where she had started the mischief, Shrew emerged from under the grocer's table and bolted for the alley. Behind her she could hear cries for the City Watch and the curses of those who had just lost their wares and dignity. She heard no sound of pursuit. A wicked smile lit up her grimy features and her eyes sparkled as she clutched her ill-gotten bounty closer to her chest. Halfway down this alley was a wall; once over this she would be in the backyard of the Three-legged Dog, a dilapidated tavern where the patrons were far too busy partaking of soursop ale and pipe-weed to care about her. She had barely entered the alley when a lanky youth stepped out of the shadows to block her path.

"Ah, Shrew, I see you've brought me my supper!" The youth's grimy features were dominated by his broad mouth, which split in a smile to reveal a row of rotting teeth.

"I've told you before! Leave me alone, Cutter!" Shrew cried as she took a step backward, looking for an avenue of escape. Fleeing back the way she had come was not an option. She felt trapped. The youth was at least a foot taller than her and considerably stronger. He was one of the Stilts gang, a band of local ruffians who had named themselves after their ignoble leader, a thin, jaundiced rogue who had developed some notoriety within the Duns. In desperation, Shrew glanced upward. Like most of the poorer dwellings within the Low Reach, the upper floors of this alley's tenements overlapped the lower floors and were supported by wooden joists, which protruded out beyond the overhang of the storey above. In some cases, the overhang was extreme and the alleys and streets became tunnel-like to the denizens beneath them.

It was a quick decision. As Cutter moved towards her, Shrew thrust one of her apples forward. "Take it!" she ordered. The ruffian hesitated a moment and then grinned as he reached out to grasp the fruit; but Shrew was quicker — dropping the apple, she grasped his outstretched wrist, which gave her all the leverage she needed to bring back her foot and swing it hard between his legs. She winced in pain as her toes drove into his crotch and then stepped aside as he dropped on all fours. Only a small squeak escaped from Cutter's surprised countenance as his legs buckled and his knees hit the ground. Without a pause, Shrew thrust the remaining apple and loaf into her shirt and used the ruffian's back as a springboard to launch herself towards an overhanging joist. "Enjoy the apple!" she called back, as she swung herself up onto the next protruding joist and then ran nimbly along the remainder until she reached the top of an adjoining wall. The wall marked the western boundary of the Three-legged Dog Tavern. Shrew allowed herself a smile as she dropped down into the tavern's cluttered courtyard and landed in a crouched position.

"Oww!" she squealed, and winced in pain as she rubbed her bruised big toe.

The courtyard was quite small and Shrew was relieved to see she was alone. The grey stone wall from which she had just leapt bounded the west and north sides, although little stone could be seen through the bindweed and purple-flowered toadflax that covered most of its surface. The rear of the tavern occupied the south side, and from that direction she could hear faint sounds of conversation and the lilt of a poorly tuned lute. She quickly made her way over the shattered remains of clay flagons and the wooden staves of former beer barrels to the back of an outhouse. Here, she pulled aside the lid of an old ale barrel to reveal a dark hole that led to a forgotten wine cellar. As she dropped into the hole, a cry carried over the wall from the alley. It was Cutter. "Shrew, you little runt, next time I see you, I'll kill you!"

With the lid replaced to conceal her hole, Shrew crouched down in the darkness and listened. Nothing — no sound of pursuit — only her panting as she regained her breath and the steady beat of her heart. The Stilts gang were becoming a problem. Soon her hideout would be discovered. She didn't want to be down here when that happened, like a cornered rat with nowhere to hide!

As her eyes grew accustomed to the darkness, a faint thread of light from the outside helped her find her small wisp lamp. This was her most treasured possession which she had discovered buried under rubbish in the yard above. It had a feeble glow, but the light from its trapped will-o'-the-wisp was sufficient to illuminate her small world within the cellar. As she carefully withdrew its cover, a pale green glow spread out to illuminate the booty on her lap. Her stomach growled and she sighed. A small loaf and an apple, but it was better than nothing. She wasted no time devouring the apple, including the seeds and core. Now she regretted losing the other apple, and for a moment considered going back to the alley to see if it was still there. She shook her head; that would be fruitless, she told herself, and a faint smile crossed her grimy features as she realised her own pun.

Shrew was very smart for her age. She did not know it, but soon she would have spent fifteen years within the city's walls. She was a little below the average height for her age and also quite skinny. This was certainly due to being malnourished, for she was permanently hungry. Times hadn't always been this bad, though. Up until a few months ago she had always managed to find scraps of food inside a cracked bowl outside the rear door of the tavern. One day, however, this regular bounty of bread crusts, meat rind and vegetable cuttings had suddenly stopped. Since then the bowl had remained empty and now lay half-full of stagnant rainwater peppered with dead flies. Shrew had guessed the truth: there had been a change of ownership, for she no longer saw the cheery red-faced man with the baggy shirt in the yard any more. As far as she was aware, the new owner, or owners, never ventured into the yard, and although she missed the food, she was thankful for that. Nevertheless, it had now forced her to totally rely on her thieving skills to provide the sustenance she required; hence her more frequent forays into the markets and shops of the local neighbourhood and her most recent encounter with the traders of Gifford's Street.

Shrew yawned sleepily and reached across her straw pallet to pick up another of her treasured possessions, a small cracked mirror in a pewter frame. Placing the mirror down close to the wisp lamp on an old wooden shelf, she inspected her grimy features and sighed. With a rag and some water from a small cup she had rescued from the courtyard, she started to remove some of the city's dirt from her face. Seemingly satisfied, she then proceeded to play with her hair, plucking and ruffling the short tawny tufts. Her appearance was quite boyish, and this suited her. She smiled to herself. One day she would be the leader of her own band of rogues, and then the Stilts gang better watch out! Her gaze settled on the loaf beside her. For a while it had been nice just to leave it, knowing it was there for later, but the pangs of hunger overcame any thoughts of being frugal. Like the apple, she ate it ravenously until only a small piece of crust remained, and then, picking up the wisp lamp from its home on the shelf, she crawled a few yards to the corner of the small cellar and placed the crust next to the grill of a drain. "For you, Mousling," she whispered, and retreated to her straw bed.

An hour passed. Shrew had covered the wisp lamp and now lay on her side, one eye lazily scanning the faint outline that marked the exit to the outside world. She could sense that twilight was gathering. Her stomach was reminding her that she needed to eat better than she had today. Tomorrow, she thought, a large market would gather in Fountain Square, just inside the South Gate. It was outside the Duns, but promised plenty of opportunities. She smiled; besides, it would give Cedric the grocer and the rest of the traders of Gifford's Street a day of peace. A scratching noise suddenly broke her thoughts. Turning her head, she spied movement over by the drain. "Ah, Mousling," she whispered, "we shall feast well tomorrow, I promise." With that, she fell asleep.

The city of Highfall covered almost the entire southern flank of the last peak in a range of mountains that were known throughout Sillaesia as the Dragon's Spine. To the west lay the mighty Swan River, which was wide and deep enough to allow sea-going galleys to unload their exotic cargoes from every corner of the known world. Further west spread the shadowy eaves of the vast and mysterious Gloamril Forest, whose gnarled trunks and twisted roots often encroached the far bank of the river. In contrast, the lands to the east were open. Beyond the stagnant and foul pools of the Mucmarsh spread meadowlands, and dotted here and there, farmsteads nestled amongst small stands of trees. On this, the last day in the last month of revival, the Sillaesian name for spring, the sun rose into a brilliant, clear blue sky and the roads entering Highfall bustled with market traffic. Many of the wagons and carts passing through the city's gates had started their journey several days before in the outlying districts. Alongside the farmers with their livestock and heavily laden wagons bearing fresh vegetables, fruit and grain, a host of other folk entered the gates under the watchful eyes of the city guard. Many of these trudged through on foot and included woodmen and trappers from the nearby Gloamril Forest, barge folk from the Swan River, alchemists and potion sellers, soothsayers, fortune tellers and even a travelling circus. The day had just begun, but already the air buzzed with excitement. Throughout the Low Reach and Middle Reach brightly coloured awnings were being erected and the shutters of shops and caravans opened as Highfall stirred and prepared for the first great market of the summer.

Shrew awoke suddenly. It seemed like her heart was beating in her ears and her body felt clammy, even though the air in the cellar was cool. It was that familiar dream again, and like many times before, it had transformed into a nightmare that ended badly. Her stomach ached, and to add insult to injury, the dream had followed its normal course and started in a great hall, where a warm and inviting hearth fire burned and crackled in front of a table laden with food. Food she could see, but never eat. She cursed under her breath and shook her head in a vain attempt to rid herself of the fragments of her dream, as if shaking chaff into the wind. Then, as she recalled the great event in Fountain Square, she breathed a prayer to Latia, goddess of luck and mischief. She needed some of Latia's luck at the market today.

A short time later, after covering her wisp lamp, she slowly moved aside the lid that concealed the entrance to her hideout and cautiously looked out upon the yard. Having satisfied herself that it was empty, she nimbly stepped out and crept to the overgrown wall opposite. Her appearance had changed. She had applied an oily black pigment to her hair so that it was now much darker than before, although it was still spiky and unruly. She wore a thread-bare grey tunic with matching skin-tight leggings and instead of roaming barefoot had strapped sandals to her feet. Around her waist she had tied an old leather boot lace that made an adequate belt, and from this hung a small bag wherein she had placed her cracked mirror and a small knife, which made up the last of her treasured possessions. She planned to travel to the market incognito, so had decided to disguise herself as a boy. She wanted to cross the Duns unrecognised.

As Shrew approached the rear of the tavern, it appeared quiet. The discordant sounds of the lute and the slurred voices of its intoxicated accompaniment had long since ceased. She moved swiftly and silently, no more than a passing shadow as she entered the alley that ran between the tavern and the vine-clad wall. This passage connected the yard to the street which ran in front of the establishment. Halfway along, where a side door provided egress to the tavern's common room, something or someone lay sprawled in her path. Shrew crept forward cautiously; she had come across bodies before whose throats had been cut merely for the boots on their feet. This one, however, still wore his footwear, a fine pair of knee-length boots which Shrew regarded with interest. It took but a moment to establish the cause of this fellow's predicament; as Shrew cautiously leant over the body, she noticed a pool of vomit. The stench took her back. He was breathing, but totally comatose. No doubt he had stumbled out of the door during the night to relieve a full bladder, but had been pole-axed by the night air! Shrew grinned at the thought and quickly felt for the pockets in the drunkard's jerkin and the purse that should lie by his belt. She frowned with disappointment and cursed under her breath when nothing was found. Taking a second to glance up and down the alley, she turned her attention to his boots. These proved difficult to remove and more than once Shrew had to pause her tugging and pulling as her efforts caused the man to stir in his slumber. She soon realised the boots were too big for her, but as the second came off his foot two bronze coins fell to the ground. Shrew's eyes opened wide. Two bronze mites! She wasted no time pocketing the small coins and then, breathing thanks to Latia, stepped over the body and ran to where the alley met the street.

Swine Street was the main thoroughfare through the Duns that connected its east and west boundaries. During the daylight hours, the street swelled with the many folk going about their business. Along its rutted cobbled length, taverns and inns proffered their meagre hospitality, pawnbrokers and money-lenders exacted their extortion and the commoners' shops provided the bare necessities. On every corner and entrance to lane or alley, tinkers, beggars and various idlers and conmen made their living. As the sun set, however, few journeyed abroad. For those that did, the pleasure houses, gambling dens and taverns welcomed their coin, but so, too, did the cut-throats, vagabonds and rogues that loitered in the darkened alleyways.

Shrew whistled merrily as she left the alley and joined the milling crowds on Swine Street. Two mites were an unexpected boon that would fund a hearty breakfast! Her whistling wasn't very good, but she did it nevertheless. It helped her get into character — after all, most of the boys did it! She quickly fell in with a large party that included a group of children close to her own age. They were heading westward down the hill towards the South Gate and Fountain Square. This suited her perfectly!

It wasn't often that she had the opportunity to talk to others of her own age and make friends. Those few friends she had known in the past had either moved on to better parts of the city or had mysteriously disappeared. She was sure many had been snatched off the streets and sent to one of the workhouses. She was determined such a fate wouldn't happen to her! Therefore, for a few minutes she enjoyed the group's company while masquerading as a youth from the Labour Quarter, north of the Duns.

As the group turned into the wider avenue of South Street, they joined a larger throng and left the slums of the Duns far behind. Suddenly, the road bent to the right. The tenements to the left had disappeared, providing her with a magnificent view of the southern end of Low Reach, all the way down to the outer wall and the great South Gate. She gazed in awe across rows of descending rooftops to the bottom of the hill, where she could see her destination, a tapestry of brightly coloured canopies and awnings that clustered around a gushing fountain. Shrew waved goodbye to her new friends and then picked up her pace, skipping the remaining few furlongs down the descending road until she entered the market.

The market at Fountain Square was just one of many similar events across the city, although it ranked as one of the largest and more cosmopolitan, with a greater mix of outsiders. Collectively, these individual gatherings, which lasted several days, made up the first great market of the Sillaesian summer.

Shrew's eyes widened in wonder at the numerous coloured canopies, flags and bunting that dazzled and caught the breeze in the bright morning sunlight. The market was a hive of activity. All about her she could hear the calls of the traders and hawkers trying to capture the attention of the crowds. These competed with a cacophony of animal sounds that included the barking and yelping of chasing dogs, the whinnying of impatient cart horses and the loud cries of a cockatoo. Her nose twitched as the inviting smell of a roasted hog wafted in her direction from its bed of smoking apple-wood. Her stomach rumbled and she remembered she hadn't eaten since yesterday. Close by, a wooden table groaned under the weight of salvers and dishes containing an assortment of various pastries and pies. The stall vendor was calling out the merits of his meat pies, and Shrew's mouth watered at the prospect of trying one herself. A group of women, who from their dress appeared to come from one of the more respectable parts of the Low Reach, now crowded around the stall, and Shrew joined them, squeezing in to get close to a small pyramid of the meat-filled parcels. Her reading and writing skills were poor, but she could see that the vendor was asking two mites for each pie. Shrew wrinkled her face in disgust; she had no intention of parting with her new-found wealth for a solitary pie. Looking up, her eyes met those of a surly youth dressed in a brown smock, who had paused unloading more of the vendor's pies from the open back of a wagon to eye her suspiciously. She threw him an angelic smile and withdrew behind the entourage of women who were now bartering for an enormous truffle tart that was clearly the pie stall owner's prize offering.

Unperturbed, Shrew melted into the crowds and moved across to a neighbouring stall, where a green-plumed parrot squawked in a cage and a scrawny mule stood tethered to a post. Below the mule, between two stone cobbles, something moved and caught her eye; and a wicked smile spread across her face. Moments later, she was back at the pie stall, where the owner was defending the price of his truffle tart. The women were intent on getting the best price possible and the commotion had attracted passers-by. With an air of indifference to the whole affair, Shrew made out to scratch her head and flicked her fingers. A dark blur arced across the table to land beside the crust of the tart. As it settled, the Weaver Beetle spread its metallic green carapace and extended its long spindly legs. A woman screamed and another fainted and collapsed backwards into the crowd. In the pandemonium that followed, no-one saw a meat pie disappear off the end of the table.

Shrew watched mesmerised at the performance in front of her, as she hungrily devoured the succulent meat pie in her fingers. Before her stood a tall, pale-skinned man, dressed in shimmering robes that seemed to hold a coloured aura about them, such that they deceived the eye. One moment they were as black as pitch, but in the next, as quick as the blink of an eye, they had changed through deepest violet to a vivid turquoise blue, like a kingfisher's mantle. In his hand he held a long reed that had holes like a flute. Moments before, he had waved it in a broad circle to create a glowing ring of golden nebulosity high in the air before his audience.

"He's an illusionist," the old man standing next to Shrew affirmed, nodding slowly. "He's not from these parts." He started to say more, but his words were drowned by a loud cry of surprise from the crowd. The illusionist had made a further pass of the reed, and tendrils of colour had emerged from its holes to form a beautiful butterfly with lace-like wings. Shrew watched fascinated as the butterfly flew in and out of the glowing ring. Up until now the illusionist had been silent, but now he let fly a staccato of strange sounds that caused blossoms of colour to erupt along his reed. These colours quickly coalesced to form a dragon-like creature, no larger than a cat, which stretched its wings and rippled its gossamer tail. A cry of awe rose from the crowd, and Shrew nearly choked on her last mouthful of pie as the dragon took flight and chased the butterfly through the ring.

For a short while one flitted and the other darted around the ring, and the crowd responded by calling out encouragement — some to the butterfly to escape and others to the dragon to hasten its chase. However, Shrew's eyes had left the colourful shenanigans that played out before the entranced crowd and had settled on a lace handkerchief that protruded from the pocket of a nearby spectator.

The crowd's cries rose to a crescendo. The dragon had finally caught up with the butterfly and closed its smoky jaws on its delicate shimmering wings. Suddenly, there was an explosion of light and the illusions vanished in a cascade of golden droplets that faded and disappeared before they reached the ground. The crowd was unanimous in applause, and Shrew withdrew her hand from her bag to clap enthusiastically; but, as the entertainer held out his cap to catch the coins that were generously thrown by the crowd, she withdrew and moved on.

A short time later she paused to browse some nearby stalls and remembered to thank Latia again as she felt the soft lace in her bag. This was an expensive handkerchief; it might bring in enough money to feed her for a week!

Her eyes caught sight of a pair of jugglers exchanging flaming torches, and she started to wonder what act she could perform that would make people eager to throw money at her. She had just started to entertain the idea, when one of the jugglers mistimed his catch and had to suffer the indignity of retrieving his torch whilst the crowd jeered. She quickly decided there might be easier ways to obtain coins. Sure enough, an opportunity soon presented itself.

Near the southern edge of the square, close to the entrance to Southgate Street and the avenue that led down to the huge gatehouse and the road out of the city, stood an open cart. Above the cart hung a sign portraying a smoking flask and the word 'Alchemie'. It was not the dark-skinned alchemist or his vast array of coloured flasks with curious contents that had attracted Shrew's attention, but one of his prospective customers. He was a tall, slim fellow, with long violet hair, that appeared to her to be one of the sylvan, a race of secretive folk that lived within the depths of the Gloamril Forest. Shrew made her way slowly through the press of people. Her eyes had settled on the red kidney-shaped purse that hung by a cord from a silver belt around his waist. She was always careful not to do anything hasty and call attention to herself. There was no need to rush, she reminded herself, as she fingered the small knife in the bag at her side. A mischievous smile briefly played across her features as she settled on a plan that would land her a purse full of coins, but she had to dismiss it as quickly as she had conceived it. There in front of her was the fat slimy toad known as Boil, an overbearing bully from the Stilts gang. He hadn't recognised her and she thanked Latia for that, but he had noticed the red purse.

She cursed with disappointment, yet at the same time was intrigued. Just how would he thieve the purse without getting caught? Then she saw the answer in the lanky form of Cutter, who had sidled up to the sylvan with a question on his lips.

"So that's how!" she muttered, as she saw their plan. Cutter would distract the fellow whilst Boil cut the cord and snatched the purse. She knew exactly where he would make his escape and made her way now to Southgate Street, which was much less crowded and where several shady side alleys offered numerable places to hide, as well as alternative routes back to the Duns.

She had just reached the street corner when a shout rose above the myriad sounds of the market. Through the crowds she saw Boil heading quickly in her direction, a look of surprise, which quickly converted to fear, spread across his face. Despite his bulk, he was moving surprisingly quickly; yet rather than conceal his prize, he appeared to be juggling it between his podgy fingers. In an instant Shrew leapt into the thief's path and snatched the purse as it arced between his fat clumsy hands. He had run on a further twenty paces before he realised his prize had gone!

As soon as Shrew plucked the purse out of its short path between Boil's hands, she realised something was wrong. It burned. It seemed to set her hand alight! She hastily tossed the painful thing into her other hand, with the intention of thrusting it into the bag at her side, and took off down Southgate Street like a frightened rabbit, with the aim of putting as much distance as possible between herself and any pursuers. The pain in her hand increased; it spread up her arm and gripped her body. Gasping, she slowed in her tracks. The purse now felt like a glowing ember freshly disgorged from the bowels of a forge furnace. The damned thing was cursed. If only she could empty its contents and be rid of it! She was so preoccupied that she failed to notice the burly mail-clad figure step into her path. Shrew looked up as a shadow fell upon her, but it was too late to avoid the heavy gauntlet that swooped down to grasp her shoulder. The next moment, another hand gripped her arm and lifted her bodily off the ground. The fierce grip immediately broke the curse and her fingers relinquished their hold on the purse. It fell, spilling its content of silver coins onto the cobbled street.

"Caught red-handed!" The Captain of the Watch looked back at the other members of his contingent and laughed. Shrew struggled wildly, trying to escape the vice-like grip, and attempted to aim a kick at her capturer's crotch, but he dodged effortlessly and took his other hand to her throat.

The other five members of the troop had gathered around, and one chided, "I would stop making a fuss, else Waylan will throttle you!" The others laughed. Shrew gasped and her eyes blurred; she could see bystanders had stopped to watch her predicament, and she was now the centre of a crowd.

"Bind his arms and pick up those coins," Waylan barked, but the latter part of his orders was already being attended to. "And careful with that purse," he continued. "There's something odd about it!"

The cord around Shrew's arms was drawn in tight and a heavy shove from behind pushed her forward. She winced in pain. The strange sorcery that had afflicted her was quickly wearing off, but her hand tingled and her eyes smarted, not least from the shame of being caught. Yet despite this, she felt some satisfaction. Her disguise as a boy had fooled them all!

"Open thievery in his majesty's streets is a serious crime," Waylan informed her as he strode ahead of her. "The punishment meted out for such crime can be very painful." Several of the soldiers laughed, and Shrew looked up to see one chopping his arm with the edge of his hand.

Waylan turned back and grinned. "Lucky for you I'm in a good mood today and I don't want the screams of a guttersnipe spoiling it. You're going to the work…" He paused for a moment and then spoke with an air of finality. "You're going to the orphanage."

CHAPTER TWO
THE COMING OF THE PRIESTS

A medley of birdsong and falling water lifted the tranquillity of the mist-soaked valley, but the figure that stood before the fern-wreathed waterfall looked out into space and appeared oblivious of his surroundings. He was tall, thin-lipped and hawk-nosed, with a complexion that spoke of warm, arid climes. Upon his forehead, under a tangled crown of coal-black hair, blazed a red tattoo, a rune, shaped to resemble the lidless eye of the serpent. For several minutes he stood unmoving, staring out across the lake in solitude, and then he turned and cast his dark eyes upon the line of horses and wagons.

Cyrus Col looked pleased. They had travelled many leagues and now were but a few days from the city of Highfall. With a sweep of his priestly robes, he made his way to the front of the line of wagons, where a warrior, clad in dark chain-mail, was dismounting from his horse.

"This location will suit us well tonight. Set up camp by the trees." The priest's thin mouth parted in a smile, revealing filed teeth and a red-stained tongue. "If any more are foolish enough to try assaulting our caravan, they will meet with the same fate."

The warrior put his hand to his chest in salute. "Yes, your Holiness. Blessed is the Void."

"Blessed indeed," returned the priest. "Tell your men to be vigilant; we are near the territories of the sylvan scum, so take these wretches to assist you." Cyrus Col gestured to the bedraggled group of cadaverous figures standing beside the second wagon and clicked his bony fingers. At the priest's command, the group jerked into motion and came forward. The warrior stepped back to let them pass. Although he was now familiar with them, he could still barely conceal the look of horror on his face. These forest bandits had attacked their caravan three weeks ago and he had seen them all slain; but now they stood again, animated corpses with rent armour and gaping wounds, whose final expressions still remained on their ashen, hollowed faces. Cyrus Col's lips curled into a smile as he noticed the warrior's discomfort. "Is it not ironic that those that sought us harm are now protecting us?" He cackled mirthlessly and then spoke sharply. "I will now meet with my brothers. So, see we are not disturbed. There is much to discuss before we reach Highfall and meet with the Sillaesian King."

The guard nodded and watched the priest walk to the largest of the five wagons. Then he cursed and pulled his fur-lined cloak about him. There was an unnatural chill in the air. He would be glad when they reached the city; then these walking corpses could finally be put to rest.

Chapter Three
A Lord in the Orphanage

An hour passed before Waylan turned his small contingent up the hill towards the place he called the orphanage. Most of that time was spent in the vicinity of the market, although Shrew was too preoccupied to care where they were or what went on around her. Both fear and anger welled up inside her, smothering any rational thought, so it was that, when two of Waylan's men forced a drunken youth to fall in beside her, she barely noticed. By the time she took stock of her surroundings, they were trudging up a steady incline alongside the massive grey stone curtain wall that separated the Low Reach from Middle Reach. Before them rose an arched gatehouse that was flanked each side by a two-storey tower. Shrew had heard of this place; she had even seen this portal before, but had never been so close. She managed a faint smile, for Waylan clearly had a sense of humour. This grim place was no orphanage. They were heading for the Middern workhouse. As the small party approached the open gates, her pale tear-streaked face stared up at the looming right-hand tower, where a brazier sent dark smoke vertically into a windless clear blue sky. The next moment they passed under the arch and entered a square compound, hazy with smoke and bustling with activity. With a swift motion of his right arm, Waylan called a halt.

"Wait here while I speak to the Matron," he called back brusquely, and swaggered off towards a wide stone stair that led up to the second floor of a wide drum turret that occupied most of the opposite side of the yard.

Shrew took a deep breath and coughed as dry sooty air filled her lungs. Her arms ached; in vain she tried to stretch them within the confines of her taut bonds. Looking up, her eyes settled on a line of nearly a dozen children who were queueing with brooms and forks next to a mule and cart. They were mostly boys dressed in loose-fitting tunics and leggings made of beige-coloured sackcloth. She guessed that the youngest child was no more than eight years old, whilst the oldest, a girl with red hair and a freckled complexion, was probably a couple of years older than herself. She could see the older girl was staring at her. Without a second thought, she raised her chin and returned the stare with an imperious frown. She had made a decision. From this moment, she would pretend to be the wayward son of a noble who had been amusing himself by parodying a vagabond for the day!

Turning to her right, she gazed for the first time on the inebriated youth standing beside her. Dirt encrusted his blond hair and he appeared to sag on his feet. His eye was bruised and blood still dribbled from an open wound on his chin.

"Sirra's breath!" Shrew exclaimed. "Looks like they beat you up good."

For a full minute the youth didn't reply, and then he spat blood from his mouth. "Get used to it," he drawled. "You obviously haven't been here before."

Shrew looked about her. The square-shaped compound was quite small, no more than thirty yards wide; it had once served as the bailey of a minor fort that abutted the curtain wall. To her left rose the massive grey stone wall; its thickness was so great that it was riddled with openings and recesses that gave egress to chambers deep within. These all appeared to be connected by a criss-cross of stairs that were hewn into its side. Besides the drum turret that occupied most of the eastern side, the remainder of the fort sprouted from the wall as a random collection of towers and buttresses that shielded a ramshackle collection of timber and stone buildings. These faced in on the remaining sides of the yard.

The sound of bellows, the ring of steel on steel and the hoarse shouts of men pierced the incessant murmurs of countless children. Through a haze of smoke, where flecks of soot danced in the rising warm air, Shrew gazed wide-eyed. Groups of children scurried back and forth under the watchful eyes of guards or overseers; these were mostly youths clad in crude leather armour, which she guessed was some badge of authority. She noticed that some even carried weapons. A small posse of boys carrying long poles over their shoulders caught her attention. Each pole measured at least five yards in length and was pierced at regular intervals by short perpendicular pegs. Shrew watched amazed at the skilful manner in which the boys manoeuvred the poles through the busy yard, but her expression changed to one of incredulity when she spotted a guard closely following them. A crossbow was slung over his shoulder and a bloodied whip hung from his belt. She watched them for several seconds until they passed beyond a row of iron cages and disappeared into one of the larger openings in the wall. It was then she spied the three children huddled before the cages, shivering in wet rags, with manacles on their ankles. Their eyes were closed and for a moment she wondered if they were fully conscious. They reminded her of drowned rats. What hell was this she had come to?

All at once the sounds in the yard seemed to hush. Waylan was returning, and behind him limped a ragged figure. Shrew squinted; the smoke irritated her eyes, and although she was determined not to shed any tears over her predicament, they started to trickle down her cheeks.

"What have you brought me?" A skinny man with long greasy hair that thinly plastered his pink scalp shuffled forward. One eye was covered by a patch of leather, but the other bulged from its socket, so much so that it reminded Shrew of a fish she had once seen.

"Honourable Malcaw." Waylan turned and looked at his one-eyed companion. "I believe this renegade is one of yours. I found him nigh comatose on soursop by Ahlune's Abbey."

Malcaw edged closer and craned his head forward. "Yes, that is indeed the one that escaped us. Congratulations, Captain, you have returned our most accomplished wall monkey."

As Malcaw roved his one good eye over the youth, two burly guards joined him on either side. Each wore leather cuirasses and greaves. As they stood and shuffled insolently either side of their master, Shrew's sharp eyes noticed the blood-stained whip looped around the sword belt of one of them. This was turning into a nightmare she wished she would soon wake up from.

The sudden appearance of the guards seemed to inflate the confidence of the fish-eyed Malcaw. All of a sudden, he let loose a string of obscenities at the sagging youth; and then, after wiping the spittle from his mouth, he struck the boy hard in the face with the palm of his bony hand, causing him to fall to the ground like a sack of stones.

Seemingly satisfied at the damage he had done to the boy's face, Malcaw turned to one of the thugs beside him. "Take this whelp and flog him a full score. Let it be known what happens to those that try to escape!"

Shrew looked stupefied. Her expression must have caught the eye of Waylan, because she noticed he was watching her curiously.

"Now what have we got here?" Malcaw's sickly voice broke their eye contact instantly. Shrew realised that the one-eyed bully was now addressing her, but before she could utter a single word, Waylan had answered the question.

"A young lad I caught filching a merchant's purse in the market today." The captain hesitated. "But… but I'm thinking we'll take him down to the barracks; I'm thinking he'll make a good errand boy."

Malcaw chortled and nodded to the thug that remained. "Aye, and I'm thinking he'll make a good chimmy spark. He's just the right size!"

Straightening herself as best she could, Shrew decided it was time to speak. Lowering her voice, she interrupted their laughter.

"I would have you know that I am known as Flarion, second son of Baron Bodrun of Gloamril Hall. I would also have you know that today's deed was a prank. My elder brother had given me a forfeit, to act as a vagabond for the day. Even as we speak…"

"Silence!" Malcaw snapped, but Shrew didn't wilt under the glare of his one eye; instead, she levelled her eyes and stared back up at him.

"Wait, let him continue." Waylan had moved up to stand beside her. "If what he says is true, there may be a reward for his safe return."

Malcaw turned on the mail-clad officer. "So that's why you wanted to take him away! You knew there might be a reward in the offing all along!"

Waylan stood his ground and dug his fingers into his sword belt. Behind him one or two of his troop murmured in disquiet tones.

"All right! All right!" Malcaw raised a hand in acquiescence and took a faltering step backward. "Let your little fonkin have his say; but I'm betting he's making it all up!"

"You doubt me?" Shrew cried, as she summoned all her courage and pulled the lace handkerchief from her bag. "See here, this is proof!" She held out the handkerchief, but as Malcaw reached for it, Waylan snatched it from her hand.

"Can you read?" Waylan shot a glance at Malcaw and then continued to inspect the lace work.

Malcaw scowled, but didn't reply.

The Captain of the Watch smiled. "Well, here in the middle is his initials." He tossed the handkerchief at Malcaw. "Seems like there may be some truth in his story after all."

Shrew quickly concealed her surprise. "Aye!" she cried. "Even as we speak my father will be sending his kinsmen to look for me. I had told my brother I would meet up with him with proof of my deed and now I am late." Shrew then managed an artful grin. "And yes, he will reward handsomely those that aid the safe return of his son, as well as pay for any damages or hurt that may have been caused." She cast her eyes towards Waylan and noticed he was looking at her closely again, but this time he wore a strange smile on his face.

Her words had appeared to have stunned everyone into silence. For a few seconds the sounds of industry within the yard seemed hushed, but suddenly the air was rent by the crack of a bull whip and the scream of its victim.

Malcaw was first to speak. He looked Shrew up and down as his thin fingers raked the stubble on his chin. "That's quite a tale for a young brat. You're either a rich fool or a smart liar. Either way, I can sense a profit. I'll strike you a deal, Captain."

Waylan, turning back from conferring with one of his men, re-joined the conversation. "Speak, Malcaw. We're all ears, but it had better be good." He paused and then gestured towards Shrew. "And I mean good for the boy, too."

Malcaw sneered and leaned forward. Shrew winced as she caught the foul stench of his fetid breath. "Little Lord Flarion will stay here with us, in a nice cosy pen." Malcaw reached forward and gently patted her shoulder. "In the meantime, you and your gallant men will seek out the truth behind this amazing tale. When you find his kinsmen, you will bring them and their gold back to me."

There then ensued a heated debate on the division of the gold, but Shrew's thoughts were elsewhere. This Waylan was up to something, but she wasn't sure if it was good or bad for her. She quickly calculated how much time she had before he returned from the Gloamril and her story was revealed as a pack of lies. A couple of days at the most, she thought, and in that time, she must find a way to escape. Then she recalled Malcaw's words of gaining profit either way and shuddered at the thought of what he had in store for her.

A tug on her body pulled her quickly from her thoughts. Waylan was removing the cord that bound her arms. It took a few seconds before proper feeling returned to them, but before she had time to enjoy the freedom, Malcaw's thug had grasped her wrists and manacled them.

"We don't want you running off and doing yourself harm!" Malcaw sniggered. Shrew looked down at the iron cuffs and then Waylan caught her eye again. He was staring in her direction, deep in thought.

She felt nervous under his stare. She was sure he could see right through her disguise.

"Look after this lad well, Malcaw. I want to see him safe and well when I return." The Captain of the Watch turned to Malcaw. "I mean what I say. Keep your goons off him." As if to make his point, Waylan moved closer to the remaining guard and eyed him menacingly.

Malcaw grinned wickedly. "Captain, you're wasting time. The sooner you find his kinfolk, the sooner we split the gold."

Waylan turned on his heel and barked a command at his troop. Seconds later they were marching back through the gatehouse and were gone.

A violent tug spun Shrew about. A chain had been attached to her manacles. The guard yanked at it again, making her stumble forward, and a broad smile split his ugly countenance. She had heard that ogres lived out beyond the eastern plains. Maybe this brute had a mother out there somewhere.

"Wait!" Malcaw shuffled forward. "Before you go down to the comfortable apartment we have awaiting your Lordship's repose, I want to see what you have in your bag." Without waiting for a reply, he pulled hard at the bag that hung at her waist, tearing it away from her belt and causing its contents to spill out. Her mirror, whose face was already scarred by numerous cracks, broke, scattering glass shards over the stony ground. Out, too, fell her valued knife and the bronze coins she had found earlier in the day.

She could do nothing but watch as Malcaw stooped forward and picked up the coins and the knife. She had just lost two of her most valued possessions.

"We can't have you poking people with this, can we?" he said with a patronising smile. "Take him down below, Rolkar, and not a word to the Matron, else you'll see no gold lining your pockets!"

A short sharp tug on her wrists jarred her into motion. She found herself trotting behind the broad back of the burly guard. He dragged her into the shadow of the great wall and into a cavernous opening in its steep sloping side. The air in the yard was warm, but here inside the wall it was stifling. Without warning, he swung right and descended a stair that coursed downward into a passage lined with flickering torches. The stair was steep and she struggled to keep her footing as he led her down into the foundations of the wall. At the end of the stair, he paused and she almost fell into the back of his hulking frame. An incessant whispering captured her attention and for a brief moment she thought they were the disembodied conversations of ghosts who languished in this foul place, but as she was pulled forward again, she could tell that they were the hushed conversations of children. The sounds were coming from behind the numerous doors that lined the passage they now followed.

Rolkar growled and beat the nearest door with his club-like fist. "Shut yer mouths," he hollered, but the sounds didn't abate, and even seemed to increase in volume. All of the doors had window-like grills and as she passed them, she swore she could see eyes framed within.

They passed an intersection and, shortly after, climbed a short stair where their passage joined another. Shrew marvelled at the extent of the tunnelling within the wall. She felt like a small ant, in a nest of termites.

"Here!" Rolkar had stopped at the first door in this new passage and drew back the bar-lock. "This is your pen." Before Shrew had time to fully realise, their short journey had ended and her captor had unhooked the chain from her manacles and pushed her through the door into the dark chamber beyond. She stood, seemingly paralysed, as the heavy door closed behind her. The scraping sound of the bar-lock being slid back into place momentarily screamed out into the depths of the wall, and then there was silence.

It was several seconds before Shrew could collect her wits. Then her eyes widened as she spotted the apparent illusion before her. A shaft of golden light lanced downward from a small square window in the far wall to illuminate the straw-covered floor at her feet. For a few moments she stood transfixed, mesmerised by the motes of dust that seemed suspended in its path, and then she moved slowly forward.

The window was part of a larger recess in the far wall and was no more than a small opening to the outside world. Shrew climbed into the recess and thrust her head forward into the square space. The warm golden glow of the afternoon sun bathed her face. She found herself looking between the mighty trunks of two trees, beyond which spread verdant parkland that was speckled with vibrant blooms and crossed by pathways that led to leafy bowers and secluded places, with statues and gushing fountains. Further away, white minarets and slender towers rose against the blue sky. So, this was the Middle Reach, she told herself. It was as grand as the stories she had heard about it, but it was a place for the middle classes, and her kind were never allowed past the guards at the Middern Gate. As she gazed dreamily at the sprawling vista, her eyes caught sight of a flock of birds that unexpectedly rose up from a copse of trees into the clear sky. A single tear ran down her cheek. She felt like a bird in a cage. If only she had the freedom of that fortunate flock beyond her window! Biting her lip and crossing her fingers, she made two promises to herself. First, she would do her utmost to escape her captors; and second, if she was successful, she would find a way to visit the park below and follow its winding paths to whatever secrets they might lead.

The storm rolled in from the north. Its leaden clouds, heavy with rain, passed over the mountains men had named the Dragon's Spine, and unleashed its fury on the Sillaesian city of Highfall. Lightning flickered in the dark nimbus over the city and thunder rumbled deeply, resonating across the three-tiered metropolis as if the gods were rolling giant mill-stones back and forth across the crystal highway of heaven.

Shrew woke up with a start. Her stomach rumbled much like the storm outside, and when she heard the rain start to fall, she remembered her thirst. Night had fallen and her pen was surely as dark as the deepest pit of Midir. She had fallen asleep on a pallet of straw and images of a familiar dream still lingered in her thoughts. As she cleared her mind of banquet tables laden with tasty treats, the wall and door opposite the window suddenly stood out in bright relief. Barely a second later, the chamber reverberated with a deafening boom that brought her fully awake. In that brief moment she spotted a jug and bowl beside the door.

In eager anticipation, she shuffled on all fours to the door and grasped the rim of the bowl. Soon after, she felt the hard crust of a loaf and a softer substance shaped as a wedge that smelt like cheese. Reaching for the jug, she could feel that it was full. Clearly her captors didn't want their new-found source of wealth to starve or die of thirst! She smiled faintly and devoured the contents of the bowl greedily, pausing only to clasp the jug to her mouth to take a deep draught of the brackish water. Barely had she finished this wholesome fare when she thought she heard sounds within the passage beyond the door. Outside, the thunder rumbled and the rain fell in torrents, but these noises were different. For a moment she panicked: was Waylan back so soon? Surely the officer could not possibly be back from the Gloamril in less than a day?

The sounds of footsteps and voices were now unmistakable. She crawled quickly back to her pallet and curled up in the straw so as to appear asleep, but kept one eye on the dark shadow of the door.

Shrew felt herself trembling as she heard the voices fall silent. Glancing up, she saw flickering yellow torchlight through the small window-like grill near the top of her door. A moment later the bar-lock squealed in protest as it was drawn roughly back and the heavy door swung inward. Suddenly her small chamber was flooded with torchlight and ghostly shadows played across its walls; but before she snapped her eyes shut, she saw a dark shape lurch through the open door and slump heavily on the floor, barely a yard from where she lay. The door was closed and the room was plunged into darkness once more. Catching her breath, she lay unmoving and tried to focus her eyes on the object that lay just inside the door. The maroon afterglow of the torches danced in the darkness before her. It was some time before her eyes could see clearly, and when her night sight returned, she could see she was no longer alone.

It was a long night. The thunder rumbled on for some time, even after the rains had stopped. She could no longer sleep, but continued to stare suspiciously at the new arrival in the room. Once or twice she heard it breathe heavily and groan. It definitely sounded human, and that gave her some comfort; but despite her efforts to stay awake, weariness finally overtook her and at last she fell asleep. When she awoke, the faint light of dawn was seeping through her window.

As the pale light grew brighter, she could see clearly what had fallen into the room. It was the drunken blond-haired youth; the one Malcaw had called a wall monkey.

Slowly, she rose from her pallet and crept forward on all fours towards the sleeping boy. She was soon crouched beside him and had never once taken her eyes off his sleeping form.

"Sweet Ahlune!" she cried. The boy's naked back was a trellis work of red welts and lacerations. Her exclamation was loud enough to wake him from his slumber.

Rolling onto his back, the boy groaned loudly. "No more!" he pleaded.

"No more what?" Shrew realised the stupidity of her question as the words trailed from her lips. From the look of his bloodied back, the youth had been flogged to within an inch of his life.

She hissed in his ear, "They've gone. It's just you, me and this prison room. I won't hurt you!"

The boy's eyes darted left and right, before they settled and focussed on her. "Who are you?" he rasped. Shrew noticed that the side of his mouth was still swollen where Malcaw had struck him.

"I am known as Sh…" Shrew hesitated. "I am known as Flarion," she corrected herself. "I am the son of Baron Bodrun of Gloamril Hall, exalted second cousin of King Wulfred and…" But, just as her words started to sound like those of a herald announcing the grand entrance of a royal procession, they were suddenly cut short.

"You don't seem very royal to me," the boy interrupted. He stared at her curiously. "I remember you. The South Gate Watch had you bound up like a trussed chicken!"

Shrew felt herself blush and then her boyish features creased in a smile. Her capture seemed funny now. How stupid she had been to let herself get caught.

The youth smiled, too, and then they both found themselves chuckling. "I must have looked silly, too," he grinned. "A sodden dronkin all doused in soursop." They laughed again, but her companion's chuckles soon trailed off and became a hacking cough. "I don't feel good," he spluttered. "They beat me really hard this time."

"So, who are you, then? That slimy rake upstairs called you a wall monkey!" Shrew looked closely at the boy's grimy features. He was older than her, flaxen-haired, with blue eyes and freckles, but his chin was discoloured and encrusted with dried blood and the right side of his mouth glared an angry red and still wept from the damage it had taken earlier.

The boy attempted another smile and winced in pain. "My father named me Wilfstan after his father, but you can call me Wilf." He paused and looked up. "And yes, I am the best wall monkey this side of the Swanny!" He looked closely at his new companion, expecting to see some sign of awe at the telling of this revelation, but was quickly disappointed by the absence of any emotion.

Shrew was staring into space. In her mind's eye she saw a small child staring, totally mesmerised by the rich, colourful portraits of a number of wild and exotic creatures within a deck of playing cards. The card she could best recall showed the strange monkey creature crouched on the bough of a tree. Suddenly, her face brightened with the dawn of understanding.

"Ha! I have it." She turned back to the boy. "I've seen your kind a few times on the east curtain wall outside the Duns. You climb the walls and clear the vine and bindweed that grows there!" Her eyes sparkled and her excited expression quickly swept away his earlier disappointment.

"You climb really high using long thin ladders! It looks dangerous," she added.

"Indeed, it is," he replied in a serious tone, and nodded slowly. "Many have fallen. Some have received major hurts and now, can do nought but beg, and some have had their life taken from them — but better that than live on as a starving cripple." He spoke with a solemnity that belied his young age. "But what would a noble's son know of that, and how would a noble's son get to see the goings on in the Low Reach anyhow?" he added with curiosity.

Shrew suddenly felt uncomfortable. She felt her disguise was slipping away and quickly attempted to change the subject.

"So, what other work do they make the children do here, Wilf?" she asked inquisitively, calling him by name and hoping she could shift the centre of attention away from herself.

Wilf slowly managed to ease his body upright, such that he was sitting with his back to the wall with the recessed window. In the meantime, Shrew had recovered the jug of water from near the door and now offered its remaining contents to the boy's lips. Much of the water spilled from his swollen mouth, but he drank with relief.

"Thanks," he whispered gratefully, taking the jug from her. "They make us do many things. The lucky ones, that's the snitches and those that have more favour with Matron, get all the best jobs. Like sweeping the streets or making candles and sackcloth." He paused and took another sip of water. "Some even get to help the smithy and the tanner, but then there are other kinds of work, work that's even worse than that done by the wall monkeys." He trailed off for a moment and contemplated the inside of the water jug.

"Like what?" Shrew queried. "What kind of work?"

Wilf swirled the water in the base of the jug as if he was attempting to conjure an image from the remaining dregs. "Like the work done by the sewer rats," he said bluntly; but before he could continue, a sound like that of a jangling steel chain interrupted their thoughts.

Wilf looked up towards the door. "They come," he said.

CHAPTER FOUR
WALL MONKEYS AND POLEKERNS

They could hear voices. Shrew looked nervously towards Wilf and then back to the small door of their prison. Metal grated heavily against metal and the sound reverberated within the confines of their dim chamber as the bar-lock was drawn slowly back. Almost instinctively, Shrew tried to hunch up and make herself as small as possible, in the vain hope she could somehow vanish into the wall. She was certain her captors had now discovered the truth and that the tale of little Lord Flarion was nought but a lie. Nevertheless, she had to admit, her performance had been quite convincing, abetted in no small portion by the men's greed!

The door swung inward and one of the leather-clad ruffians she had noticed the day before took a step into the chamber. He was followed by a younger, slimmer man who was dressed in similar garb, but who also carried a chain looped about his shoulder.

It was the first of the guards, a swarthy dark-tanned individual who bore a vivid scar across his right cheek, who spoke first. "You!" He stabbed a finger at Wilf. "You're needed up top. We're short of a climber in our wall team."

Wilf started to rise and then sank back down again in agony. The younger guard swiftly stepped forward. "On your feet, you idle pup," he commanded menacingly, "or I'll beat you with this chain before I tether it to your cuffs!"

Shrew watched on in horror. Her initial fear had subsided and now both anger and hope welled up inside her simultaneously. "I will go instead." She blurted the words out so suddenly and loudly that she surprised herself.

A silence fell upon the chamber as the guards appeared to notice her for the first time. Wilf started to remonstrate, but his words were cut short by the guard holding the chain. "I see we have a volunteer. I like that. Hold up your wrists, boy!"

Shrew immediately complied and turned to smile faintly at her companion. Wilf stared back at her, seemingly dumbstruck, as the guard attached the chain to her manacles. A second later she was pulled forward through the door and into the torch-lit corridor beyond. She had no time to look back; a yank on the chain had her moving forward again as the heavy door of her former prison slammed shut behind her.

Shrew had to squint as she was brought up into the yard. Dull, ashen clouds scudded overhead in an overcast sky and for a few seconds the pale morning light hurt her eyes. Unlike the previous day, the small compound was virtually clear of people. There were no signs of activity around the forge, or by the row of cages. Only a single brazier burned, and its sooty signature was barely noticeable in the stiff breeze.

The younger of the two guards, who Shrew had heard being referred to as Lerrin, brought her abruptly to a standstill. "By Sirra's sweet breath, where are they?" he cursed. A voice called across the yard from near the two towers of the gatehouse and his swarthy companion returned the call and grunted with satisfaction.

"They've moved out down the road, Lerrin. Malcaw wants them back by noon for another job."

Lerrin cursed again and pulled the chain, jarring her wrists. "Come, lad, your legs better be quick!"

Shrew lurched forward. She had to trot to keep up with the young guard and prevent herself from being dragged to the ground. As they jogged under the weathered stone arch of the gatehouse, she caught sight of the one that had just hailed them, a dwarf of a man burdened by a crossbow. Up from him stood another guard, similarly armed. Suddenly, she realised that the compound they were leaving was not as empty as it had at first seemed.

Halfway down the steep road that linked the workhouse with the Middern Rise, a main thoroughfare that led into the Middle Reach, they came across the work party they were looking for. The party had paused, and as Lerrin slowed to a walk, Shrew could see two lines of children standing behind an open wagon and horses. There were a number of men in the wagon. One lolled lazily, with one leg dangling over the back end, and he beckoned Lerrin over.

"Ho, Lerrin, what's that you brought me? A scrawny waif if ever I saw one. He looks like a four-peg polekern!" The indolent youth's remarks set off some snickers from the other passengers in the wagon, but Shrew's expression remained stoic. Her mind was elsewhere. She had already noted three crossbows with the five men in the wagon and she could see an older man, up by the two horses, who was obviously their teamster. The children were mostly boys, attired in the drab-coloured sackcloth tunics and leggings she had seen the day before. She counted eleven of them altogether; six queued behind the wagon on the right and five on the left. They stood either side of a small pile of long poles, whose lengths were pierced by peg-like protrusions at regular intervals. The poles looked familiar, but Shrew thought they looked too flimsy to scale the city's outer walls. She had no time to ponder further on the construction of the peculiar ladders lying before her. Her thoughts were suddenly interrupted by a forceful shove between her shoulder blades.

"Hey, you with the cloth ears, didn't you hear him? Get yer lazy carcass in line!" Lerrin's swarthy companion, with the scarred cheek, had stepped forward and now pushed her roughly, so she stumbled into the front of the children queuing on the left side of the wagon. She could feel his foul breath on her cheek as he bent over her and released the manacles from her wrists. Freedom from the chafing weight of the cuffs was a welcome relief, but before she could entertain any thought of escape, a leg iron was clamped to her right ankle. She was now tied to the other five in her line.

For several minutes, Lerrin and the rest of the guards exchanged idle banter. Shrew watched disinterestedly until the leader of the troop, who was referred to as Sicga, rose quickly from his slouched position at the back of the wagon and called out to the teamster. Suddenly, there was a flurry of activity and a voice from behind barked loudly at Shrew, "Pick up *your* end, won't you?"

Looking around, she could see the other children were lifting the poles to their shoulders, and guessed that she was required to do the same. Each line of children was managing three poles, two of them to each pole. She was to carry a pole the other end of which was being carried by the fourth child in her line. She grasped the knuckled end expecting it to be heavy, but it was lighter than she had imagined and she easily lifted it to her shoulder.

Above the hoarse cries of the men, a horse whinnied and then the wagon creaked in protest as its heavy iron-shod wheels slowly ground forward. As they slowly moved off, Shrew took a moment to glance behind and looked into the cheerless face of a surly-looking youth with ginger hair. His morose expression turned into a scowl as he noticed her stare. Crinkling her face to feign disgust, she turned back to face the rear of the wagon and noticed the leader of the troop back in his slouched position, with one of his legs swinging over the back end of the cart, as it bumped and rumbled down the cobble-stoned street. Sicga was observing her closely, but she blanked him entirely, deciding to channel all her thoughts on a plan of escape. She felt her time was running out; she had to make a break soon.

Within minutes they had reached the junction with the Middern Rise, where, even at this early hour, folk were up and about, making their way to and from the Middern Gate that led into the broad avenues of Middle Reach. The teamster had brought them briefly to a halt, which gave Shrew time to look up the street towards the great crenelated gatehouse that gave access to the next tier of the city. She had often dreamed of walking through the huge portal, but that was almost impossible for street urchins such as herself. The guards on the gate seemed to have an innate ability when it came to deciding who rightfully had business in the middle city and who hadn't.

Hope suddenly leapt into her heart. Maybe they would turn right and enter the Middle Reach. The teamster was signalling them forward, but he wasn't taking them right; their direction was the narrow street opposite, where the four-storey brick and timber houses leaned so far forward over the road their roofs nearly touched. Shrew couldn't prevent a scowl from wrinkling her features, which seemed to amuse Sicga, who was still appraising her.

"I hope you have a head for heights, lad," he chuckled, and slouched back even further into the back of the wagon.

They were entering Candle Street; she had ventured here only a few times and could recall that the folk here seemed arrogant and unfriendly. This was a more prosperous part of the Low Reach. As they proceeded along the street, they passed well-dressed shops on either side, many of which were just opening. The street would have been quite shady if it weren't for the many lanterns and oil lamps that flickered from their sconces, illuminating even the darkest areas under the low eaves and arches through which they passed. After a few minutes they entered an open area where folk were busy about a few stalls that crowded around the circular stone wall of a well. The left side of this marketplace was occupied by an inn, whose front was adorned with a myriad of coloured lanterns. Shrew recognised it immediately. It was the Will-o'-the-Wisp Inn, a well-known haunt for strangers from out of the city. But there was little time for her to enjoy the rich smell of roasted pig that wafted from its kitchens; the teamster had steered the horses in the other direction.

Leading off from the market to the right, a lane led between long open-fronted houses, which were already bustling with activity. As the wagon turned into the lane, the inviting smell of breakfast was quickly replaced by a pot-pourri of scents and odours. Soon the air was heavy with the smell of tallow and a countless number of other oils and waxes. As Shrew trudged behind the wagon, she could see the candle- and lantern-makers busy about their crafts. Beyond the line of houses, no more than a bow-shot away, she spied the imposing curtain wall of Middle Reach; in the early-morning light, under the grey windy skies, it looked drab and dismal, which adequately reflected her sombre mood.

As they drew closer, she could see there were people halfway up the wall. They looked like spiders, moving this way and that, amongst a web of ropes that were festooned across the pitted stone, up to a parapet high above. Although the pole was quite light, it was starting to hurt her shoulder and she was glad when the teamster brought them to a sudden halt beside a sloping shack that abutted the wall.

Sicga was first off the wagon. He cupped his hand to his mouth and hollered to a figure high on the parapet above. Shrew could see a man waving back. He must have been nearly a furlong away, and she could see from the pennants that whipped furiously on the battlements that the wind was fierce up there.

"Stop your gawking and mix in with the rest!" It was Lerrin. He had been behind the troop the whole way and she hadn't even noticed. The other end of her pole had already been lowered and they were all waiting for her. She heard a curse proffered from the youth behind her. As she eased the weight off her shoulder, she noticed he was sneering in her direction.

"They made you the climber and me anchor, but you look witless to me and too small to tie the lines, let alone cut the vines." His heavily freckled face sneered again under his crop of ginger hair.

Shrew shrugged, in part to return the circulation to her shoulder, but at the same time she wanted the boy to know that she didn't give a care to any of his problems. "I'm a better climber than you any day," she retorted. "That's why I got the job, carrot mop!" As she spoke, she felt the leg iron clamping her ankle fall away. Then she recalled Wilf's proud boast and added, "I'm the best wall monkey this side of the Swanny!"

"That's the spirit, lad!" Lerrin laughed. He had heard her last words and grinned. "You're going to go a long way! But for you, right now, that long way is going to lead upward, so get over to the wagon yonder and get a skreet!" He pointed to one of the two wagons that were already drawn up at the base of the wall.

Shrew found time to cast one of her dirty looks at the youth she had just called carrot mop and then swaggered towards the wagon which Lerrin had pointed out. She had seen enough already to understand what was expected of her. Now that the leg iron no longer chafed her ankle, she felt hope welling up inside her chest and thoughts of escaping her captors started to occupy her mind once more.

Looking around, she quickly realised they were in a cul-de-sac, a dead end, with no alleyways to which she could sprint for freedom. She frowned with disappointment and looked along the wall. Most of the activity appeared to be on its mid-section, and she could tell from the number of children present that at least two other troops of wall monkeys had arrived earlier. She had seen their kind at work before, although from a distance whilst near the south wall in the Duns. Now she was closer she could see the pole she had carried could be joined to others to make simple ladders to scale the walls. Together with a network of ropes, which fanned out from a number of points on the parapet high above, they enabled the young climbers to reach and cut down the vegetation that had taken root in the walls. One of the wagons was already nearly full of green fern and trailing vines, and a small company of children were fully occupied, scurrying around the base of the wall, collecting more as it fell.

As she reached the back of the wagon, a dour-looking man, clad in a leather jerkin and with a prominent scar across the bridge of his nose, handed Shrew her skreet, which was no more than a curved notched blade with a vicious-looking hook at its tapered end.

"Careful now, lad. It's as sharp as it looks. We don't want you pricking yourself with it, do we? Neither do we want you pricking others." He grinned, exposing a row of yellow teeth, and tapped with a hooked finger the haft of the crossbow that lay cradled on his lap. "Else my friend here will have something to say about it!"

Shrew balanced the blade in her hand and smiled faintly. "Don't worry, mister; I'll use it just fine." She pitched her voice as low as she could muster in an attempt to sound as boyish as possible.

"Hey! New boy, we need you over here!" Sicga was calling from the base of one of the makeshift ladders.

Shrew made her way quickly to Sicga's side. She wanted to appear keen and eager to please. She hoped that this strategy would divert attention away from her and mask her true intention, which was to escape at the first opportunity.

"It's very simple, boy. You will climb up this pole to the top peg, see?" He pointed upward and Shrew followed the line of the pole to where it rested on the mid-section of the wall. "Now look to the right of the top peg. Do you see those two ropes?"

Shrew looked up to where Sicga was pointing and nodded. She could see one rope simply trailed straight down from a machicolation in the battlements high above them. It could easily be reached from the top of the polekern. The second rope was different. It appeared taut, and trailed from a similar projection further to the right, and traced an arc across the wall to a point halfway up the length of the first. Here it was pinned amidst a tangle of trailing green bindweed several yards above the top of the polekern. There was a climber, who appeared to be of a similar age to her, already high up on the wall, grasping the taut rope with one hand and gouging at the weed with the other. The sun was now shining through rents in the drifting cloud, and its light flashed off the skreet in the climber's hand.

Sicga must have seen the expression on Shrew's face, because he laughed.

"Are you sure you're not scared of heights, lad? Well, you're to join that climber up there and clear the weed around both ropes. We'll put up another pole soon, just right of this one, to reach the anchored rope." Shrew ignored him and started for the pole, but the troop leader blocked her. "Wait!" he admonished her. "You don't climb a two-pin pole without an anchor!"

As if from nowhere, the boy she had called carrot mop appeared. His freckled face seemed to wear a permanent scowl, and Shrew was tempted to mimic the expression, but instead gazed up the length of the pole. Sicga had said 'two-pin', and she could see what he meant. Her pole was long, and now she could see why. It was actually two polekerns joined together!

"Cedrin is your anchor. He supports your pole. If it starts to slide, you call down and tell him!"

Shrew looked at the freckled boy and didn't like his expression. He appeared to be mocking her. Shrugging her shoulders, she turned towards the pole and Sicga stepped aside. Placing the skreet in her belt, she nimbly leapt up, and within a second was halfway up the first section of the pole.

"Sirra's breath!" Sicga cursed with astonishment. He stepped back in surprise. By now, Shrew had reached the top of the pole and had grasped the final peg. "Cedrin, you whelp!" Sicga screamed, striking the boy's cheek. "Anchor it!"

Shrew paused for a few seconds and looked over her shoulder. A cool breeze blew into her face. Over the red-tiled roof of the nearest building in the yard and through a gap between the eaves of two taller buildings a bow-shot further away, she could see the pennants flying above the battlements of the great South Gate. She sucked in the cool fresh air that was untainted by the pungent oily brews of the wax-makers and turned to examine the bristled rope that lay across her pole. With her left hand gripping the clawed end of the pole, she tugged hard on the rope with her right till she felt it pull; and then, grasping it tightly, she leant towards it till it took her weight. Now with both hands she pulled herself upward till she could plant her left foot on the top of the polekern and then turned her attention to the wall.

The squared stone blocks of the Middle Reach curtain wall were marred and pitted by erosion. For countless summers they had felt the stinging blast of the southerly trade winds which, in their passage to the southern coasts of Sillaesia, had picked up dust from parched lands far to the south. Yet, as Shrew looked along the breadth of the wall, she saw that deep green mould and paler lichens flourished in the crooks and crannies, whilst in the crevasses between the stones all manner of creepers and weeds had taken root in the crumbling mortar.

She soon spotted a foothold for her right foot. Indeed, she noticed that in quite a few places the stumps of hacked and sawn bindweed protruded sufficiently from the wall to give a climber an excellent footing. Now she found that she was in comfortable reach of a clump of toadflax, which was unmistakable due to its spray of delicate purple flowers. With a flourish, she withdrew her skreet from her belt and brought its saw-toothed edge down to hack at the plant. It took a few minutes, but she soon learnt how useful the hook at the tip of the blade could be for severing the smaller root fibres that clung in mats to the wall. She was so engrossed in her new line of work that even her thoughts of escape were temporarily forgotten. It was, therefore, a shock when the support from under her left foot suddenly gave way.

Her foot slipped, but she soon recovered, as instinct born out of years of traversing the dilapidated roofs and crumbling walls of the Low Reach saved her. Shifting her weight to her right foot and grasping the rope tighter with her left hand, she looked down and saw Cedrin grinning back up at her. He had deliberately made the polekern slip and move an arm's length away from her.

"Whoresop!" she screamed down at him, but none of the guards below seemed to have noticed, and she could see that Sicga had wandered off. She was about to let off a string of more verbal abuse when a scream from above interrupted her.

Looking up, she could see the cry had come from the climber above her, who was clinging to the second rope that Sicga had indicated. This rope was also attached to the same projection on the battlements as hers, but was shorter and its end was tied amidst some bindweed vines, about three yards above her head. He appeared to be slipping down the rope, with one foot scuffing the wall, desperately trying to gain grip. Something fell, and Shrew flinched as she caught sight of his skreet momentarily snagging on some bindweed to her right and then fall spinning to the ground below.

"What's wrong?" she yelled, looking up. As if in answer, a drop of warm blood hit her right arm. There was some commotion below now, shouts from amongst the guards, and she thought she heard Sicga call, but the sounds seemed muted and distant as she heard the boy call down.

"My leg," he gasped. "I've hurt my leg!" were the few words she could discern, but she didn't stop to listen. She let go of her skreet and let it fall. Then she quickly pulled off her sandals. Why she hadn't done so earlier, she couldn't fathom. She could move much faster without them. The boy was close to the end of his rope now and she could see blood dripping off the heel of his bare foot. Grasping her rope with both hands, she moved one hand over the other and seemingly walked up the wall. Her rope would take her very close to where the wounded boy's rope ended amidst a tangle of bindweed, and it was to this point that she moved rapidly.

"Hang on tight!" she called up. "I'll be with you in seconds."

The boy had reached the bindweed and was hunched up, grimacing in pain. As Shrew drew level with him, she could see that his left leg had been pierced above the knee. He looked across to her with wide eyes; he looked no more than twelve years of age. "My skreet," he murmured. "It slipped."

Shrew reached out. "Take hold of my hand," she ordered, and then wondered if she could take his weight; but the boy seemed to have his own solution to the problem.

"Just help me on to your rope," he said weakly. "I can climb down to the pole from there."

The tangle of bindweed proved useful to them both. Shrew found a good foothold amidst the vines and moved the rope so it was in reach of the boy's grasp. Then she held on to him as he moved between the ropes.

"What's your name?" she asked.

"Berin," he answered, and started to lower himself on her rope.

She became aware once more of the commotion below. A small crowd had gathered next to Cedrin, and it seemed that another climber had mounted the polekern to help Berin descend. All attention appeared to be on the injured climber.

This was her moment. Glancing up the wall, she could see she had two choices. There were only two ways up. She made her choice and grasped the taut rope just above the point where it had been pegged into the wall and quickly started to make her way along it. At intervals there were stumps of bindweed, which provided good footholds, and these boosted her progress. Within seconds she was pulling herself up the last few yards of rope and could see where it disappeared into a narrow opening where the top of the wall jutted out in an overhang. She knew these overhangs allowed the defenders on the battlements to throw missiles, or burning pitch, on attackers below who were attempting to scale the wall. Shrew hesitated, as she thought about her next move, and as she paused, a cry of alarm sounded from below and another answered close by, above her head. A faint hiss sounded close to her right ear and a missile from a crossbow struck the wall beside her; then another fell short a few yards below her. They had realised she was trying to escape and were shooting at her! In desperation, she looked up again at the opening in the stone overhang. It was too small to squeeze through; she had no choice but to make for a gap in the tooth-like merlon structures on the top of the wall. She saw her chance. A patch of bindweed and ivy lay a few yards to her right and spread up almost to the top of the wall. This was her ladder to freedom, if she could just make the leap. There was another hiss, loud, that filled her ear, and a searing pain burned her neck. She muffled a scream. It had been fired from above! Looking up, she could see there was a guard on the battlements about to take aim again. With all the strength she could muster, she pushed her feet hard against the wall and with the agility of a cat sprung towards the carpet of vines and creepers. Reaching out, she caught a thick vine and scrabbled with her free hand to find another. She could hear the guards below her barking orders, and two more crossbow quarrels slammed into the wall beneath her. Heaving herself up, she looked up at the space between the merlons and there, framed between them, was the head and shoulders of the crossbowman who had just a moment ago singed her neck. It was point-blank range. Shrew screwed up her eyes and waited for the inevitable shot that would send her to oblivion. It didn't happen. Instead, she heard a thud, and when she opened her eyes, she saw a hand reaching down to her.

"Quick, take my hand, girl!" It was a gruff but firm command, and Shrew grasped the leather-gloved hand. Within seconds she was over the wall and standing on the wall-walk between the battlements.

As she caught her breath, the first thing she saw was the body of the crossbowman slumped against the parapet of the wall. She took a nervous step back and looked at her rescuer.

"It's the first time I've seen you lost for words, Shrew."

She recognised the voice and the posture. It was Waylan, the Captain of the City Watch, and he wore a broad grin on his face. Shrew paled and took another step backwards. He knew her name. She clutched her stinging neck and turned to look for a way of escape. She could hear shouts and voices getting louder. Waylan heard them, too. Half turning, he gestured to the small tower some twenty yards behind him. "They're coming up the stair," he said sharply. "I've locked the tower door, but it won't hold them for long!"

Shrew turned to look behind her. Here, the wall-walk disappeared under wooden hoardings, but she could hear pursuit in that direction also. She felt like a cornered rat.

"Wouldn't it have been easier to let him kill me?" she retorted, and pointed to the crossbowman who had started to move and appeared to be reviving.

Waylan ignored her and moved quickly to peer over the battlements on the side that looked over Middle Reach. "You have a chance. The drop on this side is shorter and there are trees. You can jump, but be quick!"

The urgency in Waylan's voice and the hammering at the door of the tower galvanised her into action. She stepped up on to the parapet and then to a gap in the battlements on the Middle Reach side. In a different situation she would have stood awe-struck at the vista spread out before her, but there was no time. Her attention was focussed on the crown of a large elm tree, which seemed tantalisingly close. Breathing a quick prayer to Latia, the goddess of luck, she jumped.

Chapter Five
The Coming Together

Pale mist pooled in the hollows of the crumpled vale of cypress and hawthorn that stretched down to the eastern bank of the Swan River. Dotted here and there rose stumps of masonry that projected from amongst the trees like broken teeth.

Cyrus Col opened his eyes. He stood alone within a small clearing of stunted trees that overlooked the vale. Just a moment before, his thoughts had been amongst the ruins that lay scattered before him. Behind, less than a furlong away, stood the remainder of his retinue beside the wagons. The restless horses whinnied and shook their harnesses, whilst the black-mailed guards fidgeted and looked nervously up at the road that led towards Highfall's southern gate.

The ancients were no fools, he mused. In his moment of contemplation, he had felt the energy that lay hidden before him, and now he sensed his brother returning.

The silence in the clearing was broken by the emergence of a gaunt, dark-robed figure from the surrounding thicket.

Cyrus Col appeared not to notice, as his dark eyes ranged back and forth over the ruins, searchingly.

"Your revered holiness," the gaunt acolyte whispered, as he shuffled up beside his master. "It is indeed as written in the Psalm of the Shades. I found an entrance."

Cyrus Col turned; his face radiated a sanguine expression and the red rune on his forehead appeared to blaze in the early-morning light.

"It is as I expected, Cullis Ra. I doubt the fools in Highfall can remember the building of their first city, or that Armeris, son of Glossingal, built a shrine here upon a confluence of ley lines. Tell me more about what you found."

The acolyte pulled his robes closer about his gaunt frame, as if to ward off the chill air. "I found the remains of the entrance to the shrine in a hollow, half buried beneath the roots of a tree. Much is covered in moss and debris, but the visage of Folkron was unmistakable."

Cyrus Col smiled with satisfaction, revealing the filed teeth between his thin lips. "You have done well, Cullis Ra, the omniscient one clearly guided you; blessed is the dark silence in which he dwells."

The acolyte bowed his head in deference and the light of the rising sun caught his bald crown, revealing a patchwork of white scars.

"Our journey is nearly at an end, Cullis Ra. Let us return to our brothers and send forth a rider to the city to announce our arrival." Cyrus Col grinned malevolently. "Soon we will meet their ignoramus King and the other half-witted fools of the Council of Nine. We will go to them as ambassadors of wisdom and knowledge, seeking to sanctify the legacy of their past. Yet if this fails to kindle favour, we will show them the gold in our coffers and enflame the avarice in their hearts."

CHAPTER SIX
INTO THE DARK

The crack of thunder proclaimed the beginning of a storm and woke Shrew suddenly. She had been in a dream that seemed to slowly fall apart, taking her from extreme comfort, nestled in a bed of soft white down, to a state of being constantly knocked and buffeted by hard unseen forces that battered and bruised her. She opened her eyes and looked into Lerrin's leering face.

"He's awake. Look, his eyes are open!" Lerrin leaned closer, such that his soursop-laden breath spilled over her. Shrew coughed and then gagged. She felt the urge to vomit. She lay on the floorboards of a wagon, surrounded by guards from the workhouse. It was on the move, jolting from side to side and back and forth, hammering her bruised body till the pain felt almost unbearable. She tried to think back, but her head hurt. Overhead, the evening sky grew menacingly dark as the storm clouds gathered.

"You've caused us a lot of trouble!" The voice was Sicga's. "The lads aren't happy, you disappearing like that. You're lucky we haven't slit your throat and be done with you!" There were murmurs of agreement from the others in the wagon. "Aye… you've got yourself noticed by Matron, and Malcaw is beside himself!" There were a few sniggers at these last words. It appeared that Malcaw's inconvenience was amusing to the guards.

A brilliant flash of lightning rent the darkness overhead, illuminating the palisade beside which the wagon passed. As the ensuing thunder rolled over the city, the rain began to fall. Large droplets fell on Shrew's face and mixed with her tears. There was no holding back now and no façade. The tears flowed, but no-one noticed.

A short time later and the wagon passed under the arch that spanned the gate towers of the workhouse and came to a halt in the yard. The storm now vented its fury on the city and sheets of rain fell, such that water flowed in countless rivulets between the cobbles of the compound and gathered in a torrent down by the drains where the gatehouse abutted the curtain wall.

Shrew was dragged roughly from the back of the wagon and taken towards a wide stone stair that led up to an imposing pair of doors set into the second level of a wide turret. She stumbled amidst the press of men until she was forcibly pulled up and pushed through the portal.

Inside the turret, the sounds of the storm were hushed. She staggered forward and looked up. Before her a pale blue flame flickered from a copper brazier, sending moving shadows dancing across the walls of a large chamber. It was as if she had stumbled upon an old junkshop. There were bronze figurines, hearth-sized salvers and tall porcelain vases filled with flowers, but even a casual observer could see that these were just gaudy imitations. Even the flowers were artificial, and their once-vibrant colours had long since faded.

Behind this paraphernalia in the deeper shadows hung tapestries and wall hangings that every so often were dimly illuminated by brass lanterns, whose jewel-like windows threw out a feeble light from the glow-worms trapped within. Amidst all of this, the air was heavy with the pungent scent of blue dwarrow, an intoxicating herb that Shrew had come across before whilst negotiating the darker alleyways in the Duns.

"Hah, at last we get to meet the cause of your vexation, Malcaw!" The gravelly voice had come from the far side of the brazier. Shrew squinted. The rain had washed some of the dye from her hair and it had trickled into her eyes, making them sting.

"Let me flay the flesh from his back, Matron." The sickly voice was unmistakable, and Shrew shivered.

Her eyes were growing accustomed to the strange flickering light and she could see there were people just beyond the brazier. The largest reclined on a divan, whilst another stood hunched close by, like a vulture.

"Come closer, boy. I want to look at you more closely." It was the figure on the divan who had spoken to her first and who now ordered her to approach.

Shrew hesitated for a moment, but a push from behind set her moving forward. The guards had followed her inside, and now she felt surrounded. As she made her way slowly around the brazier, her eyes darted nervously left and right. There were others in the shadows and she thought she could see children amongst them. Then her eyes settled on the bulk of flesh and gaudy trappings that could only be the Matron. In the wavering light of the blue flame, she reminded Shrew of a picture of a Sea Harpy she had once seen. Straggling grey hair framed her corpulent features that glistened with beads of sweat. From head to toe she was bedecked with jewellery of every kind; yet, although it glittered and shone in the blue light, it looked as cheap as the rest of the junk that littered the chamber.

"I said closer, whelp!" The Matron's fleshy jowls tremored, as she spat out the words. Shrew winced as she was nudged closer. She could almost taste the woman's rancid breath and the stale odour of pipe-weed. She stood nervously as the Matron's dark beady eyes appraised her.

"Look at it, Malcaw!" Matron idly waved a podgy arm in Shrew's direction. "Pray tell me how this scrawny waif can be the son of a lord!"

Sounds of sniggering came from the shadows, and Malcaw fidgeted uncomfortably.

"And look, what foolishness is this? There's black stuff coming out of his hair!" With a speed that belied her size, Matron reached out and grabbed the front of Shrew's tunic, pulling her in close.

It happened so quickly that Shrew had no time to react. She gasped as the Matron pawed her body, and at last found the strength to kick out hard into the sagging paunch of her captor. It was enough for Matron to release her grip, and Shrew fell back, crying in pain. For a moment, she crouched and shut her eyes, expecting some form of retribution, but none came.

To the surprise of everyone, the Matron shook with laughter, and it was several seconds before the deep rattle in her massive chest subsided.

"Fools!" she bellowed. "You have all been deceived! This is a girl!"

It was Malcaw who spoke first and broke the stunned silence. Slowly and with menace, he pointed a long bony finger. His one eye gleamed balefully at Shrew.

"Let me take her now and give her a fitting end," he rasped, and looked towards Matron for an answer.

"Not now, Malcaw." Matron waved him to be silent. "I've seen how quickly you work, and I want answers from this one." She turned to look at Shrew, who was still crouched on the floor. "Who are you, girl? Speak up or I'll let Malcaw take you now!"

Shrew desperately wished she could disappear into one of the cracks between the floor stones, but there was no escape. The chamber was suddenly quiet except for the crackling flame and the distant sound of the rain. "My name is Shrew," she whispered.

There were murmurs in the room. It seemed that some had heard of the name before.

"Silence!" Matron boomed angrily. "She is a guttersnipe. Filth from the gutters, and that is all." She turned to look at Malcaw with a sneer creasing her face. "And to think you were foolish enough to believe this brat's tale! Your greed deceived you!"

Malcaw opened his mouth as if to speak, but voices were suddenly raised from the shadows and one called out loudly, "What if she is a spy? She was brought in with the South Gate Watch, but no one knows where she came from."

It fell quiet again as the impact of those words sank in. Matron sighed and rested her podgy arms on her knees.

"Listen!" she hissed. "If you listen, you will hear that it is still raining hard outside."

Shrew slowly raised her head. It seemed everyone was listening to the storm.

"You all know what happens when it rains this hard," Matron continued. "There will be floods and the Clerk of the Middern Gate will send one of his cronies to visit us." There were a few chuckles at her words.

"This whelp" — Matron pointed at Shrew and grinned, showing the brown stumps of her rotting teeth — "this whelp will be our sewer rat tomorrow, and if perchance she somehow survives... I will let you decide what to do with her, Malcaw."

There seemed to be general murmurs of approval in the room, particularly from some of the guards who had brought her in. Shrew looked up at Malcaw and noticed he was staring back at her. His gaunt features seemed to radiate a joyous malevolence!

"Take her away," Matron ordered, "and lock her in a topside cage 'til she's needed tomorrow."

The violent reverberations of the storm had ceased, but the rain fell heavily, long into the night. Shrew shivered and hugged herself, trying to keep warm. They had placed a manacle on her ankle and chained her within a square cage that had two boarded sides and two filled with vertical bars that did little to protect her from the wind and rain. The roof and floor were also made of wooden boards, and Shrew huddled in some straw that had piled up furthest away from the bars. She was tired and hungry. The pain in her empty stomach was nearly as bad as the burning pain from where the crossbow bolt had singed her neck. Although she tried, she couldn't sleep. So she peered out into the darkness of the yard and puzzled over what had happened that day. First, she thought of her encounter with Waylan again. How did he know her name, and was it chance that had placed him on the battlements? He had saved her life, but why? Then she thought of her jump off the wall. She remembered reaching out for a branch high up in the crown of a tree, and she was sure she had managed to grasp it; but after that everything blurred, and the next thing she could recall was waking up in the cart. She turned these events over and over in her mind and each time it ended with the cart in the storm. All of a sudden, she felt lonelier than she had ever felt before and her eyes filled with salty tears. She wept bitterly. Eventually, the rain stopped, and as the first light of dawn touched the ragged clouds on the far eastern horizon, she finally succumbed to sleep.

Something woke her suddenly. It could have been the shaft of sunlight that cut between the bars of her cage and softly lit her tear-stained face, or it could have been a sound nearby.

"Pssst!" The sound came again. She turned and saw a youth squatting down beside her cage. She immediately recognised the sandy hair and the grimy features of her former cell-mate. It was Wilf, and he was forcing a chunk of bread towards her through the bars.

"Here, take it, quick!" he whispered, casting his eyes nervously about. "I'm on an errand and will soon be missed."

Shrew reached out and grasped the bread thankfully. "Thanks," she uttered hoarsely, and immediately started to devour it ravenously. By the time she looked up, Wilf had gone.

The yard didn't stay deserted for long. Within minutes of Wilf's departure, she heard a shout and a group of boys, flanked by two leather-clad youths, jogged past her cage with polekerns on their shoulders. Soon afterwards, more children and their minders appeared. Braziers were lit and forges that had smouldered all night were stoked and fed with coals as the workhouse slowly came to life. The dry smoke that entered her cage reminded Shrew of her thirst, and she eyed the bowl of rainwater just outside her cage. It was within easy reach and she shuffled her way towards it; but, before she could reach through the bars to grasp the bowl, a heavy iron-shod boot kicked it aside, spilling its contents.

"You'll get water soon enough, little-un." Shrew looked up into the ogre-like features of the guard known as Rolkar. He was grinning inanely as he fingered a hoop of keys. "All the water you'll ever need!" The brute's face split into a wider grin and he chuckled.

Malcaw then stepped into view from behind the guard. His gaunt face peered lecherously into the cage and he whispered under his breath, "You're going on an outing now to please the Matron's wishes. When your work is done, we'll have the time to get to know each other a lot better!" The coldness in Malcaw's words sent shivers down her spine and she backed away into the far corner of the cage.

Rolkar was still grinning as he unlocked and released the clasp holding the cage door shut. The rusty hinges squealed in protest as he pulled it open and then, with a speed that belied his bulk, he reached in and freed the chain that was attached to the manacle on her right foot.

Shrew had no strength to resist when the brute's heavy hand grasped her and pulled her from her prison. She was hauled to her feet under the clear blue morning sky and pushed to a line of children who had assembled by the gatehouse. There, another chain was attached to her manacle and shortly afterwards she found herself in the back of a wagon with two older boys, who were dressed in the beige sackcloth that she had seen when she had first entered the workhouse.

Minutes later, the wagon was trundling down the cobbled descent to the Middern Rise. As its rickety boards shook and threw the wagon's occupants back and forth, Shrew looked up and noticed Malcaw was riding with the teamster up front. The boys sat opposite her, each flanked by well-armed guards wearing full leather armour. Rolkar sat on her right, nearest to the tailgate, and hummed discordantly as he played with his keys.

Shrew's head ached and each time the wagon jolted, or Rolkar's tune entered a high pitch, she winced and closed her eyes in a futile attempt to stop the pain. She ran her dry tongue over her cracked lips. There was water gushing from the drains beside the road, but there was nothing for her to drink to quench her nagging thirst.

When the wagon reached the junction with the crowded Middern Rise, it was met by a small party of city officials and soldiers. Shrew hardly noticed the boys being taken off. She was barely conscious when the wagon lurched forward and turned left into the busy thoroughfare.

It was Rolkar who brought her fully awake with a hard jab to her ribs. The wagon was passing under an old weather-beaten arch known as the Lichgate.

"No napping!" he barked gruffly. "We're nearly there."

Shrew raised her head and looked up with squinting eyes. They had entered a small square enclosed by buildings on all sides. Shrew immediately recognised the column and arched façade of the Shrine of Tommas the Lame. It fully occupied the southern side of the square. Beyond the impressive central arch, adorned with writhing stone serpents and twisted vines, a short passage led to the Almshouses of the poor and less fortunate of Low Reach. Even Shrew knew this was a sham, as very few of the occupants of these dwellings were really poor. Here lived the beggars and conmen who had the coin to bribe the Low Reach's governing council, an elitist body of rich traders and pompous officials that included figures such as the Clerk of Middern Gate and the Consul

General of the Foreign Quarter. The genuine poor lived in the Duns and the south side of the Labour Quarter, and everyone knew it!

The wagon had slowed and the teamster was calling. Water was gushing from a drain on the eastern side of the square and was forming a small lake that threatened to expand into the shopfronts and the passage to the Shrine and courtyard beyond. The wagon skirted the flood and was met by a small group of men that, from their attire, seemed to be mainly local traders and municipal workers, common labourers hired by the council for city repairs and maintenance.

Shrew watched with indifference as the wagon pulled to a halt and a spokesman for the group stepped forward to address Malcaw.

"You've come just in time. The water will soon be in the crypts. We need to quickly locate the blockage from the lower drain." The spokesperson clearly held some rank and was probably a foreman of some kind. Shrew eyed him suspiciously as he pointed to an arched recess in the wall of the Shrine at the south-western end of the square, where the water hadn't yet reached.

Malcaw had dismounted from his seat and turned towards the rear of the wagon. "Rolkar!" he commanded. "Prepare our rat for entry!"

Shrew suddenly noticed that everyone was staring at her: the guards in the wagon and the small crowd of workers and tradesmen. Rolkar rose to his feet and tugged on Shrew's leg chain. "Shift yer butt then. You're going down a hole!"

Little preparation seemed to be required. Barely a minute later, Shrew found herself being escorted to the arched recess of the lower drain by Rolkar and the two other guards who had ridden in the wagon. A new chain had been attached to the manacle around her ankle. This chain was lighter and longer, and Rolkar carried most of it looped over his shoulder.

Shrew felt as if she was walking to her execution. Her craving thirst and her aching head and body seemed distant and unimportant now. Whatever happens, she thought, nothing could be as bad as that which Malcaw had promised for her later.

As they approached the drain, Shrew's spirits lifted slightly. Below the arch and within the recess immediately above the drain sprouted a stone effigy that looked like a yawning cat. Its mouth issued a steady stream of clear water.

Malcaw's tall rake-like body was bent over the drain, as if he was attempting to peer into its depths. Beside him the foreman appeared to be uttering instructions. He waved his hands in an animated fashion and then paused as Shrew arrived.

"Is your boy ready?" The foreman nodded in her direction.

"It's a girl," Malcaw answered. "You'll find she's just the right size."

As Shrew stared mesmerised at the water that poured from the yawning cat, the two guards who had followed her stepped forward and proceeded to pull up the rusted grill that covered the drain. Soon, a small crowd had gathered around them as the shopkeepers and labourers wandered over.

The foreman looked down imperiously at Shrew. "It's a simple task," he said briskly. "You will be lowered into the drain shaft. When you get to the bottom, you will find yourself in a tunnel. Go upward in this direction." The foreman pointed in the direction of the flood that was pooling on the other side of the square. "We think you'll find some debris blocking the opening of the other drain shaft where it meets the main tunnel. Your job is to dislodge or break it up so the water can get through."

A bystander called out sarcastically, "If she clears it completely, she'll surely drown in the surge, unless your men can pull her out quick!"

The foreman dismissed the caller with a wave of his hand, but Malcaw only grinned and focussed his one eye on Shrew. "You have your instruction," he rasped. "You will be given a lantern and an awl. Just mind you don't get too wet." He chuckled and, as an afterthought, added, "We have you on this chain. Scream and we'll pull you up. I don't want anything to happen to you before our meeting tonight!"

Rolkar stepped forward and handed Shrew a small jar sealed with wax on a loop of cord. The bright sunlight made it difficult to see the faint green glimmer that emanated from within the thick glass. She looped it over her shoulder and accepted the awl he offered. The awl was no more than a short wooden pole whose end was made of hollowed brass which split into a sharp point and a curving barb. Thus equipped, Shrew stepped down into the recess around the circular opening of the drain shaft and sat for a moment on its rim. Turning her head, she managed to catch some of the falling water from the fountain in her mouth. For a few seconds she gulped the water that cascaded off her tongue, until Malcaw nudged her hard with his boot.

"Move!" he spat viciously. "We haven't got all day!"

The circular opening of the drain shaft was barely two feet across and she could see it descended on an incline. As she lowered herself into it, her heels made contact with its slick sides, but she soon felt stone protrusions that could control her descent. Turning around, she descended on her stomach, using the protruding stones as steps. The world above was no more than a blue circle now, framing the heads of Malcaw and the foreman. She was descending into a stygian darkness. From her side, the feeble light of the glow-worms in her lantern bathed the damp mossy wall of the shaft in a pale olive-green. The air was damp and musty, but not unpleasant; from below came the sound of rushing water. She had climbed down about a dozen of the protruding stones when she became aware of the shaft widening and the incline getting steeper. The glow of her lantern revealed a rusting iron handrail set into the wall and she grasped it to steady herself. Looking down, she could see a glistening platform of stone. As she lowered herself on to it, something moved quickly into her circle of green light and then disappeared into the darkness. It was a rat. Shrew wrinkled her nose. One or two rats didn't bother her, but a large number of them could prove troublesome, or even dangerous. A voice called down the shaft from above, but she ignored it. She could see she was now standing in the main sewer tunnel. Holding the awl in one hand and raising the lantern with the other, she could see that the platform she stood on was slightly higher than the flowing water, which moved swiftly past her in a channel at her feet. There was a similar platform or walkway a few feet away, on the other side of the water. Turning around, she noticed that the shaft she had descended entered the main tunnel quite high up and that the water trickling down it followed a well-worn course down the centre of the shaft, before spilling on to the platform and into the torrent.

Looking up, she called up the shaft. She could no longer see the far opening, but knew her words would carry above the sounds of water behind her.

"I'm in the main tunnel!" she cried. As if in answer, she felt the chain slacken on her right foot.

Raising the lantern again, she peered upstream and cautiously started to move along the walkway that hugged the right wall of the tunnel. The viridescent glow from her small lantern could reach no more than a few paces, so her progress was slow. After a few yards, she was forced to duck under a pair of arches that spanned the width of the passage. Between the arches she noticed a few rats busy on the opposite platform, where a drain disgorged its contents in an arc into the main stream. This drain didn't appear blocked. She paused and sniffed the air. There was now an unpleasant odour in the tunnel. She ignored it and carried on until something that looked like a large bundle of rags emerged out of the gloom on her side of the tunnel. This looks odd, she thought to herself, and after hesitating a moment, thrust her awl forward, using it like a short spear. Then she edged forward nervously. Almost immediately, she knew that this was the cause of the blockage. A sodden pile of debris covered the platform ahead and half-filled the central channel, causing the water to splash and swirl around it. There was another drain opening here, but it was lower than the others and was choked with something that looked like a sickly yellow slime. Shrew retched; there was a terrible stench in the air. As she waved her lantern before her, she could see, amidst some maroon-coloured rags, a white bone protruding. She gasped and took a step back. Something else had caught her eye. Near to the bone, something reflected the light of her lantern. Now she was curious. Fighting the need to retch again and keeping the awl in front of her, she moved slowly forward for a closer look. It appeared to be the curved end of something metallic. Using the barb on the end of her awl, she managed to hook it and pulled. It took all her strength, for it seemed to be stuck in some strange kind of sticky ooze, but suddenly it emerged from the pile and fell to the stone platform before her. Another gasp escaped her lips as she recognised the shape and form of a dagger!

Still holding the awl, she carefully placed the lantern next to the dagger so she could see it better. It was not in a scabbard. The reflection she had seen had been from the pronged metallic guard, not the blade. Shrew looked closer. The blade defied description. It reminded her of a long tapering leaf, like those she had seen growing on the ancient willow tree that grew in the centre of Low Reach's Foreign Quarter; it certainly didn't appear to be made of metal or steel like other daggers.

A noise suddenly distracted her. It was like a sucking sound and it was close by! She quickly picked up her lantern and her small hand squeezed the brass shaft of the awl tight. It must be rats, she thought. Maybe there's a giant one nesting in these rags. Then she heard voices calling. They echoed from down the tunnel behind her and they reminded her of the task that she had been sent to do. The dagger would probably help, she thought. Placing the lantern back on the stone before her, she reached down and picked the dagger up by the hilt.

"Sirra's breath!" The oath was almost inaudible. She froze, partly in fear and partly by surprise. Everything appeared to be changing. A new light seemed to have blossomed all about her, illuminating the outline of the tunnel in reddish hues so she could see much further into the darkness! Her mouth opened and her eyes widened in astonishment. Then she turned to look at the rags and debris before her and screamed in horror. Something writhed within! The ethereal glow that now permeated the darkness outlined the translucent folds of a living nightmare that roiled within a mass of fatty ooze that seemed to bind the rags and sewer debris together.

Shrew shrieked and hurled the awl into the heaving mass that seemed to be spreading out towards her! As if in response, a sound rang out that was so high-pitched it was barely audible, but for a brief moment it numbed her hearing. Dark water suddenly erupted and spurted violently in all directions, as the monstrosity moved free from the drain it was blocking.

In panic, she turned to flee, kicking the lantern into the surge of water that now rose and swirled about her ankles. Its green glow disappeared and was swept away in the torrent, but darkness didn't close in around her. The sewer glowed red as if bathed in blood.

The tunnel stretched before her like a bloody maw! She could see where she had entered the sewers, but managed only a few strides before the chain attached to her ankle pulled taut and took her right foot from under her. She slipped and fell backwards into the cold murky water that was now swirling over the platforms along the tunnel sides.

Like a drowning man clutching a straw, she gripped the dagger with her left hand and desperately clawed the water with her right, as she was dragged along half-submerged. Malcaw and the others were pulling her up! She tried to scream, but suddenly water engulfed her and she found herself being pulled into the deep channel in the middle of the tunnel. She would surely drown before they pulled her out, or the thing behind her would catch up with her and envelop her in its sticky folds! She managed to gulp a last mouthful of damp, fetid air as the water rose over her and bubbles flashed past her eyes. She prayed to Latia for salvation, but if this was to be her death, surely it would be a better way than by the hand of Malcaw and his thugs!

While her thoughts were thus engaged, she was unaware that her left hand had subconsciously moved the dagger to her right. A pocket of turbulence hit her and the chain slackened for an instant, enabling her to grasp it with her free hand. Then the chain pulled taut again and she nearly lost her grip as she was dragged under the water again. A voice in her head screamed at her to cut the chain. Without a second thought, her right hand, swung round and the dark blade of the dagger passed cleanly through the linked steel, severing it completely! A second later her head broke the surface and she took a gulp of air. She was still in the tunnel, but had passed the drain shaft that she had descended. There was little she could do but keep her head above the water and ride the flow. Her journey didn't last long. The tunnel ended abruptly. Its waters spilled out of the wall of a large circular chamber and plummeted in a waterfall into a deep pool. For a brief moment she found herself falling through space, before hitting the cold murky water below.

As she rose spluttering to the surface, she collected her wits and looked around her. There were stepped ledges at the edges of the chamber and it didn't take her long to drag her wet form on to a stone platform that ringed the pool. For several minutes she lay on her back panting, and stared up at the water cascading from the hole in the wall from which she had just fallen. The sound of the water as it hit the pool echoed throughout the confines of the chamber. As her eyes stared transfixed on the hole above, she fancied she could hear her heart beat. It was pounding in her chest after her exertions in the water. After a short while, the thunderous noise of the water lessened and the cascade became a steady flow. Shrew sighed and gave thanks to her goddess, Latia. She was still alive and no longer burdened by the chain that had tethered her. A wave of exhilaration surged through her as she suddenly realised, she was free!

CHAPTER SEVEN
UNDER THE CITY

For the first time in many hours, Shrew allowed herself to smile. She had no idea what to do next, but the exhilaration she felt at thwarting Malcaw's wicked plans and of escaping incarceration in the workhouse was overpowering. Thoughts of Malcaw brought her attention back to the tunnel opening above. Would he send someone down after her? Maybe she would see their green lanterns in the darkness? She sat up and peered nervously at the dark hole high up in the far wall. Its circular rim seemed bathed in crimson. She had lost her lantern. How was it she could still see? She cast her mind back and looked to her right hand that still clutched the dagger. Then she remembered the voice in her head and how easily its blade had cut through the steel links of the chain. Carefully and with some respect, she placed the dagger down on the stone by her side and removed her fingers slowly from its hilt. It was as if a dark shroud had suddenly enveloped her. She stifled a cry of shock. It had become pitch black. It was as if she had suddenly become blinded. Her fingers made contact with the dagger once more and, as she grasped it, her strange vision returned!

"Sirra's breath!" she cried out in astonishment. "It lets you see in the dark!"

She held it closer, but the dagger's gift of deep-sight would reveal no further secrets of itself. The blade appeared dark and featureless, and the metal guard and hilt also looked plain and unremarkable.

Shrew's thoughts flashed back to her encounter with the foul abomination that had blocked the drain. She tightened her grip on the dagger nervously. Maybe it had found its way into the pool, too! It was time to move on. But where to? Looking around, she noticed there were a number of dark openings that led from the chamber. Two were accessible from the ledge on which she sat, and she could see two more that could be reached by a narrow stone stair that wound upward against the curving wall. Water flowed or trickled from each opening to spill into the dark pool below the ledge. Shrew guessed that all were similar to the one she had just vacated. She thought for a moment. The sensible choice was to take one of the higher outlets, but not the one from which she had just fallen. It had to be the other. She rose to her feet, shivering. Her clothes were wet through and as she made to move to the stair, she noticed the manacle on her right ankle and the remnants of the chain. She paused for a moment — if the dagger had cut through the chain, then maybe — without further thought, she bent down and held the edge of the dagger's blade to the iron band encircling her ankle. It bit easily into the metal and as she applied pressure it cut through the iron like a hot knife through butter! She gasped. The blade clearly had powerful magic in it! No ordinary dagger could do such a thing! A few more cuts and the manacle fell apart. She picked the ruined implement up in her free hand and then disdainfully threw it into the pool. Only now, with the last vestige of the workhouse gone, did she truly feel free!

It didn't take long to mount the stair and reach the sewer opening she had spied from the ledge below. A few rats scurried out of her path as she stepped up on to the walkway inside the tunnel. It was similar to the previous one in that it had a walkway either side of a central channel which carried the run-off, although Shrew noticed that this one carried very little water.

Holding the dagger before her, she moved cautiously forward on the right-hand walkway. Her new-found sight allowed her to clearly see at least ten yards into the tunnel, but beyond that the rose-tinted outlines of its brickwork and curving arches quickly became blurred and merged into darkness. The tunnel curved to the left and ascended slightly. Shrew's eyes darted left and right. She was searching for signs of a drain shaft similar to the one she had descended. She passed several smaller drains that emptied mere trickles of water from moss-clad orifices half-way up the side of the wall, but these were barely a hand's length in diameter.

A few yards further on, the tunnel turned sharply to the left and Shrew approached the bend with caution. The encounter with the hideous creature in the other tunnel was still fresh in her mind. She decided to approach the bend from the left side and nimbly leapt across the channel to the other walkway. As she crept slowly around the corner, she breathed a sigh of relief. Less than ten yards ahead, on the left side, there appeared to be a major drain shaft entering the tunnel; she could make out the outline of a handrail leading upward, but there was something else that caught her attention. It was the opposite wall; a part of it seemed to reflect a different light from the rest. Shrew tried to focus on the shimmering brickwork. There was a pale violet glow in the midst of it all. Her curiosity overcame her fears. Several rats scattered left and right as she leapt back across the channel to examine the wall more closely. The glow came from a symbol that appeared to be scrawled on one of the bricks. It was almost level with her head and, as she moved closer, she fancied it looked like the outline of a hand. A voice inside her was telling her to place her hand against it. She hesitated for a moment, but before she had time to contemplate the situation, she had unwittingly placed her hand within the symbol. Almost at once she heard a faint sound like a click! Startled, Shrew quickly withdrew her hand just as a rectangular section of the wall swung silently inward and she nearly toppled backwards into the channel behind her!

When she had recovered, she cautiously peered into the opening that had just appeared in the tunnel wall. The deep-sight bestowed by her dagger revealed a short passage a few yards long which led into a large chamber. She realised at once that she had stumbled on a secret place and was intrigued. Who put this here? She hesitated for a moment. A voice inside her head was urging her to step forward and see what was inside. "Sirra's breath!" she cursed quietly under her breath. Since the moment she had picked up the dagger, all kinds of new thoughts had entered her head. Looking suspiciously at the dull blade in her hand, she stepped into the passage.

Shrew's eyes widened and a faint whistle escaped through her lips. The chamber looked like the inside of a small chapel she had once visited, although the altar appeared to be in the centre of the room rather than against one of the walls. No holy symbol or other trappings adorned the altar; indeed, it appeared no more than a raised stone plinth with intricate sculptures carved around its sides. Looking around, she could see that similarly sculptured brickwork rose from the four corners of the chamber to meet at the apex of a domed ceiling high above her head.

For a few seconds, she stood motionless. The deep-sight seemed to bring the sculptures alive. They looked like entwining serpents whose scaly bodies shimmered and writhed in a rose opalescence. Another thought entered her head. This place was very old, maybe far older than the sewer she had just left. It was then she noticed something out of place, over in the far right-hand corner.

Gritting her teeth, Shrew crept cautiously forward and skirted the altar to get a better view. It was a small table and beside it was a low cot covered in a pallet of straw. There was also what appeared to be an oil lamp on the table and a small bag neatly placed underneath it. To the left was a door inset within a low arch. There was another way out!

She took another step forward and a faint clicking sound from behind spun her round. The door to the sewer had closed! She swiftly returned the way she had come in panic, but quickly noticed that although the door had closed, there appeared to be a lever set into a recess within the short passage leading up to it. For a minute or two she examined the lever with her deep-sight. It must trigger the door mechanism, she thought, because there was no glowing hand-shaped mark on this side of the secret door. With some trepidation, she curled the fingers of her free hand around the lever and with ease drew it downward. The faintest of sounds came from within the wall, followed by an audible click, and the door swung inward, revealing the sewer tunnel beyond. Shrew allowed herself a smile and then waited. A short time later, the door closed with a faint click.

Satisfied that she could leave the chamber, she returned to the table and the cot with the pallet of straw. These were clearly new additions to this ancient room, and she wondered who could have put them there and for what purpose. She felt weary and rubbed her sore neck. Maybe she should rest here for a short time. She had not slept properly for days. With a sigh, she lowered herself on to the pallet and as she did so her eyes again caught sight of the bag under the table. She reached out with her free hand and pulled the bag onto her lap. Soon, she was searching inside it.

The first item she found was a small leather pouch that appeared to contain a long taper, some dry tinder and a flint striker. Her deep-sight didn't always show things as expected. It would be good to see things as they really were, and so she immediately set to work to light the oil lamp on the table. Soon, a yellow light was burning in the corner of the chamber that immediately banished her deep-sight. The shimmering serpents on the altar no longer appeared to move, but were transfixed, petrified in the stone of their makers. Shrew slowly rose from her pallet and looked closely. The top of the altar was covered in dust and the remains of what was once a casket. She spied fragments of bone amidst the debris and felt herself involuntarily shiver. This was no temple. She was inside a tomb!

For a few minutes she examined the rest of the chamber, but found nothing more than a couple of urns in the far corner whose contents had long since dried to dust. Having satisfied herself that nothing lurked in the shadows, other than a few small black spiders, she returned to the cot to examine the remaining contents of the bag. Soon she had a number of items laid out before her. She had placed the dagger beside them, for the light from the lamp was more than sufficient for her needs.

Shrew was ecstatic. It was as if she had found a treasure chest! There before her lay three glass vials containing viscous-looking fluids, a wineskin that felt half full, a goatskin purse containing five silver florins — a fortune for a poor waif such as her — and finally a number of small blocks of a brown substance wrapped in some kind of oily leaf. She held the brown substance to her nose — it smelt good! Suddenly her hunger returned, and she bit the corner of one of the blocks and tasted it. It appeared to be some kind of dried meat. She bit off a larger morsel. It was delicious! Soon she had dispatched two of the blocks and had removed the stopper on the wineskin. Only after she had gulped a long draught of the watery wine and eaten yet another of the blocks of meat did she pause and wonder who had left all of these things in such a place and when might they return? She didn't ponder these questions for long; a great weariness had overcome her. She grasped hold of her dagger and lay back on the straw and promised herself that she would only take a quick nap before returning to the sewer to seek a way out. After all, she didn't want the owner of these treasures returning whilst she was still here! Within a minute she had fallen into a deep sleep.

She was back in the great marble hall before the hearth fire and the table laden with food, but now the scene shifted its focus and she became aware of a young woman sitting beside her who looked on her with kindly eyes. Her companion smiled at her and for a brief moment she felt a deep love; but now her heartbeat gathered pace as darkness closed in and her familiar nightmare began to unfold. This time, it didn't last long. Unexpectedly, a bright light grew in the darkness, like a turquoise sun. It wavered, and a slim, curvaceous figure, clad in armour which hugged her body with silvery scales like those of a fish, stepped out of the light. She had long, flowing hair the colour of lavender; pale olive skin covered her exquisite features. Shrew felt this strange woman's bright green almond eyes settle upon her. Then this strange being spoke. Her tone was assertive yet also soft, alluring and compelling.

"I have journeyed with you through your dreams, child. The wickedness is delightful and you..." The voice paused. "You are so strong. You are different to the others. We will help each other, you and I."

The turquoise light faded and the strange woman's face dimmed, as if it had become masked by smoke.

Shrew awoke coughing. The lamp was flickering as it burned the last of its oil and the air in the chamber was acrid and suffocating. As her head cleared, she remembered where she was. For a moment she felt panic. Then she noticed the dagger in her hand. How long had she slept like this? She chided herself for sleeping so long and rose swiftly from her straw bed. The last vestiges of the dream were still loitering inside her head and it felt like the voice was still there, somewhere deep within the dark recesses of her mind.

She thrust the dagger into her belt and rubbed her eyes. The magical dagger was real enough and not a fancy of her dreams; neither were the contents of the bag, she noticed with relief.

Getting to her feet, she decided to keep the purse and put the other items back into the bag. This she did carefully and methodically. Soon she had placed the bag back under the table and had tied the purse to her leather shoestring belt. Stepping back from the cot, she took stock of herself. She had lost her sandals and her small bag, along with its precious contents, but she smiled when she realised that she had replaced the lost two mites with five silver florins, a sum more than a hundred times greater! Moreover, she had replaced her blunt knife with a magical dagger that she was sure was worth a king's ransom! More than all of this, though, she reminded herself that she was free and, despite everything that had happened over the last few days, was richer, not only in terms of treasure, but in what she had learnt. Yet before she could truly celebrate, she reminded herself that she must find a way out from this underworld and get back to the world above. She would return, though, and promised herself that when she did, she would see what lay behind the other door.

She snuffed out the lamplight and drew forth the dagger. Soon she was past the secret door and inside the sewer once more. She had to smile. The musty air in the sewer seemed almost fragrant compared to the stifling atmosphere in the old chamber. The deep-sight bestowed on her by the dagger clearly showed that there was a major drain shaft just a short distance from the secret door. She could see the outline of a handrail leading upwards, and there appeared to be a stair. This may be no coincidence, she thought. She approached cautiously and quickly discovered that this shaft was even wider than the one she had first descended. Ancient moss carpeted its walls like verdigris, and even the rose-like shimmer of the deep-sight couldn't mask its bluish-green hues. This shaft rose in a curve to the right, and a worn stair, slick with moisture, hugged the left side. Soon Shrew was climbing the stair that spiralled upwards. To her left hand the rusty handrail provided useful support, whilst to her right, within a deep channel beside the stair, stagnant water trickled over a bed of rotting leaves into the sewer below. A few moments later the stair levelled and she faced a semi-circular opening, filled with a door grill of iron bars, which appeared to prevent further progress. A dim light diffused through the bars, so Shrew slipped the dagger into her belt and, as her natural sight returned, tears from an overwhelming feeling of relief welled up in her eyes. Beyond the grill she could see walls on either side, but beyond their eaves, like sparkling diamonds on a velvet screen, she could see the summer stars and the horned crescent moon. She had reached the surface!

The door was no more than half her height, but it silently swung outwards when she stooped and put her weight to it. A moment later she stepped into an alleyway.

Shrew was used to hugging the shadows. Her capacity to seemingly disappear or blend into the background was instinctive. So, as she emerged into the alley, she glided silently into a shallow recess below two columns that abutted a wall. The crescent moon seemed bright and, until she was sure where she was, she wanted to stay out of sight. Nearby, the moonlight highlighted a weatherworn façade which was punctuated with a row of open archways that appeared to lead to an orchard garden. Trailing vines of jasmine climbed and crossed the archways, whilst the fragrant scent of its tiny white flowers hung heavy in the air. The scent, the tree gardens and the imposing architecture of the walls and buildings suddenly became familiar to her. She quickly realised she was in the grounds of Ahlune's Abbey, one of the oldest buildings in the Low Reach and the residence of the druid priests that worshipped Ahlune, the goddess of forests.

Somewhere far off, a distant bell chimed twice, marking the beginning of the last watch, a period of time just before dawn. Shrew smiled and crept forward. On this occasion, this was the perfect time to make her way back to her hide in the Duns. Normally, she preferred not to travel at night, a habit she had acquired from living in a place where darkness brought forth many a ne'er-do-well and where death stalked the shadows for little more than a few bronze mites. Tonight, however, she would risk the journey. She knew her way in and out of the Duns better than most. She was also better than most at remaining hidden from sight and becoming seemingly invisible; so much so that, when she emerged from the shadows of the Abbey gatehouse, she crossed the main thoroughfare of South Street completely unseen by the gate guards and the few folk who still journeyed abroad at this late hour.

South Street led down the hill in the direction of Fountain Square and offered a quicker way back to her part of the Duns; but such a route would be patrolled by the City Watch. For a moment she thought again of Waylan. There was an old Sillaesian saying that warned, "Never trust a smiling guard". There was certainly something odd about that man. Without another thought on the matter, she crossed into an alley and left the lamp-lit thoroughfare behind her, preferring to take a shadier path back to her hide.

She hugged the darkness of the narrow streets and soon entered Cheap Street, which bordered the northern-most fringe of the Duns. Sounds seemed to carry further at such an hour. The rolling dice, tumbling across an ironwood table, sounded stark against the muffled cries of the gamblers; a gasp of ecstasy from a nearby pleasure house fell clearly upon her ears. There were people about, tarrying on street corners or hurrying to some destination, but she always saw them first and avoided them. When she entered the narrow confines of Cutlers Row, however, something felt wrong. Suddenly, it was too quiet. She froze and slowly pulled the dagger from her belt. Immediately, the deep-sight returned and the narrow-rutted street and leaning houses blossomed in crimson hues. Now she could see behind the shadows under every lintel and inside the mouth of every alley. Her eyes focussed on three human-like forms huddled in a doorway, barely a stone's throw away. Their attention seemed elsewhere and they hadn't noticed her. Shrew had to suppress a grin. She had seen this behaviour before; they were waiting for someone, probably some drunken fop who had been lured into a house by promises from a harlot. She moved forward and padded past them so close she could hear them breathe and smell the reek of pipe-weed on their sordid garments.

The faint hint of dawn tinged the eastern sky when she finally reached Gifford's Street and the region of the Duns she knew so well. As she climbed the wall into the back yard of the Three-legged Dog Tavern, the distant sound of a cock crowing sailed through the cool air from the direction of the South Gate. Jumping nimbly into the yard, she thought the place looked untidier than before. Even in the poor light she could see that the rotting door on the old outhouse on the east side of the yard now hung precariously on a broken hinge. Then she noticed the lid of the old ale barrel that had once covered the entrance to her hideout was lying broken at her feet. She drew the dagger once more and the yard sprung into stark relief as her brain adjusted to the deep-sight. A voice whispered deep inside her ahead. It sounded like the woman in her dreams, and it was the same voice that had commanded her to place her hand against the strange symbol on the sewer wall. This time it seemed to be telling her to hide and stay alert. She crouched low and peered behind the outhouse. The opening to her hideout was clearly exposed, and she noticed that some old clothes and other simple possessions she had hidden there had been strewn about. She moved closer to the opening, and the acrid stench of urine wafted up, making her pull back in disgust.

"Poor little Mousling," she whispered, feeling the tears well up in her eyes. She held her breath and leaned forward to look down into the old cellar, but the voice returned inside her head and she withdrew quickly. Suddenly, a noise attracted her attention from the direction of the tavern and she slunk back into the shadow of the outhouse.

There were no further sounds, but Shrew stayed motionless. After a while she curled up and hugged her knees to stave off the chill. She was shivering, but didn't know whether it was out of fear, or the cold.

Gradually, the sky brightened, and as it did so, her deep-sight faded. She barely noticed the disappearing shadows as she wrestled with her thoughts. The voice was quiet now, but she could feel its presence; it seemed to be regarding her from within. With a look of suspicion in her eyes, she turned to look more closely at the long tapering blade in her hand. It appeared more like some kind of glass than metal and it seemed to change its colour as she swivelled it in her hand. One moment it was a deep silvery grey, like the amalgam she had seen once brimming in a crucible on an alchemy stall, the next moment it was almost black, like the volcanic glass eyes set into the dragon that spread its wings across the gable at the Brass Dragon tavern at the end of Cheap Street. She shivered and hugged herself tightly. Who had found her hideout? It had to be Cutter, or the dumpling called Boil. She cursed them under her breath. Who in the five-and-forty hells was Waylan? The curse settled on her tongue. He had appeared out of nowhere and saved her life. Then he had called her by her street name. He must have known all along she wasn't little Lord Flarion of Gloamril Hall! Another curse escaped her lips. Then who left the strange mark in the sewer and the bed and other things? She slowly shook her head and looked towards the opening leading to her former hideout. Shifting her body to relieve cramp, she thought about going inside and checking whether her precious wisp lamp had been spared, but deep inside her, the voice reprimanded her foolishness. She should remain alert; the cellar would be a trap. Tears trickled down her cheeks as she studied the rectangular opening, but then something caught her attention. A small brown mouse emerged from the neck of a broken wine bottle, where a tangle of vines trailed down to the ground from the back of the outhouse. "Mousling!" she whispered with delight. "They didn't find you!" She wiped her eyes and watched the mouse sniff the air and return to the safety of the bottle. "You have a new home, I see. You're a survivor just like me!" Shrew furrowed her brow. I need a new home, too, she thought. This place is no longer safe.

The sun had risen, but its light still hadn't found the yard. Shrew slowly rose with the dagger still in her hand. She had made a plan. First, she would buy some new clothes and something comfortable for her feet; then she would buy a breakfast that would compare with the lavish meals of her dreams! She decided she would make her way to the Foreign Quarter of the city and then, maybe on to the district known as Harbour Gate. It was far enough away from both the Duns and the workhouse, and now with silver in her new pouch she might be able to make a new start. She looked idly around the yard and spotted a ragged brown cloak caught amongst a tangle of prickle weed and purple toadflax. It was her spare cloak. Someone had tossed it out of her hide, but she was glad, as it would prove to be most useful, since she had lost her other cloak in the workhouse. She slipped the dagger into the leather boot lace tied about her waist and donned the cloak. It hid the weapon perfectly. It wouldn't be a good idea marching down Swine Street in broad daylight sporting such a trophy. She grinned. It would certainly catch attention!

There were three ways out of the tavern's back yard. Her preferred route was over the wall in the north-west corner and into the alley beyond. The other ways took her past the rear of the tavern, either through a side gate into an adjacent yard or down a narrow alley towards the front of the establishment and Swine Street. There were no sounds coming from the tavern, which was quite usual for the time of day, so she decided to take the most direct route to the street.

Wrapping her cloak about her, she padded cautiously towards the narrow alley that separated the tavern and the wall. Then she froze. A figure had stepped into the alley. She turned, deciding to climb the wall instead, but a lanky youth had just scrambled down into the yard, blocking her way. She recognised him immediately. It was Cutter! Turning again, she saw Stilts, the ignoble leader of the gang, emerge from the alley, closely followed by the rotund Boil, whilst another swarthy youth entered the yard through the side gate. They had planned this. She was trapped!

"You've nowhere to hide, Shrew." Stilts swaggered forward, a leer on his jaundiced features. "Now hand over the purse you stole from us and we might let you off with just a good kickin'."

Shrew backed away as he approached, but she could sense that Cutter was not far behind her. She was thinking quickly. "I'll give you the purse. I hid it for safety," she blurted, "but it's…" She paused. "It's not here."

Stilts's pock-marked features creased as an ugly grin spread across his face. In a sweep of his hand, he had pulled a needle-like stiletto from his boot. "Of course it's not, you little runt, but you're soon going to squeal and tell us where it is." He waved the weapon in Shrew's direction. "Besides, Sliver here always finds out the truth!"

Shrew moved a step back towards the wall. A sideways glance told her that Cutter had also pulled out a blade.

Boil let out a shrill laugh. "Look, she's shaking. She'll piss herself, just you see!"

The others hooted with laughter, but their jocularity ceased as Shrew thrust her left hand forward, clasping the pouch she had taken from the hidden chamber in the sewers.

"Here it is," she cried. "More money than you've ever seen. Take it!"

Realisation slowly dawned on Cutter's face as he recalled the apple in the alleyway, but he was too slow to bark a warning.

Stilts reached forward to snatch the pouch, but in the blink of an eye it had been replaced by a blur of silver destruction, which sliced cleanly through his wrist, hurling his severed hand into the wall in a spray of dark blood.

The surprise on Stilts's face changed to a look of horror. His thin blade dropped from his other hand, as he wailed in agony. Then, in desperation, he tried to stem the blood that squirted from the open veins in his severed wrist.

Shrew felt a wave of euphoria course through her body. Her new dagger was in her hand, red and bloodied, and the voice inside her head sang and exalted at the taste of blood. It had been a long time since it had last tasted blood, and loud noises filled her head as it yearned for more. A malevolent light filled Shrew's eyes as she turned on Cutter.

The lanky youth held up his dagger in a meagre defence as Shrew's blade arced in his direction. It was with effort that she bent the dagger to her will, for it seemed to have made up its own mind where to strike. Filaments of light crackled down its grey length as it cut through Cutter's blade, slicing it in two. Shrew felt another wave of pleasure and she found herself exulting with the blade and whooping with delight.

There was now pandemonium in the yard. Stilts's howls had broken the slumber of the tavern's occupants and voices shouted in alarm. Cutter stood frozen in shock, looking at the remains of his dagger, and then turned and bolted like a frightened rabbit back the way he had come.

Grasping the pouch, Shrew took off towards the alley. Only Boil stood in her way, but as he saw her approach, he turned in panic and collided with one of the tavern's patrons who had stepped into the yard to investigate the noise.

Shrew side-stepped them both and ran, quickly reaching Swine Street just as three more men burst out of the side entrance of the tavern into the alley behind her.

Swine Street was coming to life. A few traders were setting up stalls or opening window shutters, but they paused from their chores to watch the disturbance unfolding.

Shrew stopped suddenly in the middle of the street; there was a wild look in her eyes. The voice in her head was challenging her to go back and finish them all. She gritted her teeth and firmly quelled the thought, slipping the bloodstained blade back into her lace belt beneath her cloak. Voices rose loudly behind her, and it spurred her to run.

She took off westward and ran as fast as her legs would carry her. There were sounds of pursuit, but she daren't stop or turn her head to see who followed. Just ahead, the rutted road angled sharply to the right, as it descended the hill towards its meeting with Cheap Street. As soon as she rounded the bend, she ducked right into a narrow alley that ran under the shadows of two leaning buildings whose upper storeys seemed to merge. She was now in a warren of passageways and dead-ends, but she knew these like the back of her hand. Her heart was thumping in her chest, and eventually she slowed her pace. The sounds of pursuit had faded, but she could take no chances: from here she would make her way back to Ahlune's Abbey and to the relative safety of the sewers. No-one would look for her there, and then she could decide on her next move.

CHAPTER EIGHT
BEFORE THE KING

A flicker of contempt crossed Cyrus Col's dusky complexion as he looked up at the expansive vault that arched high above him. This was merely the ante-chamber to the throne room, yet it dwarfed his party and the palatine guards that had been sent to escort him. He loathed the sylvan and their fey kin. Countless millennia had passed since they raised this edifice high on the spine of the world and, although the architects were long gone, they still managed to infuse a sense of insignificance into his being. They had kept him waiting here over an hour, and now he was beginning to despise the Sillaesians as much as their predecessors. He turned to the Sillaesian officer standing beside him and opened his mouth to protest, but fell silent as the great adamantine doors at the far end of the chamber swung silently open.

The officer looked towards him imperiously. "The King will grant you an audience now."

Cyrus Col strode forward with his priestly retinue in tow. His robes shimmered deepest indigo and seemed to absorb the ghostly light from the amber wisp lamps that hung either side of the great doors. As he entered the throne room, he felt as if he had suddenly stepped outside. The pale blue dome, high above his head, gave the illusion that it was the sky, and a soft light filled the chamber. There were also clumps of trees and bright flowerbeds in islands of greenery that furthered the effect; yet there were also signs of great age and of a slow deterioration from a former glory. Before him, a marble walkway veined with pale green olivine and flanked by tall columns with the girth of ironwood trees led to a broad dais and the Sillaesian throne. Here, a crowd of many people, the noble classes of Highfall and their attendants, clustered around the King and his advisors.

As Cyrus Col approached, the crowd parted, creating a path to the foot of the dais.

The crack of the Seneschal's staff on the marble dais brought silence. Then a deep voice called out that echoed through the chamber.

"Highfall and his illustrious majesty King Wulfred of Sillaesia bids welcome to his most exalted reverence Cyrus Col of the Ancient Kingdom of Rathasia."

Cyrus Col took one further step forward and bowed his head. Then he looked up and focused his dark eyes on the grey-haired king, whose bulk filled the seat of the Sillaesian throne.

"I bring greetings, your majesty, from the imperial capital Merrandis, and from the high queen herself. We both thank you for this audience."

The chamber fell silent as the portly king eased his bulk forward on his seat and regarded the stranger to his realm. He studied the man closely, from the crown of black curly hair and the peculiar mark on his forehead, to the dark, shimmering robes. There was something unnerving about his presence.

"You have journeyed far, priest. To what do we owe for the pleasure of this visit?"

Cyrus Col's eyes travelled from the king to the young scrawny man with pale blond hair who sat to his right. This, he assumed, must be Prince Eustace, the heir apparent. Behind the youth stood a stern-faced man, dressed in intricately engraved armour, whose long, fiery hair lay in braids about his shoulders. So, this was the holy knight Aelmar, he mused, the subject of ballads of glory that had even reached far Merrandis. Finally, his eyes caught an ancient figure hunched in the shadow behind the throne. Their eyes met for a moment, but the gaze from the other was intense and never faltered. Cyrus Col suddenly felt uncomfortable and looked back towards the king.

"Your majesty, I have come to ask for a boon. One that might seem trivial to yourself, but that would greatly please the ancient gods, whose blessings still linger in this land. I have come to ask your majesty's permission to build a temple in their honour on the land above the river, in Everdim, to the south west of your city."

King Wulfred stroked his short-tapered beard and looked hard at the priest. There was a long silence, but before Cyrus Col could speak again, the figure behind the throne had stepped forward.

"Your majesty, if I may interrupt?" All turned to look at the bright-eyed old man, who straightened his ancient frame and then leaned indolently against his long, slender staff.

The king slowly nodded. "The audience is yours, Lord Miruvar. What have you to say?"

Miruvar smiled through his bushy white beard. "Thank you, your majesty." He turned and gestured towards the visitor. "Priest of Rathasia," he challenged, "I recognise from the mark on your forehead that you are a disciple of the Crimson Sect, a renegade brotherhood that worships the Master of Shades. Is that so?"

Cyrus Col appeared unmoved. "You speak of others, old man. I simply wish to raise a temple to the honour of Yngvi and Dysettis."

"To what end?" the king interrupted. "The old gods sleep; why disturb their slumber?"

"To receive their blessings, your majesty. The ruins of their temples lie broken and we wish to restore some of their splendour by building a new house of worship on the foundations of the old. Such blessings bring knowledge and foresight, as well as other benefits that gold cannot buy." Cyrus Col paused for a moment, and then added with a wry smile, "We have brought much gold with us, your majesty. We would pay handsomely for the privilege of building this temple."

The king's face creased with a curious smile. "Much gold, you say? Hear that, my subjects? This priest wants to buy my consent!"

There was some quiet laughter, but Cyrus Col merely bowed his head and smiled politely, before turning to signal to his entourage that stood a short distance behind him.

A silence fell as a group of robed, hooded figures stepped forward, pulling behind them a low cart, upon which rested a large casket decorated with silver filigree and blood-red garnets.

Cyrus Col turned to the king with the smile still frozen on his thin lips, and with a single gesture of his hand commanded the cart to halt.

The lid of the casket slowly opened and an audible gasp arose from the spectators as the treasures within were revealed.

King Wulfred leaned forward to better see the fortune presented before him and then exchanged quick glances with Miruvar and a number of others around his throne. Then, slapping the palms of his hands on the arms of his throne, he addressed the priest.

"Cyrus Col of Rathasia, we have listened to your request. We will inform you of our decision within the hour."

CHAPTER NINE
QUESTIONS ANSWERED

The sun had passed into the western sky and the shadows were drawing long on Unicorn Street. Shrew gazed out of the smoked-glass window at the bustle in the street outside and then withdrew again into the shady alcove beside the smouldering fireplace of the eating room. She had been in this corner of the inn for several hours and had already feasted on the largest meal of her life. She sat back in a state of well-being and fullness and regarded her half-filled cup of watered mead. After her meal of roasted boar and turnip, the few extra coppers dropped into the hand of the serving maid had ensured she wasn't disturbed.

Earlier that day she had approached Ahlune's Abbey, but there appeared to be some ceremony taking place and the guards seemed extra vigilant. She had decided to delay her plans for re-entering the sewer and, instead, had crossed South Street and turned into the busy thoroughfare known as Unicorn Street. For a while she had mingled with the crowds. Unicorn Street was lined either side by many different trading establishments and emporia. Their brightly coloured awnings and signs dazzled the eye. Here she had found a cobbler's and a tailor's, from where she had bought ankle boots and a grey tunic with matching hose. A little while later she had found the Southern Star Inn nestled between an apothecary and bakers. She had decided that this would be an ideal place to wait out the afternoon.

Shrew leaned back in her seat and admired her new outfit. Her attire was still quite boyish, but this suited her fine. She had parted with four of her five silver florins, but she thought the expense worth it. Now she felt she could mingle with the more respectable folk of the Lower Reach with impunity, for she no longer looked like a guttersnipe with an eye for the next pocket to pick. She looked inside her purse at the few coppers she had remaining. This would be enough to keep her fed for a few days, although, sadly, there would be no more roast boar. She looked through the window again at the folk passing outside. She was sure half of the Duns would be searching for her by now, and maybe even the City Watch. As soon as dusk fell, she would try and enter the Abbey again and the entrance to the sewers. She had decided that she would return briefly to the hidden chamber and take the remaining contents of the bag, before exploring the sewers for similar stashes of wealth. She would be out of sight of anyone searching for her. Then, after a day or two, she would make her way to Harbour Gate. Who knows, she thought, maybe there she could get on board one of the trading boats and journey outside the city. Shrew allowed herself to smile and then breathed another prayer to Latia. Her goddess had already bestowed great fortune on her. This was going to be a new start, and she was certain that she would enter this new chapter of her life with luck on her side!

Somewhere inside the Abbey a bell tolled, calling the faithful to gather for evening prayers; but Shrew paid little attention to it as she pulled the door grill open far enough to squeeze through into the arched mouth of the sewer. Just a few minutes before, she had passed through the main gate of the Abbey with a small party of pilgrims from the Gloamril forest. It had pained her to lose one of her few remaining coppers to the collection bowl of a venerable-looking Druid, but it ensured her entry, as well as, she was assured, a blessing from the goddess herself!

As the darkness enveloped her, she pulled forth the dagger from her belt and watched the arching walls of the sewer tunnel swiftly materialise in front of her eyes in a patchwork of rose-coloured hues. Also present were the patches of moss she had seen earlier. This smothered much of the ancient stonework and shimmered through the deep-sight, one moment appearing a coppery green and the next a cerulean blue.

Shrew carefully followed the descending stair and soon found herself back in the main sewer channel. She had entered cautiously, looking in both directions to see if anything had changed and ensuring that a few dark mangy rats were her only company.

A short time later she was back where her deep-sight clearly showed her the glowing symbol on the wall and the concealed entrance to the hidden chamber. With less hesitation than on her previous visit, she placed her hand on the symbol. There was a familiar click as the wall swung inward, allowing her to enter the short passage beyond.

The voice inside her head had been silent for a long time, but now it spoke up and urged her to be wary. Shrew glanced down towards the tapering blade in her hand. She hadn't been sure at first, but following last night's dream and the events in the Duns, she was now convinced that this disembodied voice that spoke within her thoughts was not an awakening of an inner part of herself, but was coming from the dagger!

She moved forward towards the chamber that opened up before her. The air no longer seemed as fetid and suffocating as it had when she had left it the day before. It all seemed the same, she thought, except for… Her eye caught something in her path that she could only describe as a thread, as delicate as that made by a spider. Her deep-sight suddenly brought it into sharp relief and the voice in her head called a warning, but too late — she could not prevent herself from stepping through it. There was a sound like that made when a shaken ale bottle is breached, and then a sharp pain entered her right leg below her knee.

Shrew staggered forward. The voice inside her head raged and became unintelligible. She felt her legs wobble and a dizziness as a grey shroud seemed to envelop her. She managed a few more steps and then collapsed onto the stone floor of the chamber.

Shrew opened her eyes and was immediately aware of a flickering yellow light. She felt nauseous and confused. Where was she? She had been in the inn. Maybe she had drunk too much and fallen under the table next to the fire? Then she saw a face looking down at her. It was a man, and his hawkish features and short-cropped brown hair looked familiar. Panic engulfed her as she remembered the tunnel and the trap. She tried to sit up, but her body wouldn't respond!

"Ah, you're awake. Don't worry, the paralysis will wear off soon and you'll be fine."

Shrew found she could turn her head and watched the man sit down cross-legged on the floor next to her. He was dressed in fine leather armour adorned with small clusters of overlapping metal rings. This wasn't the attire of an officer of the City Watch, she thought. It had been his voice that had given him away, that unmistakable hint of sarcasm and glibness that she had been exposed to on that long march up to the workhouse.

"Waylan," she managed to utter. "You won't take me back to the workhouse, will you?"

Waylan's unshaven features creased in a smile and he chuckled. "No, you won't be going back there. You're no ordinary guttersnipe, Shrew; neither the Duns nor the workhouses are places for you. I want to help you."

Shrew began to find feeling in her arms and managed to prop herself up on one elbow. She lay on the cot by the small table upon which the oil lamp she had lit the night before burned brightly.

She had a dozen questions she wanted to ask. "Where's my dagger?" she blurted before she had time to think.

"Back over there, where you dropped it." Waylan gestured. "It wouldn't let me pick it up. It seems like it's bonded to you!" Waylan paused for a moment in thought and stroked the bristles on his chin. "It's an ancient blade by all account, and it reeks of sylvan sorcery. How in Serreth's name did you find it?"

"I found it down here in the sewers," Shrew replied. "But before I tell you where, I want to know more about you, Waylan. You're no officer of the Watch, are you, and how do you keep finding me?"

Waylan held up his hands submissively and grinned. "I am an officer of the Watch some of the time, Shrew. Other times..." He paused. "I take on other roles. Here now, drink this. It will help take away the paralysis." Waylan proffered a small cup and Shrew took it hesitantly. "Take a sip at a time and I'll tell you all about the run-around I've had trying to keep up with you."

Shrew took a sniff of the oily liquid inside the cup and let a drop settle on her tongue. It tasted good, so she took a small sip and then another. A moment later, a pleasant feeling coursed through her body.

Waylan smiled and nodded. "At first, I thought you were a typical street urchin from the Duns; but that grand story you told about little Lord Flarion. I still laugh when I recall it! The way you stood, so pompous and bold." Waylan chuckled and leant across to the bag under the table and pulled the wineskin from it. "It was then I started to realise there was something different about you, and it wasn't just your manner. I couldn't believe it. I was looking at a girl and one of the best efforts at disguise I had ever seen!"

"You saw right through me from the start, Waylan!" Shrew retorted over the brim of the cup. "Surely, that lace handkerchief didn't have Lord Flarion's name on it?"

Waylan lowered the wineskin from his lips and laughed. "No, it didn't, but we fooled that maggot Malcaw, didn't we?"

Shrew looked puzzled. "So, you helped me?" she whispered.

"I was trying to buy you time while I checked out who you really were," he answered. "Don't believe for one moment that I went all the way down to the Gloamril Forest to check the validity of your tale. No, I went instead to the Duns and it didn't take long before I was hearing tales of a skinny young brat named Shrew who was the bane of hard-working folk up and down the length of Gifford's Street!"

Waylan gave Shrew a sly smile and brushed his lips with the back of his hand. "Where do you come from, Shrew? What's your real name, or don't you have one?"

Shrew stared blankly into the shadows beyond the reach of the lamplight. Her eyes had watered ever so slightly, but not enough to shed a tear. "Shrew is my only name, and the Duns has been my home for as long as I can remember," she replied slowly. "I often have dreams about living in another place, somewhere big and grand, but it doesn't seem real and the ending is so bad it always wakes me up." She spent a few moments describing her dream to Waylan, but made no mention of the recent vision of the strange woman who had entered her dream the previous night.

Waylan studied Shrew in silence for several long seconds, before quietly muttering, "Curious, very curious. You certainly are a puzzle."

Shrew had managed to sit up now and was rubbing the numbness from her legs. A small bloodstain had formed on the fine hose that covered the calf of her right leg and she touched it gingerly.

"Sorry about that." Waylan nodded in the direction of her leg. "But you were a hard one to catch. I guess they named you Shrew for a good reason!"

Shrew cast a black look at Waylan. "So, you set that trap for me?"

Waylan levelled his eyes at her. "It was important I caught up with you as quickly as possible. After I found out who you really were, I went back to the Middern workhouse. Unfortunately, I was delayed, but when I reached there the next morning, you were gone. Even Malcaw hadn't realised you had joined a wall team. It took me a while to discover that you had gone to the Middern Wall up by the west side of the Middern Rise."

"I had to escape that foul place," Shrew interrupted. "I took the first chance that came my way."

"You're what we call canny-like," he smiled. "A useful trait, but it nearly got you killed!"

"I have to thank you, I suppose." She looked back at him sheepishly.

"Nay, not at all. In the end, I may have stopped you being skewered by that goon's crossbow, but things didn't work out too well, did they?"

"I don't remember much at all," she replied.

Waylan took another draught from the wineskin. "I watched you jump from the wall," he continued. "You caught a branch high in the canopy of a large elm, but then you disappeared from view. I thought you had got clean away. It was only later that I found out from a friend that you had been recaptured."

"A friend?" Shrew questioned.

"Aye, I can't be everywhere at once. It's my job to know what's going on in the Low Reach, so I have a few little birds looking out for me." He winked at Shrew. "Anyway, to cut to it, this friend told me that Matron had you put into the sewers and that you had drowned."

Shrew's face lit up. "So they think I'm dead?" She beamed with satisfaction.

"Aye, they do." Waylan suddenly looked serious. "I will admit I was more than a little upset. Very few get away from me." He looked back at Shrew with a sly smile on his face and laughed when he saw her expression. "All right, I was genuinely upset, because I really believed you had drowned. There were bad floods that day because of the storm. I couldn't see how you could have survived." He paused. "I didn't have time to check for myself. I was given a number of duties that I had to attend to, and then earlier today I was summoned to…" He paused again and then added, "Somewhere important, that's all I can say."

Shrew stretched her legs and looked at him inquisitively. "But you still haven't said how you found me here!"

Waylan smiled. "Word came to me that one of our caches had been pilfered not far from where you disappeared." He gestured to the bag under the nearby table. "I also received news that Shrew had been spotted again on Swine Street. Apparently, there was quite a disturbance there this morning."

Shrew looked impressed. "You have your little birds everywhere," she whispered with genuine awe.

"At the time, I wasn't entirely sure it was you that had stolen from the cache. Nevertheless, the miscreant had to be caught, so I set a trap. I'm really glad it turned out to be you."

"The bag, the lamp and everything else, who's are they and why are they here?" Shrew felt slightly guilty now and was not sure whether she would like to hear Waylan's answer.

Waylan stroked the stubble on his chin again and took a few seconds to answer. "I guess you've heard of the Order of the Silent Knife, although some jokingly call it the thieves' guild. They're mostly former soldiers and honest thieves." He winked at her.

Shrew nodded slowly; it was as she suspected. She had heard the name whispered many times. It was a name that invoked fear in many, and even the street gangs of the Duns paid it respect.

"Down here, this underground world" — Waylan spread his arms — "we call it the Everdark. You have seen the sewers, but there are also countless tunnels and catacombs under this ancient city. The Silent Knife uses some of them and these caches are placed and marked in locations where they can assist our people."

"So you are one of the Silent Knife?" Shrew exclaimed.

Waylan provided an artful grin. "You keep that to yourself, young lass."

"What are you going to do with me?" she asked nervously.

"Did I not say I mean to help you?" Waylan smiled reassuringly. "Shrew, you are special and, whether you like it or not, more like us than you can imagine. I am going to give you directions to a safe place where good people can look after you. You must realise that you can't go back to the Duns."

Shrew looked shocked. "Can't I come with you?" she asked in a faint voice.

"Alas not. I have been given an important errand and already I have tarried here far too long. Some damn priests from the extremities of Rathasia have been given leave to build a temple outside the city. They will need some watching, and I have a lot of arrangements to set in place to see that happens. Now, try your feet and pick up your dagger while I quickly write a note of introduction to those good people I mentioned."

Shrew rose slowly to her feet and brushed down her tunic. The last vestiges of numbness had now disappeared and she could move her toes once more inside her boots. She walked slowly to the shadows by the passage and found the dagger where she had dropped it.

She stooped down and scooped it up and cried out in pain as a momentary burning sensation lanced through her arm. A voice inside her head rebuked her for her clumsiness.

"What's the matter?" Waylan called out, noticing that Shrew was carefully examining the dagger in her hand.

"It's nothing," she said. "The dagger is sharper than it looks."

"That reminds me," Waylan countered. "You need a scabbard for such a weapon."

Placing the dagger back in her belt, Shrew returned from the shadows to the pool of light by the cot and table where Waylan now stood. He held out his hand and Shrew noticed that in his palm lay a small leather pouch resting on top of a folded piece of parchment. "Take these," he ordered. "In the pouch you will find three sovereigns. These are worth a lot more than the silver florins you took, so look after them!"

Shrew provided another sheepish smile and took the pouch and parchment out of his hand. "Thank you," she said, gratefully.

"I don't suppose you can read," Waylan continued, "but that doesn't matter. You are to give the note to Jervale. He is the ostler at The Half Moon Tavern. You can't mistake him; he is both short and stout with a fiery temper, but he will see you are cared for. Give him one of the coins for his trouble and I would suggest you use one of the others to buy a scabbard some time. Oh, and a word of advice. Keep that dagger out of sight. Only use it when you really have to."

Shrew nodded dutifully and watched Waylan as he returned the bag to its place under the table and attended to the lighting of a small bullseye lantern. "I'm going to take you nearly half way to your destination, but then our paths will separate and I will have to leave you. Don't worry; the directions for the rest of the way are easy to remember. You'll have no problem finding the inn. Now follow close behind me."

Waylan extinguished the oil lamp. The shadows suddenly crowded around them. The pale cone of light from the bullseye lantern was feeble in comparison to the lamplight. Shrew likened the contrast to that of the difference between the Sun and the Moon.

Waylan made his way to the low arch at the opposite end of the chamber to the sewer passage. Here, a few steps led down to the heavy-looking door which Shrew had spied on her first visit, but hadn't explored. Waylan soon had it open, and as they passed through it into a small passage, Shrew slowly gripped the hilt of her dagger under her cloak. This time no painful shock jarred her arm; instead, the deep-sight returned in its crimson splendour, marred only slightly by the orb of bluish light that came from the lantern carried by her companion.

"We are in the ancient crypts under Ahlune's Abbey," Waylan informed her. Shrew gasped as they stepped into the broad chamber beyond the passage. Her new-found deep-sight enabled her to see more of its majesty than the feeble lantern could possibly show. Here there were fluted columns of pale lavender that sprouted intricately sculptured arches that crossed the vault above her head. She gazed in awe at their radiating patterns and the way they interlocked and entwined in a seemingly frozen embrace, yet all appeared swathed in dirt and decay.

"There are many tombs here, like the one we've just left," Waylan whispered. "All were ransacked long ago. This place is now lost to the world above. There are few ways in and most are hidden, like the door you entered."

She followed him as he turned and entered a broad arch. "We must enter the northerly edge of the catacombs. There is a main passage we must follow, but stay close and be careful not to stumble off to the left or right, or we may become separated and you'll quickly become lost."

They entered a meandering passage. Shrew quickly understood why Waylan had passed her the warning. Side passages appeared frequently, and as they passed some Shrew could see alcoves littered with bones. After a while, Waylan called her to halt. They had reached a fork in the path.

"I want to show you something," he whispered. "See here." He was pointing to the natural stone wall. They had left the stonework of the ancient masons far behind and the passages were now hewn out of the hard sandstone that supported much of the city. Shrew didn't need to look hard; her deep-sight spotted it almost immediately, and now the strange marking on the wall fairly blazed before her eyes! It reminded her of a knife pointing downward, as if balanced on the tip of its blade.

Waylan traced the outline of the mark with his finger. "Do you see it?" he asked her.

"Yes. It looks like a dagger," she responded.

Waylan nodded. "It's marking our route. The left passage is heading downward, whilst the right slopes up. The sign is showing that we go down."

Shrew watched as Waylan held the lantern up higher and looked around. "The golden rule down here in the Everdark is never take a passage leading down if you don't know where it goes. This mark was placed by my order. You'll find many more down here. Come, let's go."

They entered the left passage and followed its gradual descent. Shrew kept her grip on her dagger. She felt comforted by the fact that she could see further ahead than her guide. After a short while, she noticed the walls around her were beginning to shimmer with a different colour. It was similar to the coppery green she had seen in the sewers where the moss grew.

Waylan stopped for a moment and looked back. His face appeared like a mask of light in the glow of his lantern. "We are close to the place we call the Dovecote," he whispered.

Out of curiosity, Shrew removed her hand from the hilt of her dagger. As the deep-sight slipped away, the rose shimmers were replaced by a beautiful turquoise glow.

"The walls are glowing!" she exclaimed.

"Aye," Waylan replied. "I'm not sure what causes it, but you will notice the rock has changed. We are now out of the catacombs. Look up ahead."

Suddenly the passage opened into a vast space. It was like entering the rim of a giant bottomless barrel, fully fifty yards across, that had been sunk deep into the rock. Around its sides row upon row of galleries descended downward, wherein dark openings and ledges interrupted the pale fluorescence from the curved rock face. Shrew stepped forward to stand beside Waylan. Her mouth opened in awe; she was captivated by the spectacle.

"Behold the Dovecote." Waylan spoke in a hushed tone. "One of the hidden wonders of the Everdark. No-one that I know has descended to those lower levels and returned."

Near where they stood, a low balustrade of smooth pillars capped with fluorescing stone marked the rim, which proved this massive sink-hole was not entirely natural. Shrew gazed upwards and noticed a few further galleries curved outward above them as overhanging ledges, but these soon merged into a rippled dome that formed the roof of the cavern.

Waylan turned towards her. "It is time to part ways, Shrew. I will give you my lantern and instructions of how to reach the inn. I have accompanied you as far as I am able. I must take a different route to meet up with my fellows."

"I don't need a lantern to show my way," Shrew countered enthusiastically. "My dagger gives me special sight."

Waylan grinned. "I suspected as much. How else would you have found your way past the hidden door?" He pointed towards the far wall at an opening on the same level as them. "Follow the path right around the edge to that doorway. Then follow the passage beyond. At one point the path will get narrow as it passes through foundation stones. We call this place the Squeeze. Don't stop or loiter to look in any side passages, but continue on till the path enters a small natural cavern. There you will find that several passages lead out of it. Take the first on the left. It's the only one that appears to go nowhere, but there is a hidden door at the end, exactly like the one you entered from the sewer. Enter it and climb the stair to the surface. When you reach the surface, you will have no problem finding the inn. Remember, it's called the Half Moon and the ostler's name is Jervale."

Shrew nodded slowly. She was saddened that Waylan was leaving her. She had known few friends in her short life, and no-one as important as the one who stood before her now, with that enigmatic smile on his face.

"Are you sure you have to go chasing after priests outside of the city?" she asked, half-hoping he would change his mind.

"I will visit you," he reassured her. "Now move swiftly and be on your way. I must be on my way."

Shrew became very emotional all of a sudden and felt like hugging him, but he turned quickly and strode off towards the left side of the rim.

Without a word, Shrew sought a similar purpose and set off around the right side of the rim, towards the dark opening Waylan had indicated. The entire chamber was bathed in a turquoise light, and the deep-sight wasn't required to see the way. Nevertheless, Shrew drew her dagger from the cord around her waist. Immediately, she heard the voice within her lament, and for some strange reason she felt sadness in her heart. She shook her head and entered the opening. The passage beyond had little light and soon she was totally reliant on the deep-sight bestowed on her by the dagger.

She mulled over Waylan's instructions and as she passed the first of many side passages, she ignored it and carried on. The main passage appeared to be ascending and veering towards the left as it climbed. She passed more minor passages that branched off either left or right, until at last her deep-sight revealed masonry and a constriction ahead. It was then that Shrew heard a shuffling sound behind her. She paused for a moment and looked back. She could see nothing and there was no further sound, so she hurried forward to where the passage narrowed. It was as if massive blocks had encroached in on either side, pressing forward to try and meet. This, she thought to herself, was the Squeeze Waylan had mentioned. She was now in a tight tunnel, barely a yard in width. She passed another side passage that drove into the stonework at right angles to the direction she was travelling. It looked dark and foreboding, but Shrew paid it no heed and pressed on until she reached the other end, where the passage widened once more. Then she heard the sound again. It came from far back in the Squeeze. She grasped her dagger tightly and continued quickly on her way.

After what seemed a long time, but was likely only a few minutes, she noticed dampness in the air. The passage was ascending again. It veered suddenly to the right and opened into a small cavern. Her deep-sight outlined the contours of the cavern in rosy hues. As Waylan had mentioned, there were several openings radiating out in various directions. She turned to examine the nearest to her left and as she peered into its darkness, she spied with relief the glowing outline of a hand-shaped symbol.

A familiar voice inside her head called out a warning and almost simultaneously she heard the shuffling noise again. It seemed much closer and from the passage that led back to the Squeeze. Turning quickly, she noticed a bright blue light ripple down the length of her dagger's blade and the voice inside her head called a warning and urged her to be wary.

Another voice, that was likely her common sense, told her to run for the symbol and the secret door that must lie behind it. Curiosity tipped the balance and, instead, she strode back towards the opening of the passage and looked back the way she had just come. She could see something crouching in the middle of the passage just at the edge of her deep-sight. It appeared to be sniffing the floor and then it seemed to notice her, for it looked up and two baleful yellow eyes fixed themselves upon her. Shrew stood motionless and watched as the thing rose to its feet. It appeared to be half-rat and half-human!

She could feel her own fear now, but the voice inside her spoke in calm tones. A filament of bright light crackled along her blade, which the strange creature must have noticed, for it snarled and slowly backed away and then disappeared from view. Shrew stood her ground a little longer, but the creature didn't return. Without further hesitation, she turned back towards the short passage and quickly found the symbol that marked the secret door. The mechanism was exactly like the one she had seen in the sewer, and once she had passed through the door, she quickly closed it from the other side and turned to face the worn steps of a stone stair.

It seemed a long climb and it made Shrew think about just how deep she had been under the ground. She passed a landing and another symbol marking another door, but ignored it and carried on upward. Finally, she reached the top of the stair. She could see a circular trap-door above her head and it took little effort to push it up.

The sweet fragrant smell of flowers greeted her as she poked her head out and looked at the dawn sky brightening in the east. She had arrived at the surface, on the edge of a copse of trees, behind a small stone plinth. She climbed out and breathed a prayer to Latia for delivering her from the darkness. Then she realised where she was. Here, there were gardens and tall trees. Across the way, amongst an oasis of lights, she spied a wooden sign hung high, depicting a jovial half-moon with glowing red cheeks and enjoying a tankard of ale. She was in the Middle Reach!

THE BLACK BLOOD AND THE SILENT KNIFE

REAPEN

YEAR 5124

The Lands near Highfall

CHAPTER ONE
FOREIGNERS IN THE SOUTH

It was the last month of reapen. The harvests were done and Highfall lazed in the balmy warmth of the southern trade winds. For several days the sky had been cloudless; not even a wisp of high cirrus had marred its azure blue.

A light breeze fanned the flags and pennants that were proudly being flown atop the highest turret of the great South Gate. Here, a small band of men, clad in fine ringed chain-mail and leather, surveyed the lands that stretched southward in a haze under the late afternoon sun.

Aelmar's brow creased and his weathered features wrinkled as he squinted and focused his gaze towards the scrublands to the south-west and the flank of the Swan River by the land known as Everdim.

"I see it," he announced to the others standing around him. "The light now blazes from its dome roof. See how it shines now, as the sun catches it."

The Gate Commander, who stood beside him, was an older man; straggling grey hair blew out from behind the cheek guards of his helm.

"They say it's made of pure gold, my Lord."

Aelmar pursed his lips and stared out towards the distant temple, in deep silent thought. More than a minute passed before he turned and looked towards the Commander and then the other senior officers standing around him.

"Sylvan runners have reported a wagon train accompanied by Rathasian cavalry heading towards Everdim from the south road. An informant has told me that the wagons contain religious artefacts and a red-leafed herb. This herb is no doubt this so-called fang weed that the priests distribute to their devotees. It is strange that such merchandise requires a military escort."

The Gate Commander looked alarmed. "Rathasian cavalry in Sillaesia? By your leave, my Lord, have they not been stopped?"

A faint smile played upon Aelmar's lips. "Allay your concern, Hengrin. Let us allow events to unfold. It intrigues me to learn more of their business here, and I think we will discover more if we ask questions of them on their return journey." He turned back towards the south and looked again at the distant golden dome.

"I would like to know where they get all their wealth," he muttered. "I have my suspicions, but I don't understand their purpose."

"There's a steady stream of pilgrims, sire," the Commander replied gruffly. "They come from the city and the hamlets and villages in the low lands to the south. I've heard they pay handsomely for the blessings of the old gods."

"It is more than blessings, your Lordship. They offer renewal, a return to youth and cures for all ailments." A young officer, whose surcoat was emblazoned with the crossed talons of the Palatine Guard, stepped forward. "My father visited their temple a week ago. He came back a changed man. It was as if the burden of his many years had fallen from him. He said that one of the priests had laid hands on him and cast a blessing."

Aelmar studied the officer closely. "Indeed," he said grimly, "and at what price?"

The officer looked confused, as if unsure how to reply. "I understand he paid the priest several florins, my Lord," he stammered nervously.

"Is that all?" Aelmar asked suspiciously. "Does your father's tongue bear witness to the red stain of the fang weed?"

The young officer paused for a moment and then his face brightened in recollection. "His tongue is stained red, my Lord. It concerned us at first, but he reassured us it was part of the priest's cure."

Aelmar swept aside a strand of his long red hair that had blown across his face in the brisk breeze. "I feel uneasy," he muttered, and spat on the stone by his feet. "Damn these foreigners, they insult the memory of the old gods."

"We will continue to keep watch as you ordered, my Lord," the Gate Commander reassured him. "We will report anything unusual."

Aelmar nodded slowly and looked up at all those assembled before him. "A pearl of wisdom from an old warrior," he said. "We have one life in this world and it follows a natural course. It would be a fool who tries to change what the fates have decided."

CHAPTER TWO
REFLECTIONS OF THE PAST

Like many inns within the city basking under the blue skies of late summer, the doors of the Half Moon in Middle Reach stayed open late and its courtyard blazed with coloured lanterns well past midnight and long into the late watches.

Within the Half Moon's common room, a young barmaid paused for a moment to wipe her brow with the sleeve of her long dress. The air was warm and heavy with the sweet smell of burning pipe-weed. Its smoke hung in a blue-grey haze, wreathing the room's dark wood stanchions and drifting up to where they joined the sooty beams that supported the ceiling above.

Numerous lanterns hung from the beams, or filled sconces and niches within the walls, illuminating the shadiest of the snuggeries that led off the main room. The inn was busy and patrons were calling for their flasks to be filled, or their platter of roasted hog and sweet potatoes to be served.

"Sheri!" a woman's voice called loudly above the hubbub and chatter. The barmaid looked up and waved to the caller, a portly woman with a bun of grey hair, who stood by the door to the kitchens. "Sheri, before you retire, please be a dear and go and attend to the elderly gentleman beside the inglenook. He asked for you, as usual."

The barmaid nodded and tidied the curls of pale blonde hair that had slipped from under her cap. Then she adjusted her apron, tying it such that it pinched her slender waist and accentuated her bosom. As innocent as it seemed, her actions caught the eyes of several of the menfolk nearby, not least three young gallants from the Middern Gate Guard, who feasted their eyes upon her curvaceous figure.

Seemingly oblivious to their attention, the young woman moved deftly between two long crowded tables and approached the lone figure who sat hooded and hunched in the corner by the inglenook fireplace.

"Good evening, sire." The young maid bowed her head and waited patiently for the man to notice her.

The man looked up. "Aha, it's my favourite maid," he said, and pulled back his cowl to reveal a white bushy beard and sharp blue eyes. "I was wondering what to eat this fine evening. It seems that the roasted pig is the cook's choice, but the air is much too sultry for such fare tonight."

The barmaid smiled. "I could get Gervaillas to prepare a skewer of grilled linnet. I know that is your usual preference, sire. But I would recommend the poached skimmer-fish. It was brought up from Harbour Gate this very afternoon."

The old man smiled. "Skimmer-fish," he mused, stroking his beard. "Is it chance? On this very night those sparkling jewels of the celestial skimmer-fish will reach their zenith above the herdsman."

"Yes, sire. Volans will be shining high above our heads tonight."

The old man's blue eyes fixed on the young woman. "Indeed, it will," he whispered. For a few long seconds he held his gaze. Then he reached into his robe and produced two gold sovereigns. "Poached skimmer-fish it will be then, and also bring a carafe of Saffron Perruse."

The barmaid nodded slowly and looked quizzically at the man. "One sovereign will be sufficient for all your needs, sire."

The old man grinned through his thick beard and then looked around furtively, before whispering, "The other coin is for the most nimble-witted barmaid in all the Reaches."

"Gervail!" the Innkeeper's wife called into the heat of the kitchens. "There are two more orders of hog." Turning, she made to loosen her neckerchief, but nearly collided with Sheri, who was hurriedly returning to the kitchen.

"Sheri! There you are. Have you served the fish?"

"It's all taken care of, Rosa," the maid replied. "The gentleman sends his compliments. He wanted Gervail to know that the fish was heavenly."

"Well done, Sheri. I keep wondering why he always asks for you." The older woman shook her head and smiled. "You can retire now. We'll see you in the morning."

"Goodnight, Rosa!" the maid called back, for she was already climbing the stairs to the upper levels of the inn.

It was a tiny room, high up in the attic under the sloping roof of the inn, with a small square window overlooking the thatched stable roof, but it was all she needed. Sighing with relief, she sat down heavily on a stool beside her bed. Only a dim light from the lanterns in the courtyard outside came through the thick glass of the window, and so it took her a few moments to find her lantern and coax its flame into life. With the yellow flame flickering brightly, she removed her serving maid's cap and gazed into the pewter-framed mirror on the table, just like she had done many years before. Back then it was a smaller mirror, scarred by a trellis-work of cracks, and the bed beside her was no more than a pallet of straw, strewn on the cold floor of an old wine cellar, in the heart of the Duns.

Shrew smiled. It had been over three years since she had crawled out from the hidden passage and the dark labyrinths under the city. So much had happened since.

She remembered entering the courtyard of the inn and the many glances she had received from the folk gathered there. Fortunately, she had soon found Jervale, the ostler, by the stables. Waylan hadn't exaggerated when he described him as short with a fiery temper. She grinned. He certainly scored highly on both counts, and it was only when she produced the sovereign that he had become amicable. She could remember him ushering her through the back door of the inn and her first meeting with Gervaillas the innkeeper and his wife, Rosa. She recalled being overwhelmed by their kindness. No-one had ever treated her like that before, except maybe in her dreams, but those occasions were rare and more often her dreams were of a sinister kind. Gervaillas and Rosa had taken her in as a child of their own. Their care and attention, along with good wholesome meals and a warm bed at night, had had a profound effect on her. She was no longer a skinny waif of below-average height. She had grown to become a healthy young woman who was now slightly taller than the average. Yet, also, she was blessed with a lithe physique and a comeliness few could compete with.

Shrew withdrew the sovereign from her apron pocket and examined it in the light of the lantern. That white-bearded old gentleman was a regular visitor to the inn, and the two of them had built up quite a rapport. He always preferred to sit alone, and Shrew empathised with that — for she, too, had always been a loner. There was something about his manner; maybe it was his bright eyes that fascinated her. She had a feeling, or a sixth sense, that he was more than he seemed, so she was more than happy to exchange banter with him when the opportunity arose. He was also very generous, she reflected, as she turned the coin over with her fingers so as to let the light play on its lustrous surface.

The coin reminded her of those first sovereigns that had been given to her in that long-forgotten tomb in the Everdark. Her thoughts turned to the enigmatic character of Waylan. He had returned to visit her as promised, although two weeks had passed before he had appeared. She smiled as she recalled his entrance into the common room. It had been late morning on a blustery day, and she remembered cursing because every time the door to the courtyard opened leaves and other debris would be blown in onto the floor she had just swept. So it was that when the door opened and an extravagantly-dressed gentleman crossed the threshold, her first thoughts were of the entourage of leaves and chaff that followed him. She did not recognise him, because as she later found and for reasons he did not divulge, he had taken on the appearance and demeanour of a well-to-do merchant. Indeed, it was more the look of his companion, who followed behind, which aroused her interest more. He was young and pale-skinned, dressed in a maroon doublet of soft velvet with matching pantaloons. Yet it was not these fine clothes decorated with feathers and lace that caught her attention and remained stuck in her memory, but his long curling blond hair tied back in a filigree of silver.

A while later, Gervaillas had called her into one of the private rooms and introduced her to the merchant and his popinjay companion. She smiled as she remembered her shock at discovering that the merchant was Waylan! The young man was presented to her as Dardalloy, and it was with him that she would become much better acquainted. Waylan had not returned merely to see how well she fared in her new life. She soon learnt that he had been discussing her future with Gervaillas and Rosa. This news had come as a relief. The promise of something that didn't entail serving or cleaning was welcome indeed! She enjoyed the comforts of her new home, but had already started to miss the freedom and adventure of her old life.

Shrew placed the gold sovereign on to the table and looked towards the small window with a mischievous smile. The window opened onto a gently sloping roof and she had soon learnt that it offered an easy means to leave and return to the inn unnoticed. By the time Waylan had appeared, she had already had three late-night forays into the surrounding neighbourhood. Waylan had returned just in time, she thought. Sooner or later she would have been caught, or discovered missing from her room.

It turned out that Waylan had persuaded Gervaillas and Rosa that their new-found prodigy needed a level of education beyond that offered by the nearby school. He had told them that he had acquired the services of a well-respected tutor from Wood Grange College, a venerable institution that was well known throughout Sillaesia for its academic prowess. He convinced them that Sheri — for Rosa had wasted no time providing her with a "proper" name — could attend the College during the day and help out in the inn during the evening. The matter was settled when Waylan promised to pay all of the fees and find her an escort to and from the College.

Suddenly, a faint voice entered her thoughts and brought her back to the present. She turned and looked to the corner of the small room. There, under a loose floorboard, she had concealed the dagger that she had found in the sewers. Over the last few years, a bond had forged between her and the spirit in the dagger, for that's what it seemed. The spirit was a woman and her appearance, when she appeared in her dreams, was not unlike the sylvan folk she had seen in the city. The bond had grown so strong that she could sometimes hear the woman's voice calling inside her head, even if the dagger was not being held, although it had to be close by. The voice spoke now; it was faint, like a distant echo, but the tone expressed urgency.

"Come, child. Time is eternal, but I cannot wait for ever."

Shrew had heard similar words before, but whenever she tried to focus her thoughts to elicit further information, the voice faded. Sometimes it seemed that a barrier came down between them. Nevertheless, for most of the time she felt an empathy with the spirit and it, or she, gave her a valuable sixth sense. Over the last three years the dagger had become a part of her life and she would never part with it willingly, even if she were offered a king's ransom!

She sighed and looked into the flame that flickered in her lantern. Soon her thoughts drifted back to the College where she had spent so much time these last few years. She grinned when she recalled her first day in the dim candlelit study of the tutor Waylan had found for her. Bulric Barofey was one of the strangest men she had ever met, and one of the last she would ever want to cross. He was a giant of a man with a thinning pate of grey hair. One moment he could appear comatose, slumped in his chair like a down-and-out soaked in soursop, the next he could be up and poised with a piece of chalk, ready to hurl in her direction. She had learnt very quickly that she couldn't take advantage of his resting moments. No doubt, she reflected with a smile, such moments had been when he relapsed into thoughtful meditation rather than an alcoholic haze!

Under Barofey's tutelage, she had soon mastered reading and writing. This was followed by courses covering metaphysics and astronomy, but the subject she enjoyed the most was what Barofey called "The Multiverse", which included geography and the history of the world and its peoples.

Her time with Barofey only lasted till twice after noon, the beginning of the third hour of the afternoon. At that hour, her escort would come and collect her. When Waylan had announced that her escort was to be Dardalloy, she couldn't suppress the broad smile of pleasure that spread across her face. He looked like he was going to be fun. Yet things did not turn out quite the way she had expected. Once Dardalloy had picked up his charge, he took her over the road from the College to the cellar of a shady building that nestled under the shadow of Middle Reach's Eastern Wall. Here he transformed from escort to tutor, but his lessons were unlike any taught beneath the red-tiled rooves of Wood Grange College.

First of all, he taught her how to handle and care for bladed weapons. She had no need to bring her own dagger, for in the cellar there was a range of weapons at her disposal. Dardalloy introduced her to all manner of blades, from slim poniards to broad-bladed short swords. He even taught her how to use a strange device with quilloned barbs which could catch and break an opponent's blade.

Dardalloy turned out to be a harder taskmaster than Barofey. Shrew soon found out that there was another side to this effeminate and seemingly mild-mannered dandy. For when he moved to engage in combat, his eyes would become cold and emotionless. Shrew likened his graceful motion to that of a dancer, yet this was more a dance of death, for his finish was nearly always unexpected and delivered with lethal force and precision.

Fortunately for Shrew, the weapons they used in their training bouts were made of wood. She smiled when she recalled the numerous times she had returned to the inn, covered in bruises. When Rosa noticed a particularly nasty bruise on her wrist one day, she remembered telling her that she had caught her hand in a door. Dardalloy had mentioned right from the start that it was better her new guardians didn't know about her additional lessons. Shrew was happy to play along with this. Learning how to cut and thrust with a short sword or open a locked door with only a twisted wire were far more entertaining than her regular studies. Besides, she kept reminding herself, they were far more useful.

Unlike college, where she often moved on from one subject to another, her weapon training never stopped. Even now, three years later, she would still practice. Dardalloy would often chide her, telling her that she still had much to learn; yet just recently she had noticed that it was her tutor, not her, who was receiving the bulk of the bruises!

Shrew sighed and cast her bleary eyes at the array of crystal vials, mixing vessels and other paraphernalia that lay cluttered on her table-top. It was just as well Gervaillas and Rosa respected her privacy and rarely came to her room now. What if they were to look more closely at her perfume bottles and read her neat hand-writing that carefully labelled each one? There they would see names such as "Snakeroot", "Clerics-cowl" and "Bleeding heart". She grinned at the thought.

Her mind drifted back. Teaching her how to use bladed weapons may have been the main reason why Dardalloy took her down to the cellar, but there were other reasons, and not all required physical skills. Alchemy, herbalism, lock-picking, pick-pocketing, mysticism and the arcane arts were all introduced to her.

She proved to be a quick learner, but there were two skills at which she excelled. The first was her handling of daggers. Dardalloy had taught her the basics, but she had soon discovered her own style. She recalled him watching her, with mouth agape in surprise, as she spun a slim blade that was balanced with its steel point on her fingertip. The second skill she acquired through many hours of patience and experimentation. This was the art of making salves and poisons. Obtaining the herbs, fungi and other ingredients she needed was challenging. Fortunately, her journey to Wood Grange College took her past a small and unimposing shop that could supply most of her needs.

So it was, almost every day for three years, Barofey in the morning till two after noon and then Dardalloy till supper time. How she had found the energy to help Gervaillas and Rosa during the evenings she never knew. She did occasionally get short breaks, and she was grateful for them. These mostly came when Waylan returned to visit her. His last visit had been two weeks ago, and it had been a momentous occasion. He had taken her with him to the High Reach. She had accompanied him on other occasions, several times to the Foreign Quarter in the Low Reach and also a few times to the upper levels of the Everdark, but this one was special. It was her first visit to the highest level of the city. She recalled its splendour — the Crown Gate at the top of the Dragon's Rise and the tall towers and minarets of the Citadel of the Ancients. She smiled as she pictured Waylan in his satin breeches and his doe-skin waistcoat lined with ermine. He had explained to her that he had business with the Commissar of guild traders and that whilst he conducted his affairs, she could spend time in the magnificent gardens of the Commissar's villa. She had agreed enthusiastically, but soon after had learnt of the downside. Having discovered she was visiting an important residence in the High Reach, Rosa had made her wear one of her old dresses. "You have to look your best," she had said. Shrew scowled as she recalled the embarrassment. It was a small price to pay, however. The gardens truly were as Waylan had described, and she spent a happy hour exploring the secret paths that meandered under groves of olive trees, or that coursed through tall banks of dazzling flowers. That was until she reached a viewpoint, a break amongst the trees, which enabled her to look down onto gardens that appeared to be part of another property. A strange feeling suddenly overcame her. There was something about those neighbouring gardens that looked familiar, and this troubled her. These dark thoughts were soon forgotten as Waylan found her and announced that he was going to take her to the best eating house in all of Highfall. Shrew smiled as she recalled that night's proceedings. It was an evening without equal. Dardalloy had joined them, and together they relaxed on luxurious divans on one of the highest verandas of an inn known as the Violet Orchid. There, under a night sky, frosted with countless stars, they laughed and joked, whilst eating sweetmeats and sipping Saffron Perruse long into the night. It was then that Waylan told her she had passed her training and was henceforth an initiate of the Order of the Silent Knife.

Shrew stretched and yawned. The sounds from the common-room two floors below had subsided. It was time to stop thinking of the past. She must rouse her senses and focus on the night ahead. Her journey to the High Reach and the strange feeling she had experienced there was compelling her to return. The familiarity of those gardens had awakened her dream of richly adorned marble halls which, since her time in the Middle Reach, had faded somewhat from her memories. She furrowed her brow in thought and considered her options. She could travel openly and follow the well-lit streets for most of her journey, or she could travel out of sight. The latter appealed to her more; it was what she was used to. There was no strict curfew in the Middle Reach, but she would need some convincing answers if she was to run into a contingent of the City Watch at this late hour.

She had made up her mind. She rose from the stool beside her bed and crouched down to prise loose the floorboard in the corner of the room furthest from the door. Reaching into the space between the rafters, she grasped her dagger, which now fitted snugly in a burnished leather scabbard. A distant feminine voice entered her thoughts and berated her for ignoring her for so long. She ignored the protests and dropped the weapon on to her bed. Then she proceeded to change her clothes. She had formulated a plan to get back into the highest level of the city, but it required that she travelled carrying as little weight as possible. Once she had finished dressing, she stood back and looked into her mirror and nodded with satisfaction. She needed the protection offered by leather armour, but had compromised by only wearing a bodice of dark grey leather that fitted snugly over a tight-fitting sylvan shirt of similar colour. Below, she wore a dark grey tunic and tightly fitting hose made from a fine grey thread. Finally, lightweight sylvan gloves and boots of a coarser grey material on her hands and feet had the overall effect of darkening her entire appearance. She smiled at her reflection. Now all that was left was to fix her hair. On another occasion an application of a charcoal-based hair dye would have served her needs, but tonight a light grey cowl that could be pulled like a hood over her head would suit perfectly.

Carefully, so as not to attract attention from below, she opened the small square window. For a brief moment, she paused to check the cloth belt around her waist. Within it were concealed pockets crammed with miniature vials of viscous liquids, a folded leaf of a pungent herb and several ovoid seed pods that had originated from deep in the Gloamril. She reached back over her shoulder. Her dagger was secure, strapped in its scabbard between her shoulder blades, beneath a small backpack. Satisfied that she was ready, she climbed through the window.

A grey shadow emerged silently on to the sloping roof of the Half Moon Inn. Shrew looked up at the star-studded sky. A full moon would soon rise, so she had no time to delay. She glanced down to the courtyard below. There were a few late-night revellers loitering by the stables, but they were preoccupied, or too addled by their ale to notice a shadow momentarily blot out some of the stars high above their heads.

Shrew had crossed the short distance between the inn and the stables and now padded quietly towards the roof of an adjacent building. She was well acquainted with this route; she had taken it many times during her late-night forays into the Middle Reach. The Half Moon Inn faced the Gardens of Ahlune, the largest park within the city, yet its rear nestled close to a number of outlying buildings that were part of the urban sprawl, known as the Jewellery Quarter. She would make quick progress in this direction, using the rooftops to make her way towards the Avenue of the Ancients, the winding highway that snaked its way from the Middern Gate towards the Dragon's Rise and the Crown Gate, which gave access to the High Reach.

Unlike the dark, narrow streets and shadowy alleyways of the Low Reach, most of the thoroughfares of the Middle Reach were well lit by wisp lamps or oil lanterns. This posed a problem for those who wished to move unnoticed from one place to another. Fortunately, Shrew had quickly discovered that in the busy conurbations of the Jewellery Quarter and Artisans District, the rooftops offered an excellent means to travel unseen from one part of Middle Reach to another. She had come to the conclusion that it was safer than using the sewers and catacombs of the Everdark. On the rooftops she could move swiftly, out of sight from the folk on the streets, whereas in the dark passages below ground, one had to move more carefully and be constantly alert for all kinds of hidden dangers. Navigating through the Everdark was challenging and the routes were often circuitous, but high on the rooftops she could often see her destination.

Shrew stopped for a moment beside a tall chimney stack and noticed soot had encrusted its weathered, crumbling brickwork. She removed one of her gloves and smeared some of the soot on her face to further darken her features. Looking up towards the north, beyond the serried ranks of rooftops, she could see the tall, slender towers and pale stone walls of the High Reach. This was the direction she needed to take to reach the Avenue of the Ancients. Then she would descend from the rooftops and follow the course of the broad highway up the hill for a short distance. This was the riskier part of her journey, for it meant avoiding the light from the high-hung wisp lamps that lit the street; but she was confident that she would find some refuge in the shadows of doorways and shop fronts. Once she reached the White Cross, where there stood the imposing bronze effigy of the paladin-king Finngol the Fair — the first human to rule Highfall — she would turn quickly into the dimly lit Avenue of Wisdom and then find her way into the trees that marked the northern perimeter of Wood Grange College.

She leapt nimbly to an adjoining roof and landed so softly that she didn't disturb the colony of rooks perched above the gable, only a few yards away. The air was warm as the heat from the day still rose from the tiles and brickwork beneath her. On cooler days these roofs would be wreathed in smoke from the countless fires burning below, but tonight only a few fires burned, and she could clearly see her destination — a tall stand of elm trees which stood as a dim scar against the pale stone of the High Reach wall. She knew these trees well. They stood on the banks of a dark pool of water known as Mirror Lake. This body of water was aptly named, because it could reflect the sky so perfectly that passing clouds would barely quiver upon its tranquil surface. She had last visited this spot only two days ago, whilst paying a visit to her tutor, Barofey. As on previous occasions, she had strolled into the College gardens and sat on the banks of the lake close to the wall to eat a light lunch. Dardalloy hadn't been with her on this occasion, so she had made herself comfortable and idled away the time counting members of a family of swiftlets, small fleet birds who had made a nest in a tangle of purple-flowered toadflax, halfway up the wall. This exercise had soon brought back memories of her brief time as a wall monkey and instead of counting the darting birds, she had found herself tracing a path up the wall, from one clump of weed to another. The revelation was soon coming. Here was a covert route into the High Reach without the formalities of the Crown Gate and the perils of the Everdark!

She paused in her thoughts, checking her balance as she tip-toed across a decorated roof beam that crossed high above a gloomily lit street. Then she followed the course of this thoroughfare from the rooftops till eventually it joined a lamp-lit concourse fronted with grand buildings. This was the Avenue of the Ancients, and she smiled with satisfaction as she dropped silently into a pool of darkness beneath a shop's awning.

She moved swiftly, keeping to the shadowy margins and away from the glow of the amber wisp lamps that hung suspended above the street. There were only a few people abroad at this late hour and it was an easy matter to reach the shelter of a stand of trees that stood a mere bowshot from the imposing edifice that was Wood Grange College. Shrew halted for a moment and looked up through a gap in the tree canopy at the bright stars overhead. The boatman had now passed the zenith, which would mean the moon would soon start to rise. She calculated that she had less than an hour before its pale radiance bathed the High Reach wall.

With urgency in her step, she moved forward and soon spied the placid waters of Mirror Lake. A moment later, she emerged from the trees, close to the spot where she had eaten just a few days before. With the still waters of the dark lake to her left, she climbed the springy turfs covering its banks to the grassy slope and the massive foundations of the wall. Only now, as she stood in its looming shadow, did she realise the magnitude of the task before her.

For a few moments she searched for the signs she had seen the day before. This wall was different from the grey ashlar wall built from hewn granite that she had climbed as a wall monkey. This wall was ancient, built on foundation stones the size of wagons that knitted together so closely it was hard to see where they joined. Nevertheless, countless millennia of scouring winds, heavy rains and harsh frosts had taken their toll and in places this punishment showed. Shrew gazed up and even in the poor light she could discern dark patches against the pale ivory stone where weed and lichen had taken hold.

As she stood seeking her path up the wall, she slowly unwound a cord of twisted woven strands from around her waist and looped it over her shoulder. Then she tucked her gloves into her belt, in preparation for the climb.

A stone's throw to her left, the path of the wall changed direction, as it veered suddenly to skirt the lake. High up, silhouetting the stars, a bartizan or overhanging wall turret sprouted from this corner. Shrew eyed it suspiciously. She could see a pale light flickering from one of its slit windows. There were people up there on the battlements, probably palatine guard. There was no time to waste. Cat-like, she paused for a moment to judge her distance to a point on the wall, and then she leapt. One hand grasped the stump of a vine, whilst the fingers of the other found a narrow fissure where the ancient mortar had crumbled. She had marked her path well and in the first few minutes of her climb she made good progress, exploiting every bristle of vegetation and every nook and cranny in the stonework. Soon, she was halfway to the battlements and almost at a level with the base of the bartizan that rose to her left. But now the climb had become more difficult. For some reason there were fewer crevices in which to insert her fingers, or plant the toes of her boots. With fewer places to take root, there was also little vegetation to exploit. She now had to claw her way upward, clinging by her fingertips to the slightest scars in the rock surface. Her situation had become quite precarious and she started to question her audacious plan. All of a sudden, the dark labyrinth of the Everdark seemed a better proposition. To add to her discomfort, a breeze now fanned her body, chilling the beads of sweat on her forehead and threatening to dislodge her from the wall. She took a furtive glance downward. She was now a long way from the ground and higher than the trees that surrounded the lake. A fall would mean almost certain death! Pausing for a moment, she spied a crevice above her where two wall stones joined. If she could just reach that, she thought to herself, it would provide the support she needed. Her fingers clawed desperately upward and she sighed with relief as they found the crack between the stones. It allowed her to reach with her other hand and pull the loop of cord from her shoulder. The cord unwound and fell like a plumb line, aided by a heavy metallic device that suddenly sprung open in a flourish of scythe-like prongs. Shrew eyed the battlements above her and let the line swing till the device was spinning and inscribing a wide arc beneath her. Then she breathed a short prayer to Latia and cast the line such that the whirling prongs flew up high and over the battlements above. Shrew held her breath for a few long seconds, waiting for cries of alarm, but none came. She pulled on the line and smiled with satisfaction as it took her weight. There was no time to waste. Over her shoulder the eastern sky was brightening with the rising of the moon. Less than a minute later, she vaulted over the parapet of the battlements and landed softly on the walkway beyond.

Shrew crouched motionless for a brief moment. There were sounds drifting on the breeze from the nearby bartizan. She could hear wagers called and the clatter of dice. The guards were preoccupied, and Shrew allowed herself a smile. What was there to be vigilant for? Any invading army would have had to cross two cities undetected or climb a sheer cliff a thousand feet high to reach this part of Highfall — and who would be so foolish as to try to climb the wall anyway?

She glanced over her right shoulder and the vista took her breath away. Light from the moon had combined with a pre-dawn mist to illuminate the tops of the tallest towers and minarets of the High Reach in a pale, ghostly aura. They reminded her of candles, so tall and slender were they, and testament to the skill of the sylvan architects and stone-wrights who built them so many years ago. For a moment she recalled one of old Barofey's history lessons. This was the oldest part of the city. According to legend, it was once the seat of the fey king, Glossingal. Now, it was the home of the elite and the ruling classes. It was the seat of King Wulfred and the residence of the Council of Nine, the so-called Representatives of the People.

She gazed out once more on the unfolding spectacle. One of these towers was close by. It rose from the grounds of one of the many villas that occupied the lower region of the High Reach. Shrew pursed her lips in thought. What a view she would have from the top of that tower! Her plan from the start was to seek out such a high vantage point. From its great height she would see the layout of the High Reach, and most important of all, the location of the gardens that had invoked so many feelings during her last visit just two weeks ago. Her mind was made up. The occupants of the villa would surely be asleep. She would investigate the tower and be back and ready to descend the wall before the sun rose.

CHAPTER THREE
CALLING THE DEAD

Dawn had broken over the land known as Everdim. The air was fragrant with the scent of rosemary and witch mallow. Vaskah Shen turned in his saddle and looked back at the caravan that was slowly following his vanguard of riders. He cursed his luck for being drawn away from the balmy climes of the south for this foolish errand. The pleasure houses of Merrandis were now far behind him. It had been a long journey, and the last few weeks had been particularly nerve-wracking, as his company and its charge of six heavily laden wagons had skirted the south-eastern fringes of the Gloamril forest. A call from the front broke his thoughts and turned his attention forward. The temple had been sighted.

Under the temple's high dome, surrounded by fluted pillars of red-veined marble, five robed figures stood motionless, as if frozen in time. A humming sound that was almost imperceptible pervaded the chamber. It rose and fell in intensity, but varied little from the same monotonous pitch. From a distant corner, a bell chimed once and instantly the humming stopped, to be replaced by an eerie silence.

Cyrus Col slowly opened his eyes and regarded the four acolytes that surrounded him. Turning his head, he glanced at the arched portal and the pair of ebony doors that led out of the chamber.

"At last they have arrived, my brothers." His thin mouth curled in a smile. "Let us go outside and meet them." Then, as an after-thought, he looked at the bald-headed priest to his right. "Cullis Ra, go on ahead and administer the rabble that waits outside our gates. Ensure our visitors are not hindered. I want them to see the progress we have made."

Vaskah Shen called out to urge his teamsters forward, and then he broke ranks with the front riders of Rathasian light cavalry and spurred his horse into a canter. There were other people on the road, and soon he was passing small wagons and carts and an increasing number of peasant folk on foot. Their numbers increased as he approached the domed structure that rose before him.

There was a dark line of cloud on the horizon to the north-east. Light from the rising sun suddenly broke through its ragged edges to seemingly ignite the golden dome of the temple in a blaze of light. The crowd that had gathered before the temple's gateway looked up in wonder.

Vaskah Shen cursed when he saw the throng before him and urged his horse forward. His imposing appearance, however, was sufficient to cause the crowds before him to move aside. As he approached the gateway, a band of priestly figures rushed forward to forcibly remove people from his path. He reined-in his horse as the leader of this band, a gaunt individual with a bald head, stepped forward and raised his hands in greeting.

"May the blessings of Yngvi rain down upon you!"

Vaskah Shen looked down suspiciously. The priest had a peculiar smile; it split his face between his hollow cheeks like an open wound. "Don't fool with me, priest. I am Lord Imperiat Vaskah Shen of the Merrandis Legion. Take me to your master."

The priest bowed, revealing the trellis work of scars on his bald pate. "Follow me, my Lord Imperiat. My master follows and awaits the pleasure of meeting you."

Cyrus Col emerged into the cool air of the temple courtyard and bade his priestly retinue to halt. His dark eyes squinted as they adjusted to the light from the rising sun.

"I see our brother returns," he hissed though his filed teeth. "And he brings with him one of the Queen's lapdogs."

The High Priest stared impassively as the dark-mailed figure approached. The gold insignia and turquoise plumage adorning the figure's fur-trimmed cloak announced a commander of the Royal House of Merrandis.

At the last moment, Cyrus Col bowed his head. "Welcome to the temple of Yngvi and Dysettis, my Lord Imperiat. We are honoured by your presence and are grateful that our most exalted Queen has sent such an esteemed noble as yourself to assist our cause."

Vaskah Shen looked upon the dark-robed figure before him, at the sharp, dusky features and the red rune that flamed on his forehead like a third eye.

"You are Cyrus Col, High Priest of the Crimson Sect, I presume."

Cyrus Col's dark eyes narrowed at the mention of the brotherhood and his demeanour suddenly changed. "You have found the one you seek, Lord Imperiat. Do you bring the merchandise as arranged?"

The commander gestured towards the direction from which he had just come. "Your precious cargo follows in six wagons escorted by a score of riders and their retainers. I brought with me five of my own legion, to ensure its safe arrival, but the delivery of the merchandise was not my sole duty. There was another task that has sent me to this forsaken hole on the edge of the civilised world."

"Of what other task do you speak?" Cyrus Col raised his eyebrows in feigned surprise. Then, for it seemed he already knew the answer to his own question, he flicked his fingers at a number of passing priests and their followers, who then altered their course to join the group.

"Her exalted Majesty grows concerned with your progress, Cyrus Col. She has asked me personally to report back to her Council regarding all that you have achieved here during these last three years."

The priest's face glowered. "We have achieved much, Lord Imperiat, and you will soon see it with your own eyes." Cyrus Col turned to one of the pilgrims who had just joined the group and beckoned. "Come here, child, and tell us — why are you here?"

A young woman, who from her long gown was clearly from the city, stepped forward nervously and brushed aside a strand of long auburn hair that had fallen across her freckled face. "I am here, father, because you have the power of the gods and can cure me of the sickness that afflicts us all."

Cyrus Col nodded benevolently and cast a gleaming eye at Vaskah Shen. It was as if some subliminal signal had been passed from the priest to the woman, for she turned to the commander and spoke directly to him. "The father is one with the old gods. He has the power over life and death, and through him we have found renewal. He will save us when the darkness comes!"

Vaskah Shen appeared unmoved. He noticed the red stain on the woman's tongue and the dilation of her pupils. After a few seconds, he spoke. "So, tell me, priest, will the subservience I witness here conquer a city?"

The thin smiling lips on Cyrus Col's face curled and turned into a scowl. With a wave of his hand, he dismissed those around him. Only the gaunt priest with the crown of scars remained. "Lord Imperiat, you are a warrior and I am fully aware that it is the way with those that bear the sword that if a city stands in their way, they take it by force. As you have observed, I am a priest." He paused and grinned for a moment, displaying his tapered teeth. "I approach the problem with more subtlety."

A faint smile crept onto Vaskah Shen's face. "I see your approach, Cyrus Col. I see dregs from the city and peasants from the fields with their minds addled by the fang weed. I don't see a city about to be brought to its knees."

Cyrus Col's hawk-like features darkened. A malevolent light flamed briefly in the deep pools of his eyes as he answered sharply, "I have something to show you, Imperiat, and I promise you that you will find it is an achievement worth her Royal Highness's attention." The priest's attention was suddenly drawn to the arched gateway that led out of the courtyard. He then spoke with calmer tones. "But it can wait, as I see your kinsmen have arrived. In the meantime, my brother here will attend to all your needs. We will meet again after even-prayer."

Vaskah Shen leaned forward and looked out of the narrow-arched window that overlooked the west. The sun was setting behind a bank of cloud, and mist now gathered along the dark fringes of the Gloamril Forest. Nearby, beyond knots of hawthorn and cypress trees, the Swan River reflected the last vestiges of daylight, like a strip of quicksilver. Earlier, he had eaten with his officers. There had been no sign of the dark priest all day, and now he looked forward to their meeting. He allowed himself a smile of satisfaction. Deep down, he felt quite smug. Right from the onset he had been sceptical of this crack-brained scheme and had voiced his concerns to the Queen's Council more than once. Now the hard part of the journey was over and, unburdened by the heavy wagons, his return to Merrandis would be swift. When he was once more in the presence of the Queen, he would recount the absurdity he had witnessed here. This dark priest and his renegade Crimson Sect were out of their minds; there was no evidence that their new religion would succeed in undermining the authority within the city.

His thoughts were broken by a sharp knock on the door to his bedchamber. It was the sallow-faced priest with the scarred pate.

"My master awaits you, Lord Imperiat. Please follow me."

Despite his frail appearance, the priest moved swiftly, and Vaskah Shen had to move quickly to keep up. They passed through a long torch-lit corridor and then descended a spiral stair. Vaskah Shen looked suspiciously around him. He had been expecting an audience under the high dome of the central hall, but it appeared that he was being taken deep underground. At last the stair entered a long chamber, where shadows danced under the light of a few flickering torches. The priest slowed down, giving his guest time to quickly survey his surroundings.

Vaskah Shen scowled. This place was different from the temple above. The walls were highly decorated in relief sculptures and carvings that portrayed scenes from another age — the place reeked of antiquity. The priest signalled him to move, and he obediently followed. As they passed more of the carvings, he couldn't help but notice that some re-enacted carnal scenes that even his debauched imagination could barely comprehend. They passed under a broad arch and into a second chamber, where the walls were lined with deep recesses and occasional alcoves. As he paused a moment to peer into one of the recesses, the hollow eye sockets from a stack of mouldering skulls peered back at him from the darkness. The commander swore an oath under his breath. These were crypts, and seemingly long forgotten. What were these fools doing down here? He was about to interrogate the priest, but fell silent as he became aware of a deep throbbing sound that seemed to permeate the stone around him.

The priest slowed his pace and gestured at an ornately carved portal a few paces before them. He looked at the commander knowingly. "Do you like what you see, my Lord Imperiat?" He waved his emaciated arm to indicate the bloated figures framing the door whose bodies appeared hideously entwined in strange acts of depravity.

Vaskah Shen shuddered. This was all wrong. There was an unnatural chill in the air, and all of a sudden, he felt very uncomfortable. "Where have you brought me, priest?" he demanded. "Where is your master?"

The priest turned and his lips twisted into a grotesque parody of a smile. "My master awaits you beyond these doors. He invites you inside, my Lord."

Vaskah Shen hesitated. Then anger and impatience overcame him. "Very well, priest. I am tired of waiting and playing your cretinous games. Know, then, that I will enter in the name of Mistranna, our beloved Queen." With that, he strode forward and pushed open the doors.

The chamber on the other side was huge. The vaulting of its domed ceiling spread down to form pillars that guarded shadowy alcoves and dark, yawning openings. Before an ancient stone altar, four cloaked figures stood, silhouetted against a pale sphere of light that hovered above the broad upturned palms of a large effigy of a malformed dwarf.

Vaskah Shen halted in his tracks. He recognised the figure immediately and crossed his heart with his right hand as a ward against evil.

"Welcome, Lord Imperiat. Can you feel the energy? It pervades the air around us and seeps into the soul!" Cyrus Col had appeared suddenly from the shadows.

Vaskah Shen opened his mouth, but his efforts at making coherent speech failed. The throbbing sound seemed to come from the sphere that swelled and collapsed like a beating heart. At last he managed to blurt out a single word. "Folkron!"

"Yes, Imperiat. Your knowledge of the ancient gods is commendable." Cyrus Col's words were laced with sarcasm. "This, my Lord Imperiat, is a shrine to Folkron, gatekeeper to the vast silent darkness that is the Void, and the earthly voice for the Master of Shades."

"What are you doing, priest?" Vaskah Shen struggled with his words. "To call upon this... this demon. It's insanity!"

Cyrus Col smiled, revealing his stained tongue and pointed teeth. "Call upon? No, no, you're missing the point, my Lord. I don't call upon. I command!" The priest moved towards a nearby alcove. "Watch!" he cried.

A staccato of high-pitched sounds erupted from the priest's mouth. Vaskah Shen stepped back in shock. Something had moved in the alcove. Again, the priest sent out a series of strange sounds, but this time he gestured to the alcove and beckoned something to come forth.

Cold fear crept up Vaskah Shen's spine. From the shadow of the alcove a mass of soiled rags and bone slowly emerged. A skeletal foot placed itself down on the ground before him and he recoiled in horror. As the thing rose, the rags became a long-hooded robe, and within the hood the nasal passage and grinning teeth of a skull slowly protruded.

"Don't look into its eyes," Cyrus Col warned, and moved slowly around the horrifying apparition as he observed the man's discomfort. "You are shaking, Imperiat. Do you feel the essence of your being slowly draining from you? It is feeding on your soul through your fear!"

Vaskah Shen's face paled and then he retched. "Send it away!" he cried, hoarsely.

Cyrus Col laughed mirthlessly. "Did I not promise to show you progress, Imperiat? We have achieved much. Now turn around and see for yourself."

Vaskah Shen turned his head and stepped back in horror. The empty space behind him had now filled with rotting skeletal figures: some bore weapons and wore the remnants of armour, whilst others were insubstantial, no more than an outline of something that once had lived.

"You are mad!" the commander stuttered. "Your madness will kill us all!"

Cyrus Col laughed loudly. The high-pitched echoes of his laughter carried throughout the vast space of the chamber.

"Go back to your Queen, Lord Imperiat," Cyrus Col hissed, and approached the trembling man. "Tell her I have found crypts beneath my temple that extend underground, all the way to Highfall." The priest pointed his long-hooked finger in the direction of a high archway and a dark tunnel beyond. "I think even you realise what this means!"

CHAPTER FOUR
THE ARCANE AND THE BLACK BLOOD

Shrew hunched up close to the wall beneath an open window. Reaching the villa that she had spied from the High Reach curtain wall had proved a harder task than she had anticipated. The grounds and approach to the building seemed to be crawling with guards. She smiled; surely someone very wealthy lived here!

She was crouched on a veranda overlooked by several windows. Their shutters were open, allowing a faint breeze, no more than a blown kiss, to tease the diaphanous curtains that were half open. Near to her was a door that gave access to the building from the veranda, but it was closed.

She cautiously raised her head to look through the window. An amber wisp lamp shed its light from somewhere inside the building. She could hear soft female voices. Their playful calls and giggles intrigued her. So, too, did a crystalline bowl of luscious ripe peaches that rested on the window sill. It had been a while since she had eaten. This was a real opportunity. She had appraised her surroundings and had established an escape route, should it be needed, so without further thought she peeped into the room.

Immediately, she saw the thigh and buttocks of a naked woman, and there was another similarly unclad off to the right. The women's attention was drawn to someone lying on the largest bed she had ever seen. She sized up the situation instantly and snatched one of the peaches. Crouching back down, she sniffed the rose-coloured flesh and bit hard into the succulent fruit. Nothing had tasted better! A lascivious cry came from the room and Shrew smiled. Raising her head, she looked into the room again. Both women were now occupied, crouching cat-like on the bed as if to devour their victim. For a short while, Shrew watched the unfolding sex game with interest as she licked the juice of the peach from her fingers. Then she quickly decided to move on, for if the villa's occupants were so preoccupied, this was the perfect time in which to explore the next veranda. Besides, she had started to feel the passion in the air and didn't want to lower her guard with such distractions!

In the flicker of an eye, she had crossed to the adjoining veranda. Here, the window shutters were closed, but light from the moon allowed her to inspect them closely. Reaching into a pouch at her waist, she pulled forth a slim steel rod with a hooked end. She was about to insert it into the narrow gap between the shutters when voices drifted up from the gardens below. She froze as two figures passed by beneath the veranda. Holding her breath, she waited till they were gone and turned again to the task in hand. A familiar feminine voice inside her head interrupted her concentration by urging her to take more caution. Shrew cursed under her breath and tried to focus once more. She was seeking the latch on the inside and smiled with satisfaction when at last she found it. It was lower than she had expected, but she felt it move and faintly click as the shutters started to move open. Almost instantaneously, there was another sound, a faint twang as if someone had plucked a taut metallic wire. Gas and metal splinters blew out into the space before the shutters. She barely avoided the full blast, and as she rolled aside, she felt a stinging pain in her left arm. Cursing, she quickly reached for the source of the pain and pulled a sliver of metal from where it had penetrated her arm just below the elbow. Her action was just in time, for within seconds the metal splinter had dissolved, becoming no more than pungent smoke within her fingers! She reached quickly into one of the many small pockets in her belt and withdrew a pad of folded leaves, which she quickly pressed on to her wound. Leaning back against the wall, she felt the pain subside and sighed with relief. If the metal had dissolved inside her, she would have been in deep trouble! Looking up, she noticed the shutters wide open. There was no turning back now; she just needed to be more careful.

She glanced towards the moon. Valuable time had been lost. Reaching over her shoulder, she pulled forth her dagger from its sheath and watched as the deep-sight drew into focus and provided her with its strange perceptive view of the world. Immediately, the voice inside her head rebuked her for her foolishness!

"Very well," she whispered under her breath. "I should have been more careful, so now show me what I need to see!" Taking a last glance over her shoulder, she climbed through the open window and stepped lightly into the room beyond.

Shrew's eyes opened in surprise at the bewildering array of paraphernalia that greeted her, and even her deep-sight found it hard to unravel. The left side of the room seemed more like a library. Dusty spines of countless books protruded from sagging shelving, or lay stacked in piles, ragged pages poking out from their covers like broad yellowed tongues. In contrast, the right half of the room appeared to be an alchemist's hovel. She recognised the tools of the alchemist's trade resting upon a sturdy bench — an alembic, a distillation jar and a series of other less familiar crystalline vessels and receptacles. Stranger objects hung from arching beams or poked out of shady niches in the walls. She noticed the gaping jaws and glazed opalescent eyes of a large mummified snake and a peculiar coiled creature, encrusted with spines, which lay petrified in a stone. In the far corner of the room, the embers of a small furnace still glowed and illuminated a large glass vessel on a pedestal within which something moved!

She froze and squeezed the hilt of her dagger tightly. Even her deep-sight failed to give form to the thing that moved under the mercurial sheen of the vessel.

A calm feminine voice spoke within her and broke her thoughts. "Keep your distance, child, a homunculus is contained within. It watches you!"

Shrew felt a cold sweat; a shiver passed up her spine and she shook her head to try and clear her thoughts. The voice was right; she could sense that something was watching her! She felt a sudden desire to leave the room as quickly as possible. Beyond the rack of shelving that strained under the weight of countless tomes, she could see a door. Without further thought, she moved quickly towards it. Surely this would lead to stairs and a means to escape this room and reach the top of the tall tower? It had been her plan all along to gain a bird's-eye view of the High Reach estates. Maybe she would be able to spot the olive groves of the

Commissar's villa and nearby those familiar flower gardens that still haunted her dreams.

The door was set within an arched, stone alcove. As she approached it, her heart sank. Her deep-sight showed it to be reinforced by a lacework of metal that seemed to be burrowed deep into its timbers. Worse still, there was no obvious latch or lock. Motes of crimson light wavered back and forth across its surface and a murmur of warning interrupted her thoughts, leaving her in no doubt — the door was trapped!

Disappointment, followed by a feeling of nausea, overcame her and she felt unsteady for a moment — she reached out towards the shelving to steady herself and dislodged a thin book which fell to the floor in a cloud of dust. Glancing down, she noticed the faded crest of Highfall on its burnished cover. She recovered her balance and picked it up to examine it more closely, but barely had she lifted it from the floor when a sound came from the large vessel in the opposite corner of the room and the urge to leave became almost unbearable. Shrew turned and bolted to the window and leapt through the opening just as a high-pitched scream burst forth from the room behind her!

She landed clumsily on her left side, still clutching the book in her left hand. The pain in her arm had returned and as she sat up, she dropped the book and her dagger to reach swiftly into her belt for another bundle of folded leaves. As she quickly placed the pungent yellow herb on her arm, she could hear cries of alarm coming from several directions, including the room she had passed earlier. Her eyes darted left and right, and, reaching quickly into her belt pockets, she produced two dark objects. Their ovoid shape looked similar to that of a large beetle carapace, but at one time they had served as the seed pod for some exotic plant. Now they had another function. She took one and rubbed it vigorously between the palms of her hands until she could feel it heat up inside; then she threw it high over the veranda, in the direction of the loudest cries. The second one was accorded similar treatment and landed on the adjoining veranda. Quickly, she crammed the book into her backpack and sheathed her dagger. A long, mournful cry suddenly came from the open window, but it was silenced by an earth-jarring thump that resounded from the gardens below. A flash of yellow light momentarily banished the darkness and illuminated a row of trees. Without a backward glance, she threw herself over the balcony of the veranda, halting her fall for a brief moment with both hands before dropping to the ground in the shadows below. A loud retort announced the detonation of the second pod and grey smoke billowed out above her. As the echo of the last blast faded, the pre-dawn chorus of the birds resumed, but then was quickly drowned by the cries of men calling to arms and the screams of frightened women. Shrew smiled with satisfaction; she had sown the seeds of confusion. Under the cover of the smoke and darkness, she drew her dagger and crept into the undergrowth that surrounded the villa.

A few minutes later, with the aid of her deep-sight, she had reached the perimeter wall of the estate and could see the eerie ghost-like auras of the arcane wards protecting the brickwork. These wards would no doubt conjure a fate similar to that which she had encountered earlier. Whose estate was this that it should be guarded so? She pondered this for a moment until the baying of hounds and cries of men brought her back to reality. Her pursuers seemed to be getting closer; nevertheless, she needed to pause for a moment. The dizziness she had experienced earlier had returned. Although she had pulled the splinter from her arm before it had dissolved, it seemed that some of its poison had entered her body. She crouched down to apply the last of the fair-foil leaf to her arm as her inner voice chastised her again for her stupidity. Her expedition to the High Reach was turning into a disaster. It was time to leave — but she could see no avenue of escape. Earlier, she had managed to slip past unsuspecting guards at one of the gates in the wall, but no doubt they would not be so negligent now! She cursed her luck as she noticed that the dark veil of night was beginning to lift. Through the dark trees she could see the eastern sky was already proclaiming the dawn, and with the hounds on her trail, they were sure to find her soon! She reached into another one of her belt pockets and produced a small crystal vial. The dark liquid inside was potent — spittle of devil's crown with a tincture of blue dwarrow. At best, it would slow the poison and sharpen her thoughts — at worst, it would unhinge her mind! The voice inside her head pleaded with her not to drink it, but she could see the shadowy outlines of men in the trees and she could think of no alternative. Putting the open vial to her mouth, she quickly swallowed the contents as the voice raged her disapproval.

After following a route downhill with the boundary wall of the villa estate on her left, Shrew suddenly back-tracked and proceeded uphill. She could feel her blood coursing through her veins and pulsing against her temples as she moved swiftly, but silently, stooping low and altering her course to stay within the deepest shadows. The concoction in the vial had heightened her senses, for both her hearing and her deep-sight seemed enhanced. She could clearly sense the presence of her nearest pursuers, who were thrashing and crashing through the undergrowth, less than a stone's throw away. Their torches were like wildly dancing wisps. She could tell that they were accompanied by at least two hounds. Her left hand reached into her belt and she took out another thunder pod. Pausing for a moment, she rubbed the pod vigorously till she felt its inner fire. She waited till it began to burn and the casing started to glow before she lobbed it high through a gap in the trees. It detonated loudly, causing a flock of birds to fly up in panic from their roosts. The screams of her pursuers and the yelping of their hounds told her that her aim and timing had been almost perfect.

Now she only had one of the thunder pods left. She had two more back in her room in the inn, but they couldn't help her now. It would be a long time before she could make any more: the seeds were hard to come by and the process which transformed them into volatile capsules that burst forth bright heat and smoke was lengthy. She would save this last one till her life depended on it.

Without further thought, she continued up the hill. There had to be a part of the wall that was unprotected, but as yet she saw no avenue of escape. The pod had bought her little time. The cries of her pursuers and the baying of their hounds seemed to surround her now. She was being hunted and doubted she would receive any quarter if she was caught. Why hadn't they released their dogs? Surely, they would find her quicker? There was no time to think of such things: something had caught her attention — she could hear the sound of rushing water. A moment later she could smell and taste the dampness in the air.

She was almost on her stomach now, crawling on all fours in a bank of tall reeds. Her heart was racing and she could feel an energy surging through her body that made her skin prickle! Her deep-sight had already revealed that she was close to the shimmering surface of a small lake. On its far side, ground water bubbled from a spring to cascade over rocks into the lake's inky blackness. This could be her salvation. She felt she had the power to stay below the water a very long time. No-one would find her.

The sound of pursuit was now very close and she could see torch-light through the nearest trees. She slid into the water and felt its cold embrace. Taking a lungful of air, she sank into its depths.

Darkness enveloped her. Flashes of light flew by her eyes as air escaped from her lungs. She was aware of being pulled downward. Whether it was her dagger, the potion, or just a current, she didn't know, but a subtle force nudged her deeper. This was no ordinary lake. It seemed she was in a funnel, for she was descending to the centre of the lake at an ever-increasing speed!

Pain was building across her chest; her ears had popped more than once, when a glowing strip of bars appeared below her. She now seemed to be a passenger in her own body for, without conscious thought, her right arm had cut through one of the bars with the dagger, enabling her to slip through the grill which barred her way. Almost immediately, she felt the current take her and carry her along at great speed. The last vestiges of air that remained in her tortured lungs swept across her face in small bubbles, but a moment later her head broke through the surface of the water and she gulped and spluttered, trying to fill her tortured lungs with air.

Shrew took a moment to orientate herself. She was in a large chamber that was mostly filled with water, but there was a landing stage nearby and something that looked like a skiff moored up against it. Surely, she was deep underground; but if it was a part of the Everdark, it was totally unfamiliar to her.

After dragging herself onto the landing, she sat still for a moment, trying to recover from her ordeal. The air in the chamber was surprisingly warm, but nevertheless she found herself shivering. She was soaked;

water dripped from her hair and ran in rivulets down her face, making pink streaks where it washed away the remainder of the soot that she had applied earlier. Looking around, she quickly surveyed her surroundings with her deep-sight. Orbs like small suns dazzled overhead, whilst the water shimmered in crimson hues under their bright light. The water flowed out of the chamber under a broad arch, whilst she noticed a further means of egress from the landing on which she sat. This narrow-arched opening appeared to lead to a stair.

She took off her backpack and placed her dagger back in its scabbard. As the deep-sight faded, she was not plunged into the darkness she was expecting. The orbs overhead turned out to be wisp lamps. There were four of them hanging from the arched vault of the chamber, and although they had clearly been there a long time, they shed sufficient light such that she could start making herself more comfortable.

She set to work making a small fire within one of the many alcoves accessible from the landing. It was a simple matter. The remains of a wooden casket lay close by, and so she had a source of dry tinder. She also had two reagents in her belt that when brought together combusted to produce a small flame. Within minutes she had a small fire burning.

As she waited for the combined heat of the fire and the chamber to remove the chill and dampness from her body, she cursed as her mind raced over the events of the evening. Her plan to gain a bird's-eye view of the High Reach had failed spectacularly, and she was lucky to be alive. She recounted each mistake, analysing them in turn, trying to understand where her judgement had failed. She thought of the use of the thunder pods. She had never used them on people before, but it was unlikely she had hurt any of them badly. A few burns and momentary deafness, she thought; a far better lot than the retribution she would have suffered had they caught her! Then she recalled her descent in the water of the lake. That was madness. She could hardly swim. Whatever possessed her to do that? She looked at her dagger incredulously and shivered.

As time passed and the comforting warmth of the fire seeped into her body, she looked around. High above her head, ten arches curved downward from the apex of the domed chamber, continually bifurcating on their way down, such that the chamber walls became corrugated by a multitude of pale stone columns. The architecture was impressive, and Shrew recollected drawings shown to her in the shady library of Wood Grange College. There was little doubt that this was the work of sylvan stonemasons from a time long ago. As she watched the slow movement of the turbid water under the broad arch, she wondered where it led. Maybe there was a subterranean network of canals under the city!

She now felt more comfortable, but occasionally shivered and fidgeted as the wild concoction she had imbibed earlier still raced through her veins. It was time to move. She stood up and kicked the burning embers of her fire into the water and then shouldered her backpack. A quick look inside the skiff revealed a paddle, but nothing of use. She decided to investigate the arched opening on the far side of the landing. The staircase within its recess climbed upward towards the surface. This was the direction she wanted to go. Reaching over her shoulder, she withdrew her dagger and was soon climbing the dusty steps of the stairs. No one had been here in a long time.

Shrew could only guess, but she suspected she wasn't too far beneath the surface and still within the boundaries of the High Reach.

The stairs twisted around in their upward course, and she had barely taken a few dozen steps when they opened into a huge, dimly lit cavern.

A faint whistle escaped her lips as her mind tried to grasp the scale of the place. It reminded her of the dovecote, because of its barrel-like shape and the many rows of galleries that descended downwards; but there the similarity ended. This vast cavern was considerably larger and within its depths protruded spires and towers; no doubt once gleaming and proud, they now stood like ghostly shards, their former glory dimmed with age. She stood for a moment in awe and sheathed her dagger. Her deep-sight wasn't necessary; the pale glow of fading wisps illuminated the delicate structures like misty stars. She sighed. For some reason, she felt sad. Deep in the past, when it stood under the sky, there had been happiness here; but now it was only a shadow of its former self. Shrew found herself mourning the passing of Glossingal's kingdom and shook her head to dispel the intrusive thoughts.

She was standing on the highest gallery; it stretched to left and right as a balcony overlooking the remains of the fey city. She turned and looked along the walkway. There were many openings besides the one that led back down to the underground lake. Almost instinctively, she pulled her dagger from its sheath and staggered under the wave of emotion that hit her. As the deep-sight shone, the woman's voice in her head returned with a vengeance, lamenting the passing of the years and the forgotten deeds of Armeris and their time in Myrifel and Qinestra before he fell into darkness.

Shrew felt empathy with the woman and tried to think calming thoughts. They were two lost souls, one living and the other trapped in a shard of enchanted crystal.

"Show me the way out of here," she whispered, "and I promise to take you down to Qinestra, for I sense your yearning to behold it once more."

Within seconds of uttering her promise, she found herself staring at the third opening on her left. There was a mark on the wall next to it that glimmered and looked vaguely familiar. As she approached it, she quickly realised that it was not the slim dagger of the Silent Knife, but a sign made by the Black Blood, a nefarious organisation that mostly operated near the docks within the Harbour Gate district of the Low Reach. She looked at the glyph closely. It was clearly their mark. A blade and teardrop of blood; but next to it someone had scrawled an arrow that pointed to where the opening became a tunnel. She looked inside. The secrets of the tunnel were quickly revealed by her deep-sight. It was blocked by fallen masonry barely ten paces inside, but there was a hole in the ceiling from which hung a knotted rope whose frayed end draped over the rubble.

Shrew entered the tunnel cautiously, but couldn't help wondering why the Black Blood had been here, so far from the Low Reach. It was a good sign, though, for this must be their way in from the surface.

"It seems we will be back here after all," she whispered under her breath, and looked up into the hole from which most of the rubble had fallen. Her deep-sight showed it to be a narrow shaft that opened into a larger space beyond. There was even a light source somewhere above. She listened for a moment. There were no sounds other than her shallow breathing. Satisfied that nothing untoward lurked in the shadows above, she sheathed her dagger and started to climb. As she pulled herself up the rope, her arm started to ache again and she had to pause as the dizziness returned.

"Sirra's breath!" she cursed vehemently. Her balms and her elixir had done nothing more than briefly stem the effects of the poison. It was still working its evil in her body!

She waited a moment and then hauled herself up inside the shaft until she finally emerged inside a small square chamber that basked under the pale green glow of a wisp lamp. Looking around, she noticed dead rats on the floor. An unpleasant musky odour hung heavily in the air. She wasted no time crossing the chamber to a stone stairway that climbed up against the far wall towards a dark opening. As she reached the opening, another glyph portraying a dripping dagger proclaimed that the Black Blood had passed this way. A few seconds later, she entered a sewer conduit.

Shrew sighed with relief. She was near the surface. Every ten yards or so a faint shaft of daylight entered the sewer tunnel in a narrow column from drains high above. Now all she needed to do was to find a drain large enough for her to climb up to the surface. She decided to follow the tunnel downhill. After all, she thought, a down-hill path must eventually lead to the Middle Reach. Downhill would also have been the direction the water would have flowed, but the channel was dry. There had been no rain for weeks.

As she moved stealthily forward, a few rats scattered out of her path. Every so often she passed suspicious-looking mounds of debris and took wide berths to avoid them. Her memories of her first visit to the sewers and her encounter with the slug lion were all too vivid. Such a creature, if indeed it could be called that, was a living mass of slime that devoured almost anything in its path. If she was to meet another one of those, she wanted plenty of warning!

As time passed and no sign of egress had become apparent, Shrew began to question her decision to take the downward route. She had passed a couple of narrow side tunnels, but these appeared choked with rubbish from the city above. Her left arm was now aching almost continually and her fingers tingled; furthermore, the welcoming sight of daylight filtering down from above had become less frequent. She was on the verge of turning back when she spied a stairway climbing up from a recess in the far wall of the tunnel. Without hesitation, she crept forward. The steps climbed upward into darkness. She would need her deep-sight to probe its secrets. As she reached back for her dagger, a voice spoke from out of the darkness.

"Lo, what is this that creeps in the deeps?"

Shrew froze momentarily and then quickly pulled her dagger free from its sheath on her back. As the veil of darkness retreated and her deep-sight blossomed, she could see the wavering outline of a dark figure that was crouched at the top of the steps.

"Kurell's fingers!" exclaimed the voice. "A comely wench! Come here and let me take thee to the hilt of my dagger!"

Shrew stepped forward. Her blade was screaming warnings… "I am no wench for your pleasures. Who are you?" she countered.

"I am a master magsman," the voice mocked, "and if yer take another step closer with that bodkin… I'll skewer yer gizzards!"

Suddenly, something grabbed her from behind, pinning her arms. She felt a hand clamp down on her right breast and another slide up under her tunic. Hot breath blew down on her neck. Others would have screamed and struggled, but Shrew let her body go limp. She waited but a moment, gritting her teeth, trying to ignore the fingers fumbling towards her crotch. Then, as the pressure on her body reduced, she suddenly slipped free and rolled sideways and up onto her feet.

"Slippery bitch!" the one that had held her cursed loudly, and peals of laughter came down the stairs.

"She's a quick one, Finn," the voice from the stair cried between fits of laughter. "Yer better catch her quick!"

Shrew quickly appraised the one called Finn. He was thickset and stocky, with a neck like a tree trunk. With her deep-sight she could see he was well equipped: a leather cuirass protected his broad chest and scale-skin breeches were strapped to his legs. These were the trappings of a picaroon, a professional rogue or sell-sword, yet he also wore strange accoutrements around his waist, and from their blazing signature she could recognise miniature quarrels or darts.

Shrew stared into his unshaven pock-marked face and raised her dagger, flicking it sideways to mimic a one-cut pass across the throat.

"Cheeky whelp!" the man growled, and pulled forth a one-handed crossbow and aimed it at her chest.

Shrew was already turning her body as the trigger clicked. The bolt skimmed past her, grazing her chest and leaving a scar across her leather bodice.

She gave him no time to release a second missile. Leaping forward, she swung her dagger such that it cut the air in a wide arc that fell just short of his chest.

"Hah! You're wasting your time," he mocked, and patted the leather protecting his chest. "This armour has protections that will deflect your paltry winkle-picker."

Her first cut had been a feint. Now she swung her dagger lower. A blaze of crackling blue light leapt down the blade as it bit into her assailant's cuirass and sliced it away just below the stomach. A look of astonishment appeared on his countenance as his entrails spilled on to the floor. Then he sank to his knees and fell head first into an expanding pool of blood on the edge of the sewer conduit.

Shrew gagged, but the voice in her head sung with exultation. This was the first time she had slain a man, and it took a few seconds to grasp the fact.

Any further thoughts on the matter were suddenly curtailed. The second man was coming down the stairs.

She stepped back and readied her dagger. As he emerged from the recess into view, her deep-sight showed something red glinted from where his right eye would have been. She took another step back.

"That's a fancy dagger ye have there." He spoke glibly. "Just look what it did to poor Finn, lying there in his own guts." He turned towards Shrew, revealing a cruel smile and a horrid scar that creased his right cheek. "If you drop the dagger, I might let thee go."

Shrew raised her weapon and a blue flame licked along its glassy blade. "Come and get it," she replied.

"Oh, I will," he said reassuringly, "and then I will screw you as you bleed." In an instant, he had flicked his wrist, sending several darts heading in her direction. Somehow, she avoided two, but the third grazed her right arm.

A cold numbness spread out from the wound. She felt her grip on her dagger slacken and she sank to her knees. Looking up, she saw him approach. He had drawn a thin serrated blade that smouldered in the deep-sight, and the baleful gleam of his red eye seemed to cut through her. The feminine voice inside her shrieked and then it faded as the dagger slipped out of her hand.

Shrew gasped as darkness started to envelop her, but somehow the last vestiges of the deep-sight seemed to linger. The elixir was still in her veins and its potency seemed to counter the effect of her opponent's poison. Her attacker thrust his dagger forward, but to his astonishment it met no resistance. In the blink of an eye, Shrew had rolled clear.

"Sirra's breath!" he cursed. "You're quicker than a slippery stoat; but moving will only make things worse for you!" He chuckled. "But now your dagger is mine!" He stooped to pick up her blade and turned his head to gloat at her, just as a crossbow bolt slammed between his eyes, hurling him backwards.

Shrew leapt to her feet, dropped the crossbow and in an instant had retrieved her blade. Raising it high with both hands, she plunged it deep into the man's chest and pulled it free in a spray of blood. Then she did it again and again until his gore-streaked body stopped convulsing.

"Silence!" she commanded, and the exultation inside her head ceased. She stood up slowly and looked down at the bloody ruin at her feet. The red eye stared back at her, but it seemed to have lost its sparkle. She bent down and looked at it more closely. It was a gemstone, probably a ruby. Her deep-sight showed there was an aura about it and a faint inner fire beneath its many facets.

Her hands were already covered with blood, so it mattered not, therefore, when she set about the grisly task of removing the stone from the dead man's eye socket. The gory trophy fitted well into one of the pockets in her belt.

She rose stiffly. All of a sudden, she felt very weary. The numbness in her right arm had subsided, but her left arm still ached. The effect of the elixir was starting to wear off, and she knew that soon she would suffer a malaise as the withdrawal symptoms took their toll.

She moved cautiously towards the stairway, pausing a moment to pick up the crossbow. There, just inside the recess, was the familiar sign of the Black Blood alongside the crude depiction of an arrow that pointed upward. By the time she reached the top of the stairs, she had started to stagger. She had entered a drain-shaft and daylight was filtering in from a circular grill above her head. There were missing bricks in the wall of the shaft that formed a simple ladder, which she was able to climb. Moments later, she emerged from the shaft to step into a cul-de-sac of aged timber houses that sagged under the weight of their thatched roofs.

The sudden bright sunlight made her blink, but the street looked familiar. On her left, the sun's rays warmed the crenelated heights of the great Eastern Wall. She was close to Wood Grange College, in a back alleyway known as Binders Row. She had crossed back into the Middle Reach. The street was deserted, which was most fortunate considering her condition. She swayed on her feet and looked down at her torn hose and blood-stained tunic. There was little chance she would be able to cross town and reach the inn, but there was an alternative.

Several minutes later, she approached the shady entrance of a run-down house that stood at the end of a terrace of buildings that abutted the wall. She barely had the strength to rap three times on the door. Darkness was descending all around her. As the door opened, she stumbled forward and collapsed.

CHAPTER FIVE
THE COUNCIL OF FOUR

It was a wooden-panelled room, lit by many flickering candles, with an arched ceiling supported by huge timber columns. A dark table of polished walnut occupied the centre, from which several concentric rings of chairs filled the remainder of the room. Behind these, wall panels made from mahogany and other exotic woods reflected the light of the candles from their highly polished surfaces.

Miruvar fingered the curls of his bushy white beard and looked briefly at the richly attired man on his left, then the young blue-eyed sylvan woman seated on his right. Behind them, in the next row of seats, sat their close confidants, and further back a number of retainers.

"It seems that Lord Aelmar is delayed," he said matter-of-factly, stating the obvious.

The sylvan woman countered, "Then I suggest we start this meeting without him, Lord Miruvar."

Miruvar looked uncomfortable, but before he had time to reply, both doors on the far side of the chamber opened.

"Aha, our knight errant enters!" Miruvar looked relieved as the fiery-haired warrior strode forward and bowed before them.

"Lady Melowyn, Lord Mallory and Lord Miruvar." Aelmar nodded curtly and then slowly shook his head in mock derision. "I find that entering the back door like a thief in the night most disconcerting, but I assume from the urgency of your message, Miruvar, that the clandestine nature of this gathering is justified?"

Miruvar nodded slowly and dabbed at his brow with a grey cloth. It was a warm evening and the heat from so many candles intensified the closeness of the air inside the chamber.

"Lord Aelmar, I know this is most irregular, but we cannot possibly discuss this openly at the next meeting of the Nine. Such meetings are nearly always fractious, and when you hear Mallory's news, I think you will understand."

Aelmar's expression softened and he flashed a wry grin at the old man as he found his chair.

"I know you well, Miruvar, my old friend. Something is afoot. Now tell me, what is it that troubles you?"

Miruvar turned to his left and regarded the wizened features of the man in red velvet that sat next to him. "I will let Lord Mallory tell you for himself."

At the mention of his name, Mallory leaned back in his seat and conferred briefly with two men who sat behind him. One had hawkish features and wore grey leather armour, whilst the other wore foppish garments and a feathered cap that gave him the appearance of a dandy. Seemingly satisfied with their information, Mallory leaned forward, rested his elbows on the table and made a bridge with his fingers.

"Lords Aelmar, Miruvar and Lady Melowyn," he said, providing a nod of acknowledgement to each of them in turn. "As you are aware, we have been secretly observing the temple in Everdim for some time. Such activity has only been possible by having eyes and ears on the inside. Two weeks ago, we received a report that two very important guests were received by the High Priest. From their description, it seems they were members of the King's council, the Lords Luven and Morrdis."

"Indeed?" Aelmar interrupted. "So why tell me now?"

Mallory reached forward and took a slender crystal goblet from the table. "Up until last night we weren't sure of their identity. Last night, however, the High Priest was seen leaving Luven's manor house in Harbour Gate."

Aelmar leant forward in his seat. "Was he on his own or in company?"

Mallory pursed his lips and played with the crystal goblet in his hand, letting the red wine swirl around the bottom of the glass. "Let my man tell you himself," he offered, and glanced over his shoulder at the leather-clad individual who sat behind him. "After all, he made the report."

All attention shifted to the weathered features and keen grey eyes of Mallory's confidant. A knowing smile crept on to Aelmar's face. "Go ahead, Commander Wellen, or are you known as Waylan today, perchance? Your disguise is good, but you won't fool an old brother in arms."

Waylan cleared his throat and returned a sheepish grin. "My Lord Aelmar, as always, you see right through me. I must exude an ambience that only you can detect!"

Aelmar's smile broadened and he slowly nodded. "I trust your words, old comrade. Now tell me, what is that devil up to?"

"It was a dark night, my Lord, and Harbour Gate lay under a blanket of mist from the river, but I'm sure it was the High Priest, the one they call 'the father', that left the back gate of Luven's estate. We have been observing him for a long time now. He has a peculiar gait, and even with the cowl of his robe pulled across his face, he is unmistakable." Waylan's forehead creased in thought as he recalled the scene. "Aye, he was with Virryn and a number of the Black Blood. All told, an evil gathering."

Aelmar's face darkened. "Virryn, the assassin? Well, that answers another question. That foul blackguard is working for Luven after all." The red-haired warrior struck the table with his fist, shaking the crystal glassware and sending tremors through a carafe of red wine. "So, where did they go?" he asked.

"They boarded a flatboat out by the south dock and were soon lost in the mist, but we learned later that they had returned to the temple by the river." Waylan paused for a moment and then added, "But that isn't all I have to report, my Lord. Over the last few months there have been frequent visits made to the Low Reach by the temple's acolytes."

Aelmar scowled. "They are recruiting more followers. No longer do they wait outside our walls for the sick and the dispossessed to find their temple, they now bring their cursed art into the city. They are poisoning the minds of our people. Only the other week I heard that a father, crazed and intoxicated by the fang weed, cut the throat of his son whilst he slept. This madness must stop!"

Miruvar nodded. "We could stop them at the city gates and ban the weed from the city, but I fear that would not be easy. They have won the hearts of many of our people."

Aelmar's eyes narrowed. "Better still, we could raze their cursed temple to the ground, and remove the blemish from the fair face of Everdim."

Mallory turned his eyes away from the dregs in his glass. "There are ways that deed could be done without placing the blame on ourselves." He looked knowingly at Waylan.

"We could, but alas, it is not that simple," Miruvar sighed. "Remember that it was the King who invited this Crimson Sect to build their temple in the first place. To destroy the temple without the full support of the council would be treasonous." He paused a moment. "And clearly both Luven and Morrdis are in league with these foreigners. I can only imagine what they think they stand to gain."

At these words, the room fell silent as each turned to their own private thoughts.

It was Waylan who finally broke the silence. "My Lords and Lady, there was something else you must hear, if I may speak?"

Aelmar grunted in acquiescence. "Speak, my friend; I hope your words will help us find a way around this conundrum."

"One of my bondsmen works for the Clerk of the Middern Gate. The Clerk was enraged the other day when his request for a sewer squad was turned down by the Middern workhouse. Apparently, the squad had been assigned to Luven for more important business."

Mallory chuckled. "Has his recent entertaining placed an additional burden on his latrines, perchance?"

Waylan smiled momentarily and then his expression turned more serious. "There were eight in the squad, and only one returned. There are rumours that this one survivor returned insane and is now incarcerated in a dungeon beneath the Middern workhouse."

Aelmar looked up. "I sense evil at work. By the grace of Verrain, if that one could talk, we might learn more of Luven's plans."

"Then I might be able to help." All heads turned towards the pale-skinned sylvan woman. Her blue opalescent eyes sparkled under a fringe of pale blonde hair. "If you can bring this unfortunate to me, I may be able to heal their mind."

Miruvar smiled through his bushy beard. "Indeed, you might, Lady Melowyn; your powers of restoration are beyond compare, but the act of extracting this individual from their current place of incarceration will not be a simple matter."

"Well, my friends." Aelmar slapped the palms of his hands on the table. "It seems we have found ourselves a challenge, and also the promise of some answers. I am sure Luven's strange behaviour is connected with these cursed priests. Lord Miruvar is right, this task will not be easy, and at the moment I am unsure how to approach it."

Waylan nodded slowly and grinned. "Leave that chore to me. I know of one who would dearly love to visit that workhouse again."

CHAPTER SIX
BACK TO THE WORKHOUSE

It was a familiar experience. It had happened several times before. Shrew felt that she had been pulled into the bowels of the earth and far from the light of the sun. The only light in this strange subterranean world seemed to hang in the air: it was a diffuse, turquoise glow that illuminated the intricate lace-like structures that formed the walls around her. She felt at peace. The light was cold, but she lay on a warm and yielding surface that felt as soft as the finest down. She looked up into the bright green eyes and delicate features of a familiar face; it was the sylvan woman of her dreams.

Shrew tried to speak, but the words she intended to say slipped out of her thoughts before she could open her mouth. "You were inside my head. How is it now you are beside me? Am I dead?"

The woman bent over Shrew and a strand of her long lavender hair fell across her face and over the shimmering scale armour that clung to the contours of her breasts. A smile formed on her pale red lips. "You are not dead, child. You still have much to do."

Shrew's thoughts betrayed her again. "What is it that I have to do?"

The woman sat upright and cast her green almond-shaped eyes again on Shrew. "You have to come to me." Her words started to fade. "Look at the tome, it will show you a way."

Shrew tried to speak again, but the world around her dissolved. She blinked and looked into blue sylvan eyes that were framed by flowing blond hair. This was not the sylvan woman of her dreams! She sucked in a deep breath and opened her eyes wider.

"Aha! She is back with the living!" The voice was familiar. It was light and hearty and resonated in the close confines of the candle-lit room. She turned her head and stared into the youthful countenance of her friend and mentor, the one who had taught her swordplay and the more dubious skills attributed to the likes of tricksters and mountebanks. She had learnt them all and given them a character of her own.

"Dardalloy," she whispered, and then turned back to the bright-eyed sylvan woman who sat beside the bed upon which she lay. "Tirriel?" she exclaimed, and tried to rise up.

"Tirriel?" the sylvan woman replied quizzically, and gently laid her back. "No, my name is Melowyn. I know no Tirriel, except..." She paused and fell silent. "You must rest," she resumed. "You had some vile concoctions coursing through your veins."

"How long have I been here?" Shrew demanded. She peeked under the sheets and realised she had been stripped of her clothes. A blush must have reddened her complexion, because Dardalloy laughed.

"Since this morning, and it is now evenfall," he responded. "Your clothes are on the chair, and I wasn't present when they were removed." A wicked grin contorted his features. "And it was good to learn that the blood covering them was not your own!"

Melowyn frowned. "That was clearly obvious," she countered. "Now go tell Waylan that she is awake."

The bright columns of candle-light wavered and then danced and flickered as the door opened and Waylan, grim and weather-worn, strode into the room. His grey eyes glinted in the candle-light and settled on Shrew. "Give Ahlune thanks," he breathed. "You are awake!" He folded his arms and the stare that followed made her cower under the bedclothes. "You have a lot of explaining to do..."

An awkward silence followed. Shrew bit her lip and returned Waylan's stare. It was Dardalloy who finally broke the tension. "She's been through a lot, sire; I think she's learned her lesson."

"That I doubt," Waylan retorted. "I should remind you, Sheri..." He paused, and Shrew frowned like a petulant child. He always called her by her adopted name when he was angry. "I should remind you," he repeated, "that initiates of the Silent Knife do not go solo. They work as a team. You are no longer some wayward footpad of the Duns; you are a member of an organised guild of professionals, and you must behave like one."

"But you must admit, sire," Dardalloy interrupted, while he was examining the sleek lines of the small crossbow that Shrew had acquired, "she shook up Taro's place like a pro. There is a rumour that a shade was unleashed, for no-one saw the intruder, only a fleeting shadow amidst the trees!"

"Fortunately, that appears to be so," Waylan nodded in agreement. "Just rumours and nothing more, and thank the gods that is the case." He turned his attention back to Shrew. "The next time you want to be off on a whim, lass, tell one of us first."

Shrew managed a nod and then gave him one of her sweeter smiles. Waylan sighed. "I guess you are restless. I think I would be, too, if I were cooped up in that inn. Very well. I have some news that I might as well tell you now, and also you, too, Dardalloy. Tomorrow, assuming our 'Shade of the Night' is well enough, I want you both to visit the workhouse by the Middern Wall. I will reveal more in the morning." Waylan turned and bowed at Melowyn, who had been sitting quietly in the corner. "My Lady, I wish to thank you for your aid." He cast a fleeting glance at Shrew as he turned for the door. "Make sure you thank the Lady Melowyn for her trouble. Luckily for you, she took the time to come and restore your health, and that, I might add, was not just out of pity! It's because we both think you're going to be useful one day!"

The sound of Waylan descending the stairs beyond the room faded. They heard the outer door close as he left the house. The candles resumed their steady glow and for a short while there was silence in the room.

Dardalloy was the first to speak. "He is always on the move. Rarely does he stay in one place long. It's as if the Hounds of Midir were on his tail." He resumed his study of the crossbow and then exclaimed, "By the light of Ahlune, see here, this device takes five quarrels!"

Melowyn looked up and whispered, "It's a one-handed repeating crossbow. I can see from here that it was made by sylvan bowyers. I have seen some that can take twice that number and release all in the blink of an eye."

"That seems impossible," Dardalloy retorted, "but one day I will visit the Gloamril and see for myself..."

"Who is this Taro?" Shrew interrupted. She had suddenly broken out of her apparent sullenness.

"Stavan Taro?" Dardalloy raised his eyebrows in feigned surprise. "Stavan Taro is an enigma."

"What is that?" Shrew queried.

Dardalloy laughed. "Stavan Taro is either one or two men, for he has been seen in different places at the same time. It is a common belief that he is an illusionist, and it is well known that he dabbles in the arcane arts. Whatever he is… he is a confidant of Morrdis, and that makes him dangerous. It is said that they both arrived in Highfall together, having crossed the Great Desert from far Sellitan.

"Then that explains what I saw," Shrew muttered.

Dardalloy leaned forward and placed the small crossbow on the table beside Shrew's bed. He looked at Shrew closely. "We need to have a long talk, you and me."

"Not tonight, though," Melowyn countered. "She needs to rest, or all my hard work will be for nought." She cast her sparkling blue eyes back towards Shrew. "What shall I call you, young lady? Will it be Sheri or will it be Shrew?"

Shrew gazed back, mesmerised by the sylvan woman's beauty. "Please call me Shrew," she whispered. "I have had that name the longest."

Melowyn smiled. "Of course, then Shrew it shall be." She pulled out a bag from close to where she was sitting. "This is for you, Shrew. Your clothes are in a poor state, so I brought you these." She pulled some garments from the bag. "I have no need for them now, but they will suit you well and should also fit you perfectly."

Shrew raised herself up on to an elbow and gazed quizzically at the tawny-coloured tunic that was laid out before her. It appeared to be made of doe skin, but its surface shimmered slightly. When Melowyn brought it closer, Shrew noticed that the garment was covered in interlocking leaf designs and that every movement caused faint ripples of colour to wash across its surface. "It's beautiful!" were the only words Shrew could manage as she stared awestruck at Melowyn's gift.

Dardalloy had moved from his chair to join them. "That's the finest sylvan leather tunic I have ever seen." He shook his head in disbelief. "It looks as if it was made for a princess."

Melowyn cast a knowing look at Dardalloy and a faint smile settled on her lips. "It has some secrets," she said, as she lifted it up to reveal its underside. Shrew gasped. The scaled structure reminded her of the clinging mail that Tirriel, the sylvan woman of her dreams, wore. "It also changes its appearance," Melowyn continued, "quite subtly, so that it's hard to notice sometimes; but over time these changes will mimic the surroundings, so that the wearer can become almost invisible."

"I don't know what to say," Shrew whispered, and tears welled up in her eyes. "I don't deserve this. It's much too special!"

Dardalloy grinned. "You could follow Waylan's advice and thank Lady Melowyn," he said. "It is a wondrous gift!"

Shrew nodded and looked into Melowyn's eyes. "Thank you," she whispered. "One day I will repay you, I promise."

Melowyn shook her head. "There are no debts to be paid; besides, I have more for you." She pulled some other items from the bag: a pair of calf-length boots and leggings. Both appeared to be made of the same material as the tunic. She looked at Shrew again and smiled. "There, now you have the set. I hope these serve you well."

Shrew stared at the items laid out before her. This was an unexpected boon. As she tried to conjure a vision of herself wearing them, a sudden thought came into her head, which was quickly followed by Tirriel's distant voice. "I know my dagger is near me, but where exactly is it and where are my belts and bag?"

Dardalloy chuckled. "I have them all safe over here, and although I was sorely tempted to look inside your bag, I resisted my thieving instinct!" He walked over to the shadows in the corner of the room and brought back her bag with the dagger lying on top in its fine leather scabbard. After placing them carefully on the end of the bed, he held up a many-faceted red gemstone in his fingers, so that it flashed in the candle-light. "This bauble fell out of one of your belt pockets. It was too beautiful to leave there, all caked in dried blood, so I cleaned it. It has a hidden fire in its depths and is most unusual."

"Show me!" There was a trace of urgency in Melowyn's soft voice.

Dardalloy passed her the stone and stood back with his arms folded. "Is it special?" he enquired. "Where did you find it, Shrew?"

As Melowyn turned the stone in her fingers, her sharp eyes seemed to bore into its depths. "It's an optic, an eye-stone," she said. "Conjured to reveal secrets; but this one is maligned. It should be destroyed, as it still holds some of the wicked essence of its last host. Deep inside, I can see the ghostly image of what this host last saw." She turned and looked at Shrew.

Shrew paled. "Take it!" she whispered. "Please destroy it!"

Melowyn nodded. "I will. Now get some sleep. Tomorrow I will return with some flights that better suit your crossbow."

Shrew settled back into her bed and whispered, "Dardalloy, please tell Rosa I won't be working tonight." She yawned and soon drifted off to sleep.

Shrew was in high spirits, despite the mutterings of one of the Clerk's men that the job was not for a woman. She hung back beside Dardalloy and together they followed the three men from the Clerk's office up the long incline to the workhouse, letting them take the lead. Summer had yet to relent, and the sky dazzled with a glorious blue.

As the warmth of the dry south wind fanned her face and ruffled the feathers in the flat cap upon her head, Shrew recalled Waylan's words that morning. The Clerk of Middern Gate was sending an artificer and two assistants to the workhouse to discuss the recent shortage of child labour. She and Dardalloy were to meet the Clerk's men where the workhouse road met the Middern Rise and then accompany them, posing as officials from the Street Workers' Guild. They were to let the Clerk's men do the talking and take the opportunity to learn what was happening at the workhouse. Most importantly, and without raising suspicion, they should seek the whereabouts of the sole survivor of the missing sewer squad.

Dardalloy was also enjoying the afternoon sun and the balmy breeze. He turned to Shrew and eyed her up and down with a wry smile upon his face. "The fancy cloak and the cap suit you," he grinned.

Shrew gave him a withering stare and retorted, "Well, I notice you don't need to dress up — you're always wearing fancy dress!"

Dardalloy feigned a hurt expression, which then quickly turned into a leer. "I noticed earlier that Melowyn's armour clings to you closely. It's almost like a second skin. Is that all you are wearing?"

Shrew turned to him and gave him a wicked smile. "It's all I need," she said

Dardalloy nodded. "Then it's fortunate you are wearing that cloak. It saves all our blushes!"

Suddenly, the men up front halted and their leader, a poker-faced individual with greasy grey hair that poked out from under his cap, signalled them to come closer. "You leave me and Cedric here to do the talking," he muttered. "We deliver the Clerk's message and then we leave… and you," he said, pointing a stubby finger at Shrew, "keep yer trap shut and stay at the back."

Shrew ignored him and looked over his shoulder towards the arched gatehouse of the workhouse, which was now less than a hundred yards away. Her mind flashed back to that time over three years ago when Waylan and his small troop from the City Watch had marched her up this hill. How things have changed, she thought, and now looking back at the situation, Waylan had certainly taken a very cavalier approach to his role as an officer of the Watch. Further musing on the subject was quickly abandoned as the group started moving again. Shrew smiled grimly as she set off in the rear. Her fingers strayed to the hilt of her dagger. Maybe there would be an opportunity to right a few wrongs whilst she was here.

As they approached the gatehouse, a voice challenged them from one of the adjacent towers. The leader of their group was quick to reply, and they were soon waved through.

As they passed through the gatehouse into the compound beyond, memories of the place came flooding back, but it all seemed very different to Shrew. The buildings and great curtain wall, with its many openings and recesses, were unchanged; the blacksmith's forge was smouldering, and nearby she spied several iron cages, but all were empty. That was it, she thought: where are the children? Save for a few guards, the place was deserted!

As they crossed the compound, they were joined by two youths, clad in poorly fitting leather armour that, from their demeanour, had been given the role of escort. Shrew appraised them from the corner of an eye. One had a heavy-looking crossbow slung across his back, the sort that took a lifetime to load, and the other sported a short sword that hung scabbard-less at his side. She wondered if they had ever used their weapons in anger. Soon they were mounting the broad stairs that led to the audience chamber and a meeting with the self-appointed governor of this run-down old fort.

They were clearly expected, for the two great doors that gave access to the wide drum turret, which loomed before them, opened as they approached.

The Clerk's men entered first, closely followed by Dardalloy. Shrew deliberately entered last and watched their escort close the doors behind them. She didn't think anyone would recognise her: after all, as far as the people here were concerned, she drowned in the sewers. Nevertheless, she felt more comfortable standing in the background. For once she was happy to follow orders and do exactly as the Clerk's man had ordered.

As she surveyed her surroundings, it was almost exactly as she remembered. The chamber still looked cluttered like a pawnbroker's shop. The only difference was that the brazier in the centre of the room appeared to burn brighter than she recalled. Light from its luminous yellow flame dazzled the bronze figurines and copper urns that stood in front of the wall hangings at the edge of the chamber. Shrew gazed beyond the flickering flame and her eyes settled on Matron's bulk. On her right stood the gaunt and hunched figure of Malcaw and two other men that she did not recognise.

"Come forward." The heavy voice of Matron resounded through the chamber. "We have been waiting for you."

The Clerk's men shuffled forward. Shrew noticed their leader had removed his cap. He was the first to reply. "Clerk Farringay sends his greetings," he responded with a flourish. "He is pleased that you have allowed us this meeting so we can discuss terms for more labour."

Matron snorted, cleared her throat noisily and then spat into a copper spittoon at her feet. "Hah, honeyed words. Last time his message was more vitriolic!" As she spoke, she shifted her bulk on the divan and for a brief moment Shrew noticed the red mark of the fang weed upon her tongue.

"My master regrets any misunderstandings," the Clerk's artificer continued. "He realises labour is short and he is willing to increase the regular stipend twofold if you could provide us with two dozen sweepers, a half-dozen sparks for the round-house on Unicorn Street and a dozen…"

Matron laughed loudly, interrupting the artificer's request. "Hear that? Is he trying to bribe me now? Why not get the labour you need from the orphanage in the Foreign Quarter?"

The artificer seemed lost for words for a moment. Then he turned and gestured towards Dardalloy. "We are accompanied by two honourable journeymen from the Street Workers' Guild. They will add to the stipend if they can view and assess the labour you currently have here in the fort."

Shrew raised her eyebrows and cast a quick glance towards Dardalloy.

"The labour here is not for sale," a gruff voice broke into the conversation. It originated from a hulking individual on Matron's right. It was one of the two strangers Shrew had noticed earlier. Instinctively, her left hand sought the hilt of her dagger.

The chamber fell silent and the artificer turned to the new speaker. "Why is that?" he enquired. "And who, may I ask, are you?"

Shrew detected a smug look on Malcaw's face. Her fingers now closed around the hilt of her dagger. Slowly, the dark recesses around the edge of the chamber began to yield their secrets to her deep-sight, and Tirriel stirred deep inside of her.

"Because the labour is spoken for," the gruff voice continued. "You don't need to know my name; you just need to know that I speak from a higher authority than your Clerk. I speak for Lord Luven, High Councillor to the King. It is he who needs the labour!"

The artificer pursued his questioning. "What would Lord Luven want with child labour?"

Tirriel's voice cut through Shrew's thoughts and focussed her attention on the wall hangings on either side of the chamber. The shimmering hangings concealed human-like figures, mere smudges of crimson, but she could see their hazy breath and the weapons they bore.

"And what would the Clerk of Middern Gate seek to learn from spies?" the voice growled back. "Slay them all!"

Shadows moved at the chamber's edge, and to the left and to the right, the brazier's light flashed off metal rings and studs. Swords rasped as they left their scabbards and an abrupt hiss announced an arrow as it pierced the smoky air.

Dardalloy called to Shrew as pandemonium broke out around them. "Save yourself — it's a trap. The game's up!"

Shrew didn't need his warning. Her crossbow was already levelled, and the first man that rushed her stopped dead in his tracks with a feathered bolt buried deep in his eye. Then, in quick succession, her next three shots took down three more attackers. Two others fell back, fear written on their faces as their comrades writhed on the floor. She had a moment to look across the chamber and spotted Luven's emissary and Matron duck behind a wall drape on the far side. Malcaw followed them, but he was not quick enough to escape the bolt that slammed into his right shoulder and spun him around. Shrew watched with satisfaction as he dropped to the floor, and then turned to notice Dardalloy hard-pressed against a wall, blood flowing from a wound on his arm. Hooking the crossbow to her belt, she shed her hat and cloak and drew her dagger; a blue light blazed along its edge as she advanced on Dardalloy's attackers. Two men were fencing him in. They were large individuals, wielding heavy broadswords and well clad, wearing splint mail and stiffened leather skirts. Two more of their kind lay dead near his feet. Shrew leapt over the bodies and plunged her dagger deep into the back of the nearest of Dardalloy's assailants. Shock and surprise spread across her victim's face as he looked down upon the gory shard that now protruded from his chest. The blade drew out as easily as it had entered; a fountain of warm blood sprayed her hand and Tirriel's voice sung inside her head.

Dardalloy looked equally surprised and had to quickly parry the remaining attacker's sword. It was then that his assailant noticed Shrew and realised it was now two against one. He broke off his attack and fell back, waving his sword towards Dardalloy and then at Shrew, not knowing who to attack first.

Dardalloy had no fight left in him; he fell backwards, hitting a wall and then sliding down till he collapsed on the floor, grasping his arm.

Shrew quickly stepped in front of Dardalloy, blocking any move in his direction.

Her opponent was a bear of a man, covered almost head to toe in leather armour that was reinforced with bands of steel.

"Drop your sword," Shrew called out. "There's no need for you to die."

The man laughed, and his grizzled face split into a wide grin. "You're only a girl — a small maggot. After I kill you, I will finish off your friend."

Shrew didn't reply. She strode forward, her dagger by her side and a determined look in her eyes.

The man's grin faded from his face. For a brief moment his expression reflected uncertainty, but then he laughed and drove down on her in an attempt to cleave her in two.

It was too easy. This brute had won past battles through his sheer momentum and size. Shrew nimbly side-stepped his clumsy charge and thrust her dagger into his underbelly. The crackling blade sliced deep, cutting through leather and steel and then through fat and gristle, till his stomach burst open. He fell heavily like a slaughtered ox and lay still.

Shrew stepped back and wiped her blade. She appeared to be the only one standing. A noise by the door brought her quickly to attention. It was the guards who had escorted them in. They took one look at her and fled out of the chamber, terrified.

"Sirra's breath!" she cursed, running over to Dardalloy. "We need to get out of here fast!"

Dardalloy winced as Shrew crouched down next to him and applied a pad of Fairfoil leaves over the gaping wound in his arm. "Black Blood! It's Virryn's scum; how did they know we were here?" he gasped.

Shrew pulled a small stoppered vial from her belt pouch. "Drink this," she ordered. "It will kill the pain."

"I feel better already." Dardalloy rose to his feet and shook his head. "How did they know?" he repeated, and stared in disbelief.

Shrew stood up and surveyed the carnage. There were bodies everywhere; their twisted and dismembered forms flickered under the light of the brazier, but there were groans from a number of the wounded. "The Clerk's men are all dead," she said with an air of finality, "but a few of these Black Blood are still alive. My poison will keep them down for hours."

"Poison?" Dardalloy was curious.

"Aye." She grinned wickedly and looked into Dardalloy's eyes. "It's a virulent paralysing concoction I made from Snakesroot and Adder's tongue."

Dardalloy chuckled. "I'm glad I'm on your side!" He watched her as she carefully loaded her crossbow with more of the flights that Melowyn had delivered that morning. He marvelled at their iridescent feathers and dark crystalline points. "Come," he urged, "it's time for us to leave this place, before others return!"

"Just a moment," Shrew responded. "I forgot. There is someone we need to talk to first." She hastened to the far side of the chamber and Dardalloy followed as quickly as he could, still holding the pad of leaves to his arm. Shrew pointed. "The Matron escaped in that direction, but I felled her stooge."

They found Malcaw lying on his back. Froth bubbled from his mouth and his one good eye widened in fear as they approached.

Shrew poked him with the toe of her boot. "I bet you never expected to see me again!"

Malcaw gurgled, a look of incomprehension on his face.

Shrew leaned over him and looked down contemptuously. "We haven't the time to get re-acquainted, Malcaw. Just tell us where the sewer rat is, the one that survived an errand for Luven."

Malcaw coughed. "I don't know what you're talking about," he rasped, revealing his red-stained tongue.

Shrew crouched down and noticed the feathered flight protruding from his right shoulder. She feigned a sigh. "Let me tell you, Malcaw. I've lost count of all the times when I imagined slitting your scrawny throat." She reached over and fingered the smooth feathered shaft. Malcaw groaned and coughed up more spittle. "Think back to a time when you sent a young girl called Shrew down a flooded sewer by the Shrine of Tommas the Lame. She never returned for those foul games you had planned for her." Shrew turned towards him and studied his face; his one eye seemed to bulge out from its socket. She had never seen a man look so terrified. "Aha," she grinned. "It seems your memory is good, after all. I am Shrew and I am the sewer rat you thought you'd drowned. Now think hard, for your life depends on it…" She leant on the shaft in his shoulder and his screams filled the chamber. "Where is the sewer rat that came back from Luven?"

"She… She's in a holding pen… in the wall," Malcaw screamed. "Please don't kill me!"

Shrew rose to her feet and looked at Dardalloy. "I think I know where she is. Let's go." Turning to Malcaw, she added, "Next time you cross my path, I'll sink a blade deep into your foul heart!"

They crossed the compound quickly, and no-one barred their way. The grey stone wall loomed before them; its many openings and recesses beckoned, but Shrew veered towards the largest of them all, a broad dark hole in its steep, sloping side. As they approached it, two men, both wearing the leather trappings of the workhouse guard, stepped out to meet them. Without hesitation, the first raised his sword and charged. He barely covered half the distance between them when a feathered shaft hit him squarely in the chest and sent him sprawling backwards. Shrew drew her dagger and before the second guard could react, she had him pinned to the wall, her breath on his cheek and the point of her blade at his throat.

"Don't move a muscle," she hissed, and looked into his frightened eyes. There was something in his expression she recognised. "Wilf?" she exclaimed. "Is that you?"

The youth nodded slowly, the dagger still tickling his throat.

"So, they promoted you from wall monkey to one of Malcaw's henchmen?" She stood back and looked him up and down. "The armour doesn't fit you too well," she added glibly.

Wilf looked confused.

"Do you remember Flarion, the boy who turned out to be a girl? You helped me… remember?"

Wilf nodded and then looked at Shrew with incredulity. "How could I forget?" he said. "But they said you'd drowned!"

Dardalloy coughed. "I hate to spoil this happy reunion," he said, looking over his shoulder, "but we're going to have a fight on our hands soon."

Barely had he uttered these words, when an arrow hit the wall behind them.

"Follow me!" Wilf yelled, as another arrow hissed past them. "I know why you're here. I'll take you to the girl!"

"But won't we be trapped?" Dardalloy countered, but Wilf had already turned back into the wall and was racing down a steep stair, with Shrew in close pursuit.

"Come on!" Shrew called, and glanced back, but Dardalloy was surprisingly quick and had caught up with her, despite his wounded arm.

The air was warm and oppressive within the wall and the tunnel they followed was dark and poorly lit, but soon they entered a passage lined with flickering torches.

"This way!" Wilf urged. He led them down another steep stair and stopped suddenly beside a heavy wooden door. "She's in here!" he cried. "Wait, I have a key!" He paused to fumble with a ring of keys on his belt.

Dardalloy looked at Shrew; the one torch in the passage illuminated the concern on his face. Faint cries and shouts drifted to them from the way they had just come. "Hear that?" he hissed. "We're being followed!"

"I have it!" Wilf cried, and opened the door of the cell.

"You go in first," Shrew ordered, pointing at Wilf, and then drew her dagger. Her deep-sight blossomed and the dark interior of the cell transformed such that she could see that it was no more than a small pit with walls arching in from both sides. There before her was the girl; heavy chains hung down from the pit sides to cuffs on her wrists. Shrew guessed that she was of a similar age to her when she was last in this foul place.

"There's a key here somewhere to unlock her chains," Wilf ventured, looking at his ring of keys; but Shrew cut him short.

"There's no time for that!" she snapped. She took her dagger to the manacles and for a few seconds blue light blazed in the cell as the crystalline blade sliced through the metal.

"Sirra's sweet breath!" Wilf cursed out loud. "How did you do that?"

"They're getting closer!" Dardalloy whispered urgently from the passage. "We need to make our stand where the tunnel is narrowest."

"There's no need for that," Wilf replied. "If you two can help the girl, I can lead you to a safe way out!"

The girl could hardly walk, and mumbled incoherently, but Dardalloy swept her under his good arm. "I can manage her," he said.

Shrew took up her crossbow. "Then I'll take up the rear." She smiled.

They passed through a labyrinth of passages. It seemed that this mighty wall was riddled with tunnels, much like an ancient oak that has suffered through the blight of worm. They journeyed downward, and Wilf took up a torch from a sconce to light the way. Halfway down a passage, he suddenly stopped and placed the palm of his right hand on a stone block in the wall. Shrew could feel a slight vibration beneath her feet; no doubt the reverberations from the movement of hidden counterweights, as a section of the wall swung outward and golden light from the late afternoon sun came flooding in.

"I found this by accident," Wilf declared proudly. "No-one else knows it's here. It's an old postern gate that opens into the Middle Reach. I can close it once we step through."

Stepping through the gate, they emerged into a thicket of alder. Brushing aside the toothed leaves that hung before them, Shrew breathed in the sweet air. They were in the Garden Park of Ahlune, and she knew it well.

"We're safe!" Shrew sighed with relief.

Dardalloy smiled. "Aye, it's not far to my place from here. Follow me."

CHAPTER SEVEN
A SHIFT IN THE BALANCE

A gentle breeze, warm and heady with the scent of musk lily, fanned the broad veranda. Aelmar leaned against a marble balustrade and looked out across the gardens below. It was evening and the sun had now disappeared behind the villa and was settling into a bed of cloud. Long grey shadows stretched across the olive groves and dimmed the banks of flowers that bordered the many pathways of his garden. Just a few moments before, he had bade goodnight to Hengist, the last of the Palatine officers with whom he had just shared a hearty meal. Now, as he stood all alone, the doughty spirits of his comrades, which had been so up-lifting, were replaced by troubling thoughts.

"Oh, Ellamae," he breathed, "you would know what to do." He walked over to the bronze bust of a woman that stood under the pale-yellow light of a wisp lamp. He gently touched the smooth contours of her face and then let his fingers trace the cool, flowing tresses that cascaded down to her shoulders. "Why did I ever leave you behind when I took up my sword for the eastern marches?" He shook his head. Only a few hours earlier he had received word from Miruvar that Rodderic, one of the remaining members of the Council of Nine, had pledged his allegiance to Luven and Morrdis. Rodderic was a wealthy trader who owned several estates in the High and Middle Reaches. He was also the King's Chancellor and Keeper of the Treasury. Aelmar frowned as he recalled that it was Rodderic who had been the most vociferous in supporting the building of the temple, on the grounds of the vast sums of wealth it would bring. Aelmar breathed in deeply and let out a long sigh. He needed time to think. He was certain that Rodderic would sway the King's vote, and even if Berenbold, the King's Minister, came to his side, the weight of the King's vote would shift the balance in favour of Luven. There was nothing more he could do. The King's vote was an ancient decree, originating back to the time of Finngol the Fair, the first human king of Highfall, which stated that the King's vote counted thrice! Aelmar was sure of the outcome. Luven would have six votes and he would have five, and that was based on the assumption that his side won Berenbold's favour. He shook his head. The odds were stacked against him, but somehow, he must persuade the King that the Cult cannot be allowed to continue its practices; or else these Rathasian priests and their vile fang weed would be free to continue their corruption of the city. He clenched his fists and stared resolutely in front of him. First, he would go to the private chapel and seek wisdom from Verrain. He would ask the God of Chivalry and Justice to intervene and plant good sense into the mind of the King. Then he would try and sleep.

"Damn it!" he cursed loudly, as he strode through the lamp-lit upper hall towards the chapel. This villa was much too big for a single man; he preferred his small apartment in the Citadel. Right now, he knew the few servants he still retained would be dousing the lanterns and covering the wisp lamps below, but they weren't proper company. When Ellamae had been here, things had been different; the place would have been bustling with activity, and a veritable army of servants would have been on call to attend to their every need. It was at times like this that he yearned for the companionship of his men.

By the time he reached the small chapel, he was still mulling over his next move. Tomorrow, he would confer with Miruvar and Melowyn. Their collective wisdom might find an answer. He bowed to the tall statue of Verrain that stood proudly above the altar and then knelt in silent prayer. Many minutes passed before a distant bell chimed, marking the beginning of the first watch. He rose wearily and made his way towards his bedchamber.

Aelmar's sleep was restless. He had woken up several times to see the stars framed in the far window, but now the pale orange glow of a harvest moon flooded into his bed chamber. He closed his eyes in an attempt to drift back to sleep, but then he opened them again. Something had disturbed him, and he was sure a shadow had passed over the moon — yet there was no cloud in the sky. Suddenly, he was wide awake, but he lay still and closed his fingers around the haft of a slim dagger that was hidden under his pillow.

Long seconds passed. It was so quiet. He would have heard a pin drop had one fallen, yet all was silent. Indeed, it was so silent, it seemed unnatural. He could sense that he was not alone.

He was ready when the attack came. Two curving blades struck where he had just lain. Aelmar was on his feet and hurled his dagger in the direction of movement. A loud curse told him that his dagger had hit more than a fleeting shadow, but something of substance. He backed off and pulled away the cover of a wisp lamp — now his attacker was revealed in the pale glow of the amber light.

"You had your chance," Aelmar taunted. "Now give me one of those cloak-hooks you carry and we can fight on even terms."

His attacker made no reply. Instead, he, for it appeared to be a man, expertly spun each blade in his hands, cutting the air before him as he advanced. He was slim, wiry and quick. There was no sign of race or skin colour, as dark leather covered his body, from calf-length boots to a hood that obscured his face. Aelmar had no doubt that this was a professional assassin.

"So, it seems Virryn has sent one of his stooges to do his master's dirty work," Aelmar quipped, as he circled the room in an attempt to keep his distance from his attacker. If he could reach his dressing room, he thought, he might have a chance. Grasping a chair, he threw it at his attacker and sprinted for the door of the dressing room, where he knew he would find a weapon. He reached it and had almost got through, when he felt a sharp pain in his left arm. Without hesitation, he reached back and pulled a dart free from his left shoulder and hurled it back in the direction of the oncoming assassin. The dressing room was smaller than his bedchamber, so it took him only a few seconds to reach the table under the far window. His left arm felt cold and stiff, but he could still move his right arm. He grasped the short sword that lay on the table and stepped back against a nearby chair to await his attacker. For a brief moment he considered calling for help, but then dismissed the idea. It was unlikely the few servants who still remained in the building would hear him.

The assassin entered the room slowly. He didn't seem as quick as he had been a few moments before and Aelmar noticed with satisfaction that his dagger had indeed found its mark, for several spots of blood coloured the marble floor behind the intruder. He raised his sword and waited for the assassin to attack, but, instead, the man paused in the centre of the room.

Aelmar's lips curled in a half-smile. "It's always the same with you people," he said dryly. "You always want the odds stacked in your favour; but now the odds are even, you've got to decide whether you still have the edge. You know I'm one of the most experienced swordsmen in all of Highfall. How lucky do you feel tonight?"

For the first time, the assassin spoke. It was a low whisper and his words were laced with malice. "I don't have to make my move just yet," he hissed. "The paralysing poison in your veins will soon render you immobile, and then those odds you talk about will be in my favour!"

Aelmar slumped back into the chair behind him. "This is a predicament, is it not?" he chuckled. "For as I sit here slowly freezing, you are bleeding all over my floor." He paused and stared into the shadow under the man's cowl and detected two eyes glaring back. "So, it's just a matter of who can last out longest, is it not?" Aelmar raised his eyebrows and smiled.

Several hours must have passed, yet Aelmar still held his sword in readiness. The veins stood out against the back of his hands as he grasped it tightly. All before him appeared misty and blurred. His senses were numbed and his mind was wandering, but he was aware of a coming darkness that would soon engulf him. Suddenly, a golden light blossomed before him — it pierced him with its warmth and he tried to laugh at the ridiculousness of the situation. So, this was the passing, he thought, and before me must surely be the passage to the Golden Halls of Empyrean.

"Breathe," a voice commanded. "The warmth of the emanation has entered your body." The pleasant warmth was replaced by pain, and Aelmar let out a hacking cough. The voice continued in a strange tongue, "Lirra ca, sol vesperia!"

Feeling was gradually returning to his aching limbs. Aelmar's right hand released its burden and his sword clattered to the floor. He found he could also move his head and he focussed his eyes on a line of silver buttons that adorned a fawn-coloured cassock. Slowly, he followed the buttons upward till his eyes met the concerned gaze and bearded face of a young flaxen-haired man.

"Lord Aelmar, can you speak?" The young man spoke softly and smiled. There was a golden aura about him that was slowly fading.

"Who are you?" Aelmar rasped. He noticed the body of the assassin lying close by in a pool of blood.

"I am called Deakin," the young man replied. "I am an acolyte of Berenbold, the King's Minister and High Prelate of Celestine."

"Then it seems you came just in time, Deakin," Aelmar responded, whilst massaging life back into his left arm. "What did you do to that fellow?" Aelmar nodded in the direction of the body on the floor.

"He had already passed on," the young priest replied. "Therefore, all my energy was directed at saving you. Besides, it was for the best. If he had still been alive when I arrived, I would have been obliged to save him, too."

Aelmar coughed and straightened himself. He was suddenly aware of hushed whispers and noticed that a small crowd of his servants had gathered behind the young priest. "Deakin, I am grateful for your timely aid, but why are you here?"

"I am a messenger," Deakin replied. "I came here to tell you that my holy master, the High Prelate, will vote with you at the next gathering of the Nine. The work of the Rathasian cult is an abomination before almighty Celestine and his beloved daughter, Ahlune. Such works are unholy and threaten the people of our fair city."

Aelmar smiled. "I thank you, Deakin. The message of support from your master warms my heart, but I am afraid we are too late."

CHAPTER EIGHT
GOING TO GROUND

The storm had rolled in from the Sillaesian lowlands, the dark clouds burdened by water from the Southern Washes. As evening fell, a bank of towering cumulonimbus clouds cast a deep shadow across Highfall, bringing premature darkness to the city. Finally, after an hour of ceaseless rumbling, the heavens opened and sheets of rain fell, cascading off slate roof and sedge thatch alike, to drench the streets and back alleys below. Trickles gathered into small streams, filling the cracks and fissures of the cobbled streets, to finally race in torrents to the drains.

The parlour within Dardalloy's house was cloaked in shadow, save for a few pools of light where candles burned. Shrew huddled within the light of one of the brighter candles and stared intently into a book as the rain hammered the smoky lead-glass window beside her. Over the other side of the room, Dardalloy reclined on a low divan, nursing his wounded arm, which now rested in a makeshift sling. Nearby, the mute girl they had rescued from the depths of the Middern Wall lay deep in slumber on a couch; and beside her, Wilf snored fitfully from an old armchair.

Following their escape from the workhouse, they had taken a circuitous route back to Dardalloy's house, which nestled under the shadow of the great Eastern Wall. The shock of betrayal had hit them hard, particularly Dardalloy, who still couldn't fathom how the Black Blood had discovered their plan and had been waiting in ambush. Following their return, Waylan had not appeared as he had promised, and Dardalloy's contact with other members of the Silent Knife, some of whom had visited the house earlier that morning, had failed to reveal his whereabouts. Now it was evening again, and Dardalloy was on edge.

"You've been engrossed in that tome you found for some time," he called from across the room, his voice barely audible above the noise of the rain. It was several minutes before Shrew took her eyes away from the pages of the book and studied her friend. His usual calm and happy-go-lucky demeanour had long since vanished. He looked nervous and his eyes darted furtively from left to right as if he was seeking answers in the shadows.

"Waylan would not have betrayed us," Shrew replied, reading his thoughts. "You know that as well as I." She turned back to her book. "Come, take a look at this. I think you'll find it interesting."

Dardalloy sighed. "Must I?" he groaned. His arm hurt when he moved, but he reluctantly rose from the relative comfort of his divan and shuffled over to her seat by the window.

"Here." Shrew pointed and placed a finger down on a diagram that filled the open pages of the book she had been studying.

Dardalloy peered at the intricate patchwork of lines and curves that sprawled across its ancient yellow pages. "What in Parvi's name is that?" he exclaimed, as he tried to make sense of the complex geometry before him. "It looks like the scribble of a madman!"

Shrew snorted. "Can't you see it?" she cried. "Look at this shape, see how lines appear to sprout out of it, darker on top and fading to the bottom. It's the Dovecote! It's a map of the Everdark!"

Dardalloy took a step back in astonishment. "How in the five-and-forty hells did you figure that out?" he said incredulously.

"It just came into my head," Shrew answered. "It's obvious, isn't it?"

"Obvious?" Dardalloy raised his arms in disbelief and winced in pain as he did so. "Where did you find this tome?"

Shrew couldn't suppress the broad grin that spread across her face. "It came from Stavan Taro's library, but I doubt he'll miss it. It was covered in dust and it doesn't look like it's been opened in years."

Dardalloy smiled. "I've never seen a map like this before," he said. "If you search hard enough, you will find maps of the City's sewer system in the great library at Wood Grange College, but there's nothing there charting the under-city that lies beneath this mountain. You have found a real treasure; far more valuable than that ruby you gave to the Lady Melowyn."

Shrew couldn't help but feel smug, and it showed on her face. "It was a lucky find," she said. But deep down she knew it was Tirriel who had guided her to the book. There was no luck about it. She was certain that Latia, her goddess of luck, had played no part in its discovery. She sat in silence for a moment. Maybe it was also Tirriel who had guided her to Stavan Taro's estate in the first place! Maybe it hadn't been her idea to get a bird's-eye view of the High Reach after all. Suddenly, she felt uncomfortable, and the expression on her face changed. Dardalloy noticed and was about to speak when a sharp knock came on the front door of the house.

Shrew quickly broke out of her thoughts and picked up her crossbow. The sound had woken Wilf, and Dardalloy pressed a finger to his lips to warn him to stay silent. He nodded, having quickly assessed the situation, and watched with interest as Dardalloy made several quick gestures to Shrew in a sign language he couldn't understand.

Shrew winked reassuringly at Wilf as she moved into the shadow behind the door that led to the hallway and front door. They could hear Dardalloy issue a challenge and then the creak of the door and the sound of the rain. A few seconds later, Dardalloy returned. He was followed by two figures covered in grey hooded travelling cloaks that dripped rainwater and glistened in the light of the candles. As Shrew stepped out from behind the door, Melowyn had lowered her hood and was arranging the long tresses of her golden hair.

Dardalloy looked relieved. "This is the Lady Melowyn," he said, and looked at Wilf, who sat with his mouth agape. "And this honourable gentleman is Cyr, a pathfinder from the Gloamril Forest."

Shrew bowed her head in greeting. "Welcome, my Lady, and good sir," she said cheerily. "I'm so glad it was friends at our door; we daren't leave the house!"

Melowyn returned the greeting and surveyed the room. "I see you have the child," she said; "and who's the young lad?" Her blue eyes had settled on Wilf.

"He's a former guard at the Middern workhouse," Shrew answered. "Without Wilf's help, we wouldn't have escaped with the girl."

Melowyn paused and looked closely at the young man for several long seconds. "I sense we can trust you, Wilf," she said at last in a kindly voice. "Thank you for your help." She turned back to Shrew and her blue eyes sparkled as she looked her up and down. "Did my gifts serve you well?"

Shrew smiled bashfully. "Very well, my Lady. I didn't receive a scratch. I still don't know how to repay you."

Melowyn walked swiftly over to the girl from the workhouse, who still lay asleep on the couch in the corner of the room. "You already have," she responded. "You wouldn't believe how many are looking for this child right now. Luven will be sending every scoundrel and cut-throat he can lay his hands on to find her. It is no longer safe here. We must all leave immediately!"

"We were waiting for Waylan," Dardalloy exclaimed. "He said he would return."

Melowyn looked up. Concern was written across her delicate sylvan features. "Alas, he will not come. He has been arrested on suspicion of murder and has been imprisoned in the Citadel. That's why I came here as quickly as I could. Come now, or else we might all meet a similar fate."

"Then we must rescue him… I will rescue him!" Shrew cried. She could see the shock on Dardalloy's face.

"No, Shrew!" Melowyn interrupted, and then her voice became calmer and more controlled. "You will serve him better by helping me get the girl out of the Middle Reach and into Harbour Gate. We have a barge there waiting to take her across the river; then we will head straight to Swanmere and the safety of the Gloamril." She paused and then looked sympathetically at Shrew. "Come here and help me rouse the girl while the others prepare to leave. We will not be returning here."

"My Lady," Dardalloy intervened, "I confess I am troubled by the news that Waylan has been imprisoned. When there is time, I would be grateful if you could tell me more about the circumstances."

"Of course," Melowyn replied, and hurried over to the girl.

Dardalloy moved over to the window. "It's still raining heavily. I assume you came here on horseback?" He turned and looked questioningly at Melowyn, but she was now speaking softly to the young girl, who now sat on the couch, rubbing her eyes.

Cyr spoke for the first time. The sylvan pathfinder had an imposing presence, and Shrew couldn't help but marvel at his grey leather armour and the fine rings of mail that adorned it. He answered with a voice that had a musical quality. "We have brought four greys from the Eltharion stable; they are by the side of the house."

Shrew had joined Melowyn and now both of them supported the girl as she took a few tentative steps. She looked confused, rather than frightened. "They are swift steeds," Melowyn added. "And Aily," Melowyn said, looking at the girl, "will ride with me, whilst Cyr will accompany us as escort."

"You managed to get her to speak?" Dardalloy exclaimed incredulously. "She's been silent since we took her from the workhouse."

Melowyn nodded and smiled again at the girl. "She's going to be fine, but I notice your arm will need attending to. I had planned that you and Shrew would take the other mounts and follow us at a distance, but I didn't realise you would have company." She smiled at Wilf, who was standing awkwardly beside the armchair.

Dardalloy had extinguished the candle by the window. "Did anyone see you arrive?" he asked, as he attempted to look through the thick smoky glass of the window and the streaming rain.

"We didn't notice anyone," Melowyn replied. "A curfew has been declared, and most folk are off the streets or hurrying to get home. Have you not heard?"

"We have been waiting here since yesterday evening, seemingly cut off from the world," Dardalloy answered, and turned away from the window. "I spoke to one from our order this morning, but he made no mention of a curfew. When was it declared and why?"

Melowyn gently steered the girl into Shrew's arms and sighed. "I apologise, I should have realised you wouldn't have heard, especially after seeing your reaction over the news about Waylan." She paused for a moment to consider her next words. "Aelmar sent a message to me this afternoon. Last night, attempts were made to assassinate three members of the Nine. Those attempts on Aelmar and Miruvar were unsuccessful, but I understand that Mallory was slain."

The room fell suddenly silent. Melowyn continued, "Suspicion has fallen on Waylan for Mallory's demise. That is why he is incarcerated in the Citadel."

Dardalloy started to speak, but Melowyn raised her hand and cut him short. "I need to finish," she said. "Aelmar also told me that an emergency meeting had been held that included the King, Rodderic and himself. A decision was made to disband the Council and impose a nightly curfew that will commence tonight at the chime of the first watch. Notices are being put up across the city, and public criers have been despatched to proclaim the news."

"Then the curfew will begin within the hour!" Dardalloy exclaimed.

"That is why we need to hurry," Melowyn replied. "The streets will be deserted soon and it will make it easier for Luven's accomplices to spot us. Aelmar made it quite clear in his message that all of us are in danger. It is possible that the Black Blood already know who took the girl."

Dardalloy turned again to peer through the window. "Are you sure no-one saw you arrive?" he queried. "There's some fellow loitering under the shadow of the pawnbroker's awning across the street. He's difficult to spot in the rain, but he's there for sure."

Shrew left the girl with Melowyn and hurried across the room to where Dardalloy stood in the shadowy alcove by the window. Close by lay the book she had been reading and also her small backpack and crossbow. She reached inside her backpack and Tirriel's faint voice murmured inside her head.

"Show me," Shrew commanded, as she pulled out her sheathed dagger and belt. Dardalloy pointed and Shrew followed the line of his finger. "You have keen eyes, Darda," she said, nudging him in the ribs. "Now step aside, you're in my way." She moved forward whilst buckling her belt around her waist.

Tirriel's voice now rang clear and cut across her thoughts. "Time is eternal, child, but I cannot wait for ever!"

Shrew ignored the voice that intruded her thoughts and leaned forward towards the window. As her deep-sight grew, shapes, bathed in crimson, emerged out of the darkness and, as she grasped the hilt of her dagger, all that lay beyond the window coalesced into recognisable shapes. "It isn't easy looking through this glass, but I can see three," she said, speaking in a low voice, as if fearing her words would carry beyond the window and the rain. "One leans against the corner of the pawnbroker's shop and two shelter under the roof of a lean-to down the alley. One carry's a crossbow and all have swords."

No-one replied. The significance of her words had silenced them all. It was Dardalloy who finally spoke. "I'm thinking they've been here for some time, my Lady, waiting for us to make a move. I doubt very much that you drew them here."

Melowyn sighed. "I didn't want it to come to this, but now it seems we will have to fight. I see no alternative."

"I have an alternative," Shrew announced, before anyone else had time to speak. "Darda, does the stove still burn?"

Dardalloy looked curiously at Shrew. "It does, but how will that help?"

Shrew ignored the question and picked up her crossbow. She examined it for a moment and then pulled a small package from one of the many pouches that circled her belt. "I am going to cause a distraction," she announced, and proceeded to attach the package to the first flight in the loading mechanism of her crossbow. "Cyr," she called to the tall sylvan, "when you see a blue light appear in the alley across the street, go to the horses. Soon afterwards there will be a loud explosion that should startle and distract those outside. That's the signal for all of you to leave."

"Well, where in Serreth's name will you be?" Dardalloy demanded.

Shrew grinned and pointed upwards. "I noticed you have a skylight that opens onto your roof. Now that reminds me. I'll need my cloak as it's still raining."

A comical expression spread across Dardalloy's face, but before he had time to pursue the matter, Melowyn interrupted him. "We haven't time to bicker. Shrew, are you sure about this?"

Shrew nodded. She had donned her weapons and swept up the book and her other belongings on the table and was packing them into her backpack. "I'll make my own way to Harbour Gate and meet you all there," she replied with a confident smile.

Melowyn returned her smile. "Very well, Shrew. Wilf will take your horse, if he is able. I would like you to go straight to the Will-o-the-Wisp Inn by the Traders Gate. I want you to seek out Lord Miruvar and tell him of the situation. He is easy to identify. He has hair as white as snow and a thick beard to match. We had planned to meet him there, but now, I fear, we must ride with speed directly to Harbour's Gate. He will know what he should do. Are you really sure you know what you are doing?"

Shrew nodded and turned once more to Cyr. "I will only be a few minutes. Watch for the blue light!" Then she took a last look at Dardalloy. "Don't fall off your horse, Darda!" She smiled reassuringly at him and pulled up the hood of her cloak. Then she left the room to look for the stove and then the stairs that led up to the skylight.

The roof tiles of Dardalloy's house appeared slick from the rain. Shrew had managed to crawl on to the wet roof and now inched her way forward towards the gable end that overlooked the street. The rain had eased and she breathed a prayer of thanks to Latia in gratitude. Right now, she needed luck on her side. She could see the roof of the pawnbroker's shop and now the awning, but it hid the man below. Grasping the hilt of her dagger, she let her deep-sight return. He was still there, and so were his companions further up the alley. Now all she needed to do was to make them come closer together. She had impressed Tirriel to stay silent and spent a few seconds mulling over the plan in her head. She checked to her left, down the slope of the roof. That was her exit, should she need it. Then she released her hand from the dagger and drew forth her crossbow. Her nostrils caught the acrid smell of the moonglow as it smouldered in the small package affixed to the end of her first flight. Licking her lips, she took aim.

A small jolt, a brief hiss and then a blue light flared in the alley opposite the house. It crackled and sparkled for a moment and then made a peculiar whimpering sound as its light faded. "Go on, go look at it!" she breathed. She could see that the lanky fellow under the awning had moved and now had his back to the house, but he hadn't moved further into the alley as she had hoped. "Mother of Midir!" she swore under her breath, and released the second flight. It transfixed the man's neck and he dropped like a stone.

Now there was a commotion. Beneath her she heard the horses, whilst in the alley the fallen man's companions were calling and drawing their swords. They were calling to others further up the alley. These others had been waiting beyond the reach of her deep-sight!

She let out a volley of curses and reached into her belt for the thunder pod she had just prepared. It had been primed by the stove and needed only a quick rub with her hands to turn it unstable. There was no time for a further prayer. She threw the pod into the path of the oncoming men. It detonated loudly with a blinding flash that illuminated the length of the alley and the street. There were screams and cries from every direction. Amidst the chaos, a number of horses came into view below. Two of the steeds surged forward, urged on by their riders, and then rode away into the night. Two horses remained, and she noticed one of the riders struggling to gain control of their mount. She cursed again as a number of armed figures blundered out of the smoke that had billowed out of the alley. They had spotted the horses and moved to cut off the riders' avenue of escape. She moved quickly and slid down the slope of the roof, screaming at the top of her voice, calling attention to herself. Rolling on to her stomach, she caught the broken guttering hanging crazily below the roof line, which was enough to control her fall to the ground. Her actions had distracted the men who were advancing towards the horses and it provided a window of opportunity for the two remaining riders. Within an instant they had taken flight, and Shrew found herself confronting one of the men from the alley, who stood directly in her path. He charged at her with such momentum that it took the three remaining flights from her crossbow to bring him down. Then the darkness, the drifting smoke and the confusion all came to her aid. She used them all to her advantage, and using a lifetime's experience of evading trouble, she seemingly vanished and was gone.

The storm had passed and now a few of the brighter stars were twinkling through rents in the cloud. Shrew crept silently under the shadow of a small stand of Linden trees. She had made it safely to the Garden Park of Ahlune and was close to the rearing buttresses of the great Middern Wall. Far off, a distant chime rang out from a bell that was situated somewhere over the wall in the Low Reach. It was answered by another chime close by. Shrew paused in her tracks. The chimes marked the beginning of the first watch. Only a short while ago she had heard calls from the direction of the Artisans District, warning of the impending curfew. Now it had started and, if she was caught by the City Watch, or any of the other patrols sent out to uphold the King's proclamation, she would be questioned and almost certainly arrested. Shrew grinned. They would have to catch her first.

She bent down low and padded silently out from the darkness beneath the trees to where a path ended at a small stone plinth which carried a simple bronze sundial. She stopped and listened for a moment. A light breeze stirred the leaves in the nearby trees. Further away, an owl called into the night. Satisfied that she was alone, she crouched behind the stone and prised up a secret trap-door hidden in the turf to reveal a dark opening. Within seconds she had dropped inside and found the top of the stair that would take her down to the Everdark.

Before descending, Shrew paused a brief moment to unsheathe her dagger and let the deep-sight define her surroundings. Tirriel's voice re-awakened in her mind. "Is this the time, child?" Shrew found herself hissing a terse response. "Not now. Soon!" Then she closed the trap-door behind her before descending the winding stair. This was the same route she had taken that fateful night when she had first entered the Middle Reach, except on that occasion she had been climbing up the stairs from the Everdark below. She smiled as she recalled how nervous she had been. Now such a journey was routine, as long as she stayed to the paths she knew. She passed a landing and continued down, passing the familiar sign of a dagger. Its blade was pointing down and fairly blazed on the wall under the scrutiny of her deep-sight.

A short time later, she reached the end of the stair and a short passage that led to a door. Beside the door was an iron lever set into a recess in the wall. She wasted no time in pushing down the lever and opening the door. Then she stepped through the doorway and into a cavern beyond.

The cavern was like a hub with several passages radiating from it — she took the first passage on her right and proceeded cautiously. Now she would need her wits about her, for she had just left the relative safety of a secret passage used by the Silent Knife and had stepped into a more frequented route. She knew the Black Blood and other nefarious groups used this passage, for it was one of just a few routes that enabled access to the Middle Reach from the Low Reach. Shrew moved forward cautiously and followed the passage as it descended. She had the advantage of her deep-sight and was confident she would detect the presence of others before they discovered her. It didn't take long before she entered the place known as the Squeeze, where the passage narrowed considerably. At this point she knew she was passing through the huge foundations of the Middern Wall, and she tried not to think about the countless tons of stone pressing down upon her from above. Beyond the Squeeze she entered a region she called Rat Man Alley, where numerous side tunnels cut away from the main course. She had heard tales of creatures that were half-man and half-rat, and rumours were rife in the Silent Knife that this was where they could be found. Shrew was sure she had seen one once, when she had first passed this way, but had never taken the time to check the voracity of the claim.

Tirriel's voice cut through her thoughts. "We are close to the descent, to Qinestra, child, the place your kind calls the Dovecote."

Shrew slowed her pace. Mixed emotions of joy and sorrow threatened to overwhelm her. "You remind me every time we draw near!" she snapped. "This time our road doesn't pass by the Dovecote." As if to stress her point, she suddenly turned right, into a narrow passage that immediately started to ascend. Shrew bit her lip. She could feel Tirriel's pain and found herself muttering under her breath. "You will see Qinestra soon. I promise."

The ascent became steeper and steps appeared in the stone floor. Shrew focussed her eyes as far as her deep-sight would allow, until the faint violet glow of a familiar symbol appeared amidst the maroon outlines of the left-hand side of the passage. She approached it swiftly and placed her hand over the symbol and into a slight depression in the wall. There was a faint click and a portion of the wall immediately swung inward. She stepped through the secret door and seconds later, after ascending a ladder, she emerged from a trap-door that was set into the floor of a large cellar.

Shrew caught her breath, dusted herself down and then removed the cover from a feebly glowing wisp lamp that stood nearby on a table. She looked around with satisfaction and sheathed her dagger. Remund always kept this room clean and tidy. It was one of the main cache rooms that the Silent Knife maintained within the city. Somewhere here, she remembered leaving several garments for a future visit. She uncovered another lamp that shone brighter than the first and found some towels and a basin with a jug of water. At last, she said to herself, I can clean up and remove some of the charcoal from my hair.

It didn't take long for Shrew to find the clothes she sought, and a little while later, after scrubbing her face and tidying her hair, she had transformed into a well-to-do young lady, complete with lace-trimmed gown and jewellery. In normal circumstances she would not have been out of place in one of the more prosperous areas of the Middle Reach, but now she sat on a stool and hungrily devoured the last remnants of a ration pack. Suddenly, a noise disturbed her and in the blink of an eye her dagger was back in her hand.

"Who's down there?" a voice called from the top of a narrow set of stone stairs that rose against the far wall.

"Rem?" Shrew called, recognising the voice. She wiped her mouth with the back of her hand and watched an elderly man in a leather surcoat and breeches descend the stairs.

"Shrew?" Remund peered at her from under his bushy eyebrows. "Ah, it is you! And by my mother's word, you look beautiful. Like a proper lady. I've never seen you like this before!"

Shrew did her best to control a blush and gave him the sweetest and most angelic smile she could muster. She liked Remund and the smile was genuine, but she felt that before the evening was out, such smiles might have to come often — so it was worth the practice! She stood up and greeted the man with a friendly hug and then stood back and looked at his tanned features and drooping moustache with a look of concern upon her face. "Rem, have you heard about Waylan?"

Remund was silent for a moment. He rubbed the back of his neck and looked down at his feet in thought. "Aye, lass. Maykn has stepped in whilst Waylan is gone."

Shrew nodded. She knew Maykn. A wily and canny rogue, if ever there was one, but one that was also ambitious. She doubted he would risk losing his new position by making the effort to free Waylan. She sighed and looked at Remund. "Rem, I need your help. I haven't got time to explain, but I need to get to the Will-o-the-Wisp as soon as possible."

Remund frowned. "Well, lass, there's a curfew at the moment and there's the City..." He paused for a moment and then started grinning. "There's that stalwart bunch of fine young men called the City Watch." He winked at Shrew. "They'd jump at the chance to escort a beautiful young lass such as yerself, especially in such dangerous times!"

Shrew lifted the side of her voluminous gown and slipped her dagger into a sheath that was strapped to her thigh. Then she straightened her garment and looked up into the wide eyes of her companion. His expression seemed to be trapped halfway between embarrassment and surprise. She raised her eyebrows and then smiled. "In such dangerous times, Rem, this lass doesn't journey anywhere alone."

CHAPTER NINE
THE WILL-O-THE-WISP

Shrew gave one of her alluring smiles to the Captain of the Watch, who stood stiffly in front of his men and bowed courteously towards her. Somehow, Remund had managed to draw the attention of the City Watch. When they heard that there was a lady sheltering in his house who needed to get back to her lodging, they dutifully obliged to escort her. It was only a short walk from Remund's house near the Lichgate to the Will-o-the-Wisp, but Shrew couldn't help but smile. Remund's plan had been a stroke of genius. She had reached her destination in style!

"My thanks again, Captain, to you and your gallant men." Shrew's eyes sparkled at the assembled troop as she lowered the hood of her cloak to reveal the blonde ringlets of her hair. "Next time I will plan my journey more carefully."

The Captain bowed again. "It was a pleasure being of service, ma'am."

Shrew stood for a moment, expecting the men to move off, but they stood watching her. Clearly, they wanted to see her safely in the inn before they continued their patrol. She smiled at them again and turned towards the front of the inn. It had to be one of the most beautiful inns in all of Highfall. The entire frontage was adorned with a myriad of coloured lamps that cast spectral hues over the length of its dark timber and red stone brickwork. Above the main doors, a sign depicted a glowing blue wisp trapped in a jar. It had a childish face, like a sprite, with pointed nose and a wicked smile.

As Shrew stepped forward to enter the inn, the Captain suddenly appeared beside her. "May I escort you in, ma'am?"

She touched his arm. "Thank you, Captain, but I will be fine from here." She stepped across the threshold into an ante-room lit by the pale unwavering glow of a few wisp lamps. An ostler emerged from the shadows and on seeing the apparent wealth of his next guest, called upon a small army of servants to attend to her needs. Shrew found herself being ushered away from the main common room, towards a staircase that led to a more salubrious part of the establishment, which was reserved for wealthier patrons. She turned to the ostler and halted her entourage on the stairs.

"I would like a private word," she said, drawing the ostler aside. "There is a reward for you if you can help me."

The ostler, a bow-legged man with a thinning pate, wasted no time in dispersing the servants. "How can I help, my good lady?" he enquired, rubbing his hands together in eager anticipation.

Shrew whispered in his ear. "I am seeking a friend. He is an elderly white-haired gentleman who also has a beard." She paused as she recalled Melowyn's description and then added, "His hair is as white as snow. Have you seen him?"

The ostler thought for a moment. "I know the gentleman you speak of. He is in the common room, but he is not alone. He is with another gentleman who looks like a cleric of sorts."

Shrew reached into a pocket in her gown and pulled out a silver coin. "Take me to him now," she instructed, "then this florin will be yours."

The title of common room was a misnomer. It was no single room as such, but a chain of interconnecting spaces, on different levels, connected by either stone or wooden stairs. The walls were festooned with objects of all shapes and sizes. Farm implements, battered armour, soot-stained and faded canvases of long forgotten people and creatures, even unusual curiosities from across the Western Sea, all competed for space. Amidst all of this paraphernalia hung glowing wisp lamps and lanterns of every design, colour and size. Their pale light shed rainbows of colour through the haze of the pipe-weed smoke that hung in the air and diffused into every snug, nook and cranny. As Shrew followed the ostler, she couldn't help but liken the place to the smoke-wreathed caverns of a Dragon's lair.

"This way!" The ostler raised his voice in order to be heard above the laughter and chatter from the many patrons that filled the establishment. It was busy, despite the curfew, and Shrew was glad when they descended a short staircase and entered a quieter area beside a large hearth.

"Over there." The ostler nodded towards a shady side-room, where only one amber wisp lamp shed its feeble light.

Shrew dropped two silver florins into the palm of his hand. "Thank you," she said. "The extra florin is to see that we are not disturbed."

The ostler bowed. "As you wish, my lady. I will instruct my staff."

Shrew nodded in appreciation and then turned and approached the snuggery. Two robed and hooded figures were engaged in deep conversation, hunched over a table. She coughed politely, but it was a full minute before one looked up and noticed her presence.

"Aha, it's my favourite maid!" The man pulled back his cowl and Shrew immediately recognised him.

"You!" was all she could utter. There before her was the white-bearded old gentleman who she had waited upon numerous times in the Half Moon Tavern.

The old man stroked his beard and smiled. His deep blue eyes that had fascinated her so many times twinkled, reflecting the light of the lanterns. "I haven't seen you for ages," he said. "I assume that's because you work here now?"

Shrew gained her composure and tried to think of what to say. Eventually, the words came. "Lord Miruvar," she said, bowing her head. "Lady Melowyn sent me." She looked warily at the old man's companion. "My news is important. May I join you?"

Now Miruvar was lost for words. He looked towards his companion as if seeking an answer, and then back to Shrew. "Well, of course," he said finally. "My apologies, my dear, please be seated. Let me introduce you to my friend, Deakin."

Miruvar's companion threw back his cowl and Shrew's eyes widened when she looked into the handsome features of a young man with short-cropped blond hair and an immaculately trimmed beard. "My lady," Deakin whispered. He nodded his head slightly, but his eyes remained fixed upon her. "Here," he said, as he started to rise from his seat, "please sit next to me."

"Well, well!" Miruvar said, grinning through his beard as Shrew sat down opposite him. "Now, let me recall. Your name is Sheri. Am I right?" He slapped the table with the palm of his hand and looked at Deakin. "This girl has intellect. She has a mind as sharp as a…" Miruvar paused for a moment, trying to seek a suitable word.

"A dagger?" Shrew ventured, and smiled. "Sheri is my adopted name," she informed them. "My other name is Shrew."

Miruvar opened his mouth to speak and then the words froze on his tongue as realisation dawned. He looked at Deakin. "By the light of Ahlune! You know who this is?" he finally said. "This is the girl Melowyn talks about. This is Wellen's protégé!"

"Wellen?" Shrew queried. "I assume you mean Waylan?"

"Exactly!" Miruvar cried. His face had turned red and his blue eyes sparkled, shining even brighter. "Who would have thought," he chuckled. "The most nimble-witted barmaid in all of the Reaches is also the scourge of the Black Blood!"

A look of amazement appeared on Deakin's face. He now looked at Shrew differently. The expression on his face reflected both wonder and disbelief.

"Waylan is locked up in the Citadel," Shrew declared. "If no one else will help, I will get him out on my own."

Miruvar put up his hands as if to ward off the very idea. He looked sympathetically at Shrew. "Don't think we have been idle over this matter, or are not as concerned as you." he said in a low voice. "But don't go trying anything on your own. I promise something will be done."

Shrew leaned back in her chair and looked hard at Miruvar. The intensity of her stare seemed to suggest that she was trying to bore into his thoughts.

"I promise," he repeated. "Now, I think it's time for a drink." He raised his hand and clicked his fingers to attract the attention of a nearby maid. "I think we should celebrate this fortuitous meeting."

A short time later, the maid returned, carrying a tray with a carafe and three crystal glasses.

Miruvar's eyes sparkled once more. He took the carafe and poured out equal measures into the glasses. "Saffron Peruse," he said. "The year fifty, fifty-five was an excellent vintage. Now, let us make a toast to absent friends." He raised his glass and they all joined in the toast. Shrew had to admit the wine was one of the best she had ever tasted.

Miruvar drained his glass and looked towards Shrew. "Now, my dear, you had a message for me?"

Shrew nodded, and after checking the maid no longer loitered near the table, leant forward and whispered, "Melowyn has the girl and has made directly to Harbour Gate. She is in the company of three others. She plans to go on ahead without you and said you would know what to do."

The old man grinned and filled his glass with more of the wine. "I know this already, but thank you," he beamed. "Just like the Silent Knife, I, too, have my scouts and messengers. In fact, those same informants have told me of a new legend in this city." He looked up at Shrew with a twinkle in his eye. "A shade in the night that can make the very air explode!" Miruvar smiled as he took another sip of his wine. "You've caused quite a stir, young lady."

"So, what will you do?" Shrew asked.

Miruvar put down his glass. "I think the question is — what will you do?" he countered. "Virryn's hounds will be out there looking for you. You've rattled them. They want revenge." He paused and thought for a moment. "I suggest you come with us. We will be staying here tonight, but tomorrow we'll take a barge to the hamlet of Tilterdown. It's north of here, on the other side of the Swan River. Then we will travel inland to Swanmere; it's where Melowyn will be waiting with the others. The Council of Nine has been dissolved and this city has become dangerous for anyone opposed to Luven and his friends from the Crimson Sect."

Shrew nodded. "Thank you for your kind offer." She looked across to Deakin, who returned a welcome smile. "I will stay here tonight and may follow you eventually, but tomorrow I will depart on another quest. It will not take long, maybe only a few days, but it will fulfil a promise to a close friend and will also take me far away from Virryn and his assassins... which reminds me." She turned back to Miruvar. "How did you survive the assassin's blade?"

The old man sat silent for a moment and then quietly answered her question. "Well, I didn't kill him. He quite capably killed himself."

Shrew looked confused. "Is that a riddle? I don't understand."

"Let me show you something," Miruvar replied, as he reached into a pocket in his robe. "Look closely at this coin," he said, and held out a gold sovereign in the palm of his hand. "Can you see its colour changing?"

"No!" Shrew answered sharply, shaking her head.

"Then look again more closely," Miruvar suggested. "Can you see it glow with an inner fire?"

Shrew leaned forward and examined the coin more closely. "Why isn't it burning your hand?" she exclaimed suddenly. "There are flames all around it!"

Deakin chuckled. "Can't you see what he's done, Shrew? He's thrown a suggestive-illusion!"

Miruvar closed his fingers over the coin and then opened them again. Shrew gasped. The flames had gone!

"Hah, so you're an illusionist," she said, accusing the old man. "That was a trick!"

"Call it trick, if you like," Miruvar said, putting the coin back into his pocket, "but it killed the assassin." He looked kindly at Shrew. "Let me explain. I suggested to this intruder that he was on fire and that he could extinguish the flames by jumping from my balcony into the cool waters of the fountain below. Unfortunately, there was no fountain, there was no water — but there was certainly a long fall!"

Deakin laughed and Shrew found herself laughing, too. "I never would have believed you, if you hadn't shown me the coin," she said, wiping the tears from her eyes. Suddenly, she yawned. "I'm sorry, I really will have to go and find a bed soon; it has been a long day." She paused a moment in thought. "But before I forget. Could I ask you to give a message to Dardalloy for me, please? He's with Melowyn."

Miruvar smiled and stroked his beard. "Of course. What is it?"

"Tell him I am going to descend into the Dovecote and that I will be at Remund's place on my return."

Chapter Ten
The Road to Helmscrag

Aelmar raised his hand and called his contingent of riders to a halt. To his left, Highfall rose up out of the lowlands and up the mountain slopes like a beached ship whose masts were white towers, and the clouds above, its tattered white sails. To his right, the landscape was dotted with stands of sycamore and oak, and, beyond two or three nearby farmsteads, he could see the distant grey outline of the small hamlet of Tilsh.

"We rest here only for a few minutes," he called back. "I want us to reach Bristlefair by noon."

The nearest of his companions, a middle-aged man in grey plate mail whose breastplate was engraved with the crossed talons of the Palatine Guard, drew his armoured warhorse alongside him and saluted. "Sire, we left so hurriedly this morning, could you spend a moment briefing me more on the nature of our mission?"

Aelmar smiled grimly and nodded. "You deserve some explanation, my friend. In fact, gather the men around and I'll address you all. A stretch of the legs and a moment's relief from the saddle will be good for us all."

Aelmar dismounted from his horse and was soon surrounded by the small group of men that had accompanied him from Highfall. There were eleven altogether, and he made the group a perfect dozen. He stood silent for a moment and looked into each weathered face. These were all veterans, hardened fighters and scouts. Each one returned his stare. He could see both respect and fealty in their eyes, and suddenly he felt proud of them. He paused for a long moment at the eleventh man, a scout whose features were barely visible under the shadow of the hood of his cloak. Then he surveyed the group as a whole.

"I'll make this short," he said, folding his arms. "I don't want to delay us unnecessarily, and I'm sure you're all looking forward to a tankard of ale and a wench on your lap at Bristlefair!"

There were a few chuckles from the men. He smiled and continued to address them. "You all know that we are on our way to Helmscrag, on an errand for the King; but there's more to this that you need to know."

He paused and looked at Hengist, the officer who had approached him a few moments before. "There have been strange goings-on in Highfall of late. The other night I had to fend off an assassin; although, as you can see, he wasn't successful!"

There was louder laughter now and Aelmar waited a moment for it to subside. "The King's order was passed to me by Lord Rodderic, the Royal Treasurer. The King has become more reclusive of late and recently announced that Lord Rodderic would act as his voice for the Council and matters of state. This has troubled me, but I was not surprised when a sealed message, supposedly from the King, was delivered to me by Rodderic in person. He informed me that it was the King's wish that I should deliver it to his brother, Prince Morkere, the Castellan of Helmscrag Keep. I have the message here." Aelmar gestured to his horse. "It is still sealed and safe in my saddlebag."

Aelmar brushed aside a wayward strand of his long, fiery hair and then continued. "Rodderic told me that the King was concerned for my life and that he feared that I could become the target of another assassin. So, he was sending me to Helmscrag to put me out of harm's way." Aelmar chuckled. "Out of harm's way, indeed! Does Rodderic think I am a half-witted fool, that I do not realise what his real intentions are?"

The men had fallen silent, and Aelmar could see that he had their undivided attention. The only sounds came from the wind tugging at their cloaks and the calls of distant birds. He stroked the bristles on his chin and looked towards the walls and towers of Highfall, deep in thought. "I have had time to ponder Rodderic's actions these last few hours," he said quietly. "This has nothing to do with the King at all. It's all down to Rodderic and certain members of the former Council. They want me out of the City. The more I think about it, everything becomes perfectly clear; they want me out of the way permanently! For, with the dissolution of the Council, I am the only one who stands against them and their new acquaintances, the Crimson Sect priests from the temple at Everdim."

There were murmurs amongst the men and a few voices were raised. Hengist stepped forward. "Sire, are you suggesting that Lord Rodderic fraudulently gave you an order, making it seem it was from the King? That is treasonous!"

Aelmar raised his hand and the men fell silent. Then he moved to his horse and retrieved a scroll from his saddlebag. He held it aloft so all could see the seal and that it had been unopened. "This is the message. Who dares open it?" he challenged.

For several long seconds, nobody moved — then Hengist stepped forward and took the scroll from Aelmar's hand. "Sire, I've known you a long time and we have fought together and trusted each other with our lives. That trust is with me now!" With that, Hengist broke open the seal and unrolled the parchment. For a brief moment he inspected it, and then held it aloft for all to see. It was blank on both sides.

The realisation of what the blank parchment meant slowly dawned on the whole party.

Hengist was the first to speak and voiced the concerns of the others. "This message is a ruse. The parchment is clearly blank and unblemished. I can detect no trace of secret writing. We've been duped and are walking into a trap. We've got this far, but it seems to me, we're not meant to reach Helmscrag!"

Aelmar nodded. "I have to agree," he said, and paused for a moment to think. "Now, if I was planning an ambush," he reasoned, "I would not want it too close to Highfall. Neither would I want it more than a day's ride from the city. It must be planned for where the road enters Blogar's Wood, just a few leagues east of Bristlefair."

"Then let's prepare our own ambush!" one of the men shouted. There were cheers and others made similar cries.

Hengist raised a hand and signalled for silence. "Sire," he said, turning to Aelmar, "let us return to Highfall and confront Rodderic and his treason."

Aelmar looked at Hengist and shook his head. "No, we would be intercepted before we reached the Middern Gate. Rodderic is tame compared to the likes of Luven and Morrdis. I'm sure both of them would prefer that I was out of the way permanently." He thought for a moment.

"I think I have a better plan, but it would mean us splitting into two groups." He turned and looked at the rest of his men.

"Listen up," he called loudly, so the rest of the troop could hear him. "We will continue our journey north and leave the Helmscrag road before it enters Bristlefair. I want two scouts a furlong ahead at all times. Tonight, we will camp close to the North Star Inn on the road to Holwine and then at first light tomorrow we will split into a group of three and a group of nine. Hengist will lead the nine and go east towards Helmscrag on the more northerly route, avoiding Blogar's Wood." He paused and looked at his friend. "You are still taking the more dangerous path. Use your scouts and keep off the roads where possible. Tonight, I'll put the blank parchment to good use and pen a real message for you to give to Prince Morkere."

Hengist smiled and nodded. "May I ask where you are going, Sire, and who your two companions will be?"

Aelmar turned and gestured towards a burly warrior, who was clad almost head to foot in dark splint mail. "I will take Ryrkell," he said, nodding at the man. Then he looked at the hooded scout who he had paused at earlier. "My group will be travelling to the Gloamril Forest to meet up with the other Council members who have left the city. There, we can count on the friendship of the sylvan people and plan our moves against those who seek to plant chaos within Highfall's walls. My group will take the Holwine pass and from there go on to Tilterdown. We will need a good scout who knows the eastern eaves of the forest well. Are you up for this task, Waylan?"

The scout pulled down his hood. His face was bruised and bloody, but he managed a thin smile. "Aye," he croaked. "Count me in."

ESCAPE TO THE GLOAMRIL

GOLDFALL

YEAR 5124

The Gloamril Forest west of Highfall

CHAPTER ONE
AN INAUSPICIOUS MEETING

A gentle warm breeze blew across the broad veranda from the crowded harbour below. It carried the sharp and delicate scents of exotic herbs and spices, mixed with the oily redolence of skimmer fish and the fragrance of Melusine musk, that combined to tantalise the senses. Cyrus Col stood wrapped in meditative thought, barely aware of the cries of the barge folk and the crews of the larger schooners and brigantines who busied themselves about the vessels that lay berthed along the quayside of Harbour Gate. His dark gaze tarried for a while on the brightly coloured sails and their strings of rigging, before settling on the far banks of the river and the dark shadow under the eaves of the great forest beyond. The time was drawing near. Soon, all would fall: these petty fools around him, and even Mistranna, his arrogant Queen, who had sent him here, all but banishing him from her kingdom. The beginnings of a smile formed on his thin lips as he envisaged the coming of his Master and the everlasting darkness. It was written in the Psalm of the Shades.

Loud laughter disturbed his thoughts. A growling voice called to him from inside the room and he turned to face the others.

"What is so interesting, Cyrus, that you ignore the entertainment put on in your honour?"

The indigo robes of the High Priest swirled and appeared to blur for a moment as he turned and faced his audience. He looked towards the one that had just spoken: a tall, immaculately dressed man who sat slouched in a large padded chair with two scantily clad women sprawled at his feet, their naked breasts pressed against his knees and their arms entwined about his body.

"My Lord Luven." Cyrus Col inclined his head and smiled, revealing his filed teeth and red-stained tongue. "We of the Crimson Sect partake of different pleasures, but we thank you for your lavish and unsparing hospitality."

"You must share with us the pleasures you speak of," Luven ventured, and his lips parted in a broad grin beneath a thin black line of a moustache. "We are intrigued."

Cyrus Col nodded, whilst casting his dark eyes on the others that lounged within the decadent splendour of the room, a room where furs littered the floor and crystal glasses brimming with ancient vintages rested upon delicately carved wooden pedestals and sparkled under the baleful light of a dozen ghostly wisp lamps. "Very well," the priest countered, looking first to Luven and then to the rotund, olive-skinned southerner known as Morrdis, who lounged beside him. "I will show you something that gives me pleasure!" His eyes settled on one of the women at Luven's feet. "You!" he cried, and beckoned her with a long, bony finger. "Come to me, girl."

Luven raised an arm and pushed the woman forward, and with a lazy wave of his hand gestured to her to go to the priest. She stood slowly and cast a salacious smile back at him, before moving to stand before the priest, with her hands resting on her hips.

Cyrus Col looked closely at the girl. "Open your mouth and let me see your tongue," he commanded. She shrugged and slowly let her blood-red tongue slide suggestively out between her pouting lips. Laughter erupted in the room, but Cyrus Col appeared unperturbed. Indeed, the corners of his lips curled to form the beginnings of a smile. "So, you like the fang weed?" he inquired, nodding slowly. The woman shrugged her slender naked shoulders once more. "I can see that you do," the priest whispered under his breath, "and that will make my work so much easier. Now, look into my eyes. Imagine they are windows to a faraway place." The room fell into silence, and after a few seconds the girl's hands slipped away from her hips. Her eyes were now transfixed upon the priest.

"Ha!" a voice suddenly called out from the audience. "Do you need to hypnotise your women in order to make them perform for you?" There were a few chuckles from the room, but Cyrus Col raised his hand to silence the audience and continued to focus his attention on the woman. "Now!" the priest suddenly cried, and the woman's body jerked. "Go to the brazier by the wall and pluck out a glowing coal from its fires!"

Without question, the girl turned on a heel and dutifully strode over to where the brazier blazed beside the opening to the veranda. Without hesitation, she stooped and pulled out a fist-sized glowing mass from within the fire and held it aloft so all could see.

A woman screamed and cries of shock and alarm came from many in the room. Luven leaned across to Morrdis and uttered words in his companion's ear, yet Morrdis appeared unimpressed. Slowly, he pulled himself out from his repose and called for silence. "Our friend from Rathasia has cast a powerful suggestion," he declared. "See how the harlot's fingers are beginning to char. It is not an illusion. Can you not smell her burning flesh?"

Cyrus Col smiled knowingly. "Precisely; but what suggestion can withstand pain such as this? The art of beguilement and use of suggestion can seduce and trick the mind, but excruciating pain will always break its hold. This is a more intimate form, where the subject's feelings and sensations are being controlled. Look at the angelic smile on her face, yet the heat melts her flesh!" The priest cast a long bony finger at the girl. "She is terrified, but I bade her to smile. She wants to drop the coal, but I command her to hold on to it! Now, that is power, my friends, power over the mind. That is my pleasure!"

Luven nodded and smoothed the thin moustache on his long face. "I understand, Cyrus, but wenches of this quality are hard to come by, and this room now reeks with the stench of her burning flesh. This has been an enlightening yet also a very expensive lesson. This whore is now useless to me."

Cyrus Col's lips curled, but the sneer that was beginning to form on his dusky features quickly transformed into a crooked grin. "I cannot let my host suffer loss. Let me make amends." His grin broadened as he approached the girl and clamped his hand tightly on the wrist below her burning hand. An unnatural chill descended upon the room as a stream of invectives spewed out through the priest's lips. There were muted sounds of surprise as the bright glow of the burning coal faded and a growing darkness coalesced around the girl's hand. The priest cried out a final word and was silent. A cold breeze blew into the room from the veranda and stirred the velvet drapes that covered the walls. Suddenly, a shrill scream pierced the silence and the girl collapsed, writhing in agony at the priest's feet. Cyrus Col looked up at his audience. "You will notice the flesh of her hand is restored, but it came at a high price."

Luven had risen to his feet. "What kind of price?" he demanded. "What do you mean?"

As if in answer, a peel of laughter came from Morrdis, who now rose, slowly clapping his hands. "No cost to you, Luven, my friend, be assured!" the olive-skinned southerner chuckled. "Our friend just called out to the Void in the corrupted Cyridian tongue. The cost will not be in the form of any physical token or treasure. The cost will be on his soul!"

The dark eyes of Cyrus Col narrowed. "You are very perceptive, Morrdis, and how do you know the ancient tongue of the masters?"

Morrdis ran the palm of his hand over his smooth, hairless pate and smiled. "I am from Sellitan, and those from Sellitan have long memories."

The Rathasian priest's eyes widened. "Sellitan is no more. It is lost, buried under the sands of the Great Desert. If you truly are from that city, you must be over a thousand years old!"

"You doubt me?" Morrdis raised his thin eyebrows. "Let me introduce you to Stavan Taro, who also hails from that far city." With these words, he gestured to the youthful albino who sat sullen-faced amidst a group of women in the corner of the room. "Stavan Taro can answer any question you might have concerning Sellitan."

For a brief moment, Cyrus Col appeared lost for words, but he soon recovered his composure and forced a thin smile. "Then I must show greater respect, particularly if you both hail from Sellitan. The blood of the masters must flow through your veins."

Stavan Taro brushed aside the women that fawned playfully about his feet and stood up to reveal his lithe physique. The maroon silks that covered his body matched his red piercing eyes that fixed themselves on the priest. "Respect is returned," he responded in a thin, delicate voice. "The power of necromancy, which you have so adeptly displayed, is a difficult art. One that few mortals could ever hope to attain without the favour of the…" The albino's words trailed from his lips as he studied the priest. "Without the favour of the gatekeeper," he continued. "Through him you summoned dark energy from the Master of Shades!"

"I believe I have under-estimated my new friends," Cyrus Col hissed through his filed teeth. The words of the dark priest then became more controlled. "Yet that fills me with more confidence for our newly forged alliance."

The taut olive skin on Morrdis's face crinkled in a smile as he bowed his bald head towards the priest. "Well, now we know each other better," he said, catching Stavan Taro's eye, "I think it is time to cement this newly forged alliance and bring our new Council into session. We have much to discuss."

"We wait for our sixth member!" Luven called, turning his attention away from the tormented woman who lay sprawled at his feet and who, but a moment before, had held the burning coal. She was clutching her wrist and staring at her hand with a look of disbelief painted upon her face. "But I have been informed that he will be here shortly," Luven added, "so let us move into the long room and await his arrival at the table."

Cyrus Col looked down the length of the ebony table and let his long fingers play with the crystal goblet before him. There were four others seated at the table, but a number of their retainers stood by the walls and servants milled in the shadows by the main door. The wily Luven sat to his left and the olive-skinned Morrdis to his right. Opposite sat the pale-skinned albino, Stavan Taro, whose liquid eyes stared at him like open wounds. Cyrus Col's lips twisted in a parody of a smile. Let the albino try and read my mind, he thought to himself. Let him gaze into my eyes and lose all reason in the dark emptiness of the Void.

The prolonged silence was suddenly broken by a hacking cough from the dour-faced, grey-haired man they called Rodderic, who sat to the albino's right. He must be the bean counter, Cyrus Col reflected, the one whose fingers play with the king's gold. When the darkness comes, his kind will be the first to taste death, the priest thought to himself.

Suddenly, there was a commotion by the door. The servants parted, clearing a path for a richly dressed man, who strode into the room.

"Aha," Luven called. "Our sixth councillor has arrived. Welcome, Lord Mallory. Your place is here, to the left of Stavan Taro."

Cyrus Col turned his attention to the newcomer. So, this was the one they called the Fox, he mused as he appraised the man, noting his expensive velvet trappings and his furtive glances. The man was artful and cunning, he had been told, and the title seemed aptly bestowed. The man had just successfully feigned his own death. Surely, he was the most dangerous of all those present in the room.

Mallory adjusted the collar of his jacket and cursed. "It's warm in here, Luven." He glanced across the table to his host. "The sooner we finish our business, the sooner we can retire to more comfortable surroundings."

A smile appeared below Luven's thin moustache. "Of course," he said. "But first I must introduce you to His Reverence, Cyrus Col, High Priest of Yngvi and Dysettis and ambassador to Her Exalted Royal Highness, Mistranna, Queen of Rathasia."

Cyrus Col slowly rose. His dark eyes met the cold and emotionless eyes of the Fox and for a moment there was a meeting of minds. I was right, the priest thought to himself, this man masks his true intent. He is even more dangerous than the albino.

Mallory extended his hand and his leathery features creased in a patchwork of lines as he smiled broadly. "At last we meet," he said, but no hand was extended in return. Mallory's smile remained frozen on his face as he eased himself back into his seat. "Well, let us dispense with the formalities of greeting then and waste no more time." He cast a quick glance at Luven and made a bridge with his fingers. "Let us proceed with our business."

Luven cleared his throat. "Let us start by clarifying the situation in Rathasia. Cyrus, have you received word from Merrandis?"

Cyrus Col took his eyes from the Fox and addressed Luven directly. "The legions of Rathasia have reached the border crossing at the Bow Bridge, south of Mereond. No doubt the sylvan scum will have alerted their Sillaesian allies and their warnings will have already reached the king's ears."

Rodderic coughed and wiped the spittle from his lips with his sleeve. "King Wulfred has been informed that a Rathasian army is camped outside of Mereond, but he now sits upon his throne in torpor, craving the fang weed. His Voice of Reason and his Shield have fled the city. But to that part of his mind that still harkens to counsel, I have assured that Rathasia means no harm."

"Well!" Luven interjected. "Then you might also tell him that it is the sylvan who feed him lies. Remind him that the sylvan bitch who calls herself Melowyn also betrayed him!" He paused for a moment in thought, smoothing the fine hairs of his moustache with forefinger and thumb. "And I assume that the palatine guard now answers to your commands?"

Rodderic smiled. "Of course; now Aelmar is no longer a thorn in our side, it has been a simple matter winning the hearts and minds of the palatine. The lure of gold is very strong and can overcome even the most loyal!"

"That is comforting to know. We don't want a civil war. We want the people to think we're on their side." Luven paused and looked to the priest. "I apologise, Cyrus, you were informing us of the army's progress. When will it reach Highfall?"

Cyrus Col's dark eyes cast a quick glance at the pale features of the albino. "When the darkness comes and not before," he snapped. "Then, as the might of Rathasia lies arrayed before the gates of Highfall, the elite Merrandis Legion will enter the city through the catacombs beneath the temple."

Luven nodded. "There, you have the first part of our plan, Lord Mallory," he explained. "Now you know why we emptied three workhouses of their sewer rats. It took several weeks for the right path to be found through the Everdark. Children can squeeze through the narrowest of passages!"

There was laughter around the table, but Mallory's features were creased in thought. "What darkness?" he questioned. "Is this some sort of sorcery, conjured by our friend?" He gestured to Cyrus Col. "Or, perchance, is he saying that the army will arrive at dusk?"

Before anyone could reply, Stavan Taro's thin voice spoke loudly and shrilly in prophetic tones. "A dark body from the Void will eclipse our Sun before it rises on the fourth day of the first month of half-light. A long period of darkness will follow the night. The portent is there in the heavens, to those who know the stars."

Mallory nodded. "Thank you," he whispered. "It's strange no word has come from others, especially the sylvan sky-watchers, for they monitor the heavens with unerring zeal. I assume the extended darkness will mask the Merrandis Legion's departure from the main force?"

Cyrus Col laughed; the points of his filed teeth gleamed in the wisp light. "The darkness, which Stavan Taro has so accurately predicted, will provide a greater boon! It will end with the demise of the greater force beneath Highfall's walls!"

Mallory looked uneasy for a moment and glanced at Luven. "Sirra's breath!" he cursed, and then looked at Cyrus Col. "Now I understand! The darkness is the end time prophesised by his red-tongued priests and whispered in awe by the pilgrims that still loiter within his temple walls. Does this darkness bode well? I ask you all to think on this!"

A secretive smile had settled on Cyrus Col's face, but Luven merely smiled. "Cyrus promises that the darkness will work in our favour, and Stavan Taro has said it will be temporary. The plan remains the same." Luven paused and smoothed his moustache whilst he considered his next words. "Our Black Blood and your Silent Knife will destroy the Merrandis Legion in the Everdark. Their officers will be taken hostage, as we agreed. Mistranna will be forced to pay a high price for their safe return."

There were murmurs of approval from round the table.

"Then remind me," Mallory questioned, "what's in it for the priest?"

"Revenge!" Cyrus Col snarled; the red rune on his forehead seemingly blazed as his dark eyes fixed on Mallory. Mallory met his gaze and felt a clammy coldness down his spine; for a brief moment, the priest's eyes had turned black — as black as the stygian darkness within Midir's deepest rift.

Luven appeared slightly amused. "Revenge, Cyrus? Pray, tell us more. I thought you were in this for the power? You will have a seat on the new council of Highfall!"

"First and foremost is revenge!" Cyrus Col growled. "Mistranna thinks to use me to her advantage. The Crimson Sect is a pawn in her plans for the conquest of Sillaesia, yet in Merrandis and the other capitals of her realm we are shunned and persecuted. She has forsaken the old gods and now chooses to venerate that vile witch, the Goddess of Fates, whose crooked towers foul our cities." Cyrus Col spat out a string of unintelligible curses and looked to Morrdis and then Stavan Taro. "And as citizens of long-lost Sellitan, you both know well the fate that awaits those that forsake the old gods."

A silence followed this sudden outburst. The priest's very words had seemed to cast a shroud over the room; even the light from the wisp lamps appeared subdued.

Stavan Taro was the first to speak. His pale face appeared to hover ghost-like in the shadows and he spoke again in prophetic tones. "This darkness is truly from the Void. The priest has called upon the Master of Shades to exact his revenge!"

"It matters not!" Luven interrupted. "The destruction of the Rathasian army in front of our gates and under our feet, in the Everdark, is all we need to be proclaimed saviours of the city. Rodderic has already put plans in place. The King will be replaced by his weakling son, and we will become Highfall's new council, its new leaders, with the spoils of war at our feet!"

Mallory raised his glass. "Bravo!" he exclaimed. There was a slight hint of sarcasm in his voice. "I raise a toast to the new council of Highfall!"

"Then we can depend upon the Silent Knife?" Morrdis questioned.

A wry smile broke out across Mallory's weathered face. "You can depend on the Silent Knife that remains loyal to me," he replied. "As we speak, the last few troublesome elements are being taken care of. Wellen, or Waylan, as he was also known, has been replaced. He now languishes in the Citadel dungeons. My new captain is Maykn."

Luven nodded. "Excellent!" He paused for a moment as he considered his next words. "And you have taken care of that one they call the Shrew?" he asked.

The smile faded from Mallory's face. "That guttersnipe from the Duns?" he laughed quietly. "She is but a girl, and by all accounts, has abandoned the order and fled the city, for she is nowhere to be found."

Luven nodded again. "Nevertheless, if you should find her, bind her and bring her to me. Virryn would like to meet her."

"You have my promise…," Mallory responded, but before he could finish, movement at the door interrupted him.

"Aha!" Luven cried. "My captain returns. Good timing, Virryn. You must have heard us mention your name!"

The servants at the door shrunk aside as a group of men pushed their way past the door. At their head, a thickset man, whose leathery face was criss-crossed by welts and scars, strode forward.

Cyrus Col grinned as he noticed Mallory's sour expression. So, he thought, the Fox has some taste, after all!

"What news?" Luven barked. "Did you find the girl from the workhouse?"

Virryn swept aside the ragged edge of his cloak, revealing a row of slim daggers that hung from a bandolier across his chest. "I did," he replied gruffly. "I found them all."

"You captured them?" Mallory raised an eyebrow. "For that would not be like you."

An ugly grin split Virryn's face. "A barge of corpses now burns off the Gloamril. The girl's secrets have gone to Midir. Her body lies pierced by a score of arrows, alongside those of her protectors!"

Chapter Two
Qinestra

Shrew stood on a stone balcony on the rim of the Dovecote and bathed in its turquoise glow. She wasn't sure whether the euphoria she felt was truly hers, or that of Tirriel's, the woman whose essence lay trapped within her dagger and whose thoughts often mingled with her own. Such thoughts had made her realise that Tirriel wasn't sylvan, she was fey — one of the ancient race, a distant forebear of the sylvan.

Earlier that morning, she had taken a carriage from the Will-o-the-Wisp to the Half Moon Inn in the Middle Reach. Once in her room, high up in the attic of the inn, she had changed out of the finery she had worn the night before and donned a grey skirt, white chemise and blue cotton bodice. She had decided that it was time to lower her station and change into clothes that were more befitting of a serving girl. Then she had taken a basket and placed within it the last remaining flights that Melowyn had given her for her crossbow, along with a bundle of various items that she felt might be useful. On top of these she had placed some food parcels and, finally, she had draped a cloth over all the contents of her basket. She had decided that she would attract less attention to herself if she returned to the Low Reach as a maid on an errand. After all, she had made similar trips before, when the inn required certain delicacies that couldn't be found in the local markets. Unfortunately, her unannounced visit to the inn didn't go unnoticed. Gervaillas caught her coming down the stairway towards the common room. It was then a delicate matter of backing slowly to the courtyard whilst countering his remonstrations regarding her erratic comings and goings. He knew she had a business arrangement with Waylan and Dardalloy, but he still felt she was his responsibility. Eventually, she had managed to placate him by promising to return before the week's end. As she left the inn, she remembered breathing a prayer of thanks to Latia that it was Gervaillas, rather than Rosa, who had accosted her on the stairs! Her return to Remund's house by the Lichgate had been uneventful, save for some hearty banter from two Middern Gate guards, but their interest had not been on the contents of her basket!

She had arrived at Remund's house shortly after the bell in nearby Ahlune's Abbey had proclaimed mid-morning, by sending two loud chimes ringing across the Low Reach. Rem wasn't at home and she recalled that his place looked a little less tidy than usual, but she hadn't the time to check his whereabouts. She had made her way directly to the hidden cellar and had quickly changed into her leather armour. She recalled the urgency of her actions and now, as she stood gazing down into the deep shaft of the Dovecote, at the many openings and recesses that perforated its walls, this same urgency welled up inside her again.

"Sirra's breath!" she cursed. "Be patient! I am nearly ready!" She pushed the mysterious old book she had found in Stavan Taro's tower back into her backpack. She had just reacquainted herself, for perhaps the hundredth time, with the fine traceries on the yellowed map that marked the lacework of tunnels surrounding the Dovecote shaft.

"No need for that now, child," Tirriel's voice cut through her thoughts. "The way will become instinctive, for I am your guide."

"Nevertheless," Shrew retorted, "I would like to know the path ahead." She lifted her backpack over her shoulder till it rested comfortably on her back and then checked her crossbow that fit snugly in a leather holster by her side. Then, as if to labour the point that she would leave in her own time, she checked the calf of her right boot for the envenomed needle concealed within, and then ran her fingers over the corrugated band that she wore over the leather sleeve of her left arm. Here she had lodged the latest additions to her arsenal: a set of slim darts made from basilisk bone, where the hollowed tip of each feathered missile contained a payload of toxins that she had carefully concocted high up in the attic of the Half Moon Inn. Finally, she pulled up the hood of her cloak to cover her head and smiled with satisfaction. Grasping her dagger in her right hand, she breathed a quick prayer to Latia and slowly set off along the stone balcony towards an arched opening set into the wall. Beyond, she knew that a stone stairway wound its way downward and that from time to time she would pass windows and balconies that opened into the Dovecote shaft that would let her check her progress.

Shrew paused. She had passed through several levels and this was the third descending stairway, but now it had ended abruptly and before her the crimson outlines of a long chamber beckoned. It was so long that even her deep-sight could not pierce the darkness at the far end. She had discovered that the natural fluorescence of the Dovecote now only extended a short distance from the shaft, maybe ten yards at the most, and that her dagger's deep-sight was becoming increasingly more useful. It was time to look at her map again, for this chamber radiated outwards, away from the Dovecote, and she knew that the way to Qinestra was through the base of the shaft. Tirriel's familiar melodic voice now cut through her thoughts.

"This is the beginning of the deceptions," she said matter-of-factly. "Now you must trust me and not your map!"

Shrew looked suspiciously at the buttressed walls of the chamber and then up to where stone arches criss-crossed to form a vaulted ceiling. Then her eyes settled on the flagstone floor. At the limit of her deep-sight, she could see that some of the flagstones were set in a pattern of some kind.

"I see it!" Shrew whispered excitedly. "Some of the stones are set fractionally higher than the others. They give off a peculiar glow in my deep-sight." The musical sound of Tirriel's laughter filled her head.

"It's the first and the simplest of the defences surrounding Qinestra," Tirriel informed her. "But you will soon see that it has claimed the lives of many foolish souls who came here in search of fey treasure."

Shrew moved cautiously forward and passed the arched openings of two passages that entered the chamber from the left and right. With the aid of her deep-sight, she could see that both led to stairways that ascended. So, more ways converge on this place, she thought, and made a mental note to study her map later.

Tirriel was quick to remark on Shrew's thoughts; her voice seemed much clearer and stronger than before and rang out with ebullience. "There is only one way down!" she cried.

Shrew didn't reply. She stepped forward and had soon reached the beginning of the strange pattern set in the floor. She took a deep breath and then nimbly stepped between the glowing flagstones. There was a brief respite, a break in the pattern for a few yards, and then it continued once more. Shrew paused for a moment where the floor seemed safe and looked about her. "So, what harm befalls the foolish that fail to see the pattern?" Shrew muttered under her breath.

Tirriel laughed. "Look at the walls, child!" she exclaimed. "Don't you see them?"

Shrew had noticed sooty patches on the smooth stone walls, but now, as she took a few seconds to study them more closely, she saw them for what they truly were. They were the blackened shapes of distorted humanoid figures, smeared onto the walls such that they appeared no more than shadows.

"What did that to them?" she whispered out loud.

"You don't want to know." Tirriel's rejoinder was swift. "It may affect your concentration!"

Shrew pursed her lips and then seemingly skipped through the remainder of the pattern. As soon as she was clear, she halted for a moment, for in front of her stood an impressive arched opening. It appeared to be draped in vines and leaves, but her deep-sight revealed that it was nothing more than cleverly crafted stone.

"This is the work of sylvan stone-wrights," Tirriel informed her. "Even in the depths of the world they carved their beloved trees."

"Did these sylvan also make these so-called deceptions?" Shrew asked, nodding back the way she had just come.

"They did," Tirriel replied. "Armeris brought them here during the last days. They built the tall towers that touch the sky and they also laid stone deep in the earth to hide Qinestra from the world."

"What last days? Your last days?" Shrew pursued. She was now extremely interested in the history that unravelled in her mind. A history that was long forgotten by the world above.

Tirriel sighed. "You ask many questions, child. The last days were several thousand years of your time. It was the time when the fey retreated from the lands of Myrifel and finally left this world. Now let us tarry no longer; I am growing impatient. Through this arch you will find a stairway that will take us down to the ring. It is a large chamber that surrounds the shaft your people call the Dovecote."

Shrew quickly found the stairway. It was broad and descended in a gradual curve to her right. It seemed that no-one had passed this way for a long time, for every step she took created a fine cloud of dust which sparkled in her deep-sight. On several occasions, she crossed short landings where other passages joined the stairway, and every so often shafts of light would strike the stairs from openings in the right wall. One of these opened on to a balcony that projected into the Dovecote shaft. She sheathed her dagger and let the crimson outlines of the surrounding structures fade. She wanted to view the shaft in its natural light and, from this vantage point, see the progress she had made.

"Sirra's breath!" she cursed under her breath, and stepped backwards. "I still can't see the bottom. It seems to descend forever!"

Tirriel's voice cut through her thoughts. "You are seeing another deception, child."

Shrew was startled. "How is it I can hear you so clearly now, without the dagger in my hand?"

Tirriel's melodious laughter fell lightly through her consciousness. "Because we are close to Qinestra, child. Now draw your dagger and look again."

Shrew grasped her dagger and with some trepidation stepped forward and cast her eyes down the long shaft again. Her deep-sight tore through the turquoise haze, bringing each balcony and recess into sharp crimson relief, burning away the last vestiges of a seemingly endless shaft. "It was just an illusion!" Shrew cried. "The shaft ends soon. There is a light, glowing blue-green, like a small sun, and beneath it I can see towers, buildings... maybe even a city!"

"Qinestra!" Tirriel's voice sung in her head. "Soon you will see much more!"

"By the light of Ahlune!" Shrew whispered, and stepped back into the relative safety of the stairway passage. "My deep-sight can see much further now. It showed me a city similar to what we saw under the High Reach, but so much larger!"

"It is part of the same," Tirriel informed her, "and it extends far in all directions. Highfall is but a blister upon its upper surface. Now let us continue down to the ring. There we will find the white stairway that will take us down to the city."

Shrew thought for a moment. "Will we find fey people down there?" She mouthed the words, but no sound left her lips.

Tirriel was quick to reply. "No, child. They have long since departed from this world. Now, let us be on our way."

Shrew gripped her dagger and proceeded down the curving stairway. Her eyes roved over the steps and as far as the curve of the walls allowed, looking for signs of anything that might betray a hidden danger. A side passage suddenly materialised in the left wall, barely twenty yards ahead.

"Ignore it!" Tirriel snapped.

As she drew level with it, she couldn't help but glance inside. "Mother of Midir!" she cried out loud. Within the passage, overturned casks spilled mounds of coins across the floor stones. Further inside she could see large iron-strapped chests with their lids flung open to reveal jewel-encrusted armour and weapons of every kind.

She hesitated. This was real. Her deep-sight showed it!

"Ignore it!" Tirriel's voice screamed loudly in her head. "It's another deception. Move on!"

Shrew shook her head and continued on her way. She was shaken. If her deep-sight was deceiving her, then who or what could she...?

"Trust me!" Tirriel urged, intercepting the stream of thought. "Do not be like the fool who last possessed your dagger."

"What happened to that fool?" Shrew found herself asking, as she continued her descent down the stairway.

"You saw his remains in the sewer, when you first set eyes on me," Tirriel replied. There was some amusement in the fey woman's voice, but her tone soon changed to one of disdain. "He was a pitiful wretch who deserved his fate. His mind was so polluted, so burdened by greed and earthly needs, that my voice barely touched his consciousness." She fell silent for a moment and then continued in a more congenial tone. "You are different...," she purred. "You are so much like me; so sweet, yet also so wicked, in a childish way. That you can hear me so clearly within your thoughts means that our minds are working in synergy."

Shrew's face tightened in concentration. "I don't understand," she replied tersely. "All I know is that your voice is so much clearer since we've come down here, and my deep-sight can see further."

"I told you before," Tirriel reminded her, "it is because we are so close to Qinestra. Now trust me and take heed, for everything here is not as it seems!"

Shrew fell silent and bent her will towards her deep-sight, letting her gaze wander back and forth across the stairway, in search of the slightest anomaly that could reveal another deception. Several minutes passed before she felt the need to speak again.

"The stairway ends and there is a landing ahead," Shrew whispered. She was finding it easier to speak than respond by thought alone. "The landing looks real, but the stairway before me is wavering in my deep-sight; it's as if I'm seeing it through water!"

"Focus on the landing," Tirriel replied. "Do not let your eyes be drawn to the stairway. Move swiftly and do not falter!"

Shrew breathed through gritted teeth and moved forward quickly. She was starting to have doubts about this foolish venture. She didn't relish the prospect of having to come back this way. "There's a large room beyond the landing…," she whispered. "It's weird; it looks very familiar."

"Nei…!" Tirriel groaned. A string of incomprehensible words flooded Shrew's thoughts before the warning became intelligible. "Walk swiftly through the centre of the room. Don't stop and don't question. The deception has fed on your deepest thoughts. I will do what I can to fight it!"

Shrew reached the landing and stepped over the threshold of a great hall, where warm firelight flickered across long tables prepared for a great feast. "Sweet Ahlune!" she cried. "Oh, mother… No, it cannot be!" Tears welled up in her eyes and she hesitated.

"Keep moving. Stay on the path!" Tirriel's voice rose above her thoughts and she could feel her raw emotions being tempered by the fey's presence.

Shrew blinked back her tears and focussed her eyes down the walkway, past the marble colonnades that flanked each side, to the door at the far end. She strode forward and proceeded to walk briskly with her eyes set on the door, but the temptation to turn her head and look at the table nearest the hearth was overwhelming — she felt a presence there, warm and loving.

"Sweet Ahlune, save me," she cried, as the tears now flowed in rivulets down her cheeks. "I must see her one last time."

"Fight it!" Tirriel screamed. "Keep going... Don't look or you're lost!"

Shrew hesitated as she drew level to the spot where she knew her mother usually sat. The temptation to glance across, just for a split second, was overpowering. At that moment, something bright burned inside her head and suddenly she found new resolve. "Forgive me, mother," she sobbed, and hurried forward towards the door. She didn't stop till she was through the doorway and back on the broad stairway once more.

"I have to stop a moment," she gasped, wiping the tears from her face. "I don't think I can go much further."

"We have passed through the deceptions," Tirriel reassured her. "The ring room is very close."

"I am glad," Shrew sighed, and slumped down on the stairs to rest. She sat in silence for a few moments, and then added, "I remember Waylan once said that he knew of no-one who had descended the Dovecote and returned. Now I can believe him. I couldn't have passed through those deceptions without your help. What you did back there saved me."

"You did it all by yourself," Tirriel replied.

"Yes, but I would have turned and looked for her... my mother," Shrew said mournfully. "If it were not for your intervention."

"The sylvan and their forebears, the fey, are masterful in creating deceptions and illusions," Tirriel said, changing the subject.

"My deep-sight failed to see them for what they were, though," Shrew replied. "Why was that?"

"The deep-sight, which is bestowed upon you by the power of the dagger, can only show what is real," Tirriel explained. "Those last deceptions were fabricated within your mind. They feed off the desires and dreams of those they seek to deceive."

"I don't think I will be able to face them again," Shrew whispered, ruefully.

"You won't have to," Tirriel assured her. "When the time comes, I will show you another way back to your world."

Shrew shrugged. "I will be glad to return to the surface and feel the wind on my face once more," she said quietly. "But I made a promise to take you to Qinestra, and I am curious to see the ancient fey city for myself. So, let's be on our way." Shrew rose to her feet and then slowly and cautiously proceeded down the stairs.

A few minutes later, the stairway widened, admitting a further passage that entered from the left. Then, a short distance further, she spied a pale glow ahead.

"We are very close!" Tirriel cried out excitedly.

Shrew sheathed her dagger and the crimson deep-sight changed to a soft turquoise. A great arch loomed before her that appeared to be adorned with tangled vines, and beyond spread an enormous chamber, the centre of which was occupied by a bright orb, like a fallen turquoise star, that seemed to be the source of all the light.

"The ring room!" Tirriel announced triumphantly. "Now keep to the left side and stay away from the centre."

Shrew could see that the advice was well given, for there was no floor in the centre of the chamber. There was only a gaping circular chasm and, in its centre, hovered the orb, casting its pervasive turquoise glow up the Dovecote shaft and down on to the city below.

"What is that thing?" Shrew whispered nervously. It looked like a giant Will-o-the-Wisp. She wondered if it could detect her presence.

"Il'yil," Tirriel said. There was deference in the tone of her voice. "She still faithfully illuminates our way to Qinestra, just like she did so very long ago. Now let us make haste to the white stairway. I have waited so long for this moment."

Shrew skirted the curving edge of the chamber and passed several more stairways. The ring room was clearly a hub, and other passages radiated from it like the spokes of a wheel. Its floor had an unusual lustre and appeared to contribute other colours to the pervading turquoise light.

"There's the stairway!" Tirriel cried. "Set into the floor… What was that?"

"I felt a shadow pass over us," Shrew cried. Her voice sounded hollow and lost in the vastness of the chamber. She lowered her voice. "I don't know what happened."

"Il'yil's light dimmed a moment," Tirriel answered. "I don't know why. Quickly, go to the stairs. I think the answer will lie below."

The white stairway was a peculiar construction. From the ring room, it plunged into empty space into a vast cavern and then descended to the city below, as a spiral within a spiral, through a lace-like construction that appeared to defy all physical laws. Shrew was used to scaling the high walls and buildings of Highfall, but this descent made her feel distinctly uncomfortable. The stairway appeared flimsy; it was as if it was constructed of gossamer threads, delicately spun of white silk. Worse still, there was no handrail; yet after a few tentative steps, Shrew found she could descend with ease.

Now, for the first time, she saw the city in its entirety — laid out in a turquoise haze as far as she could see. Below her, slender towers reached up like lances and came so close, she felt she could almost touch them. Further away, massive stone pillars from the cavern roof thrust down through the haze, like giant stalactites, and beyond them, other caverns opened wide as the city continued.

Shrew stood mesmerised for a few seconds and then moved again as Tirriel's concern urged her forward. Within minutes, she had reached the foot of the stairway and entered an olivine concourse that led up to an impressive archway around which constellations of wisps faintly glimmered.

The turquoise glow and the intricate lace-like structures around her seemed familiar. It puzzled her for a moment, but then she realised that she had been here in her dreams. "Sirra's breath!" she whispered. "For all the trouble, it was worth coming to see this."

"Hush! Listen!" Tirriel interrupted her. "Do you hear it? Do you feel it?"

Shrew paused and listened. "It's very faint," she whispered. "Like a beating heart. It appears to be coming from behind us, from over there." She pointed to a large structure flanked by statues that protruded from a spur of natural rock.

"It's coming from the Crypts of Everdim!" Tirriel cried, and a tirade of fey curses followed, filling Shrew's head. "What devilry is this?"

Shrew drew out her dagger. "What's buried in there?" she asked inquisitively.

"Beyond those gates lie the resting places for those that did not take the journey," Tirriel answered. "There also lie the mortal remains of many sylvan, and with them those first humans who perished during the sundering of Myrifel."

Shrew shuddered. "If only the dead lie there, then who or what is causing that sound?"

Tirriel was quiet. Shrew could sense the fey's thoughts, but could not perceive them.

Then, without warning, the pervading light grew lambent and momentarily flickered.

"Shey'fa!" Tirriel broke out of her thoughts. "Energy is being drawn away from Il'yil. Something is feeding off the ley! Go towards the crypts, child. I need to know more."

Shrew grasped her dagger tighter. "I will go to the entrance," she replied, "but don't ask me to go inside." As she drew closer, her deep-sight outlined two great gates that stood back inside the fey structure. They were open. She peered in cautiously. The deep-sight painted a crimson image that reminded her of the maw of a giant creature. From deep within came a regular thump that reverberated through the ground at her feet. It seemed as though this creature had a heart!

"We must enter," Tirriel urged. "I need to be sure."

Blue light crackled across the glassy blade of the dagger. Shrew scowled. "I don't like this," she whispered, as she stepped forward. "Something feels wrong." She was now staring down a long tunnel which had numerous niches and alcoves in the walls. Her deep-sight showed there was an intersection ahead.

"To the crossways," Tirriel commanded. "That should suffice."

Now, there was no mistaking. As Shrew moved forward, she could feel the tremors pass through the stone around her. The reverberations were coming from deep within, but from what?

"Yrrch!" Tirriel's cry interrupted her train of thought. "I sense a Dromolich!"

Shrew froze. She could hear a shuffling noise, and suddenly an overwhelming dread enveloped her. She looked around in fear and grasped the coldness of the nearest wall to steady herself. As her senses heightened and her panic grew, the stale air of the crypts, heavy with the dust of countless millennia, threatened to suffocate her.

She grasped the hilt of the dagger tighter and Tirriel uttered calming words, settling her fears. As her panic subsided, her deep-sight pushed back the darkness once more, revealing a pale and insubstantial skeletal figure, adorned in decaying robes from an ancient, long-forgotten age.

"Control your fear, child," Tirriel urged. "It feeds on fear and will try and use it against you."

Shrew raised her dagger. A blue light danced and crackled along the keen edge of the blade and the Dromolich, an apparition of the Void, turned its grinning visage towards her and looked upon her soul.

"You have the power, child," Tirriel cried. "You have my strength, my agility and my cunning, honed over ten thousand years." The voice became louder and then fused with her thoughts. "And you have no fear!"

Shrew's lips flared and she snarled as she stepped forward into the path of the apparition before her. "I have no fear, spawn of Nilhahn!" she spat, and then, in a language unintelligible to her, screamed a stream of arcane invectives at the creature.

The ghostly figure paused and then, like a snake, its jaws distended, opening impossibly wide to spew forth impenetrable darkness; but it was too late to counter the blazing dagger that tore through its chest. Shrew spun around to deliver another blow, but the Dromolich was gone, only shreds of its robe and dust laying at her feet. Now there was a deathly silence, save for her beating heart and a faint thrumming that came from out of the stone around her.

"It is gone and I have my answer," Tirriel announced. "Someone or something is drawing energy from the ley where it enters Everdim. We must leave here at once and go to the Well of Stars at the centre of the city."

"Sssh! Hear that?" Shrew hissed, and turned to look around. She had heard a sound like a rattle, and now more noises were coming from the niches and openings in the walls around her. "Mother of Midir!" she wailed, as a skeletal arm reached out of the darkness from one of the niches and clawed the air.

"The dead are stirring!" Tirriel cried. "I sense necromantic forces. Move swiftly, child, back towards the white stairway!"

It took less than a minute for Shrew to reach the stairway, and immediately she began to climb; but Tirriel's cries filled her head, calling her to stop.

Shrew cursed loudly. "I have seen enough," she cried. "I would prefer the deceptions to those things in your crypts."

"This stairway is not the way!" Tirriel cried vehemently. "We must go to the Well of Stars! Follow the green path to the tallest group of towers. Do as I say!" Shrew felt her body involuntarily jerk with the force of the woman's command.

Shrew cursed under her breath as she steadied her feet. She could see movement by the gates to the crypts. "Mother of Midir!" she cried out in horror, and turned to ascend the stairway again; but a fierce pain lanced through her head, causing her to stumble.

"Impetuous child!" Tirriel shrieked. "I am trying to save you. Now, take the green path... quickly!" Then, in calmer words, the fey woman added, "Did I not tell you that I know of another way to the surface?"

"I seem to have no choice!" Shrew cried, and then leapt from the stairway on to the path below, and ran as fast as she could towards the cluster of towers that stood higher than the rest. These towers stood directly under Il'yil's turquoise glow and were further away than they had first appeared. It took several minutes before she drew near to the tallest tower and she found herself running between lace-like arches that rose up either side of her, to merge high overhead. It was like the nave of a long cathedral, but instead of candles, pale wisps glimmered, caught within the grey lattice that formed the walls. She continued onward, not daring to look back until a tall gateway rose in front of her. Then, she glanced back for a second and was relieved to see that nothing followed her. Then she turned towards the gates and marvelled at their intricate structure. They appeared as a mesh of interlocking silver spirals and stood half-open.

"Pass through!" Tirriel ordered. Shrew caught her breath and stepped through the gateway. She entered a huge chamber with solid walls and fluted pillars, whose domed ceiling appeared to be frosted with stars. Before her were three further gateways. They were tall and narrow and appeared to have no gates barring access. A soft white light issued through the central gateway, which rose slightly higher than the others.

Shrew suddenly felt a wave of emotion pass through her — regret, sadness, despair and finally the exhilaration of finding that which was lost. "Ah'lua ai Taccivae!" Tirriel purred. "So long I have waited. Go forward, child. Go through the middle door and do not fear the light, for I will speak for thee!"

Shrew caught her breath and swayed on her feet as she tried to collect her own thoughts. She closed her eyes for a moment and concentrated, focussing on her own identity and her personal thoughts. "Where is the way to the surface?" she suddenly blurted. "It is not through this door!"

There was a long silence. Shrew could feel the presence of the woman in her head. She tried to speak, but only tears trickled down her cheeks, triggered by an emotion she didn't understand. Eventually, a quiet voice entered her thoughts. "Go through the left gate," it said. "I must give you something, and then I want you to listen."

"I will listen," Shrew whispered. "I can feel there is more that I should know." She tightened her grip on the dagger and passed through the narrow arch of the left gateway. The chamber beyond was bereft of light of any kind, but her deep-sight clearly showed statues lining the walls to the left and right. "What is this place?" she said in a hushed voice. "Why bring me here? It looks like a mausoleum!"

"Standing before you are some of the greater lords and ladies of Myrifel," Tirriel answered solemnly. "Some have gone to the new world we call Taccivae; and those that didn't, doubtless lie interred within the Crypts of Everdim."

Shrew walked slowly between the tall figures and marvelled at their beauty. They appeared so real, with their flowing hair and delicate features; it was as if they had suddenly become frozen just the second before she had entered the room. A shudder went down her spine, for their glassy eyes seemed to follow her as she moved!

"Stop here!" Tirriel commanded. "Now look to your right and behold Faeril. She beguiled many a mortal and fey alike with her beauty. Now she has gone to Taccivae and one day, if fate permits, I hope to meet her again."

Shrew stood mesmerised. This fey woman reminded her of the Lady Melowyn, but there was something extra, something almost god-like in her stance.

"Look to her waist," Tirriel said, directing Shrew's gaze. "There hang Silfa and Sceral, two weapons forged long ago, before your kind came to Sillaesia. These daggers are shards of sky crystal that don't follow the rules of your world. Now sheath your dagger and go to them. Hold their handles and close your eyes. Let me introduce you to them!"

Shrew gasped as the deep-sight faded and darkness enveloped her. Her hands reached out for the handles of the weapons, and when she found them, she cried out in surprise. They were warm!

"Now open your mind, child," Tirriel instructed her. "Let them into your soul!"

A flurry of emotions swept through her. Fear hit her first, followed by gut-wrenching horror, sadness and then finally joy. Shrew clung to the weapons for what seemed like a long time. Eventually, she opened her eyes and it was no longer dark.

"Sirra's breath!" Shrew breathed. The weapons had separated from the statue and she now held them freely in her hands. She stood staring at the lustrous blades, and as she examined them closely, she swore she could see pale white flames flickering within them.

"These are your new friends," Tirriel informed her. "They have agreed with me that you will make an excellent host. I have instructed them how to get to the surface, and they will guide you. It is a one-way route, and once you pass the concealed door there is no return. It is the route taken by Armeris after he trapped me in the dagger before the Well of Stars."

"Why do I need them to guide me?" Shrew asked. "I have you... don't I?"

"I have something important to reveal to you," Tirriel whispered faintly, "but first we must go back to the gate where the light shines. Now, tuck Silfa and Sceral into your belt and take out your dagger once more... we will need it."

Shrew walked briskly back to the great domed chamber, to where the central gateway loomed, radiating its soft white light. She suddenly remembered the dead creatures that had issued from the crypts, but they had not followed her here.

Tirriel read her thoughts. "Do not fear, child. Such spawn of Nilhahn cannot enter here. Now let me speak for you, so you may enter."

Shrew waited, clutching her dagger, and then suddenly found herself issuing a stream of orders in the fey tongue.

"Now go through," Tirriel said softly. "Then listen to what I have to say."

Shrew stepped forward, and as she passed through the light that gathered around the gateway, she felt a tingling sensation. Her hair seemed to lift on her head, and it felt like something crawled across her skin. Once she was through, she stared in wonder. The space before her appeared distorted and stretched, such that light itself was being pulled apart into its spectral colours to form a glowing ring. The centre of the ring was as black as the darkest night and was peppered with stars.

"Sweet Ahlune," Shrew whispered, and then she noticed a fainter sphere of light around the whole construction, and within it, upon the flagstones before the ring, she could see the curled-up form of a body!

"You gaze upon the Well of Stars," Tirriel said solemnly. "It is the portal to Taccivae, our new home beyond the Void. I was the guardian of this portal, this opening that took our people to a new world — but I was not alone. Armeris, second son of Glossingal, also took that role. He stayed with me and we waited for the last of our people. We were to wait five hundred years for any late-comers, but Armeris grew restless. He talked about Myrifel and the world above, and begged me to go with him to the surface. He talked about ruling the humans that now dwelled on the surface and rekindling the empire that once was, but I refused. I had pledged I would protect the portal till the five hundred years had passed."

Shrew nodded. "Is that your body before the Well of Stars?" she asked.

Tirriel didn't reply, but continued relating her story. "One day, Armeris approached me and begged me to accompany him for a short visit to the surface, but I refused. In answer, he plunged a dagger into my chest. It was no ordinary dagger, but one enchanted to draw out and capture a living essence. Later, while on his way to the surface, he threw the dagger and my essence into a drain, and it was many years before anything found me. Of all those that possessed the dagger, only you could I truly reach!"

"What do you want me to do?" Shrew asked quietly. As she spoke, a ripple of light disturbed the stars towards the rim of the Well.

"Shey'fa!" Tirriel cursed loudly. "The drain on the ley is also affecting the portal." The fey woman paused a moment before speaking again. "Can you see that fainter green light that surrounds the Well?"

"Yes!" Shrew answered quickly. "Your body lies just inside it. What is it?"

"It's difficult to explain," Tirriel replied, softly. "It's part of the portal itself, and time passes differently inside it compared to the world outside. Now please listen. I want you to pass the blade of the dagger through that wall of green light, close to where my body lies, so I can reach it. Do not let your hand pass through it. Do you understand?"

"Yes, of course," Shrew responded, "but… you are dead!"

Tirriel laughed. "No, I am not, child. Now, do as I say."

Shrew bowed her head and cautiously approached the edge of the green light, whilst keeping her eyes away from the deep depths of the Well — it unnerved her. Then she knelt a few feet from Tirriel's shimmering body and slowly moved the dagger towards the diffuse green barrier that lay between them. Tirriel's body stirred.

"Sweet Ahlune!" Shrew whispered, and watched in amazement as the fallen woman slowly raised herself up. Her lavender hair lifted from the floor, and as she turned towards Shrew the long tresses fell across the fine silver mail that girded her shoulders. Tirriel looked exactly as she had appeared in her dreams! Shrew felt her hand shaking and quickly steadied it as she pushed the blade of the dagger through the green barrier. It was then that Tirriel raised her head and reached out to grasp the dagger. Shrew looked into her dark almond eyes.

"Elou' eserai! Farewell, child!" Tirriel's voice grew faint. "As a gift to you, I give you a memory of your father. I found it buried deep within your mind. Now go and let your new friends guide you..."

Shrew gasped and let the dagger slip out of her hand and into the slender fingers of the fey. Her eyes blurred with tears.

Tirriel's almond eyes now sparkled like brilliant emerald, and it seemed there was a glowing aura about her body. She looked towards Shrew and smiled, but in her mind's eye, Shrew could see the face of her father, and in that instance, knew who she was.

CHAPTER THREE
BY THE LAUGHING WATER

Beams of golden sunlight shone down from the leafy canopy above to cast speckled patches of light upon the dry rutted road. It was mid-morning, and although the sun had risen several hours before, the forest was dim, save for occasional breaks where the tall trees of red- and orange-tinged maple and yellow linden thinned. Aelmar narrowed his eyes and scanned the path ahead, before raising his hand to bring his two companions to a halt. Motes of light drifted across their path, twinkling as they passed through the shafts of sunlight. Further ahead, he could see the bridge.

"At last!" he said with satisfaction. "We may yet make Swanmere before evenfall." He turned to the hooded figure on his right and smiled reassuringly. "You look better for the rest, Waylan."

"I had a proper bed for the first time in weeks," Waylan retorted. "It may have had a straw mattress and sheets with worn threads that depended on an army of bed bugs to hold them together, but it provided the best night's sleep I've had in ages!"

The tall warrior behind them grinned. "I had a wench to warm mine," he said gruffly. "A big lass, with thighs the size of a swanny barge's fenders!"

They started to chuckle, but Waylan raised his hand and signalled them to be silent. "Talking of lasses, I think I see one in the tree ahead, by the bridge, or are my eyes deceiving me?" he whispered.

"You have keen eyes," Aelmar replied quietly, "but all I see are the trees thinning before the river and the bridge, nothing more. Do you still think we're being trailed?"

"Aye, sire," Waylan nodded. "I do! Remember the quiet fellow in the inn last night? He sat in the corner by the door, brooding over the top of his flagon for most of the evening."

"What of him?" Aelmar returned. "He looked like a dour-faced woodman to me. What did you make of him, Ryrkell?"

The tall warrior shrugged and looked back down the forest road.

"His face seemed familiar to me," Waylan continued. "Yet it was only after we left Tilterdown this morning that I remembered. He is one of the Cutlers Row gang, and they have declared fealty to the Black Blood."

"Let them come," Ryrkell growled, and spat on the ground. "But given the choice, I would rather go seek Waylan's lass in the tree. I need another bed companion tonight."

Aelmar laughed and slapped Ryrkell's broad back. "Aye," he said, "but be careful what you ask for. This is the Gloamril, remember!" He stopped for a moment to remove a folded piece of parchment from his belt. "On another matter, this is the missive which I obtained from the innkeeper this morning. I have no doubt that it was written by Miruvar; I recognise his cursive strokes."

Waylan scratched the stubble on his chin in thought. "Aye, when you showed it to me earlier, the writing did look familiar. Could there be a hidden message buried within, that he was trying to convey to you?"

Aelmar chuckled. "It wasn't meant to be given to me! It was meant for someone called Shrew, but as that individual hadn't been forthcoming, two florins were sufficient to prise it from the innkeeper's hands."

"Did you say Shrew?" Waylan looked up in surprise.

"You know of him?" Aelmar exclaimed, and stopped in his tracks.

"She is one of my folk," Waylan replied. "A youngster and still only an initiate, but she is very smart and canny-like. How in Serreth's name did Miruvar know her? Please read the message again."

"Here." Aelmar held out the parchment. "Check it for yourself. All it says is this… 'Don't tarry, it isn't safe. We met trouble. Trust no one and take the road south to Swanmere. We will be lodging there.'"

Waylan took the parchment and held it in a pale beam of sunlight to study it, but only to note Miruvar's elegant scrawls. He shrugged and handed it back. "As I said, sire, she is smart. If she is following Miruvar, she will find him."

"Don't worry on that score," Aelmar smiled. "I told the innkeeper that there would be a greater reward waiting for him if he were to look out for this person and see that they get safe passage to Swanmere. I was intrigued by Miruvar's concerns over their safety. That wily old sage always surprises me, particularly when it comes to where he pins his trust."

"Pssst!" Ryrkell was signalling to them. He had wandered on ahead and was pointing towards the bridge further up the road. "Your eyes didn't deceive you, Waylan. There's a young-looking lass in the rowan tree, by the edge of the road!"

Waylan drew his finger across his lips and through a quick gesture indicated that he would take the lead. Just a short distance ahead, the forest halted by the banks of a river. Here, an old crooked bridge, with viridian moss powdering its ancient grey stones, arched like a hunch-back over its waters. Beside the bridge, on the near bank, stood a mature rowan tree, burdened by sprays of scarlet berries. On one of its boughs reclined a slender maiden. She was no larger than a young child; cascading ringlets of long amber hair fell about her shoulders. She wore a gown fashioned from velvet red Hibiscus petals and a smile that slowly spread across her pale elfin face. As they approached, she paid them no attention. Instead, she busied herself, preening her long green fingernails.

"Keep your weapons sheathed," Waylan hissed. "Leave me to do the introductions." He approached the tree slowly and then bowed with an exaggerated flourish. "My lady, the sun shines brightly on this, our fortuitous meeting. You honour us with your presence."

In an instant, the girl looked up and focussed her yellow luminous eyes on Waylan, and then like a wary cat, turned her head swiftly to regard each of the others in turn. Suddenly, the ground trembled and the trees swayed either side of the road, as their roots stirred beneath their feet.

"Hush, Stump!" the girl cried, and slapped the bough of the rowan. "This one is politeful and the others seem so, too." She sat up and rested her chin in the cup of her hands and a petulant expression formed on her face as she studied each of them again in turn. "You smell bad. You look

227

ugly, but you are politeful and respectful. Should I let these menfolks pass, Stump?"

The ground trembled again and Ryrkell growled under his breath, but the heel of Aelmar's boot caught his shin and quickly silenced him.

"My lady" — Waylan bowed again — "we seek to follow our dear friends who may have passed this way: an elderly man with white hair and beard and a fair sylvan lady with golden hair. They may have been in the company of others."

"Well!" The girl's brow creased in thought and an impish grin curved her lips as she shook her head disapprovingly. "The fair lady is most vexed, you see. Menfolks should tremble, that they seek to do her harm. She came through the trees like a vengeful breeze and left deceptions over and upon the great waters." She studied their confused expressions and laughed, pointing a long slender finger at each of them in turn. "So, let me think. What gift would best befit an answer to your question and let you all pass safely over our bridge?"

Aelmar coughed politely and stepped forward, but before he could open his mouth to speak, the girl's eyes suddenly brightened and a look of childish glee spread across her face. "I have it!" she cried, settling her finger on the red-haired warrior. "You will give me a lock of your hair!"

Aelmar smiled. "It would be an honour, my lady; but first I have another token you should see." He reached beneath the mail shirt that covered his chest and pulled forth a locket, a clear crystal on a silver chain, within which was framed a lock of golden hair, that dazzled in the sunlight.

The girl's gleeful expression froze on her face. It was several long seconds before she spoke, but her voice had changed. "You have the favour of the Lady," she cried in an ethereal voice. "There are no ways you could have stolen that from her. It is given and can never be taken."

"Indeed, it was bestowed on me by the Lady Melowyn," Aelmar replied curtly. "Just in case I met an impetuous sprite, like yourself. Now tell me your name. I command you in the name of the Lady."

The girl shrunk back into the shadow of the tree. "My name is Misk," she said sullenly. "And now you know my name, I suppose I should be forced to answer your question?"

"I am not forcing you to do anything," Aelmar answered dryly, "but it would be helpful if you could tell us if you saw our friends pass this way. Knowing that they passed by here on their way towards Swanmere would warm our hearts. Right now, we are being trailed by brigands, bad menfolks that want to harm us and our friends. It would not be safe for you to tarry here, either!"

"Tsk!" Misk snorted through her small upturned nose. "We can smell their foulness from here. Stump will go give them a greeting they will remember a long, long time. Won't you, Stump?" She laughed merrily and slapped the tree. "You, silly old goblin!"

The ground heaved and the rowan shook, scattering its berries onto the road. Aelmar stepped back as the ground behind the tree rose up and the gnarled and mossy form of a humanoid creature stood up and shook its massive frame. Its legs had the girth of tree trunks. Sinew and muscle bulged from its arms, and the veins that covered them stood out like creeping vines.

"By Verrain's grace," Aelmar breathed. "The girl has a troll." He signalled to his companions to fall back, but they were already moving out of the path of the creature as it strode onto the road. It paused for a moment and looked down on them with small glowing red eyes. Then it lurched forward down the way they had just come, brushing the trees either side of the road with its massive shoulders.

"Go, go, go!" Misk jumped up and cried out excitedly. "See them off, Stump — and don't eat them all!" Then, just as quickly, she sat back down again, crossed her legs and yawned. "You menfolks make me so yawnful. Why are you still here?"

"Our friends?" Aelmar reminded her. "Did they pass by here?"

Misk pouted and then narrowed her eyes and wrinkled her brow as if in thought. "Of course they did; didn't I tell you?" She winked at Aelmar. "They crossed the bridge just here and went over the laughing water towards Trillshey. There was one old manfolk with a white bush of hair on his chin instead of his head. I could have fixed his problem…" She paused for a moment and her brow creased again in thought. "And there was a young one, with short yellow hair. He had the favour of the Lord Celestine upon him, so I let them both pass."

"How long ago was this?" Aelmar inquired, but before Misk could reply, a rending sound and distant screams came from down the road.

"Aha!" Misk clapped excitedly. "I think Stump has just met your brigands. You had better be on your way quick, before he comes back; sometimes he gets confused." She tilted her head to better position her pointed ears in the direction of the commotion. "They passed here two days ago. No more and no less. Now shoo! All of you!" She dismissed them with a brush of her hand.

"My thanks to you, Misk, and to your friend. We bid you farewell." Aelmar bowed his head and then gestured towards the bridge. "Let's be on our way. We'll need to be swift to make Swanmere before evenfall."

As they crossed the bridge, Aelmar caught up with Waylan, who had forged on ahead. "'Tis all a bit strange," he muttered. "Melowyn wasn't with Miruvar. It seems she encountered trouble of her own... if the sprite's tale is true."

Waylan shook his head. "You cannot trust the small fey folk of these woods, sire. They are fickle, mischievous creatures, but flattery and gifts can sometimes get their attention. It was fortunate you had that talisman with you. It loosened her born-name from her tongue. Once you had that, she was compelled to listen to your request."

"In that case, I believe the sprite's words," Aelmar replied. "Melowyn met trouble on the Swan. I wonder who was travelling with her and whether the girl from the Middern workhouse was in her company? I'm trusting we'll find the answers we need when we reach Swanmere."

"The mystery will soon be unravelled, sire, assuming no further denizens of this be-witched forest wish to make our acquaintance."

"Are you still with us, Ryrkell?" Aelmar called, and looked back over his shoulder and smiled at the hulking warrior who trudged behind them. Then he turned back to Waylan. "Aye!" he growled. "We could do without further mischief from the locals. Indeed, once we get to Swanmere, I want us to hatch some mischief of our own!"

CHAPTER FOUR
RETURN FROM THE DEEP

It had been a steep climb through dark places — a difficult route with deep fissures and narrow bridges spanning huge gulfs, where there was no going back. Sometimes, the walls of the tunnel pressed in so close they threatened to suffocate her. At other times, the path she followed took her into caverns so vast she could not see their ceilings or fathom their plunging depths — they made her feel small and insignificant. At last, she recognised the familiar brickwork of the upper levels of the Everdark and the handiwork of man.

Her face, soiled with the dust of countless millennia, was streaked with the paths of dried tears. The memory of her father had unlocked the door to a wealth of memories, some happy and some so heart-rending they had made her weep. Her sadness had slowly transformed into anger, and now she was in a foul mood. The long, curved daggers in her hands reacted in empathy. They glowed and crackled with a white fire, chilling the air as their spirits exchanged words in a dark language that only served to blacken her thoughts. Strange images of bat-like wings and scaly coils set against a backdrop of moonlight flashed in her mind, like scenes from a back-street lantern show. Sceral and his mate Silfa had once been living dragons — frost dragons that had soared high over the snow fields of the far north; but it was a long time ago and long before man had ventured into Sillaesia. Of this she was certain. They had told her.

After several minutes following a broad passageway, which had a curving ceiling and occasional buttresses supporting its walls, she spotted something familiar. Etched into the masonry of a buttress, just a few yards away, a rune bearing the likeness of a slim dagger glowed in her deep-sight. Its blade pointed upwards, and beyond the buttress she discovered a narrow passage whose floor rose up to form steps that climbed steeply. Shrew paused to sniff the air. Her nostrils flared ever so slightly as they detected faint scents that had drifted down from the world above. Her new weapons had truly bonded with her as Tirriel had promised; not only had their presence given her the deep-sight, but also a heightened sense of smell. She commanded the blades to sleep and slipped them into her belt. She placed Sceral beside her crossbow and Silfa on the opposite side, and then took off her backpack to reach her water-skin and drained the last of its contents. The climb had been thirsty work. Wiping her lips with the back of her hand, she quelled her anger and allowed herself a rueful smile. She would soon be back on the surface with her arsenal of weapons intact. Her crossbow still held its five flights and the band on her arm still held its six bone darts. She spent a moment recalling the long climb. The only time she had needed to defend herself was when she had inadvertently brushed a sleep-stalker web on the final part of her ascent. She had met these giant spiders before. Their poison could quickly render their prey unconscious, but she had learnt their weaknesses during previous forays into the Everdark. In fact, the spiders had proved most useful, for they had presented her with an opportunity to try out her new blades. The ancient fey weapons did not disappoint her. They had quickly tuned to her thoughts and within seconds had cut a chilling path, severing legs and splitting spider thorax, to leave the beasts shattered and broken in a frosted ruin. Shrew grinned and tapped the small vial that rested in one of her belt pouches — the spiders had proven to be useful in another way: they had provided some venom that would be valuable in the days ahead. Shouldering her backpack, she entered the passage with her deep-sight showing the way.

A short while later, she encountered another dagger rune where the stairwell entered a broad passage. The air was clammy and she recognised the rib-vaulting of the ceiling as that belonging to an important thoroughfare in the Everdark, known as the Smugglers' Run, that led from Harbour Gate to the Traders' Quarter. She guessed she was close to the docks, and her suspicions proved correct when she found another rune. This sign was a crude facsimile of a saw-toothed blade and a teardrop of blood. It was the mark of the Black Blood. She cursed under her breath. She would need to be careful, as such scum were bound to use this route frequently. From memory, she knew this passage descended in an easterly direction, and for a brief moment considered checking the map in her backpack, but quickly decided it was not safe to loiter. She would proceed eastward. She was sure that she would soon find a northerly passage marked by the Silent Knife and that it would lead her towards the Lichgate and Remund's house. She was hoping that Miruvar and Deakin had managed to pass on her message to Dardalloy and that he would be waiting there for her.

The passage she sought appeared sooner than she had expected. She was glad to leave the Smugglers' Run; this new passage would be less frequented. Yet no sooner had she congratulated herself for finding the northerly route she sought, when a rancid odour assailed her nostrils. The air fairly reeked of sweat-stained leather. Then she heard voices and quickly slowed her pace. There were people up ahead, confident or reckless people, as they did not seem at all concerned about making a noise and revealing their presence. A brief moment later, she detected the faint glow of their lanterns, and as she slowly edged around a bend in the passage, she saw their lights ahead. The lanterns bobbed up and down as they walked, and she sighed with relief as she saw they were moving away from her. She picked up her pace and began to catch the thread of their conversation. They were arguing about the split of booty. She grinned wickedly — these were Black Blood scum, for sure. She pulled the hood of her cloak forward in case any stray light should fall in her direction, and moved swiftly towards them, taking care to stay out of the reach of their lantern-light. She was invisible to them, but her deep-sight showed their bodies clearly, despite the glare of their lanterns. She counted at least five of them, and now her acute sense of smell detected the reek of soursop and the musky scent of the fang weed. Definitely Black Blood, she thought. The Silent Knife were instructed to resist the lure of the fang weed. Now why are they going this way?

There was a fork in the passage ahead. She knew that the narrower path went right past the secret door that led to the hidden cellar of Remund's house.

"Shey'fa!" she whispered under her breath, and startled herself when she realised, she had just cursed in the fey tongue. The group had just veered to the right and entered the narrow passage. She hastened after them, hoping to eavesdrop on their conversation. One voice in particular sounded familiar and this irritated her, because she couldn't put a name to it. This voice was also the most vocal and appeared to be leading the group. A cold shiver crept down her spine when she suddenly recognised it — it was Maykn, the one who had replaced Waylan. She always knew he was an untrustworthy rogue! He was promising the others bags of Rathasian gold when the long darkness came. Shrew frowned; what darkness was this? A bad feeling came over her. He was leading the others straight to Remund's house! She needed to find out what was going on. Was Remund involved with the Black Blood, too?

Sure enough, the group came to a blundering halt. Maykn's voice cried out once more. "It's here! Let me open the door. Help yerselves to the ale and weed, but don't touch the old man; Virryn wants him alive."

Shrew slowed her pace; now here was an opportunity! The group were crowding around Maykn. She would join them. It would be risky, but in their addled state she doubted any of them would notice. She pulled her cloak over her shoulders so that it concealed her weapons, and as an afterthought plucked two darts from their resting place on her arm. Maykn had already activated the secret door and the others had started to follow him through when she silently crept up behind them. Even better, she thought, the last one is a skinny fellow, not much taller than myself.

The passage beyond the secret door was narrow and the men had to shuffle in one at a time to take the ladder that led up to Remund's cellar. As the last of them started to ascend, two darts plunged into his neck below his ears, each delivering its own inimitable payload of toxins. Barely a squeak escaped from the man's lips as he collapsed in a heap at the foot of the ladder. Shrew wasted no time and quickly removed the man's cloak. This is a crazy idea, she thought, as she quickly donned the cloak and then, as an afterthought, breathed a prayer to Latia. She would need the Goddess of Luck on her side for sure. She wrinkled her nose in disgust as she started to ascend the ladder — the garment stank of stale soursop. Suddenly, a voice called down and she froze. "Last one up, throw the lever by the door!" It was Maykn. She turned and kicked the contraption with her boot such that the door slid back into place, sealing the cellar from the Everdark once more.

When she emerged from the trap-door and stepped into the cellar, her pulse was racing. She expected to be accosted at any moment, yet a furtive glance from under the shelter of her hood showed she needn't have worried. The cellar was poorly lit. The feebly glowing wisp lamp that had been present on her last visit failed to banish the darkness from the corners of the room, and everyone present seemed preoccupied with their own personal needs. The group she had followed made up half the numbers in the room, and she guessed there were around a dozen all told — drinking, smoking, chewing fang weed or slumped comatose alongside their empty flagons. The door at the top of the stairway to the ground floor was open and there were likely more of them upstairs. She bit her lip; she had entered a nest of vipers, but there was no better way to find out what was going on. She closed the trap-door and sat down next to an individual who was slumped against the nearest wall. His jerkin glistened from spilt ale and he was snoring deeply. Better to have a sleeping companion than one who would ask awkward questions, she thought. She picked up the man's empty flagon and held it up as if to take a drink. It hid her face perfectly. Peering over its brim, she sized up the situation.

Maykn and an older man were man-handling a cask on to the table in the centre of the room. "Get me some flagons!" he hollered. "Dags, get out some of that blue dwarra yer have stashed away. I could do with a snuffle."

Someone groaned. Shrew's attention switched to the source of the sound and then spotted a cage-like structure in the corner opposite the stairway. Someone was strung up inside!

"Dags, shift yer lazy arse!" Maykn hollered again. "And leave that monkey alone. I told yer that Virryn doesn't want him messed up."

Shrew's eyes widened. Remund was in the cage and trussed up such that his arms hung either side of his drooping head like claws. She cursed under her breath as she realised the situation. The weapons at her waist stirred as she wracked her brain for a way out of this situation. She wished the calm and reassuring voice of Tirriel was still with her.

"Virryn's not 'ere, so it ain't goin' to matter," a drawling voice answered from the darkness beside the cage. "Yer can't deny us a bit o' fun," the voice mocked. "Anyways, you ain't a Blackun, so I ain't takin' orders from you!"

Maykn dropped the cask on to the table, trapping the fingers of the rogue next to him. There was a shriek of pain and loud cursing as Maykn pushed the man aside and strode over towards the cage. Shrew watched with interest as the wiry loud-mouth known as Dags leapt nimbly away from Maykn's oncoming charge.

"I don't take crap from sewer filth!" Maykn roared. "Give me the dwarra, else I'll take it me-self!"

The disturbance had woken some of the sleepers in the room and voices cried out in protest, complaining about the noise. Shrew nervously eyed her sleeping companion; he stirred for a moment, but then sank back into his rhythmic snoring. Shrew sighed with relief. Even the howling hounds of Midir wouldn't wake this one!

"In Serreth's name!" a voice suddenly boomed down the stairs from the room above. "Can't I leave you sons of whores a moment without you fighting?" A giant of a man appeared, silhouetted at the doorway. Even in the poor light, Shrew could see his decorated leather armour and knew he was no lowly footpad. He had to be Virryn's lieutenant, the one the Silent Knife had nicknamed Cagun the Callous.

"It was Maykn causin' the trouble." Dags pointed a long accusing finger. "He's givin' orders like he owns the place."

"Save yer bitchin'!" Cagun barked. "I want five of you faggots who can stand up here now! I got a job for yer. Not you, Dags, nor you Maykn. You two can cosy up like sweethearts and be maids to the old man."

There were a few chuckles and Shrew could see Maykn glower in the light of the wisp. She had already come to the conclusion that Maykn considered himself to be a leader amongst these men, and now he had been humiliated in front of them. She stayed hunched up next to her drunken companion and prayed that five others in the room would respond to the order. She started to plan her next move should a finger be pointed in her direction, but Cagun soon found his volunteers. Some of the men had clearly been cooped up in the cellar a while and were glad to leave. Once they had all filed out, the room became very quiet.

Shrew's fingers slid over the haft of Sceral and her breath became shallow as she waited for someone to move or speak.

Nothing happened. Surprisingly, it was Dags who eventually broke the silence. "That whoresop," he swore under his breath, and then spat on the floor. "'Tis time he got his pretty jerkin dirty 'stead of playin' boss, like Virryn." He paused and reached into his shirt and tossed a small bundle on to the table. "'Ere... get this dwarra lit."

At the sight of the blue dwarrow, Maykn and the older man with bruised fingers eagerly gathered round the table.

Shrew watched as Maykn broke up the blue dwarrow stems, dropping their fibrous fragments into a small crucible. Next, he set to work with a flint and a steel blade he had drawn from his boot. An intense mote of blue light suddenly flared in the crucible and the herb crackled as it sent a thread of pungent grey smoke spiralling upward.

"Gather round, lads," Maykn called, and soon he was joined by Dags, the old man and two others who had roused and picked themselves up from the floor at the prospect of a draught of the mind-altering herb. The light in the crucible flared again, and to Shrew the shadows of the men seemed to cavort around the room, like dancing demons drawn up from the depths of Midir.

She peered again over the brim of her flagon and counted the men in the room for what was perhaps the tenth time. Besides the five around the table, indulging in the smoke that lifted from the crucible, there were two others asleep — the one next to her and another slumped in the shadows further away. She prayed to Latia that no others would suddenly appear from the trap-door, for they were unlikely to miss the body of the one she had dispatched earlier.

"I need time!" she whispered under her breath. With time, the dwarrow might dull the senses of Maykn and the others; but she knew the herb was unpredictable and could do the complete opposite. She had to speak to Remund and find out what was going on, and the sooner the better. She started to count the men once again and sized up each in turn as the grey mist of the blue dwarrow slowly filled the room.

Deep guttural sounds filled her head. Silfa and Sceral were calling her. "Shey'fa!" She was cursing in fey again! Had she fallen asleep? She reached into one of her belt pouches and pulled out a small vial. Raising it to her lips, she bit off the cork stopper and swallowed its dark contents.

A warm feeling enveloped her as the potent elements in her concoction found their way into her blood and coursed through her veins. It was ironic that she had used blue dwarrow in this mixture, but rather than dull her senses, it sharpened them and raised her awareness. That dwarrow those fools had lit was tainted. Chances were that Dags had acquired it from some unscrupulous bargeman over by Harbour Gate. She couldn't help but grin. No one stirred. The drug, whatever it was, had floored them all. Even Maykn had collapsed; his body lay sprawled over the table.

She rose slowly and quietly lifted the trap-door that led back down to the Everdark. Then she drew Sceral out of her belt and padded silently over to the cage, where she could see Remund slumped forward, caught amidst a trellis-work of chains. There was a massive bolt lock on the door to the cage and further locks inside. She looked closely for subtler devices — tell-tale signs of traps, such as fine thread or wire — but she could see none. Neither could she see any sign of the keys that would open these locks. She guessed Cagun carried those. Strange, she thought. She had recognised another member of the Silent Knife amongst these Black Blood. What was happening, and why had they trussed up poor old Remund? She mouthed a silent oath and set to work to see if Sceral's glossy blade would cut through the bar on the main lock; but a negative reaction from deep inside her suggested this blade was not like her last. She sighed and tucked the blade back inside her belt. She would have to try another strategy.

Remund was unconscious. Shrew watched him for a moment as her fingers felt their way along the many pockets of her belt until she found the items she was seeking. Holding each up against the dim light of the wisp, she admired first the asymmetric contours of a thunder pod and then the coarse orange spines of a pricklewort seed. She re-pocketed the former and then, without a second glance, reached between the bars of the cage and crumpled the husky seed in front of Remund's face. She wrinkled her nose, for even in this fog of cheap-grade dwarrow the sharp smell of the pricklewort cut through the senses, watering the eyes and prickling the nose.

Remund sneezed and started to regain consciousness. His eyes flickered open and he coughed loudly and wheezed. "Water!" he rasped. "Gimme water!"

Shrew looked back and quickly surveyed the room, but despite the noise it seemed that no-one had been disturbed. She sighed with relief. By her knee was a small cracked jug full of water. Without a second thought, she thrust it quickly between the bars and brought its spout to Remund's mouth. The cool water cascaded over the man's lips and splashed on to the floor of the cage as he swallowed it greedily. "Shush!" Shrew hissed. "You'll wake the dead!" She withdrew the jug and moved herself closer to the bars. "Rem!" she whispered. "It's Shrew!"

At the mention of her name, the old man's bushy eyebrows rose in recognition. "Shrew? Serreth's bleedin' bones!" Remund cried. "How did you get here? You gotta leave now!"

"Not before I know what's going on!" she admonished, trying desperately to keep her voice calm and quiet.

"The Black Blood are running the joint, can't yer see? And they're looking for you!"

Shrew shook her head and tried to grasp the old man's jacket through the bars. "Rem, what of Waylan... Dardalloy... are they okay?"

Remund's eyes widened in fear as, simultaneously, Silfa and Sceral barked a warning. Shrew ducked, sensing the air cleave above her scalp, as the blade intended for her neck skittered harmlessly off the cage. As she rolled clear, she saw the rogue known as Dags recover a broad-bladed dagger and turn to face her.

"Traitorous scum!" he snarled. "Think yer gonna let 'im go? Now I'm gonna shave the flesh off yer bones!"

Shrew leapt to her feet and both Silfa and Sceral flashed in her hands — a blast of frost blew out from each weapon, instantly stopping Dag's advance.

"What the fa...?" A string of obscenities spewed from the rogue as he staggered backwards, blinking away the ice that had formed on his face.

The noise had roused others in the room. Maykn raised his bleary eyes from the table and took a few short moments to assess the situation, before bursting forth with a hoarse cry of recognition. "It's Shrew, you fools; the Shade of Highfall. Don't let her escape!"

Shrew had back-stepped nimbly towards the trap-door; her daggers each trailed a thread of smoky vapour as she waved them threateningly before her. Dags rubbed his reddened face and approached more warily now. Other men were stirring, rudely awakened by the commotion. They swore openly and reached for their weapons.

"Come, Shrew," Maykn coaxed, as he slowly eased himself out of his chair. "There's no longer any need to fight. Those of yer friends that ain't dead or locked up have fled. You'd be better off joining us."

"Don't listen to him, Shrew!" Remund called from the darkness of the cage. "Flee!"

The old man's remonstrations were abruptly cut short when Dags's boot slammed into his cage. "Shut it, yer whoresop! Else I'll cut out yer blabbering tongue!"

Shrew's expression suddenly changed. She smiled provocatively and placed both daggers in her belt. Then she rested her hands casually on her hips.

"So, tell me, what exactly would I gain by joining the likes of you?" she asked.

Maykn smiled artfully. "Well... you would get yer life, to start. Then, if yer good, I might let ye sleep with me. After all, yer boyfriend is rotting with his friends on the bottom of the Swanny, so he can't do much for yer!"

Loud, raucous laughter broke out in the room, but it was quickly silenced when the door at the top of the stairs opened and a gruff voice called down, "What yer doin? You sops got dwarra down there?"

A voice called back, "Aye, and we got a wench..."

Shrew then added her own voice. "Aye, and the wench ain't interested." She tossed the thunder pod she had held earlier in a low arc over to the table and into the crucible which still held the glowing remnants of the blue dwarrow. The pod detonated with a loud, deafening bang, instantly filling the room with thick, acrid smoke.

There was an eerie silence after the explosion, but by the time it was replaced with cries and screams, Shrew had reached the bottom of the ladder and the tunnel that led to the Everdark. Her ears rang and she knew it would be several minutes before her hearing would return to normal, but her sight was good. She clutched Sceral in her right hand and the deep-sight now opened the way before her, banishing the darkness and overlaying the Everdark with a reddish aura of enhanced seeing. She should have been congratulating herself on her escape, but the words of Maykn fell heavy on her heart. There was nothing to celebrate. One or more of her close friends were dead, and deep inside she feared that Dardalloy had not made it to the Gloamril.

"Shey'fa!" she cursed again. She should have gone with Melowyn and the others. Maybe her presence would have tipped the balance in their favour. She brooded on this for a moment, and then another unpleasant thought hit her. Rem had mentioned that the Black Blood had been looking for her. Her mind switched to Gervaillas and Rosa. A cold feeling crept down her spine — they would be in danger. Her mind was made up. She would make haste to the Middle Reach and the Half Moon Inn.

CHAPTER FIVE
THE STAR AND THE SHADE

The air was fresh and the wind gusted, sending the fallen golden leaves dancing hither and thither under the first great outlying trees of the Gloamril Forest.

Vaskah Shen, Lord Imperiat of the Merrandis Legion, was not in the best of moods. He sat on his horse, pondering his current misfortune. His return to Merrandis, with its lakeside villas and pleasure houses, had been postponed. He scowled when he recalled his haste to alert his Queen of his findings at the temple at Everdim. The messenger bird had returned quickly with instruction for him to join the Vexxis Legion, which had just departed from Mereond. He was to offer his services to the Legion Commander. He squirmed in his saddle as he remembered the moment when he discovered that the Commander was no less than Imperiat Sonn, a favourite of the Queen and a narcissist, intent only on furthering his own ambitions. Vaskah Shen despised him. He could probably see too much of himself in the man. Now he rode at the rear of the column, with the supply wagons, in order to get as far away as possible from Sonn and his entourage. As he cast his eyes back into the darkness of the forest, he fancied he saw a flash of light that flared for a brief moment. He looked again and it was gone. No doubt a shaft of sunlight had caught a falling leaf, he supposed, but nevertheless he kept a wary eye open. Only two days ago, a large band of sylvan had accosted them. They had appeared suddenly from out of the trees — mauve-haired, with lithe bodies clad in tight green patchwork leather, bearing leaf-bladed spears and grey, curving longbows. Their captain had issued a warning — to turnabout and return to Rathasia or expect dire consequences. This brazen call had been met with jeers from the men in the column; but before any official response or action could be taken, the sylvan had melted away and vanished within the trees. Vaskah Shen shook his head. Why be concerned? There were one thousand well-armoured cavalrymen in this column and an equal number of light horses who could shoot their bows from the saddle. Behind them, no more than half a day's ride away, came the larger Rathasian force comprised of fourteen legions of veteran soldiers. Who would dare to oppose them? His thoughts were suddenly interrupted by a shout from a rider who approached, at the gallop, down the flank of the column. Within seconds, he was unrolling a small strip of parchment — it was another message from Merrandis.

"Phirrir protect me!" he breathed. It was an order from the Queen herself! He was to join the Merrandis Legion at Wineport and then lead it to the Crimson Sect's temple at Everdim. Vaskah Shen shuddered, and had the rider stayed to observe the Imperiat's reaction to his message, he would have seen the Imperiat's face turn pale with dread.

The hour was late, and the night sky above Everdim was filled with countless stars. To the north, where the shadowy battlements and towers of Highfall interrupted the line of the horizon, the Milky Way rose into the sky, shimmering with the pale light of numerous star cities. It spread overhead in a broad arch until it disappeared in the mists of the Southern Washes and the Western Sea.

"Can you see it?" Cyrus Col demanded from the darkness, his face lit by the ghostly yellow light of a wisp lamp.

"The harbinger has entered the house of the hunter," a thin voice replied. It came from the gaunt figure who stood beside the astrolabe, an elaborate brass instrument of circles and curves. "It moves slowly, your Revered Holiness. It is observable through the optic when it passes in front of other stars."

"Excellent!" Cyrus Col exclaimed. His jubilation was evident in his voice. "You are blessed, Cullis Ra. You are witnessing the coming of a dark star from out of the Void. It is time to wake our captain from his eternal sleep."

Cullis Ra bowed his head, revealing the white scars that criss-crossed his scalp. "It is written in the Psalm of the Shades, your Holiness."

Cyrus Col nodded slowly and smiled, revealing his filed teeth and crimson tongue. "Indeed it is, my faithful one. On the fourth day of the first month of half-light, the night will not end. Now gather our brothers. We shall meet at the altar."

There was but one light in the huge chamber, and it pulsed like a resting heart-beat, brightening and dimming, then brightening again as it drew in energy from the powerful ley lines that intersected under Everdim. It hovered as a translucent sphere above the upturned palms of an effigy of a mis-shapen dwarf who squatted amidst a pile of bones upon a crumbling altar. The leering visage of the dwarf seemed to peer into the depths of the sphere as if seeking some mystery that lay within.

Cyrus Col stood before the altar with his thin arms outstretched, as if imploring the statue to heed his supplications. A litany of dark words passed his lips. Either side of him stood his acolytes, robed in black with crimson trim, their faces hidden beneath their pointed cowls.

His words became louder and were joined by a humming sound that emanated from those beside him. It grew and fell in intensity, but varied little from the same monotonous pitch. From out of nowhere a breeze picked up, stirring the dust upon the altar. Cyrus Col turned his dark eyes to the sphere and began the closing words that would seal the invocation. Suddenly, a brisk wind picked up the dust and bone around the feet of the statue and raised it into a swirling mass, lifting his cloak and whipping it around his body.

"Aluk Nilhahn est dromoch ei Folkron!" Cyrus Col's body shook as he coughed and retched the final words from the Psalm of the Shades. Before him, the swirling mass coalesced to form a skeletal apparition of something vaguely human. Within seconds, it had taken a more substantial form, yet the shimmering mail that covered its chest failed to hide a decaying ribcage and the face-plate of its gleaming helmet failed to hide two rows of yellowed teeth, now only broken shards protruding from a grinning skull. Two baleful white lights smouldered and smoked like boiling quicksilver within its eye sockets. This dreadful apparition was not human — it was fey!

Cyrus Col straightened his body. Sweat glistened in beads upon his forehead and the red rune that emblazoned it. His lips curled in a smile of satisfaction. "Welcome back to the domain of the living, Prince Armeris. The Master of Shades has need of your service once more."

CHAPTER SIX
FLIGHT TO THE FOREST

Shrew shivered in the darkness. There was a chill in the air. It was a marked contrast to the balmy warmth that had bathed the city prior to her journey down to Qinestra. She shivered again and drew her cloak closer to her body. This was not the stinking garment she had acquired from the secret passage beside Remund's cellar, but one from a cache of items that had been deliberately hidden in the Everdark by the Order of the Silent Knife. She had also taken a flat velvet cap that now sat askew upon her head, a small bag of coins, a fresh water-skin and some dark oily rations that looked and smelt suspiciously like dried fish. She chewed on the latter as she observed the Half Moon Inn from the refuge of a group of small trees that stood on the edge of Ahlune's Park. For the last few hours, she had sat with her back resting against the bole of one of the trees — waiting. The inn stood in an oasis of light; its coloured lanterns blazed like a cluster of luminous stars. They were so much brighter than the pale lamps that lined the road and the faint glow from wisp lamps that leaked out from shuttered windows. Red, green and blue lanterns were festooned over the courtyard of the inn; other lanterns hung from various places around the building and several illuminated a wooden sign, depicting a red-cheeked half-moon relaxing on a bed of cloud whilst supping a tankard of ale. She did not share the same happy mood. Bad thoughts crowded inside her head, which, no matter how hard she tried, she just couldn't shake off. As a light rain started to fall, some of the raindrops trickled down her face and mixed with her tears. She hadn't felt this bad for a long time. Until now she hadn't realised just how strong her feelings were for Dardalloy, but now he was gone she missed him dearly. All she wanted now was to be warm and snug, tucked up in her soft bed, high in the attic of the inn; but something — maybe a sixth sense — held her back. The inn always attracted folk well into the late hours, but those that gathered there now seemed to be idling, as if waiting for something. She decided to wait until they dispersed.

She must have dozed for a while, for she woke up with a start as a chime rang out from the bell-tower by the Middern Gate. It was quickly followed by a second chime.

She mumbled a curse under her breath. It was the call for the last watch. It was later than she thought.

She turned her attention once more to the inn. One side of it fronted on to the Middern Rise, a major thoroughfare that wound upward through the Middle Reach. A stone arch wreathed with ivy gave access to the inn's courtyard and the main entrance to the building. There had been a small crowd outside the inn earlier, but now only a small group loitered under the arch, seemingly vigilant and barring access to the courtyard.

"Sirra's breath!" she hissed between chattering teeth. "I can't stay here all night." She adjusted her cap so that it shielded her eyes and was tilted in a jaunty fashion, like that adopted by the barge folk down in Harbour Gate. Satisfied with her appearance, she rose and crept along a line of trees, before emerging from their cover, taking a path that took her away from the archway and up the street towards the High Reach. She had no intention of taking the front entrance. As Waylan used to say, "A rogue's prerogative is always through the back door." She bit her lip, expecting to be accosted at any moment, and prepared herself for a sprint — but no challenge came. She cursed silently. Maybe she was being paranoid and maybe the Black Blood had given up looking for her, thinking her lost in the Everdark. But she had little time to enjoy this pleasant thought. A moment later, a loud cry from behind told her she had been spotted!

Like a frightened rabbit, she bolted. The street was lined with flickering oil lanterns and occasional wisp lamps, but there were shady refuges between the frontages of the buildings that overlooked the Park. She quickly found some shadow, out of the light of the street, and then a side alley between two tall buildings. More voices called out behind her, and a dog barked from a back yard close by. She knew this alley like the back of her hand. Within seconds, she had grasped some bindweed that had spread itself up the side of a tall building. Few could have climbed it, but she was adept at the task, and from the straggling vines had quickly found a balcony, and from there the roof of the building. From this high vantage point she momentarily looked out across the dark urban sprawl of the Jewellery Quarter to where it climbed the hill towards the High Reach. Then she turned and ran lightly along the ridge of the roof, back in the direction of the Half Moon Inn. Her heart was racing, but as the sounds of pursuit faded, she slowed her pace. A few minutes later, she dropped down into a pool of shadow between the back of the inn and the stables. Normally, she would have climbed up on to the stable roof, for it was an easy matter to reach the window of her room from there, but she felt that the current circumstances demanded a more cautious approach. She thought it possible that the Black Blood had the place surrounded. She decided to check the courtyard first from the shelter of the shadows. She knew people were there, as she could hear their voices. They were low and subdued and so different from the laughter and convivial banter of the usual patrons of the inn. Maybe she should eavesdrop on their conversation? She paused a moment. Silfa had become alert — the female dragon's warning broke her train of thought. Then came the faintest disturbance of the air, perhaps caused by an exhale of breath from behind her?

In an instant, she spun round. Someone was there! She reached out and grabbed them.

"Shhhrew," a man's voice hissed from the darkness. Shrew eased the pressure of her clenched fist against the warm throat of the intruder, letting the point of her needle withdraw slightly from the underside of his jaw. "Shrew, it's me," the voice hissed again, urgently.

Shrew looked more closely. Her deep-sight showed her a soldier, fully clad in the ring mail armour of either an officer of the Watch, or one of the Palatine guard.

"For Parvi's sake, Shrew! It's me, Dardalloy!"

Shrew shook her head slowly. "Dardalloy is dead," she retorted, and increased the pressure on the man's throat once more. "Give me a good reason why I shouldn't push this poison into your gullet?"

"Is it a virulent paralysing concoction made from Snakesroot and adder's tongue, perchance?" the man retorted croakily, but there was still a suggestion of sarcasm in his tone.

Shrew whispered incredulously, "How did you know?", and looked into the man's eyes. "By the gods… it is you!" She lowered her weapon and slid it back into the calf of her boot. "Oh, Darda! They said you had drowned!"

"Who said I had drowned?" Dardalloy muttered, rubbing his throat. "I believe I'm alive, but narrowly, so it seems." He gestured to where the needle lay concealed within her boot.

Shrew muffled a sob and then threw herself at him, hugging him tightly and nearly tipping him off balance. "What's going on?" she whispered in his ear. "Maykn said you were drowned. He's with the Black Blood now." She pulled away and looked him up and down again. "And what are you doing here dressed as a…?" Her question was quickly cut short by footsteps approaching from the courtyard.

"Some of the men have heard us," Dardalloy warned. "Keep your weapons covered under your cloak and do exactly as I say!"

"I need to see if Gervaillas and Rosa are safe," she pressed.

"There's no time!" He pulled off her hat. "Now untie your hair quickly… Trust me!" He stood in front of her just as two armed men strode round the side of the stables.

For a moment, they looked surprised, and then one grinned lecherously. "Ah, Captain, Sir. Sorry to interrupt yer business. We thought we heard intruders."

"You can wipe that smirk off your face, soldier," Dardalloy replied quickly. "I found this maid hiding behind the stables. She's scared witless. Says some hulk took advantage of her."

Shrew edged into view, a doleful expression on her face that was half concealed by her hair that now fell to her shoulders. She could immediately tell from their attire and their demeanour that these men were no more than City Watch, press-ganged from the dregs of the Low Reach. She felt a wave of relief, but this was short-lived. The conversation had attracted others that included less savoury-looking characters. Their leader appeared to be a lanky individual wearing a fine leather cuirass and greaves.

"I'm taking her up to the Citadel," Dardalloy continued. "I will get her checked over by the physician there. We'll soon find out if she speaks the truth."

"That's a lot of trouble for a scullery slut, ain't it?" It was the tall man in finely decorated leather armour. She recognised his gruff voice immediately. It was Stilts, the gang leader from the Duns. It would seem he had come up in the world, despite the fact he now only had one hand. She glanced quickly at the hook on the end of his right arm. If he recognised her now, the game would be up. She bent her head and prayed to Latia that the shadows would hide her face.

"It's no trouble," Dardalloy replied, placing his hands on his hips and bringing his right hand close to his sword. "I was leaving for the Citadel with my men anyway."

"By Kurell's cheatin' bones, she's a spy!" Stilts insisted, his pock-marked features creased in a scowl. "Been sneakin' about in the shadows, I warrant ye."

Another man stepped forward and spoke out. "Nay, she's no spy." He was a youth dressed in the livery of the Middern Gate Guard. "I recognise her. I've seen her working here in the inn."

"Aha!" Dardalloy slapped his thigh. "Then that settles the matter. She's no spy and she's coming with me." He gently guided Shrew towards the stables whilst calling to others to prepare his horse. The rest of the men started to disperse and returned to their business in the courtyard. It seemed to Shrew that they had been here for some time, as she noticed bedrolls under a makeshift awning and even a table or two covered with platters and the remnants of half-finished meals.

Dardalloy barked further orders. A number of men in similar armour to himself were mounting their steeds and preparing to ride. "You're getting on this horse," he whispered in her ear. "And you'll be sitting with me!" Before she had time to argue, he mounted the horse and reached down to pull her up. Taking care to keep her weapons hidden beneath her cloak, she grasped his hand and he pulled her up to sit in the saddle behind him. "Now hold on tight," he instructed, and then quickly took control of the steed, steering it out of the courtyard. As they passed under the stone arch, Shrew looked back for a brief moment and caught Stilts staring after them with a peculiar look on his face. Was it a look of recognition? But then he was lost from sight and they were on the main road.

"I have a bad feeling," Shrew called to Dardalloy, as the horse broke into a trot. "The tall one that accused me is known as Stilts. He's a cut-throat from the Duns. What's his kind doing in the Middle Reach?"

"Sirra's breath, Shrew!" Dardalloy cried. "Where have you been? Don't you know what's been going on? It's chaos now in Highfall. There's an army approaching our gates and a new council has taken charge of the city." He paused for a moment in thought. "Did you really descend into the Dovecote?"

It was several long seconds before Shrew replied. "I did," she affirmed. "And I think I was down there far longer than I realised."

"Gods!" Dardalloy exclaimed. "We were getting worried. No-one in living memory has gone down there and returned. They sent me back to find you, thinking I would know your haunts best. Seems I did, for it was only a matter of time before you showed up at the Half Moon."

"Who's 'they'?" Shrew queried, as she tightened her hold on Dardalloy's waist as if trying to squeeze the truth from him.

"Lady Melowyn, the Lords Miruvar and Aelmar, the honourable Deakin, Waylan...."

"Waylan!" Shrew interrupted. "How did he get free?"

At that moment, one of the three riders accompanying them called out in alarm. "Captain, we're being followed!"

Dardalloy reined in his horse and swung it around. They had reached the White Cross, where several major thoroughfares from various quarters of the Middle Reach met. In the centre of this meeting of ways rose a statue of the proud paladin-king Finngol the Fair. Dardalloy brought his steed to a halt under its shadow. Down the hill, where the road snaked past the edge of Ahlune's Park, Shrew could see a body of horsemen moving swiftly in their direction.

"On to the Citadel!" Dardalloy cried, spurring his horse forward towards the broad avenue that climbed up towards the Crown Gate and the High Reach. "Mother of Midir!" he cursed. "It's Luven's filth, and no doubt your friend Stilts is among them. I guess he's had second thoughts about letting you go."

They rode quickly, knowing that their pursuers weren't far behind. Dardalloy signalled to the nearest rider that accompanied them. "Daegin, I'm going to the High Reach. Take Lain and Harry and go straight to the Citadel. They won't pursue you there. It's the woman they're after."

"But Captain," the rider called back, "we can hold them on the Rise. At least long enough for you to reach the gate."

"Do as I say!" Dardalloy yelled, raising his voice so that he could be heard over the wind, which had now become a stiff breeze as they drew close to the looming heights of the High Reach wall. "Go on ahead. I have a better idea." He pulled hard on a strap, releasing the flaps of two saddlebags that were thrown across the hindquarters of his horse. Out spilled a mass of thorns, covering the road in their wake with a carpet of jagged spikes. "Star thistles!" he cried. "See how they like those!"

"I see you came prepared," Shrew said drolly. "And how long have you been a Captain in the Palatine Guard?"

"We can catch up on things like that later," Dardalloy countered. "If we get out of Highfall in one piece! You'd better start praying to your lady luck that my paperwork gets us through the Crown Gate."

"Well, why in Serreth's name are we going to the High Reach?" Shrew blustered. "We should go deep into the Everdark, where no-one will find us!"

"We're not getting ourselves holed up like a cornered rat," Dardalloy replied, tersely. "We're going to the villa of the Commissar of guild traders and then on to Swanmere. So, no more questions. If anyone asks, just tell them you're a maid who was visiting her family in the Middle Reach and got caught by the curfew."

Shrew swore under her breath. Swanmere! That was outside the city. Mother of Midir, that was somewhere in the Gloamril. She had never been outside the city in her life!

They rode swiftly past the approach to the Citadel of the Ancients, a monolithic structure with many turrets that thrust out from the High Reach Wall. Here they parted company with the other three riders and continued on up the broad highway known as the Dragon's Rise. Before them rose the imposing structure of the Crown Gate, a ring of eight white towers that rose skyward, like tapering prongs from a radiant crown. There were two towers on the Middle Reach side, and between them hung an enormous pair of gates made from darkest adamantine. As they approached, Shrew could see that the larger gates were firmly closed, but a glimmer of light issued from a smaller wicket gate, and silhouetted before it stood some guards.

Dardalloy hailed the men as he pulled on the reins of his steed to bring it to a halt. "Good morrow!" he cried. "May Verrain bless you! I bid enter with the authority of the Commissar."

One of the men by the gate stepped forward and uncovered a wisp lamp. The glowing amber light of the wisp reflected off his coat of scale mail and Shrew noted from his badge that he was a sergeant of the gate guard. The man peered at Dardalloy from under his conical helm. "Good morrow to you, sir. Please pass me your papers and, if they are correct, we can speed you on your way."

Dardalloy smiled and produced a roll of parchment. Shrew watched the sergeant unravel the papers and scrutinise them under the light of the lantern. Suddenly, a sound made her look back over her shoulder. There was movement further down the road; horsemen were making their way swiftly up the Dragon's Rise. Their pursuers must have regrouped.

"Shey'fa!" she cursed under her breath; "they'll be upon us soon!"

"I'm sorry, sir, these papers bear the seal of the Lord Aelmar," the sergeant announced. "He no longer has authority in the city."

"Is that so?" Dardalloy countered, with a look of disappointment on his face. "Has every man here forgotten so quickly what the Lord Aelmar did for this city?" He raised his voice so that it carried beyond the gate.

"Mother of Midir!" Shrew hissed through clenched teeth, as her hand reached for her crossbow beneath her cloak. "We're running out of time!"

At that moment, another man appeared in the light of the wicket gate. His apparel suggested one of superior rank. "I recognise that voice," he boomed. He stepped forward and light from the wisp flared on his breast plate, revealing the crossed talons of the Palatine Guard. "My old companion, isn't it?" He stepped up to the horse and patted its steaming hide. "And with some young hussy in tow." Shrew detected jealousy in the man's demeanour. The sound of the hooves of their pursuers now seemed deafening in her ears. "Let them through!" he barked.

Without a word, Dardalloy urged the horse forward and steered it through the narrow gate. As soon as they were through, he dug in his spurs and the horse leapt forward.

"Don't think I will stop your friends," the man called after them. "Go hide from them, Dardain, just like you did from me!"

"What was all that about?" Shrew questioned, as they passed through a second gate and out from under a massive arch that linked two further towers.

"A past I wish to forget," Dardalloy retorted.

Before them, the startling vista of the High Reach ascended up the first peak of the Dragon's spine. Great edifices rose palely amidst shadowy gardens, and solitary wisp lamps glowed from within the many windows of rambling villas; monuments of extravagance and wealth, yet also testimony to the skill of the sylvan and their fey forebears. Above all, tall, slender towers of pearlescent marble climbed to dizzying heights to pierce the pre-dawn sky. Even now, the tallest sparkled, caught in the first rays of sunrise of the new day.

"So where now?" Shrew demanded. "We're trapped in the High Reach. We can't get to Swanmere and we can't hide in the Commissar's villa. They will root us out in no time. We must go down into the Everdark. Have you forgotten? I have a map!"

"I told you to trust me!" Dardalloy snapped, as he urged the horse to greater speed. "Look to your right. There's the gatehouse for the Commissar's villa. We're nearly there."

"It's just as well," Shrew retorted. "They're back on our tail again and getting closer!" As if in reply, an arrow hissed low over their heads. She started to reach for her crossbow, but was forced to grasp Dardalloy's arm as their mount veered sharply right to pass through the open gates of the villa estate. "Warn me if you do that again!" she yelled, as a number of the Commissar's retainers scattered at their approach.

"Hold on tight!" he shouted, as he took the horse off the main concourse and away from the villa complex. The new path meandered through the Commissar's gardens, and they were soon forced to slow their pace. "Our mare is tiring! We may have to dismount soon and run for it."

"Run?" Shrew screamed. "Where to?"

"The sky tower!" Dardalloy cried, pointing to a slim white tower that rose like an ivory needle from within a stand of gnarled and twisted olive trees. Its girth was little more than five yards, but its height must have surpassed this at least fifty times. Shrew's mouth fell open — there was no suitable expletive that would do justice to the foolishness of such an answer. "Come, Shrew, move!" Dardalloy leapt from the horse, breaking her state of disbelief. Within a second, she was hard on his heels.

This was now a race to the tower. Their pursuers were drawing closer and they could now hear their cries and taunts. Another feathered shaft zipped past them, ending its trajectory suddenly in the bole of a tree.

"Surrender yourselves," a voice called. "There's no escape."

"This way," Dardalloy urged, and plunged into the shadow beneath a copse of trees. Here there was a hidden trail, and Shrew wondered how her friend knew of its existence — had he been here before, or had luck played her hand and Latia was now smiling on him instead of her? They made quick progress under the twisted cover of the olive trees and soon emerged into a clearing where marble steps gently ascended to an arched opening in the base of the tower.

"We're trapping ourselves!" Shrew protested, but sprinted after her companion, for he was already mounting the steps.

Once inside the tower, Shrew caught her breath. She expected to see a spiral stairway, but there was none. They were in an empty room that was bathed in a turquoise glow that seemed to emanate from the walls around them. It reminded her of the luminescence of the Dovecote and the light that seemed to adhere to the lace-like structures of Qinestra. To her surprise, there was no ceiling, just a tunnel of open space that filled the entirety of the tower. She couldn't be sure, but it appeared to end high above in a dark circular opening.

"To the middle," Dardalloy cried. "Into the circle!" There was a circle etched into the floor in the centre of the room. Shrew followed his instruction and nimbly leapt into it.

"Steady yourself, we're going up." Barely had he uttered the words, when the floor within the circle started to rise swiftly upward. Within seconds, it had risen ten yards and continued to climb.

"Mother of Midir!" Shrew cried. "There're no ropes! What sorcery is this?" At that moment, calls of frustration and cursing rose from below — their pursuers had arrived at the tower. Several missiles were cast, but clattered harmlessly off the underside of the rising platform.

Dardalloy laughed loudly and then exchanged a few insults of his own at the men below. Then he sat down and grinned broadly at Shrew.

"Sirra's breath, Darda!" Shrew exclaimed incredulously. "How does this thing work? What is it?"

"It's a levitator," her companion replied matter-of-factly. "No-one knows exactly how it works. It was built a long time ago by the fey or the first sylvan of Sillaesia."

Shrew cautiously approached the edge of the levitator platform. It was about eight feet in diameter and so there was a sizeable gap between its rim and the apparent illusion of the moving wall.

Dardalloy smiled. "Don't worry, you can't fall off it; there's an invisible force extending across the gap. If you look closely, you can see where it meets the wall."

The levitator continued its smooth ascent and the cries of the men below faded. Shrew folded her arms and resigned herself to watching the glowing turquoise wall as it passed by. Dardalloy was right: every now and then a tendril of blue light would flick out from the platform and lash the wall, causing a momentary scintillation. It was beautiful.

"We're nearly there!" Dardalloy broke her thoughts. "Look up."

The dark circular opening which she had seen from the ground was quickly approaching. It was surrounded by blue radiating streaks of light and reminded her of the pupil of an eye. The uncanny resemblance didn't stop there. As they drew closer, the opening slowly expanded to accommodate their platform, behaving like the iris of an eye when exposed to darkness. They entered the opening and ascended a shaft until they reached a large circular chamber; here, the levitator platform came slowly to rest. Four arched openings led out of the chamber to a broad platform that appeared to surround the top of the tower. Light from the rising sun cast brilliant shafts through two of the arches, illuminating a large contrivance, half machine and half beast that appeared to sprout broken bat-like wings.

"Quick! Off the levitator," Dardalloy ordered. "We haven't much time. We can't prevent it from returning to the entrance below."

"Then we may as well throw ourselves off the tower and end it now," Shrew complained sarcastically. "Stilts and his cut-throats will be up here soon."

"Stop bitching and help me push this on to the viewing platform," Dardalloy cried, as he rushed over to the strange contraption. "And yes, you're right... we're going to throw ourselves off this tower!"

Shrew let out a string of curses. "What is that thing?" she shouted, as she hurried across to help him. The contraption appeared to resemble something that was a cross between a chariot and a large bat. It was a trellis work of wooden staves, much of it covered with a membrane of stretched skin.

"A Wind-Rider!" her companion shouted, as they pushed it through the nearest arch and into the bright sunrise of the new day.

"You're mad," Shrew remonstrated.

"You'd better start praying to Latia that I'm not," he retorted. "Put your hands through these loops, lean your body against this board and hold on tight... *very* tight. I'm extending her wings!"

"Gods save me!" Shrew breathed. In the corner of her eye, she noticed Dardalloy pull hard on a small lever. There was a click and a jolt, and suddenly her breath was taken out of her lungs and her stomach was left far behind. She closed her eyes, sucked in a mouthful of air and screamed at the top of her voice. When she opened her eyes, she screamed again — the world had suddenly opened up in all directions. The stone patchwork of the city lay below her, and beyond, a vastness of green stretched out to the horizon, all under the great blue dome of the sky. "Mother of Midir!" she yelled. "I never knew the world was so big!"

Dardalloy's laugh was barely recognisable above the wind. It whipped across their bodies and wailed as it wrestled with the Wind-Rider's wings, like a banshee's keening.

She looked down and saw the mighty battlements of Highfall's western wall pass underneath them. She fancied she could see a group of guards look up, and despite her fear of the situation she couldn't prevent a smile forming on her lips as she imagined the look on their faces — they must be wondering what kind of strange bird they were seeing!

"Hold on tight!" Dardalloy shouted. "We need more height; I'm bringing her round." The Wind-Rider turned in a wide circle and Shrew felt it rise as a warm updraft lifted them higher into the blue sky.

"Not too high," she pleaded. "We might hit the Sun!"

Dardalloy roared with laughter. "Have you forgotten your astronomy lessons so quickly?" he berated her. "You cannot possibly count the number of leagues we'd have to travel before we met with such calamity!"

She smiled. Of course she knew, but she needed to find some comedy in their situation. It was just too crazy. She turned her attention again to the landscape that moved beneath them and watched as they passed over the western wall a third time. Shortly after that, they were over water. Beneath them stretched the Swan River, its glassy surface broken by diverging lines of expanding ripples that sparkled in the sunlight and trailed in the wake of barges and brigantines plying their way to and from Highfall's busy harbour.

"We're losing height," she warned, but this time she wasn't joking. They had left behind the warm updrafts of the mountain foothills and the city and were now gliding in a shallow descent towards a vast expanse of forest that stretched as far as the eye could see.

"Behold the Gloamril Forest!" Dardalloy informed her. "Have you been here before?"

"Of course not!" she snapped. "I told you. I've never been outside the city in my life. I've seen it a few times from a distance, but never as close as this. Sirra's breath, it goes on for ever!"

They passed over the western bank of the river, where the trees of the forest crowded to the water's edge. Shrew watched in fascination at the kaleidoscope of colour beneath her. It was goldfall and, as the season suggested, many of the leafy crowns beneath her were golden, but others remained green or dazzled with various colours from orange red through to a pale powder blue and violet.

"We're not going to reach Swanmere," Dardalloy declared. "But, if we could stay aloft just a little longer, we may reach the West Way, the road that leads to Swanmere."

Shrew instinctively flinched as the tree tops suddenly appeared to rush up to meet them.

"Hang on tight!" Dardalloy cried. "We're coming down — there are clearings ahead…"

They skimmed over a broad tree top and Shrew found herself screaming again. Now the ground was rushing up towards them — a small patch of meadowland broken by clumps of trees. She prepared herself for a hard and painful landing, but at the last second the Wind-Rider reared upward and their speed reduced dramatically. In the end, the landing was surprisingly slow and gentle. She even had time to slide off the board of the Wind-Rider and judiciously plant her feet in the soft springy grass of the meadow.

"You've done this before, haven't you?" she said accusingly, casting a suspicious eye at Dardalloy as she stepped away from the Wind-Rider.

Her companion nodded and a sheepish grin formed on his fair-skinned face. "I used to race against Merris, the eldest son of the Commissar," he confessed.

"Really?" she said, and as they walked together towards a solitary old beech tree she turned and faced him. "Really!" she said again with an emphasis of tone. Then suddenly, she tripped him up and fell on top of him, pushing him into a patch of soft grass. "You just scared the living daylights out of me!" She looked into his startled eyes and then kissed him gently on the lips. "Thank you," she said.

Golden sunlight dappled the soft moss and grasses where they lay side-by-side between two great roots that arched out from the ancient beech and curved around them, seemingly to hug them in an arboreal embrace.

They had lain there for over an hour, watching the sun slowly rise above the wall of the forest till it disappeared within the leafy canopy over their heads.

"You are much like Waylan, aren't you?" Shrew mused. "Masquerading as a Palatine officer one moment and the next a crippled beggar from the Duns. I guess the ways of the master have rubbed off on his lieutenant?"

Dardalloy chuckled softly and plucked the stem of a vivid scarlet flower. "Don't feel so smug, young lady." He smiled and planted the flower in Shrew's hair, which had now become tawny coloured, as her natural blonde tresses shone through the last vestiges of her dusky hair dye. "One moment you're a stunningly attractive courtesan, seemingly at home in the most extravagant of the pleasure houses, and the next some scallywag urchin thieving apples in Gifford's Street. Well, that's what Waylan told me!"

Shrew's face wrinkled in feigned displeasure. Then she laughed at the thought. She had read once of a mythical creature called a doppelganger, which could take on the appearance of any living thing it chose. She smiled at Dardalloy — they were both very much like a doppelganger. Then she grew more serious. "Talking of Waylan, you haven't told me how he escaped. Just how did he get out of the Citadel, one of the most guarded places in all of Highfall, and then get himself all the way to Swanmere?"

"That's easy to answer," Dardalloy replied, rolling on to his side to look at her more closely. "Lord Aelmar and some senior officers of the Palatine got him out and he left the city with them."

"Who told you?" she retorted.

"Lord Aelmar told me, but then I also saw Waylan for myself, in Swanmere." Dardalloy paused for a moment in thought. "He was very quiet. He seemed a bit different."

"I guess you would be, too, if you'd been locked up in that place," Shrew muttered, and then suddenly looked troubled and quickly turned to look more closely at her companion. "One last question," she said quietly. Her eyes roved over him and then looked deeply into his. "The Black Blood that I had the pleasure of sharing a room with told me you and the others were slain... drowned in the Swanny river. Tell me the truth, Darda — you look real enough and you behave just like you used to... but it is really you, isn't it?" Her hand moved an inch closer towards Silfa, her fey blade that hung on her right side; but the dragon soul simply dozed, disinterested.

"Shrew!" Dardalloy cried, looking genuinely hurt. "I'm not a doppelganger, if that's what you're inferring. I'm the real thing!" He sighed as he saw Shrew relax. "When we get to Swanmere, you can ask the Lady Melowyn about her powers of illusion. She conjured the most marvellous visions, fooling our pursuers, such that most of their arrows fell short. She called them deceptions, or something like that."

"I've heard that word before," Shrew whispered. "So, you all reached Swanmere safely?"

"Well, a few of us picked up light wounds, nothing serious, but it must have troubled your boyfriend. He left us when we reached the forest."

"Wilf isn't my boyfriend," Shrew countered. "He's a friend. We helped each other out when we were held in the workhouse."

Dardalloy slowly raised his hand and put a finger to his lips, bidding her to be silent. "I shouldn't have picked that flower," he whispered, nodding towards a mound a few dozen yards away. "We're being watched."

Shrew squinted. At first, she saw nothing, but then she saw them. They seemed to blend in and be almost a part of the wildflowers that crowned the mound. "Who are they?" she breathed. "Fey?"

"Of a kind," her companion answered. "They are known as Sprites — small folk who inhabit these woods. It's time to leave," he whispered. "They don't look too friendly."

Dardalloy rose slowly to his feet. "When you journey in the Gloamril," he said, "always remember to bring presents." He bowed in the direction of the mound. "Polished nuggets of blue glass will please many of these folk, but some are more discerning and won't settle for anything less than a cornflower sapphire." He untied a small bag from his belt and poured its sparkling contents into the open palm of his left hand. Suddenly, they were surrounded by fluttering wisps of light and all around them, amongst the banks of flowers beyond the mossy reach of the old beech, colourful sylph-like figures emerged, some in groups and others singly.

Shrew gasped in wonder as she watched a small troop of them march solemnly up towards her companion.

Dardalloy bowed again. "May the light of the Lady Ahlune never dim," he said gently, offering the glass to the first in the troop, a stern-looking fellow with delicate pointed features and a shock of turquoise hair.

There was a moment of pause and the next second Dardalloy's hand was knocked such that the blue glass flew high in the air and then fell like sparkling blue rain amongst the crowds assembled. Laughter, shouting and spontaneous singing erupted all around them.

Dardalloy nudged Shrew. "Now we can leave. Follow me... quickly."

They swiftly left the merriment behind and plunged into the shadow of the forest. They soon found a trail bordered by fungi and toadstools of every shape and hue. Some sunlight filtered through, sometimes faintly and at other times as glorious shafts of golden light that illuminated their path ahead.

The merriment of the sprites must have been infectious, because Shrew felt like singing with joy. Everything was new and different. She had wandered under trees in Ahlune's Park, but they seemed mere saplings compared to the giants of the Gloamril. She breathed in deeply, savouring the air. It was fresh and sweetened by the breath of the living forest — the smells, the taste, it invigorated her senses. "Look!" she suddenly exclaimed. "Mugglewort! It's growing on that fallen tree. You're going to have to wait a moment, Darda. I must have some of its leaves."

Dardalloy chuckled. "Be quick," he admonished. "I want us to reach Swanmere before dark, and mind you don't disturb a sprite!" Shrew hesitated a moment and Dardalloy chuckled again. "Don't worry, I'm sure they won't miss a few leaves."

Within minutes they were on their way again. There were occasions when the trail divided or crossed another, but Dardalloy always seemed to instinctively know the way. "We're avoiding the inn," he said in a low voice. Shrew nodded. It seemed that the majesty of this ancient forest demanded a form of reverence, like a holy place, that words should be spoken quietly or not at all.

After walking for about another hour, Dardalloy paused in his tracks. "See the light breaking through the trees over there? We're close to the road, and if I'm right, about a half league west of the Wizard's Teacup, an old inn. Lord Aelmar encountered Black Blood spies at the inn in Tilterdown. He recommended we stay clear of such places."

They walked in the direction of the light and soon came to the edge of the road. Dardalloy raised his hand, signalling a halt. "Best to wait and check all's clear before we step out," he whispered.

"So, this must be the West Way," she said quietly, as she joined him. The road was quite broad, four or five yards at least, and looked fairly well maintained. The surface was clear of vegetation, being covered in flagstones, but many were now broken and well worn, having borne the passage of innumerable travellers over the years. To her left, the road descended and disappeared in a tight bend, shored up on either side by banks of earth and root. Suddenly, something caught her eye.

"We're just to the west of Cutpurse Corner," Dardalloy whispered, noticing that she was staring intently in the easterly direction. "It's a well-known haunt for highwaymen and bandits."

Shrew grasped the hilts of her daggers, waking Silfa and Sceral from their deep slumber. Immediately, the world around her began to change, as if a veil was being lifted from her eyes. Reality now looked very different as she gained the dragons' deep-sight. "Mother of Midir," she breathed. "There's so much life in this forest! I can see it all, even with the sun glow."

Dardalloy looked at her quizzically. "What are you doing?"

"Looking at two figures just inside the forest, up on the left bank of the road... by the corner," she added. "Looks like two men. It's a good place for an ambush or for watching the road."

"I can't see them," he muttered. "Are you sure?"

"Leave this to me," she answered, and stepped out into the road. Then she set off towards the corner, with Dardalloy's appeals for caution still ringing in her ears.

When she had approached to within ten yards of the hidden figures, she stopped. Her heightened sense of smell, bequeathed to her by her daggers, had picked up their scent, and now she could also hear them whispering. Her intuition had been correct: they were well-armed men dressed like typical rogues, and from their whispers, she could glean that they were acting as look-outs for Cagun, a name she knew too well. She turned and looked directly at them.

"Looking for someone?" she said, with her hands on her hips. There was silence. "I'm talking to you two," she said, raising her voice.

Suddenly, there was the sound of trampled wood and undergrowth. Up above the bank, a man emerged out of the thicket. He wore a leather jerkin, typical of a woodman from the forest, but he also wore a mask below his cap and carried a sword. "Who in the hells are you?" he bawled. "You look like a wench that needs a good poking!" He patted his groin and grinned lecherously.

Shrew's lips curled in a wicked smile. "You're Black Blood scum, aren't you? I've heard that the Black Blood are sons of whores whose tools are only fit for their own arses," she called back.

The grin on the man's face quickly faded. "You foul bitch!" he shrieked. "Gurd, did you hear that?" Another man appeared behind the first; he was bigger, and besides leather, wore loosely fitting chain mail and carried a huge axe — but he only growled in response.

The smaller man looked back at her and made a further gesture with his groin. "You're just a wanton whore and when I catch you, my tool is going to split you in two!"

Shrew raised her eyebrows. "Really? Oh, do come down and show me how," she said sweetly. "I'm waiting."

At that moment, several things happened at once. The larger of the two men leapt down the bank. He was surprisingly agile for his size. Simultaneously, Silfa and Sceral appeared in her hands as Dardalloy approached, yelling from her rear.

"Leave this to me, Darda!" she screamed, as she avoided the large rogue's incoming axe. Despite his agility, the larger man couldn't recover from his initial momentum. His axe had cleaved thin air and buried itself in the road. Now he could do nothing to stop Silfa and Sceral from plunging deep into his back to emerge from his chest like bloody thorns. Without pause, Shrew pulled the blades free and stood aside as the man toppled and slumped motionless to the ground.

The remaining rogue suddenly halted in his tracks. He had descended the bank with sword ready, expecting his companion to swiftly despatch all opposition. Now he found himself outnumbered and facing a woman who fought like a demon. He stumbled backward as Shrew advanced towards him with both her blades spitting globules of frost and dripping blood.

"Who are you?" he shrieked.

"I am the Shade of Highfall," she answered.

"Gods protect me!" he cried, and then turned and fled.

"In Parvi's name... Shrew!" Dardalloy said, walking up to her. The look of shock on his face had been replaced by amazement. "Swanmere is six hours away at a goodly pace. That's plenty of time for you to tell me all about your journey into the Dovecote and exactly how you got those daggers."

CHAPTER SEVEN
THE COUNCIL AT SWANMERE

Almost ten leagues west of the Swan River, the land rose and the sprawling forest was forced to negotiate an escarpment that ran almost north to south. Over a long period of time two ancient rivers, whose waters originated deep in the forest to the west, had eroded and cut through the escarpment to produce a spur, a tongue of land that protruded out into the lowlands. Thousands of years ago, the sylvan had recognised this strategic position and had built a fortress town on the spur. Since then, humans had been accepted into their community, and over many years the population of this cosmopolitan town grew to become the home of nearly five thousand souls. As the town expanded, it spilled over the spur and on to its southern flank; elsewhere in the lowlands, to the north and east, the forest gave way to a mere of shallow lakes and marshland and, because of its abundant swan population, it became known as Swanmere.

The sun had just set and the shades of evening were gathering. Aelmar stood leaning against the dark-wood balustrade that surrounded the viewing balcony. He was looking out towards the darkening east, where the shadowy outline of Highfall stood proud from the mountains and appeared to float upon the horizon like a ship upon a grey-green sea.

"I grieve leaving Highfall," he said, looking to his two companions, the white-bearded old sage and the young flaxen-haired cleric, "but looking back, I had little choice; and, indeed, the ruse played by Rodderic may in the end be to our advantage."

The young cleric's attention had been drawn to the magnificent panorama that rolled out before them, but after hearing Aelmar's words, he turned and looked sympathetically at the fiery-haired warrior. "The message Rodderic gave to you to deliver to the King's brother, Prince Morkere, was it completely blank? No word or mark whatsoever?"

Aelmar nodded. "Aye, completely blank," he answered. "But I made good use of that parchment, Deakin. I penned a message to the Prince, and have since learned that Hengist reached Helmscrag safely and delivered the message."

The white-bearded old man entered the conversation. "If I recall an earlier conversation we had, in that message you spoke of the dissolution of the Council and the concern you had regarding an alliance between Luven and the Crimson Sect. Did you warn the Prince of the Rathasian army?"

Aelmar shook his head. "Not in that message, Miruvar. At that time, the warning sent from Mereond hadn't arrived here in the north. I only learnt that the army had crossed into Sillaesia when I arrived here; but I promptly sent Prince Morkere a further message warning him of this new threat."

Miruvar stroked his bushy white beard in thought. "Hmm… It's an unlikely coincidence, isn't it? The timing of this ill-conceived alliance and the appearance of an army from the very same country that spawned the Crimson Sect and their unholy religion."

"Aye. I have had the same thought," Aelmar agreed. "The two must somehow be connected. We have been in Swanmere a while now, nearly three weeks, waiting for Prince Cendil to arrive from Yuarith. It has given me plenty of time to think on this matter." He fell silent for a moment, before continuing. "When we first arrived here, both of you may recall that my plans were set on dealing with these priests, particularly the one they call 'the father'. The appearance of this Rathasian army, however, has changed the whole situation, and I am now making new arrangements."

Miruvar's expression changed to one of concern. "Be careful, my friend, this may not be an army of invasion. They may have been invited!"

Aelmar frowned. "Aye, they may have been, but to what end? When Prince Cendil arrives, we will discuss the mobilisation of a sylvan army that, if necessary, could deliver a blow to the Rathasian force from the west. I have already sent a further message to Prince Morkere asking him to be prepared, for he could simultaneously engage the Rathasians from the east."

"What of your forces in Highfall?" Miruvar asked. "Are they still loyal?"

"Many of the regular forces have no doubt been seduced by this new alliance, but the Palatine are still loyal to me. I remain in contact with two of their three senior commanders."

Miruvar nodded and the three of them stood in silent thought; but before any of them could renew their conversation, their attention was drawn to a group of sylvan approaching them. At the head of this entourage walked the Lady Melowyn, resplendent in a turquoise gown that glittered with fiery gemstones of both ruby and jacinth. "Oh, there you are," she said, smiling, and bowed her head in acknowledgement. "I have good news. Prince Cendil will arrive tomorrow."

Aelmar bowed. "That is good news, my lady."

Melowyn's blue opalescent eyes shone beneath her fringe of pale blonde hair. "And I have more good news," she said, beaming. "Dardalloy has returned. He found Shrew and he's brought her with him."

The town of Swanmere displayed a veritable mix of architectural styles. In the older part of the town, on the spur, the most prominent style was seen in the sinuous timber structures of the sylvan. These complex constructions seemed to weave around and blend with the natural forest and had a similar likeness to the lace-like structures of the fey. The largest of these stood in the centre of the town and was known as the Manerel, or star hold, for at night it gleamed of wisp-light, like a city of stars.

Aelmar followed Melowyn through the great open doors of the Manerel and into the well-lit hall beyond. A crowd had gathered, and he immediately recognised his erstwhile companions Ryrkell and Waylan, looking lost and uncomfortable amidst the numerous local dignitaries. This was the eve of Ahlune's day and there was to be a banquet to celebrate. Aelmar smiled and turned to Miruvar and Deakin. "Two banquets in a week. We should visit Swanmere more often."

Miruvar grinned through his bushy white beard. "Agreed. There will almost certainly be a banquet to honour Prince Cendil when he arrives. Let us hope they think we're important enough to attend." The old man paused for a moment, then his bright blue eyes lit up in recognition. "Aha!" he cried. "My favourite barmaid and the scourge of the Black Blood!"

Aelmar turned around. Dardalloy had indeed returned, but who was the woman with him? His eyes widened. "Ellamae," he mouthed silently. He saw her now, in his mind's eye, as she was that fateful day when he left her. For a brief moment, it was as if he was in another place. The conversation around him had become muted and he was with his wife, his beautiful wife he hadn't seen for more than sixteen years. "Ellamae," he found himself saying again, but this time louder.

"Oh, I see you've found Dardalloy and Shrew," Melowyn said gaily, as she joined them once more. "We shall be walking through to the main hall soon." Suddenly, she paused. "Ah…" — she looked at Aelmar — "have you met Shrew before?" she said inquisitively.

Aelmar shook his head. He had never been lost for words like this before; he struggled to speak as the woman, who looked uncannily like his lost wife, stared at him curiously.

For a moment, Shrew was stunned — she saw the face that Tirriel had found within her forgotten memories — but she recovered quickly and spoke first. "Do you know who I am?" she cried accusingly. "I am your daughter. Did you search for me… for us? Did you think I was dead?"

The questions hit Aelmar like a hammer. "By Verrain's grace," he said quietly. "I am so sorry; I did think you were dead." He shook his head again, and Shrew could see tears in his eyes. "Believe me," he continued, "if I had thought there was even the slightest chance you had survived, I would have crossed the Great Desert to find you."

The sound of conversation in the room now seemed quieter, and it was Melowyn who spoke next, her voice soft with compassion. "I think you both need to have a quiet conversation somewhere private." Suddenly, she looked concerned. "Shrew! There's blood on your cloak; do you need aid?"

Shrew shook her head. Tears were now running down her cheeks. "The blood isn't mine," she responded. "We met trouble on the road."

Melowyn smiled warmly at Shrew. "You know how to look after yourself, don't you!" she said, nodding her head. Then she turned to Aelmar. "I can see the resemblance. She is your daughter, isn't she? Now I look, it's so obvious. You should be proud of her!" She put a slender arm around Shrew and then offered her other arm to Aelmar. "Come," she said, "let us seek a quiet place; we can join the others later."

They sat within the steady glow of a turquoise wisp lamp. Shrew sat beside Melowyn, clutching her hand as she faced Aelmar, her father. She needed someone familiar close by.

Aelmar shook his head in disbelief. "I pray this isn't a cruel dream," he said. "I thought you were dead, but now it appears that I cannot fully trust the testimony of those who claimed to have seen what befell you and your mother. I was far away when the events I am about to describe took place. I had been sent east, far from Highfall, to stop an incursion of ferals. You would have been barely two years old when I left. I still remember your tousle of blonde hair and rosy cheeks." He shook his head as he recalled the scene. "I kissed you both and said goodbye. It was a painful parting, having to leave you and your mother, for what I knew would be many months. I had not the slightest forewarning of what was about to transpire." He paused for a moment, raking his fiery hair as he carefully chose his words. "The old King, Wulfred's father, was quite mad. Some called him eccentric, but those in the Palatine who were closest to him saw his true nature. One of his strange quirks was an interest in the arcane and in inviting workers of the arcane arts to his court. You may have heard of Morrdis and Stavan Taro? They arrived in Highfall about this time, but there was another who was called Molock. I may be able to recall more about these strange guests another time, but all I can tell you now is that whilst I was away this Molock became enamoured with your mother, Ellamae. Your mother was so special..." Aelmar frowned and hesitated a moment. "Should I call you Shrew, or by your given name, Jaylee?"

Shrew blinked and fought back the tears; she was determined not to show any more emotion. "Nearly everyone knows me as Shrew," she said firmly.

Aelmar nodded and smiled kindly. "Shrew it is," he said. "Well, I was saying that your mother was special, not just because she was a wonderful wife and mother, but because she had a natural affinity for the hidden arts. I think she had the blood of the fey in her veins. Anyway, it attracted this Molock." Aelmar fell silent for a moment and looked out beyond the wisp's circle of light. It was as if he was seeking answers from the darkness.

"What did this Molock do?" Shrew asked coldly.

Aelmar turned his head to look at her once more. "All I have are pieces of a puzzle, fragmentary testaments from those few servants who survived when Molock and his mercenaries came to my villa. You were with her, but I presume you were too young to understand what was happening."

"When I was younger, I had bad nightmares," Shrew answered. "But they don't disturb me so much now." It was now her turn to become reflective and fall silent. She looked up into the eyes of the red-haired warrior who sat before her. It was truly him. After all this time, she was looking at her father. She couldn't believe it — but it was him for sure — Tirriel had shown her. Tears welled up in her eyes. "Tell me all you know," she urged.

Aelmar pulled himself up in his seat and leaned forward to look closely at her. "You look so much like your mother," he said. "I wonder if you have the strange powers she had." He shook his head. "I'm sorry," he whispered. "Let me tell you what I know. When Molock and his band of sell-swords came to our villa, they wrought much violence and abducted you and your mother. A few of my retainers saw them leave, but could do nothing to stop them. I think it was his intention to take you both back to the far south from whence he came. I do not know for sure, but I do know that they managed to leave the city and by then they were being pursued." He stopped, and Shrew could see the sadness in his eyes. "They had reached a place called the Tiel Cross, a meeting of ways to the south of the city. It was there that your mother summoned all her powers. I can only assume that's what happened, for I cannot think of any other explanation. Those brave souls from Highfall that rode in pursuit were falling behind, but they were close enough to see a bright light suddenly envelop Molock and his men. When they reached the spot, the earth had crystallised and still glowed with the intense heat of the conflagration. They counted the charred corpses and even identified Molock from his adamantine headband, but there was no sign of either you or your mother. They told me later that your ash must have blown away in the wind." He paused and looked incredulously at Shrew. "But now you are here!"

"I grew up in the Duns," Shrew answered. "I remember nothing of a bright light. My earliest recollection is of scavenging for food in the dirt."

Aelmar looked shocked. It was some time before he spoke. "Then all I can think of is that you were separated from your mother before she left the city."

Melowyn finally felt it was time to join the conversation. "That would make perfect sense," she said quietly, and gently squeezed Shrew's hand. "They would have taken the road out of the South Gate, and that runs close to the place they call the Duns. Maybe they found you a burden and dropped you there."

Aelmar studied Shrew intensely. "By Verrain's grace," he whispered, "it's a miracle. Somehow you survived. If only I had known." He lowered his head in shame as Shrew rose from her seat and extended her hand towards him.

"I am home, father," she whispered.

Aelmar looked up. It had been more than fifteen years since he had last shed tears, but now as he stood up, tears ran in rivulets down his weathered cheeks. He tenderly took her hand in his and then gently hugged her.

It was Ahlune's day, the last day in the last month of goldfall, and the morning sun shone brightly in a cloudless sky. The call from the town gate had come shortly after sunrise announcing the arrival of Prince Cendil and his escort.

Most of the residents of Swanmere had risen early and had come excitedly to the main street of the town to watch and cheer the royal procession. Shrew stood with her father, Aelmar, and the other exiled members of the Highfall council and their retainers. Only the Lady Melowyn was absent. As a cousin of Prince Cendil and a princess of the royal house of Yuarith, she stood beside the Lord Mayor of Swanmere, waiting to greet the royal party.

Shrew was fascinated. She was familiar with the sylvan folk and she counted Melowyn as one of her best friends, but this was the first time she had seen so many together. They looked so noble in their grace and posture. They resembled the fey, with their elfin features and luxurious manes of hair, but they seemed a shadow of their distant kin. She recalled how Tirriel's emerald eyes glowed and how her lavender hair shimmered with an aura of light. In contrast, the sylvan appeared earthlier and less ethereal. The nobility had passed and now came their escort — row upon row of grim sylvan warriors clad in patchwork leathers whose colours shifted between grey and green so as to deceive the eye. So these, she surmised, were the fabled sylvan runners, elite warriors who were said to be born of the forest and who could travel fifty leagues in a day. She looked on with awe as they passed, and watched the sunlight flash from their leaf-bladed spears and the plumage of their long arrows glow with iridescence.

Her musing was suddenly interrupted by a familiar voice. "Beautiful, but deadly, aren't they? See, there are even women amongst them." It was Waylan. He smiled. "Well met, Shrew. So, you're the daughter of the great man?" He nodded towards Aelmar. "I knew you were special almost from the first moment we met. It seems a long time ago since you ran into me in Southgate Street."

Shrew turned and looked into the grey eyes of her old friend. They seemed tired and his face drawn. "What's happened to you, Waylan? Did you really murder Mallory? I can't believe what they're saying."

Waylan winced as if recalling something painful and shook his head as if to rid the thoughts from his mind. "Be careful where you place your trust," he whispered. "Not all is as it seems."

Suddenly, a hand slapped Shrew's shoulder, rudely interrupting her thoughts. She swung around and found herself looking into Dardalloy's handsome features. "Pardon me, your Highness," he said with an impish grin, and raised his hands as if he dared to touch her. He greeted Waylan with a nod and then looked her up and down. "Well, what *do* we call the daughter of the King's Shield?"

Shrew kicked him hard below the knee. "You can bow next time," she chided, as she watched him bend to rub his bruised leg.

"The Council is now assembling in the Manerel!" a voice called, interrupting them.

Dardalloy straightened and turned to Waylan. "We must go at once," he said. "Lord Aelmar has asked us to attend him in the Council." He paused and looked at Shrew. "He asked that you wait back at our lodgings. There will be a hot meal and bath waiting for you there."

"What?" Shrew started to protest. She looked around for her father, but he had already departed. "Mother of Midir," she swore under her breath. "I wager he also asked for me to go and put on a dress."

Dardalloy chuckled. "Aye, I forgot to tell you that!"

There was little time for formalities. Prince Cendil took his seat at the high table of the Manerel and his counsellors took chairs either side of him. Aelmar then took his seat on the opposite side of the crescent-shaped table and Melowyn joined him to his left and Miruvar to his right. Finally, as was custom, the Lord Mayor of Swanmere entered last and, as the host, sat at the head of the table. All around the edge of the great hall their retainers gathered and either sat or stood, waiting to be called. Above all, beams of sunlight entered through clear crystal windows in the vaulted ceiling, to cast a spectral glow over the entire proceedings.

It was the Mayor, an elderly man with thinning white hair, who spoke first. He rose and then bowed towards the Prince. "Your Royal Highness," he said humbly, "we are greatly honoured to receive you and your escort on this special day, the day of our protector, Her Holiness, Ahlune."

The Prince nodded graciously. His long, braided silver hair shone like white gold in the sunlight. "Thank you, Lord Mayor," he said in a delicate yet precise tone, and then turned his elfin features and piercing grey eyes towards Melowyn and Aelmar. "I bring warm greetings to the town of Swanmere and to our noble friends from Highfall." He smiled, and then continued in the sylvan tongue, "Aluu, elowár Melowyn."

Aelmar bowed his head and noticed Melowyn was smiling. Her face was radiant. It must have been a while since one had addressed her in her native tongue, and it must have meant so much more, given that the Prince was a cousin and one of her family.

"Your Royal Highness," the Mayor continued, "if I may respectfully ask you to open our Council."

The Prince leaned back in his chair. "Of course," he said. "Let us now discuss the matters at hand; but first, let me introduce Mage Master Valorrin, on my right, and Sky Watcher Maezil, on my left. They are here to assist us." He paused for a moment and looked across the table towards Aelmar and the other representatives of Highfall. "Please accept my apologies for taking so long to get here, and let me explain the reason for our delay. I received your messages concerning the advance of the Rathasian army, Lord Aelmar. The audacious nature of their incursion into Sillaesia suggests they are indeed a real threat. I had already received word from Mereond of the army's crossing of the border, but then other issues were brought to my attention. I fear these other issues could potentially turn out to be greater threats than the Rathasian army. For that reason, my departure from Yuarith was delayed."

Silence suddenly descended upon the great hall of the Manerel as the impact of the Prince's words fell upon all those present. Miruvar raised his bushy eyebrows and looked questioningly at Aelmar, and then turned to Deakin, who sat to his right. A few whispered conversations began, but they were soon silenced as the Prince stood up and gestured to the white-haired sylvan sitting beside him, the one he had just introduced as Sky Watcher Maezil.

"Sky Watcher Maezil Tarnarith is one of my most respected astrologers," the Prince declared, as he retook his seat. "He will tell you all we know about the first of these issues."

The white-haired sylvan slowly raised himself up from his chair and bowed towards Prince Cendil. He was clearly old, even for a sylvan, who were known to live for many hundreds of years. His robe was a deep blue, like the deepest twilight on a clear summer night, and it was peppered with small gems that seemed to twinkle like stars. Maezil Tarnarith cleared his throat and then began to speak in an ominous tone. "At the fall of reapen, when Scawba was at its zenith, my sky watchers observed an anomaly in the house of the wolf. Thereafter, we followed it for many nights until it crossed into the house of the hunter. It now grows daily and will soon eclipse our Sun. On the fourth day of the first month of half-light there will be no daylight — only perpetual night."

There were audible gasps from many within the hall. Miruvar moved his hand from stroking his beard and raised it to attract attention. "Surely," he cried, "an eclipse of the Sun is a temporary phenomenon. It lasts but a few minutes."

The old sylvan's dark eyes looked upon Miruvar and the others seated at the table and slowly shook his head. "We don't know how long the darkness will prevail. This anomaly does not have a planetary course; it comes to us directly from Nilhahn, from the Void."

"Then it must have been summoned," Miruvar replied. "Such entities cannot cross into our world without being called, and therein lies the conundrum. Only someone with unearthly power could open such a gateway."

Prince Cendril nodded. "I agree," he said. "Or someone who has unearthly assistance." He turned to the sky watcher. "Thank you, Maezil, you may take your seat." The Prince paused for a moment to carefully consider his next words. "This leads me onto the next issue," he continued. "We have received reports from some who dwell in the eastern bounds of the Gloamril that a subtle change has taken hold of the forest. Workers of the arts, such as the druids and enchanters, have noticed a draining of the ley, the underlying energy of all things."

Now cries of astonishment broke out, followed by heated conversation in the hall. Aelmar rose slowly to his feet. The presence and aura of the tall, fiery-haired warrior had an immediate impact, and very quickly the commotion subsided. "I may have an answer," he said loudly, so that his voice carried to the far corners of the great hall. "At least an answer to the first of these issues, and maybe even the second."

The Prince nodded and signalled for Aelmar to speak.

Aelmar returned a nod and smiled grimly before continuing. "The red-tongued priests of the Crimson Sect, led by that shadowy figure they call the father, prophesise of a coming darkness that will consume the world. Salvation, they say, will only come through the father, although what form this salvation will take, I do not know."

The Prince leaned forward in his chair. "Lord Aelmar, this Sect came from Rathasia, did it not? And did King Wulfred give them leave to build a temple upon the scarred lands of Everdim?"

"Aye, that is true on both counts," Aelmar answered, "but both the King and his Council have paid dearly for that rash decision. Of course, I speak for those Council members represented here and not for the renegade councillors under Luven who choose to consort with these priests."

A sudden realisation dawned upon the Prince's face. "A confluence of major ley lines lies under Everdim!" he cried. "It lies below ancient crypts that have been there for millennia."

"There you have it," Aelmar exclaimed, as he sat down. "The priests are drawing energy from the ley to summon an abomination from the Void. Yet why has Queen Mistranna sent half her legions into Sillaesia at this time? Is it because of this summoning and the coming darkness?"

"It cannot be a coincidence," the Prince answered. "The legions are clearly in league with these priests. I fear they plan to take Highfall, but by what means, I do not know."

Aelmar shook his head. "Mistranna knows that Highfall's walls and defences are impregnable. They have withstood the might of greater forces than hers. This summoning must aid her somehow. I dread to think what that might be."

Miruvar coughed. "Excuse me," he said, wiping his beard with a handkerchief. "I think we all know what *that* might be, but daren't suppose." He paused and turned his attention to the fair-haired young cleric who sat beside him. "Deakin, I understand you've investigated this so-called Crimson Sect on behalf of your holy master, the High Prelate. Is that true? I trust your holy master still fares well in Highfall?"

Deakin nodded and smoothed the edges of his neatly trimmed beard. "The last I heard, my holy master was in good health, but held under guard within the Cathedral. As for the Crimson Sect, you may recall that their High Priest, Cyrus Col, openly professed to King Wulfred that they worship the old gods, Yngvi and Dysettis. Yet it doesn't take much research to reveal that they also venerate the gatekeeper, Folkron the Deformed."

"That is my fear," Aelmar interrupted. "Folkron is the way to the unspoken one, the Master of Shades. Surely, they wouldn't be as foolish as to summon that one back from the Void. It would be the end of all things!"

A palpable dread fell upon them. The hall fell quiet once again. It was Melowyn's soft musical voice that eventually banished the silence. "If I may speak," she said. "Whilst we are all agreed that the Crimson Sect appear to be the perpetrators behind this summoning, I believe we have all overlooked something."

Prince Cendil looked up. He had been silent for a while, his mind locked within a deep train of thought, but now his face brightened. "Dearest cousin," he said, "please tell us how we have erred."

Melowyn shook her head. "The fault is my own. I should have spoken earlier. When I left Highfall, I brought with me a young human girl who had been incarcerated in one of the city's workhouses. She had been one of many children they cruelly call sewer rats, who had been drafted by Luven and those we now call the renegade council, to seek a hidden passage under the city. It took many days to heal her disturbed mind, but now she is fully restored and dwells here in Swanmere with an adopted family."

The Prince looked interested. "A hidden passage, you say? Did she give you any further information?"

Melowyn nodded. "She did, but only very recently. Let me quote her exact words, for I remember them well — 'We were taken into the dark beneath the houses by bad men and one strange man with a red mark on his head. They wanted us to find a path to the man's temple. We found it, but we also found monsters, dead things that moved.'"

Prince Cendil mouthed a silent oath. His eyes glared and his brow creased with anger. "The fools," he cried. "They have entered the Crypts of Everdim!"

Aelmar slammed his fist on the table. "A hidden passage from the temple to Highfall?" he questioned loudly. "Under our walls and defences? Then that is why Mistranna confidently brings her legions to our front door!"

The hall erupted in loud exclamations of surprise and dismay. Then it quickly became a hive of heated discussion. It was only when both Aelmar and Prince Cendil rose from their seats and stood together that the noise finally subsided.

It was the Prince who spoke first, loudly and clearly, silencing any remaining conversation. "So, it appears that this renegade council and their allies from the Crimson Sect have found a path through the Everdark and into the crypts that lie under Everdim. This is very disturbing news."

"I don't understand," Aelmar exclaimed. "Are Luven and his renegades giving Highfall to Rathasia? Surely the way is now open for Mistranna to move her legions through the passage and into the city!"

Prince Cendil shook his head. "That won't be as easy as it seems," he replied. "I think I should tell you more about Everdim and the crypts that lie beneath, for they have been disturbed before."

Aelmar bade the Prince to continue and returned silently to his seat.

All eyes now turned to the silver-haired Prince. For a few moments he looked sad and lost in recollection. At last he spoke. "Long ago, tens of thousands of years or more, the fey discovered powerful energies under the eastern Gloamril that extended under the river and into the lands beyond. There was one special place in those lands, east of the river, they called Aylission. It was close to their beloved city known as Myrifel, which in those days was a jewel upon the face of the earth. There they laid their dead to rest in magnificent tombs that looked up at the stars. As time passed, the fey people withdrew from the surface of this world and retreated to a place they called Qinestra. The tombs became buried, becoming crypts under the earth. Finally, legends recall that the last fey, Prince Armeris, son of King Glossingal, built a shrine in that land, a symbol of mourning for the departure of the fey from this world. Others, however, say that it was built in grief for his lost beloved. Nevertheless, there he raged in sorrow and so also slowly passed from this world. His sadness seeped into the land, extinguishing its former beauty such that thereafter the name Aylission was forgotten and it became known as Everdim. Over time, a blight descended upon the lands and it attracted all kinds of evil. The old crypts were re-opened and sylvan and humans were laid to rest there, alongside the remains of those who had come before. Many then came and went — men from the far south, who erected their foul temples and conducted profane practices, until they were finally driven out by Finngol, the first King of Highfall. Finngol sealed the crypts, for it is said that he found the dead were restless there and declared that they should never be disturbed again."

The hall was deathly silent. This was a story few had heard. Then one voice called out and addressed the Prince. Aelmar turned his head and saw that Dardalloy had stepped forward.

Dardalloy bowed. "Your Highness," he said again, less loudly than before. "The names you just mentioned, Armeris and Qinest…" He hesitated, trying to recall the Prince's words.

"Qinestra," the Prince prompted him. "What of them?"

Dardalloy looked embarrassed. "I heard those names spoken only yesterday, as I journeyed here with my friend. She also mentioned someone called Tirriel…" Dardalloy paused and whispered to himself, "And now she will kill me for telling you all this."

"Tirriel?" The Prince repeated the name several times over, as if trying to recall something long forgotten. He looked up at Dardalloy. "Who is this friend of yours? Is she here, in Swanmere?"

Aelmar rose from his seat. "Your Highness," he said respectfully, "she is my daughter, Jaylee, although she prefers to be called Shrew. We will summon her here immediately, although I find it hard to believe that she would know much about such things." He looked questioningly at Dardalloy.

Prince Cendil shook his head in disbelief. "Intriguing," he said. Then he turned and addressed the hall. "We will take a break and continue when we have the Lady Shrew here with us."

The large oak tub was nearly full of steaming water and soap. Shrew felt like she was in heaven, or at the very least, the blessed realm of Empyrean. She hummed the catchy tune of old Jack Willow as she raised her toes out from beneath the water and wiggled and stretched them to burst a few bubbles. This was the best soak she had had in months. She reached out and delicately lifted the long-stemmed crystal glass from the table beside the tub and took another sip of the Vinye Viriesse, a rare vintage wine from the Deep Gloamril. Money well spent, she thought, as she looked at the empty bottle and the empty pouch beside it, which had formerly held a handful of florins and sovereigns.

There was then a soft knock at the door to her room. The door opened slightly and a woman's voice called through the crack. It was her maid. "My pardon, Ma'am, there's a gentleman downstairs to see you."

"Tell him to go away," Shrew called, and took another sip of her wine.

"He insists it's important, Ma'am," the maid replied.

Then a familiar voice called out and Dardalloy's face appeared at the crack of the door. "Shrew!" he exclaimed. "They need you at the Council in the Manerel."

Shrew sighed and carefully placed the wine glass back on the table. She then slowly sank under the water. A few seconds later, she quickly resurfaced and flung a towel at Dardalloy's face. "What have you been saying?" she cried. "Wait for me downstairs!"

Dardalloy looked sheepish as they strode up the hill towards the Manerel. "It's a nice inn, isn't it?" he said, as he tried to start a conversation for the third time. "Well, anyway, I think you look stunning in that new gown. Did you get it at the market?"

Shrew's dour expression softened very slightly. "It's a sylvan gown," she retorted. "Made from the silk of the emerald mayfly."

Dardalloy smiled. "Well, you've certainly turned a few heads," he said, as they approached the open trellised doors of the Manerel. Then, for the fourth time, he apologised. "I'm sorry I divulged your secrets, but they need your help."

"Let's forget it," Shrew countered. "Just keep my bag safe."

"What's in it?" he asked, as he tested its weight.

"You'll find out soon enough," she responded. "Now let's get this meeting over with; then we can go back to the inn and try more of their wine."

Dardalloy grinned. "I look forward to it," he said. "But first, let me escort you to the Council."

As they entered the great hall at the centre of the Manerel structure, people stepped aside to let them pass. There were expectant looks on their faces, and Shrew started to feel a little nervous. What did they want of her? She stopped short of the high table and found herself standing in a diffuse column of sunlight, which had entered through a window high above in the vaulted ceiling. Having hurriedly left the inn, she had left her hair untied, and now it gathered at her shoulders, gleaming like pure gold in the morning light.

Before her, seated around the high table, were the assembled Council. She recognised many of the faces, but there were also strangers; these were mostly sylvan, and one of them looked very important. That was the Prince, she thought. She felt a little uncomfortable, and not knowing quite what to do next, put on one of her most angelic smiles and curtseyed.

The Prince rose slowly from his seat. "Lord Aelmar, this must be your daughter, Shrew, I presume?" He turned back towards Shrew and bowed his head. "Pardon, my Lady. I am Prince Cendil of Yuarith. Can I say that you are the most beautiful human I have ever had the pleasure of meeting?"

Shrew smiled at the Prince again and felt some of her confidence return. She could see tears in her father's eyes and noticed Melowyn was smiling at her — even old Miruvar's eyes twinkled. "Your Highness." Shrew bowed her head and then boldly looked the Prince in the eyes. "I thank you for your kind comment. I am here because the Council required my presence. How may I help?"

"I understand you have useful information that could help us?" the Prince answered, and then looked in the direction of Dardalloy, who stood several paces behind Shrew and was still clutching her bag. "Are you familiar with the names Qinestra and Myrifel?" he continued. "And do you know of their connection to Everdim?"

There was an awkward silence. Shrew continued to stare at the Prince as she pieced together fragments of Tirriel's words and memories, as well as her own recollections regarding those things she had seen with her own eyes. Someone coughed in the hall and it brought her quickly back to the present. At last she spoke. "I know of the fey city of Mirifel," she announced clearly and confidently, "but I know more about Qinestra, for I have seen it with my own eyes."

There were gasps of surprise from all around the large hall. "That's impossible!" someone cried out in a sylvan accent, and she heard similar calls that shed doubt upon her words.

The Prince held up his hands and the commotion in the hall finally subsided.

Shrew stood unmoved and looked at her father. He sat quietly, but had a concerned look on his face. She smiled at him knowingly and then turned back to address the Prince. "Your Royal Highness, I expected some would question the veracity of my claims, so before I say more, I have something to show you." She signalled Dardalloy to bring her the bag. Moments later, she lifted her daggers, Silfa and Sceral, out of the bag and held them aloft for all to see. Channelling her thoughts, she awakened the dragons from their sleep and the lustrous blades erupted into life, glowing with a white inner fire and chilling the air around them. "Your Highness," she continued, "these are fey weapons which belonged to Faeril of Myrifel and that were given to me by Tirriel, High Warden of Qinestra."

For a brief moment there were audible gasps, but then the hall fell deathly silent. Even the Prince seemed lost for words. Their eyes were transfixed on the legendary weapons in Shrew's hands. It was Miruvar who spoke first. Pushing back his chair, he rose slowly to his feet and leaned on his staff. "Let there be no doubt," he proclaimed loudly. "You can be assured that the Lady Shrew speaks the truth, and I know that others here will also vouch for her." He smiled at Shrew through his bushy beard. "Let her tell you now what she knows." He winked and nodded at Shrew, before slowly regaining his seat.

Prince Cendil finally found his voice. He was visibly shocked by what he had just seen. "I agree, Lord Miruvar," he managed to say at last. "My Lady, please continue. I apologise for any doubts this Council may have had."

Shrew nodded and then stood in silent thought for a moment. Silfa and Sceral grumbled, but she calmed them with soothing thoughts, and soon they were dozing again. The burning light within each dagger dimmed and faded.

"Ahlune protect us," the Prince whispered in astonishment. "You have spirit blades?"

Shrew smiled and nodded again. "You mentioned Everdim, your Highness," she said, changing the subject. "While I was in Qinestra with Tirriel, I came across a pathway that led into the Crypts of Everdim. Tirriel was concerned that something deep in the crypts was feeding on the ley, drawing off its energy for a malign purpose."

The Prince shook his head and breathed a sylvan curse. "You have confirmed our worst fears," he said quietly. "Is there more you can tell us?"

"Tirriel was so concerned, she made me enter the crypts," Shrew replied. "I remember hearing a beating sound that seemed to carry through the stone walls, and then I encountered a foul creature from the Void." She paused for a moment as the horror still lingered in her mind. "The dead have come to life," she whispered.

"By the grace of Verrain," Aelmar growled. "Necromantic forces are at work. I wager it is the Crimson Sect — they have breached the crypts below their temple."

The Prince raised his hand for silence as others round the table clamoured to speak, and then turned and addressed the stern-faced sylvan who sat silently on his right. "Valorrin, I know you understand necromancy and summoning better than I. What have you to say on such matters?"

Valorrin nodded respectfully at the Prince and rose to his feet. He appeared unlike any of the other sylvan. His hair was as black as coal and was short. It was almost spikey in texture. Shrew studied him closely as he prepared his words. She guessed he was half-sylvan, but what the other half was, she couldn't fathom. "Your Highness," Valorrin began, "it appears that the summoning has started. It has called forth the anomaly in the heavens, but it is not yet ended. It has barely started. The energy drain on the ley is still small, and the beating sound — well... think of it as a knocking at the door. Those that summoned the anomaly from Nilhahn are still in the early stages of their ritual. It will end with the darkness."

"Then there's still time to stop it!" the Prince cried. "Cyr!" he called across the table to the tall sylvan that stood behind Melowyn. "You are a pathfinder and know the eastern Gloamril well. If I am not mistaken, there was once a fey tower in this part of the forest called Faerun, and if I recall correctly, it was connected to Everdim. Do you know of it?"

Cyr stepped forward from out of the shadows and bowed. "Your Highness, there is a fey ruin, barely a league south of the hamlet of Tricksey. It is known as Farren by the locals, but they will not approach it, for it is considered to be cursed. This must be the remains of that tower."

Prince Cendil nodded. "Thank you, Cyr. Well, it seems our mission is clear. We must find a way into the Crypts of Everdim and stop the summoning before the darkness occurs and the Master of Shades is let loose upon this world. The tower seems our best hope. We have less than four days."

Aelmar stood up. "This mission is not for a large force," he said determinedly, "but one for a small, skilled party that can act with stealth and subtlety." He raised his voice so all could hear. "If you agree, I will gladly volunteer to lead such a party." There were cries of support from all around the hall, and only the Lord Mayor's hammer, repeatedly banging the table, brought the hall to order.

Finally, Prince Cendil managed to speak. "I thank you, Lord Aelmar, but as the threat affects both our interests, I suggest we send five of your choosing and five of mine. In that respect, we will have a party endowed with a broad range of skills. I nominate myself, Valorrin, Cyr and two of my most able sylvan runners, Taylen and Hygil. Last, but not least, because of her unparalleled restorative skills, I choose the Lady Melowyn — if she agrees, of course."

Aelmar nodded. "I agree with those terms, your Highness, but as time is short, I will have to select my five from those here in Swanmere. I choose Ryrkell, Waylan, Dardalloy, Deakin and the Lord Miruvar, if he is able."

Miruvar stood up more quickly than his age would suggest possible. "Oh no you don't!" he thundered. "You will select Shrew. She is the most able present!"

Prince Cendil smiled. "A good choice," he said. "Lord Mayor, we will need your help with preparations. If Lord Aelmar agrees, I suggest we depart at first light tomorrow; that will give us the remainder of this day to gather the equipment we will need. We will then have three whole days in which to stop the ritual." The Prince paused for a moment in thought. "But, before we dissolve this Council, I have one last question for the Lady Shrew. Where is this Tirriel you have spoken of now?"

Shrew smiled at the Prince. "I believe she passed through the Well of Stars and left our world," she said softly. "I think she has finally found Taccivae."

THE COMING OF THE DARK

HALF-LIGHT

YEAR 5124

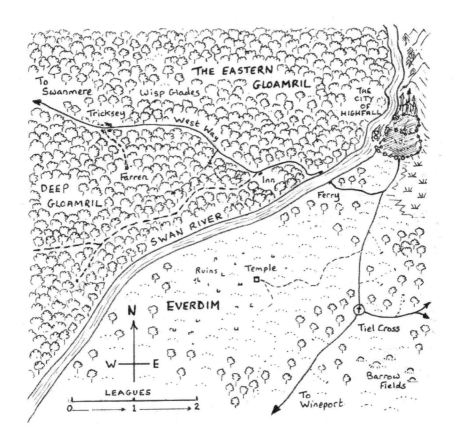

The lands close to Everdim

CHAPTER ONE
FARREN

Shrew drew the hood of her cloak further over her face, as droplets of rain fell from its brim. A fine drizzle fell, and the forest appeared cloaked in a blanket of mist that made it difficult to see more than fifty yards in any direction. The party had left Swanmere later than planned. By the time they had passed through the town's gatehouse and reached the open road, it had been daylight for several hours. It had been decided, at least for the first stage of their journey, that they would be accompanied by the entire sylvan contingent that had come from Yuarith. She had heard the Prince tell her father that their large escort would hide their small group from prying eyes and give them added protection. Shrew was thankful for her oilskin cloak. It was practically impervious to the continuous rain. Just a few moments before, her father, Aelmar, had left her to go forward, up the line of sylvan warriors and pack horses to find Prince Cendil. For the last few hours, they had shared each other's company, although the conversation seemed very one-sided. Aelmar wanted to know everything about her, from her time in the Duns to her adventures in the fey undercity of Qinestra. Now she was on her own, she had time to think about the journey ahead and the provisions she had brought with her. By a stroke of luck, she had found a herbalist's shop in the town, that nestled within the folds of an enormous ancient tree, along with other emporia that traded the fruits of the forest. This small open-fronted shop had a plentiful supply of Mestina pods, as well as other useful exotic herbs from the Deep Gloamril. This was a boon. Mestina pods had many uses, but through long periods of experimentation, Shrew had found a completely novel and disruptive use for them.

A familiar voice called, and she turned around to see Dardalloy hurry forward to join her. "Need some company?" he asked with a cheery tone in his voice. "We are close to Tricksey. Fancy stepping up to the front of the line?"

Shrew sighed. "I guess so," she replied resignedly. "My inventory-taking can wait till later. Hopefully in some place that's warm and dry."

They strode forward together and soon reached the front of the column. Amongst the vanguard, Shrew noticed Prince Cendil, resplendent in his shimmering mail armour, despite the drizzle and the poor light. There, too, were other familiar faces, and she recognised the Lady Melowyn, hooded and cloaked, like herself.

Out of the mist emerged the shape of a peasant's cot, then another slightly larger building of wood and thatch that seemingly leaned against some trees. The Prince raised his hand and a barely audible high-pitched sound rang out that brought the column to a sudden halt.

"We are on the outskirts of the village," Dardalloy whispered. "I think we part company with our escort now. Look, Prince Cendil is giving instructions to his commanders."

Shrew could see that a group of sylvan had gathered around the Prince, and her father was among them, too. She folded her arms and cursed under her breath as she prepared herself for the possibility of a long wait. The sylvan folk were renowned for deliberating over the smallest of details. "There's an inn in Tricksey," she hissed. "It will have a log fire, hot stew bubbling in the pot and maybe some acceptable ale."

Dardalloy peered back at her from under his hood as water ran in rivulets across his cheeks and dripped from his nose. Shrew couldn't prevent her lips from spreading into an artful grin. The look on Dardalloy's face was priceless, and one she wished she could preserve in her memory for a long time. "I had set my mind on a path of abstinence from goodly fare, at least for the next few days," he muttered, brushing his nose with his sleeve. "Now you've just spoiled it and reminded me of what I'm missing."

"Maybe we won't have to wait," Shrew exclaimed. "Look!" From out of the mist, a group of figures emerged, led by a tall sylvan. Shrew recognised the pathfinder known as Cyr immediately. Behind him she noticed Waylan, accompanied by Ryrkell and a few others, several sylvan and a shorter human. "Come." She tugged at Dardalloy's sleeve. "Something's happening. The scouts are back. Let's go listen."

A small group that included the Prince, Melowyn and her father was now gathering around the scouts. As she approached them, Shrew's eyes widened. She recognised the short human who now had Waylan and Ryrkell standing each side of him. "Wilf!" she cried. She turned to Dardalloy and lowered her voice. "What's he doing here? I thought he had returned to Highfall?"

"I didn't say he'd returned to the city," Dardalloy whispered close to her ear. "I said he left us when we reached the forest. It was his choice."

They reached the group and found that Cyr was addressing the Prince. Shrew took a sideways glance at Wilf and noticed he was trembling. From his expression and the way his eyes darted nervously left and right, she guessed he was more scared than cold and wet. Suddenly, their eyes met. She nodded and smiled at him, hoping her acknowledgement would give him some comfort. He looked like he'd just crawled out of Midir's deepest rift.

The Prince's voice brought her mind back to the matters at hand. "Well, that's settled then," he said. "We part company with the escort here." He pointed at the newcomer. "So, who is this lad you've brought back with you?"

"I believe his name is Wilf," Cyr replied dutifully. "He is an acquaintance of the honourable Dardalloy and the Lady Shrew. He ran into us a few furlongs south of the village. He was in a distressed state, saying he was being followed, but we saw no sign of pursuit. We sent runners back the way he had come, but the forest only spoke of one passing that way."

"I'm not lying!" Wilf cried out. "They had dogs and nearly caught me; but something scared them and I got away. They're looking for something."

Prince Cendil nodded. "We didn't say you were lying, Wilf," he said kindly. "Who had these dogs?"

"Black Blood!" Wilf blurted. "They're in the forest, the other side of the village."

The Prince raised his eyebrows and looked questioningly at Aelmar. "Are they looking for your people, perchance?"

Aelmar slowly nodded and stroked the red stubble on his chin. "Quite possibly," he answered. "We've been holed up in Swanmere some time now, and it's been no secret that remnants of the old council have sought refuge there. I'm surprised Luven's assassins haven't played their hand before now."

"More the need to get moving to Farren, then," the Prince affirmed. "Someone, get the lad something to keep out the rain. He's going to have to come with us."

Melowyn stepped forward with a cloak in her hand. "Wilf can walk with me," she said gently, and exchanged knowing glances with Aelmar and her cousin, the Prince.

Aelmar nodded. "Very well," he said. "Let's get our group together and leave for Farren immediately, avoiding the village. If any village folk are about their business, let their attention be drawn to the escort. We don't want word of our intentions reaching the ears of the Black Blood or the Crimson Sect."

"Agreed," the Prince said, and signalled to the commander in charge of the escort. "My runners will continue along the West Way. Their presence should at least distract, if not deter, anyone seeking to find us."

Dardalloy turned to Shrew. "Your hot stew and ale will have to wait," he whispered with half a smile. "It will be iron rations from now on."

The weather in the Gloamril forest was prone to change quickly. By the time their small party had grouped together and left the last outlying woodman's cot behind, the clouds had parted and the incessant drizzle had stopped. The sun now shone brightly in the south from a wide stretch of blue sky and it felt quite balmy, despite it being the second day of half-light. This was not unusual for the Gloamril; it seemed to have a weather all of its own. The appearance of the sun had lifted the party's spirits and Shrew found herself recalling an old Sillaesian saying — 'When the snow doth pile against Highfall's walls, summer still sings in the Gloamril'.

They followed an old track that at first wound around copses of young trees and passed through small patches of lush meadow. Here, the woodmen's hands had been busy, but within a short time the path they were following took them under the broad eaves of the ancient forest. Now they walked two abreast in a green twilight world where the sun rarely found the forest floor. Now and then, Shrew caught sight of motes of light drifting between the trees. These, she reasoned, were wayward wisps, the small lanterns of fey-kind. There was little conversation. It seemed everyone was immersed in their own thoughts and thinking of the mission ahead. Cyr had taken the lead and Waylan took up the rear. After a while, Shrew decided to speak to Wilf and sidled up alongside him.

"You're looking rough," she hissed. "What's happened to you? Why did you leave the others after you'd crossed the river?"

Wilf eyed her nervously and shot a glance behind. "They're following us," he croaked. "I know who they are."

"Black Blood," Shrew replied, and gently reached out to console him, but he flinched and drew away. "Steady, Wilf," she said with genuine concern on her face. "They can't hurt you now."

Melowyn quickly intervened as Cyr brought the party to a halt. "He's in a state of shock, Shrew," she said with a reassuring smile, and held out her hand to the petrified youth. "We will be making camp soon; then we can all relax."

"Sooner than you think," Aelmar said, as he joined them. "Cyr says there's a clearing up ahead and a shrine to Celestine. There's water there. It's a safe place to stop for a short while."

Shrew nodded and opened her mouth to speak, but decided to hold her tongue. Instead, she merely smiled at her father. Declaring that the presence of an inn would have been more welcome news, would not have been a good idea.

Cyr was right. Within minutes they had emerged from the forest and into a secluded dell that was bathed in the golden light of the afternoon sun. Shrew had never seen anywhere so beautiful. Everywhere was a vibrant green that glistened with the sparkling drops of the fallen rain. Wild flowers, the blooms of the season of goldfall, had opened their petals towards the sun and seemed to glow in indescribable hues of violet and blue. On one side of the dell, a craggy rock-face protruded from a bank of moss and lichen, and before it stood a human-like statue, with outstretched arms and upturned palms, staring up at the sky. Clear sparkling water bubbled from a spring at the statue's feet and spilled over stones, to collect in a circular pool.

"We are blessed," Deakin breathed, and dropped to one knee. "Here, indeed, is a hallowed place, a shrine to his radiance, our Lord Celestine."

Prince Cendil bowed his head. "Elui éathassil cei Ahlune," he said quietly. "Exalted is the father of Ahlune."

Aelmar made a sign of respect and then joined Cyr to check the perimeter of the small clearing. Seemingly satisfied, he re-joined the main group. "We should spend a short time here to refresh ourselves," he said, as he looked to the Prince for his approval.

The Prince nodded. "We are close to Farren now," he replied. "A short rest here at this blessed spot will lift our spirits."

Shrew nudged Dardalloy and unshouldered her backpack. "You can be useful," she said glibly. "I need some blood root, and there's some growing over there by that tree; and, while you're there, you can collect some of the leaves of those blue violets."

"Wait one moment," Dardalloy interrupted her. "I'm not picking flowers…"

Shrew paused and puckered her brow. "They could save your life," she retorted, and watched him as he shrugged his shoulders and smiled meekly, before doing as she bade. Looking over towards the statue, she noticed that Deakin was carefully filling some small bottles with water from the spring. Reaching into her bag, she pulled out her water-skin and wandered over to join him. As she approached, she noticed he was repeating the same words over each bottle he filled. She stopped and stood silently beside him, fascinated by what he was doing. At last he stopped and became aware of her presence.

"This is holy water," he said, looking up at her, smiling. "This spring has been blessed with starlight sent from his Celestial Radiance, Lord Celestine. This is pure living water. It embodies good and is a bane upon evil."

Shrew studied the handsome features of the young priest. "Is it safe to drink?" she asked tentatively.

"It couldn't be better," he answered, grinning through his neatly trimmed beard.

"Then he won't mind if I fill up my skin?" she asked, holding up her water-skin. "I would hate to be struck down by a falling star for being disrespectful."

Aelmar had overheard their conversation and joined them. He looked sympathetically at Deakin. "Please forgive her," he said. "She's just like her mother. At times I found that Ellamae's impeccable politeness merely hid the fact that you were at the butt-end of one of her jokes." He smiled and looked fondly at Shrew. "I'm glad I have you. You're special in your own way, but you remind me of her every day."

Deakin smiled at Shrew. "I am sure Lord Celestine would be pleased if you took some water from his spring. Maybe you could offer a small prayer of thanks in return?"

Shrew found herself blushing as she bowed her head graciously, under the eyes of her father. Her intended banter with the young priest hadn't quite gone to plan. She whispered her thanks to Deakin and then nodded politely at her father, before walking around the edge of the pool to a spot where she could catch the water as it bubbled out of the ground.

Aelmar drew his sword from the sheath strapped to his back. "Honourable Deakin," he said, as he presented the weapon in the upturned palms of his hands. "This is Argalon, a holy sword forged from sky metal and imbued with the will of Verrain. I would be grateful if it could be immersed in the holy waters of Lord Celestine."

"You need not have asked, but I appreciate your politeness and respect, Lord Aelmar," the young priest replied, as he gestured to the pool. "I would also be honoured to offer a blessing. I have heard marvellous tales of your great deeds with that legendary sword."

Shrew watched with interest as Aelmar stepped forward and submerged the sword blade into the depths of the pool. Then she watched Deakin raise his hands and begin his blessing, but when it became clear that the procedure could take more than a few minutes, she soon lost interest. Her eyes wandered over to the rest of the group and then she suddenly realised that with the exception of the Lady Melowyn, who was speaking to Wilf, all of the sylvan stood together at the far side of the clearing. Her eyes opened wide as she realised, they weren't alone. A group of sprites had joined them and the tallest among them, a slender girl clothed in a spray of green leaf and purple flowers, stood talking intently to Cyr and the Prince.

Shrew rose and returned to her backpack, placing the water-skin beside it. Now she saw that Ryrkell and Waylan had also noticed the newcomers. She bit her lip and decided to wander over and see these creatures more closely. They fascinated her. The Prince saw her coming and beckoned her to join them.

"This is the Lady Shrew," the Prince said, introducing her to the tall sprite. "She is the one who has the favour of the fey."

A twisted smile settled on the sprite's delicate elfin face that fairly shone amidst a dark shock of tufts and curls that reminded Shrew of thorns. She looked like a young mischievous girl, barely in her teenage years, but the depths of her luminous eyes belied wisdom beyond that of mortal man. "Well met, Shrew," she said, in a voice that recalled a sensation of twilight and green leafy bowers. "You are clearly a gem amongst menfolk."

"And Shrew, this is Brier," Prince Cendil interjected, so as to complete the introductions. "She is Queen of the Nightshade and oversees this region of the Gloamril."

"I am honoured to meet you, ma'am," Shrew said, lowering her head in deference.

The sprite Queen gave a gentle laugh and smiled. "And you are much more politeful than those burdensome oafs who come here to cut down our trees."

Prince Cendil looked briefly across the clearing to where Aelmar and his party had now gathered. "Brier has brought us news," he said, returning his attention to Shrew. "We must assemble the others."

Soon, the entire party of sylvan and humans had gathered together. Shrew noticed the looks of wonder on those city dwellers, Deakin and Wilf, who, like herself, had never ventured so deep into the Gloamril before and seen the small folk of the forest at such close quarters. They reminded her of children as she watched them chat and laugh beside their Queen.

Satisfied that everyone was present, Prince Cendil acknowledged Aelmar, before turning to the others. "We are honoured," he said, "to have been graced with the presence of Brier, Queen of the Nightshade, who has kindly agreed to escort us the remaining distance to Farren. I have accepted her kind offer, as it appears these woods are no longer as safe as we thought. A group of humans were preparing to ambush us further up this track. Queen Brier tells me they will trouble us no more, but also thinks there might be other groups abroad with similar intent."

Aelmar stepped forward and bowed graciously before the sprite Queen. "Thank you, my lady," he said courteously. "We are most grateful for your aid, but we are also concerned that these bad people knew of our presence here." He turned to look questioningly at the Prince.

Prince Cendil looked worried and shook his head. "It can only be the Black Blood; but for them to know where we are going and get ahead of us does raise some awkward questions."

Aelmar cursed under his breath as he adjusted the sword strap on his shoulder. "We must get moving," he growled, and then raised his voice so all could hear. "Let's prepare to move. We'll be following our new friends." As the group dispersed and prepared to depart, Aelmar approached the Prince and whispered close to his ear. "The Black Blood are receiving information on our movements, but it's unlikely it was someone at the council meeting who tipped them off; there wasn't enough time."

The Prince nodded. "I am loathe to say it," he whispered, "but it could be someone in our party. What of the young lad, Wilf? Could it be him?"

Aelmar shook his head. "Melowyn has had her eye on him constantly and has used her skills to reveal his intent. He is harmless; the poor lad is traumatised."

"Well, then, I can't think it could be any of the others," the Prince confided. "It seems more likely that the Black Blood have the assistance of someone skilled in the arts."

"That I can agree with," Aelmar answered. "The sooner we get to Farren, the better."

The final furlongs to the fey ruin took longer than expected. The sprite Queen and her entourage led the party along a meandering route, that skirted deep dells and hidden hollows. At one point they entered a place where the tangled, twisting roots of old trees appeared to claw the earth, and here, caught amidst thorny thicket and snake-like creepers, Shrew could see human remains. So, this is what happens to those that incur the wrath of the Nightshade, she thought. At last, they stepped out from the shadow of the forest and into a leafy glade. There before them rose an opalescent tower, its delicate architecture partly concealed by rope-like vines and cascades of deep red Amaranthus. To the west, the leafy roof of the forest was broken, revealing a blue twilight sky that was tinged salmon orange by the last rays of the setting sun. In its midst shone a solitary bright star.

"Ahlune's tear, the evening star, shines upon you," the sprite Queen declared. "It is a good omen."

"It is, indeed," Prince Cendil replied. "Thank you, Brier. We will not forget your assistance."

Shrew studied the base of the tower. Was it her imagination or were the vines and bindweed that festooned and draped across its entrance, moving?

"We have protected Faerun for countless seasons," Brier said, as she gestured towards the tower. "We thought that one day the fey might return from the depths of the earth and come to live amongst us once more, within the forests of Myrifel."

"They may still come, ma'am," Shrew found herself saying. "They long for the light of this world and the clear nights under the stars in the sky." Then she fell silent, surprised at her own words. Were these words her own, or were they those left behind by Tirriel, released from a shared memory deep within her mind?

Brier looked quizzically at Shrew and then smiled. "You do, indeed, know the fey," she said. "Then you shall have this." The sprite Queen reached out to Shrew and opened her fingers to reveal a ring in the palm of her hand. It appeared to be made of tiny silver leaves that were woven together. "You are young and quick-witted; it will serve you best. Take it and put it on one of your middle fingers," she said with an enigmatic smile.

Shrew carefully picked the ring out of the sprite's hand. It looked too small and delicate to fit her. "Thank you, ma'am," she whispered, and gasped in wonder as the ring seemed to grow to accommodate the size of her finger. It fits perfectly. "Oh, thank you," Shrew said again, but loudly so all could hear. "It's beautiful!"

"It's more than an adornment, Shrew," the sprite Queen quietly informed her. "It provides some protection against beguilement and deception. By opening your eyes, it will serve you all in the days ahead. Now, let me show you all the inside of the Faerun tower."

The vegetation that had lay matted and festooned across the entrance of the tower had parted, like curtains, to expose a double door with swirling patterns that reminded Shrew of the lacework architecture of Qinestra. As they approached, the patterns on the doors seemed to brighten. It may have been the last rays of the setting sun catching their curves, or it may have been a hidden mechanism, for at once the doors drew silently inward.

"Here you will find peace and may rest," the sprite Queen proclaimed, as she took them through the entrance and into the building.

The large chamber inside the tower seemed pristine: there was little sign of decay. The floor appeared to be made of onyx, a green chalcedony flecked with earthly browns. Upon a pedestal in the centre of the chamber stood the proud statue of a woman, bathed in golden light, who looked skyward, with her arms stretched outward in supplication. She appeared so real, with flowing hair and delicate elfin features that reminded Shrew of the statues of the Lords and Ladies of the fey that she had beheld with Tirriel. Her eyes left those of the statue and settled on the apex of the ceiling, high above, where crystal lamps collected the last of the sun's rays and sent them downward in a broad column of golden light.

"We stand in the light of Ahlune," Shrew found herself whispering, and Deakin muttered a prayer beside her. "I don't know how I know, but this statue reflects the living likeness of Ahlune herself."

"We will leave you now, Prince Cendil," the sprite Queen said, as she gathered her entourage around her. "Here you will find the downward path that will take you to Everdim. May Ahlune protect you in the difficult days ahead and give you the strength and fortitude to defeat the darkness that threatens our lands."

Prince Cendil bowed. "We thank you and your kind folk again, Brier," he said. "Rest assured, we know the importance of our mission. We must not fail."

It had fallen dark outside, but within the tower there was a faint glow of violet luminescence that appeared to emanate from the circular wall that surrounded them. Shrew had rolled out her sleeping mat and now sat on it and watched as Valorrin unsheathed a wisp lamp that cast a warmer amber glow upon their party. Eventually, when they were all settled in a circle around the comforting light of the wisp, Prince Cendil addressed them in a hushed voice.

"This may be the last time where we will have the time to speak openly about the journey ahead," he said, looking around the circle. "So, I thought we should take this opportunity to discuss any concerns we might have, or anything we think the rest of us should know. So, who wishes to speak first?"

There was a long silence before, at last, one of the sylvan runners, a slim, fair-haired individual who Shrew had learned was called Taylen, raised his arm. "Your Highness, what are we likely to be confronting?" he asked politely. "We know there are a few priests and maybe some followers, but what else? Legends speak of undying things inhabiting the depths of Everdim. Is this true?"

The Prince nodded. "A good question," he replied, and turned to Shrew. "My Lady, when you spoke before the Council, you mentioned that you'd entered the crypts and encountered a creature from the Void. If the memory doesn't pain you, could you please relate to us exactly what you saw?"

Shrew noticed that everyone was now staring at her and was glad that they probably couldn't see her blushing in the wisp light. "I sent a creature back to the Void from whence it came with my dagger," she said firmly. "But then I heard noises that rose above the beating sound that echoed through the passages. All around me there were bones, piles of them, and old bodies lying in holes and openings set in the walls." She shuddered as she recalled the memory. "They started to move and I ran. I ran as fast as I could!"

There was a further silence as everyone considered her words. Prince Cendil smiled grimly. "Thank you, Shrew. You were very brave, and to know you despatched that creature with only a dagger should give heart to those older and more experienced among us. Yet, also braver still, that having seen these things, you have agreed to join our party, knowing more than any of us, what dangers lie ahead."

"As brave as her mother," Aelmar said, and looked at Shrew proudly. "As for the matter of these things in the crypts, in the past, Waylan and I encountered deceased bodies that had been brought back as undead by the necromantic powers of feral shamen. We dealt with them then and we will deal with them again."

"And I have made a long study of the art of healing," Deakin added. "Particularly with regard to neutralising necromantic practices such as raising the dead."

Prince Cendil nodded. "I am heartened that we have such experience among us. Those of us from Yuarith, including the Lady Melowyn, also have skills in many of the arts." He looked across to his cousin and smiled.

"Then it seems we are well prepared," Aelmar concluded. "But, for all our experience and skills, we should remember one thing. Our mission is to break the summoning so that the Master of Shades cannot return to this world. If it means slaying the perpetrators, so be it; but we should avoid conflict unless absolutely necessary. Is everyone agreed?"

There were murmurs of agreement from all around the circle.

"Well, from my experience," Ryrkell grunted, "a good axe needs little art, just a strong arm and a good aim." He grinned broadly and nudged Waylan, who sat beside him.

Waylan smiled, but seemed a little subdued. He shook his head, as if to rid himself of a bad thought. "Aye," he said, winking at Ryrkell. "Better tell us when you start throwing that axe of yours around, because we'll all need to duck!"

Waylan's comments brought forth some hearty laughter, and Shrew found herself chuckling. In a few days, she thought, this will all be over. After all, what could a few mad priests and a bunch of mouldering skeletons do against companions such as these?

Prince Cendil raised his hands. "I think we should consider getting some rest," he proposed. "But before we find our sleeping mats, I would like to ask a question to our newly joined companion. I think it is only fair to him."

Shrew noticed that everyone had turned their attention to Wilf, who sat huddled next to Melowyn.

The Prince studied the youth closely. "Wilf," he said softly, "we do not expect you to come with us tomorrow. I know you chose to come with us because you feared for your life, but you didn't know where we were going. I can arrange with Brier for you to be safely escorted to the gates of Swanmere, if you so choose. What do you wish to do?"

Wilf looked embarrassed, but he was quick to reply. "I stay," he said solemnly, and looked towards Shrew. "Give me a sword and I will fight."

"Very well," the Prince smiled. "Hygil has a spare sword; I'm sure he will lend it to you." He gestured to the sylvan runner who sat next to him and then turned his attention to the rest of the party. "Now let us all get some rest. We will need no watchers tonight. The tower is once more in the embrace of the forest."

CHAPTER 2
THE ROAD TO EVERDIM

Shrew woke suddenly. She had just had a strange dream where Silfa and Sceral had approached her as fey-kind, with a woman who looked very much like herself, but older. The woman spoke to her. She was certain it was her mother, but she couldn't remember what she had said. She sighed as she stared up into the darkness at the pale violet glow that outlined the walls. She shivered. It was cold. She moved on to her side and tried to return to her dream; but now she was wide awake, and sleep seemed impossible.

A familiar voice whispered close by. "Your teeth are chattering. Are you cold?"

She recognised the voice. It was Dardalloy. "What do you think?" she hissed back, and gritted her teeth.

The next moment she felt his body close by and sudden warmth as he pulled her under his cloak. She didn't resist and let him put his arm around her. Sleep now came easily, but there were no more dreams.

Her state of peaceful repose, snug within a cocoon of warmth, was suddenly rudely interrupted by voices. Shrew opened her eyes and yawned. The inside of the tower was bathed in golden sunlight and people were already on their feet.

"Come on, lazy bones," Dardalloy chided her. "There's time for a quick bite to eat and then the real adventure begins."

She sat up and rubbed her eyes, before delving into her bag for the leaf-wrapped iron rations. Once she had found her breakfast, she quickly took out all her other items and laid them next to the bag. It was time for a final inventory check. As she bit into the sweet-tasting block of dried fig and fish, her eyes roved back and forth over the small vials and packets containing her herbs and mixtures. She looked ruefully at the thunder pods. Three had discoloured and showed signs of being ready to prime; the other seven, unfortunately, still needed more attention. She sighed and swallowed the last piece of her breakfast. The three discoloured ones would have to do. She picked them up gently and slipped them into separate pockets within her belt.

People were gathering in one area of the tower, where a circular pattern that shone like silver had been etched into the green crystalline floor. There was no more time. She quickly repacked her bag, leaving the bundle of spare flights for her crossbow till last. A faint smile crossed her face; she might need these in a hurry! Rising to her feet, she slipped her arms through the loops of the harness that would strap her daggers to her back and picked up her small crossbow, which she pushed into the holster that lay against her left thigh. Finally, she attached her water-skin to her belt and shouldered her backpack. She was ready.

As she approached the rest of the party, she noticed that they all now stood within the silver circle on the floor. The Prince was beckoning her, so she quickened her step to join them. Once inside the circle, memories of the tall tower in the High Reach and the levitator platform came flooding back. Looking up, she stared into the sparkling eyes of the statue of Ahlune. Its angelic face seemed to be smiling down at her.

"Now!" the Prince called, and Valorrin slammed his staff down into the centre of the circle. Threads of bright light radiated out in channels to the edge of the circle, like spokes of a wheel, and slowly the entire circular platform began to descend. At first, they descended through solid stone, but then the stone vanished and they found themselves floating downward in empty space, surrounded by the same violet luminescence that had illuminated the tower the previous night.

"Sirra's breath!" Shrew heard Dardalloy swear under his breath. "Look down there. It's huge… and there are so many different paths."

They had entered a vast chamber and were quickly approaching a central circular platform that rose as a column from a deep, seemingly bottomless chasm. Around the edge of this platform, bridges radiated outward, spanning the chasm in slender arcs to connect with dark openings set in the far walls of the chamber.

Shrew counted. There were twelve bridges, twelve pathways and, therefore, twelve different choices. She hoped someone knew the right path. The levitator platform slowed its descent and came to rest in the centre of the giant column. Immediately, her companions dismounted from the levitator and spread out to examine the bridges. Shrew hesitated. Something didn't seem quite right. She looked around suspiciously and considered drawing her daggers to view the chamber with her deep-sight, but there was no need. As she focussed her attention on one of the nearest bridges, it blurred and wavered. "Mother of Midir!" she cursed under her breath — they weren't real!

"Stop, all of you!" she screamed, and her voice echoed through the chamber. Looking around, she noticed Dardalloy was standing precariously close to the edge of the column. Another step forward would send him plummeting into the chasm. "Darda!" she called. "Step back. Your bridge is a deception, it's an illusion. It's not there!"

Valorrin held up his staff and waved it in a circle above his head. "The girl's right," he cried. "Everyone... move back!" A red light suddenly erupted from the tip of his staff. It blazed brightly for several seconds and, under its intense glare, all but one of the bridges slowly dissolved into nothingness.

Aelmar joined Shrew and gently squeezed her arm. "Good call," he whispered. Then he turned to the Prince. "Well, that solves that dilemma," he said, dryly. "Our way is now clearly obvious."

Shrew looked down at the silver ring on her finger, the gift that was given to her by Brier. It was now shining with an inner light. The sprite was right. The ring protected the wearer from beguilement and deception — somehow, it had revealed the illusionary bridges to her.

"Let's move on," Prince Cendil cried. "We have a lot of ground to cover today. Tread carefully, and be on your guard. The fey were masters of illusion and deception. They would have protected the way to Aylission and their crypts."

The party grouped together in a column of pairs, just like they had done in the forest, although Shrew found herself near the front now, alongside the spikey-haired mage master and his enchanted staff. Prince Cendil and the sylvan pathfinder, Cyr, took the lead. Behind Shrew came the two sylvan runners, the fair-haired Taylen and the quieter Hygil. It seemed that Shrew had become an honorary sylvan, for the other human members all made up the rear of the contingent with her father and Waylan, covering their rear.

The solitary bridge was thankfully very real. They crossed it silently but cautiously, and approached a large, ornate arch that sparkled in the light of the mage master's wisp lamp. The Prince signalled a halt and the party paused for a moment, admiring the craftsmanship. The arch was composed of an intricate trellis-work of natural crystal that the fey had hewn out of solid stone. Shrew studied the structure carefully and gently blew a faint whistle through her lips. She had to admit it was impressive. Most comforting, though, was that it looked as real as the bridge. Looking over Cyr's shoulder, she gazed into the violet haze of the tunnel ahead and then noticed the Prince was looking questioningly at her.

"It's fine," she said quietly, and nodded reassuringly at the Prince. "It all looks very real to me."

"Unsheathe another lamp," the Prince ordered. "And let us proceed."

They entered the tunnel that ran straight ahead with a slight incline. It was wide enough to have allowed the entire party to walk side-by-side, but they kept to their pairs. The amber-coloured wisp light revealed a curving ceiling and polished walls that were covered in lace-like patterns. Here, their shadows appeared to play a game of tag, darting and chasing one another as their lamps moved to and fro. The tunnel seemed to go on for ever. After a period of time that seemed like hours, with only the muffled sound of their boots and equipment breaking the deathly silence, Shrew summoned the courage to speak.

"The brightness of the lamps is spoiling my vision," she said quietly. "Let me go in front, just out of their glare, so I can see further ahead."

The Prince glanced momentarily at Cyr, who nodded and then gave Shrew his own approval. "Keep in sight," he instructed.

Shrew nodded, and within a blink of an eye had moved out of the wisp light and into the violet haze beyond. Almost immediately, something caught her attention. "Check up here," she called back to the party. "There are black smudges smeared across the walls."

"Stay where you are, all of you," the Prince called. "There could be another deception nearby."

"It looks like soot," she whispered, as both the Prince and Cyr joined her. "And look, up here," she continued. "There are shapes like the shadows of people. I saw something very similar in the Everdark, on my way down to Qinestra."

"There appears to have been tremendous heat here once," Cyr said, looking at the walls and the floor.

Shrew glanced up the tunnel. "Shey'fa!" she cursed under her breath, and then cried out a warning: "Look ahead!"

Coming towards them at high speed, its flames licking at the very walls, came a fiery conflagration.

"Protect yourselves!" the Prince cried loudly. "Get down low on the floor and cover your head!"

Shrew stood frozen as both Cyr and the Prince dived to the floor. "It's not real," she whispered to herself. The fire came on, and now she could feel the heat before it. "It's not real," she said again, and dismissed the rapidly approaching flames as an apparition. Now it was upon her, but it tore apart before her eyes and blew into her face like a warm wind. "It's not real!" she yelled, and turned to watch it dissolve into nothingness as it continued along the tunnel.

Now the tunnel was filled with cries and screams of pain. Most of the party was strewn all over the floor and many were rolling and slapping themselves, trying to extinguish imaginary flames that burnt their bodies.

"It's not real!" Shrew cried again, as she ran amongst them.

Only Melowyn and her father were on their feet, seemingly unaffected by the deception. Melowyn had pulled back the hood of her cloak and her golden hair now spilled over her shoulders. Shrew stopped in her tracks, surprised by the woman's calm composure. To Shrew, Melowyn looked like a goddess of serenity. Her face was a mask of peace and her arms were out-stretched, with the palms of her hands facing downward. The woman's lips mouthed a strange language and her words fell softly upon the fallen party members. An aura of golden light slowly spread out into the tunnel, banishing fear and silencing the groans and cries of pain. Exhausted by her exertions, Melowyn staggered as if about to collapse, and Aelmar had to reach out to support her. "Thank you," she whispered gratefully, as she found her feet. "The deception was powerful. It altered reality and only the most potent deceptions are capable of that. Let's check if everyone's all right."

Shrew looked around. The sylvan members of the party were the first to recover and were soon on their feet, but the humans took longer; maybe they were more susceptible, she thought. Besides her father and, of course, herself, Deakin was the only other human on his feet. He was now administering what help he could, now that Melowyn's powerful enchantment had successfully removed the deception from those who had fallen under its influence.

Shrew found Dardalloy sitting up and rubbing his arms. "I was sure my arms were alight, and my fingers, they were burning like sticks of tallow," he complained. She crouched down next to him and smiled sympathetically. "It was all in your head," she whispered, and looked around. "Mother of Midir," she cursed. "It's still playing with my mind. Look, the dark smudges on the wall are gone! I was sure they were real." Reaching back over her shoulders, she grasped the hilts of her daggers and Silfa and Sceral stirred in their sleep. The world around her blurred and then crystallised sharply, highlighting the seen and the unseen with the ruddy hues of her deep-sight. "The tunnel gets wider ahead," she called out. "Maybe we'll soon be clear of these deceptions."

"I sure hope so," Waylan muttered. He staggered forward, rubbing his head. "And if I could just get this damn woman out of my head, things would be a whole lot better."

Ryrkell laughed. "I've known you a long time; what day passes without you thinking about some lass, whether it be in or out of the city?"

Waylan growled in response and joined Dardalloy and Shrew.

Soon, the party was back together again, although some still looked shaken by their experience. The Prince approached Melowyn, who was attending to Wilf and thanked her. "A'luviel, Melowyn," he said in the sylvan tongue, and then spoke in the common tongue so all could understand. "We are lucky to have a master of enchantment and restoration amongst us," he said, smiling at Melowyn. "Without her intervention, some of us would have surely perished. Such magic can kill." There were murmurs of appreciation from amongst the group, and then they were on their way again.

Shrew was right. The tunnel was getting wider. She had withdrawn her hands from her daggers and let her dragons fall back into their primeval slumber. The deep-sight had faded, and now she could see a golden glow filling the tunnel, just a short distance ahead. It looked eerily like sunlight.

It was a warm light and it raised their spirits. Within minutes, they had entered the edge of a vast circular chamber lit by clusters of crystal lamps. It was indeed sunlight, filtering down through channels of glass from the world above. Shrew pursed her lips and whistled through her teeth. She was familiar with the architecture of the fey, but this was magnificent. Their path descended a series of steps into a shimmering metropolis of fey towers and skyways, with their flying buttresses and lace-like parapets. At any moment she half-expected to see Tirriel and others of her kind emerge from the shadows of the buildings, but she knew that couldn't be. She sighed — nothing more than memories lingered here now.

Prince Cendil strode forward with Cyr. "This must be the real Faerun," he said reverently. "The tower we entered merely marked its presence on the surface. If the legends speak true, there are gateways here that lead to Myrifel, Vaelun and Aylission."

"Where are these gateways likely to be?" Aelmar asked, stepping forward.

For a moment the Prince stood staring down towards the sprawling landscape of towers, and then replied softly, "They will be in the centre. We will know them when we see them. Let's move on."

They descended the steps and were soon on a main thoroughfare that appeared to head straight towards the centre of the town. It was eerily quiet, but they were not alone. Shrew spotted a small green spider that appeared to have added its own silken web to the fine stone lace-work of the fey. A short distance further on and she spotted something move in the shadows of a doorway. Dardalloy spotted it, too. It looked like some sort of rodent, white and furry with red eyes, like an albino.

"What a peculiar creature," he whispered, not daring to raise his voice lest it disturb more of the town's inhabitants.

"Looks like a rat," Shrew hissed. "You should go visit Rat Man Alley down in the Everdark some time. They get big and peculiar down there." She winked slyly at Dardalloy and moved up to the front of the party. There she found Cyr had gone ahead and was signalling them.

"He's found the gateways," the Prince cried. "He's pointing to that tower!"

Before them rose a tall pyramidal structure. Shrew looked it up and down. Its prominent position in the centre of Faerun certainly marked it as the most likely candidate for a meeting of ways. As they drew closer, she could see that there were shimmering circles at the base of each visible side of the structure. They were dark with an iridescent sheen, like oil shimmers on a rain puddle. "Sweet Ahlune!" she whispered under her breath. They were smaller, but looked very similar to the Well of Stars that she had seen in Qinestra. Indeed, when she looked closely, she noticed the presence of a green aura, so similar to that through which she had passed the dagger to Tirriel!

Aelmar stepped up beside her. "Well, would you look at that," he breathed, stroking the fiery stubble on his chin. "I've seen some strange unworldly things, but these... are these the gateways you spoke of?"

"The fey called them portals," Valorrin informed him curtly. "They fold space and connect interdimensional loci at the cost of temporal extensions. Now, if you'll excuse me, I need to identify the portal we need."

Prince Cendil overheard the conversation and joined them. "What the Mage Master is saying is that they allow you to travel great distances instantly, but the time that elapses from the moment you enter the portal to the time you exit it, is often longer than you think."

"Are you planning for us to use one of these to continue our journey?" Aelmar asked, with a look of concern.

"We have no choice," the Prince replied. "We only have two more days to stop the summoning, so we must take the risk. Besides, from here, there's no other way."

"What is the risk?" Shrew asked inquisitively. "I thought it was just a matter of stepping through and reaching the destination."

"I don't think there's any physical risk to ourselves," the Prince answered. "The risk is that we arrive late at our destination and after the summoning has taken place. Have you heard those old stories about people being taken into the fey realm, staying there for days or weeks and then returning safely, only to find on their return that years have gone by?"

There was a thoughtful silence before Aelmar finally shook his head. "Then every second counts," he growled. "Let's get moving."

Valorrin and Cyr had moved to the opposite side of the tower. Cyr now called and waved his arm, beckoning everyone over. "This one's to Aylission," he cried. "It will take us into the crypts."

"Everyone together!" The Prince raised his voice so all could hear. "We move in as a group, in our pairs. No one lags behind."

Shrew looked tentatively at the faint stars that shone within the shimmering disc before her. Cyr and the Prince had just stepped into it and vanished. Now it was her turn with Valorrin. She breathed a short prayer to Ahlune, stepped forward and closed her eyes for a brief moment. Then she stumbled forward into an all-consuming darkness. The air had changed — it was now dry and oppressive — and she felt panic, but then saw a dim light. Almost immediately, an amber light blossomed, illuminating the elfin features of the Mage Master. Someone bumped into her from behind. She recognised the scent of oiled leather — it was Dardalloy.

"Unsheath another lamp," the Prince commanded. As the hood was removed from the wisp lamp, a brighter light blazed, banishing the long sweeping shadows and illuminating a dusty corridor, whose walls were lined with ledges and darkened alcoves. "Is anyone missing?"

"We can't go back," Valorrin said quietly. "Not from here, anyway."

Shrew looked around her. She counted twelve others. They had all made it through, and the Mage Master was right: there was no return portal here. It all looked vaguely familiar. Nearby, a grinning skull looked out from an alcove, the amber light from the wisp lamps reflecting off its patinated cranium.

"We are in the crypts," the Prince confirmed, "in the middle of what appears to be a subsidiary passage, as it runs straight. Legends recall that all the main thoroughfares are curved except for one. That one is special. It is the central highway that intersects all the others. We will need to find it, for it will lead us to the Sacellum, where I'm sure the priests are preparing their summoning."

Shrew slowly drew her daggers. The last time she had entered these crypts, she had encountered an apparition from the Void and seen the dead rise up from their place of rest. She turned away from the wisp lamps and looked into the darkness with her deep-sight. This was an ancient tunnel, peppered with holes and niches. Bones filled every opening and dust covered the floor. She moved further from the others and into the darkness, away from the bright orbs of the wisps. No more than fifty paces ahead, she could see that the tunnel joined another.

"Shrew!" She recognised Dardalloy's voice. "Where are you going?"

She turned and squinted in the bright light of the wisp lamps. The others were preparing to go in the other direction. She hastened back to them. "There's another tunnel the other way," she called, as loudly as she dared. "It's not far."

The Prince swiftly replied, "Stay where you are; we'll take a look." She heard him mutter some other instructions, before he addressed the group as a whole. "Everyone, back to your pairs; we'll proceed the other way." Soon she was joined by the rest of the party, and she sheathed her daggers as the light from the wisp lamps returned. She caught Dardalloy's eye and gave him her '*I told you so*' expression. He nodded slowly, smiled and indicated that she should take the lead. She shook her head and within seconds had fallen in beside Valorrin. She was more than happy for Cyr and the Prince to take the lead. There was more than a stifling atmosphere in the crypts. There was a palpable dread. She could feel it weigh heavily upon her and was sure the others felt it, too.

Sure enough, their tunnel opened into a broader passage. Here, the carved vaulted ceiling reminded Shrew of interlocking bony fingers. It was likely that this was once an important thoroughfare, as stone columns lined its curving walls, which resembled tall skeletal figures. They stood like sentinels, guarding deeper recesses, with long arms that reached upward to support the ceiling.

"This looks promising," the Prince whispered. "But listen! Quiet, everyone. Can you hear it?"

Shrew stood still, barely daring to breathe. Then she recognised the beating sound that she had heard once before — a slow, deliberate pulse that reverberated through the crypts.

"Your Highness," Valorrin whispered, "we still have time. That sound suggests the summoning is still in progress."

The Prince conferred briefly with Cyr and Valorrin, and then addressed the party. "We must go to the right," he said. "The sound is coming from that direction; but, before we move forward, we would kindly ask for the cleric, Deakin, to accompany us at the front." He looked at Shrew. "My Lady, it would be safer for you to be further back."

For a brief moment, Shrew looked quizzically at the Prince. Then she nodded. "As you wish, your Highness," she said politely, and turned on her heel. She smiled at Deakin as he passed her, and then took the cleric's former position in the line. Straightening herself, she focussed her eyes up front, seemingly ignoring her new companion on her right. "You'd better behave yourself, Darda," she whispered through her teeth. "Don't even think about doing anything silly."

They entered the broader passageway, only pausing for a moment as Valorrin passed his wisp lamp to Cyr and cupped one hand over the end of his staff. He muttered a single word and his hand glowed red as bright light sprang from its gnarled tip. Now they could see many yards ahead and that the passage curved gradually to the left.

They moved forward slowly and cautiously, passing countless openings either side of their path. Occasionally, Cyr or Valorrin would pause for a moment to cast their light into the darker recesses. Such openings ranged from mere niches crammed with skulls to grand arched side-chambers guarded by carved effigies from a bygone age. At last, the monotony of the passage ended abruptly as it entered into a great circular hall whose furthest reaches remained beyond the scope of their lights.

They found themselves on a balcony, where to either side the curving chamber wall was punctuated by elaborate arches that marked the openings to other foreboding passages. Below the balcony, the deeper levels of the crypts extended into darkness. This was clearly a nexus of ways.

"Look here!" Cyr called their attention in a loud whisper. "The dust here has been disturbed recently." The pathfinder knelt down and studied the stone floor carefully. "It was very recently... by Ahlune's grace, cover the lights!"

Barely had he finished speaking, when the deathly silence of the hall was interrupted by the hiss of loosened crossbow bolts and loud cries that echoed through the crypts.

Shrew instinctively reached for her daggers, rudely awakening Silfa and Sceral, who roared inside her head as she flung herself to the side and against a wall. The deep-sight came quickly, whilst all around her pandemonium broke out. They were being attacked, but by whom and from where?

She sheathed Silfa and drew out her small crossbow. Her deep-sight showed movement from under an arch to her left. The partial outline of a human-like figure became visible and she quickly raised the crossbow and fired off her first flight. Then, a crackling sound, followed by a blaze of light, streaked across the chamber, like a wayward firework; it barely missed her and landed in a shower of glowing sparks. She quickly identified the perpetrator, a robed figure, who stepped out from the passage with light blazing from a hand. It illuminated others close by and presented her with a multitude of targets. Praying to Latia to guide her aim, she levelled her crossbow and let loose her remaining four flights in quick succession. Three flights clearly found their targets, but the last flight deflected wildly off the robed figure. She muttered an oath, but then felt some recompense when she noticed her strike had caused the light to disappear from the outstretched hand.

Cries of pain and shouting had now spread across the balcony as her companions were engaging with their assailants. Pausing for a moment, she considered lobbing a thunder pod into the fray, but changed her mind. Within the blink of an eye, she had slid her crossbow back into its holster and unsheathed Silfa. Now armed with both daggers, she crept stealthily forward. Her blades glimmered faintly and trailed a freezing mist behind her as she made her way towards her target — the robed figure who was casting magic. Whoever, or whatever they were, had to be stopped. More fire sprouted from the caster's hand, and with her deep-sight she could see the vague outlines of a cocoon of mist surrounding their body — it was some form of shield. "Mother of Midir," she swore under her breath — no wonder her flight had been deflected.

Her fixation on the caster nearly caused her undoing. Silfa roared a warning and her immediate step backward avoided the incoming thrust of steel that flashed before her eyes. From out of the shadows, a man stepped in front of her. His leather trappings and long knives, slick with vile toxins, proclaimed his identity. "Black Blood scum," she hissed, as, in a blink of an eye, she side-stepped his second lunge and pirouetted around him, driving Silfa deep into his side, below his ribs. As he tottered on his feet with his mouth agape in shock and surprise, she deftly plunged Sceral into his back and through his heart, before turning to face the caster again.

The fight didn't appear to be going well for the rest of her party. During the time she had been distracted, the robed figure had successfully cast another fiery missile that had burst in a shower of sparks amidst her companions. The dim light of fallen wisp lamps and small fires created a chaotic scene, but she could see the unmistakable silhouette of Ryrkell, swinging his axe in an attempt to cleave the caster in two. His axe rebounded off the protective shield, and the force hurled the giant warrior aside. Yet his action had succeeded in drawing the caster's attention, and Shrew saw the opportunity.

Hugging the wall, she merged with the shadows and swiftly moved behind her target, whose shrill male voice cried out to cast another spell. Her daggers had dimmed, but as she leapt forward, they suddenly erupted into life, blazing with blue-white fire and freezing the air in their wake as they plunged downward. Her dragons roared inside her head and for a fraction of a second the blades lit the chamber with a dazzling light, as they pierced the magic user's shield and drove deep into his neck. Stepping back, she pulled the daggers free, releasing warm blood that spurted over her hands, as she kicked the falling body aside. Then, looking up, she prepared to defend herself, but nothing challenged her. Looking around, she saw her father draw his sword from the last remaining foe and send the body plummeting to the levels below.

Ryrkell had gained his feet and, picking up his axe, nodded approvingly at Shrew. "Nice work, lass," he said gruffly, and brushed his charred surcoat with his free hand. "That bastard was tough."

Shrew responded with a grim smile and bent down to wipe her hands and daggers on the dead caster's robe. Looking up, she could see bodies everywhere. It was carnage. Back where they had entered the chamber, she noticed movement and then the unveiling of a wisp lamp. Its amber glow spread halfway across the chamber, silhouetting some of her companions.

Aelmar spotted her and sheathed his sword. "Are you all right?" he called.

He strode briskly over and slapped a hand on Ryrkell's back. "Did my eyes just deceive me," he said, still looking at Shrew. "Did you just slay the sorcerer?"

Shrew sheathed one of her daggers and, with the other blade, bent down and cut a cord from around the caster's waist. Pulling the cord, she grabbed hold of a pouch. "Give credit to my daggers, Silfa and Sceral," she said, as she inspected the pouch.

Aelmar's face was in shadow, but Ryrkell could detect the beginnings of a smile on the old warrior's lips.

"You know these were Black Blood?" Shrew added.

Her father nodded. "Aye, I think that's clear." He paused to look around. "We'd better get back to the others," he growled. "We've likely taken casualties, and they may need our help."

A horrible feeling crept over Shrew. She immediately thought of Dardalloy and then Melowyn, Wilf and her other companions. She quickly followed her father to the wisp light. When they reached the lamp, they found their companions in a huddle around a body on the floor. Melowyn stood up, her eyes glistening in the lamp light. "I couldn't save him," she said. "We've lost him. I must join Deakin and give time to the others."

Shrew looked down upon the body of the sylvan mage, Valorrin, who lay on the floor where he had fallen. A crossbow bolt protruded from his forehead. Looking around, she caught sight of Wilf and then Deakin and Dardalloy administering aid to Waylan. She sighed with relief; everyone else appeared to be alive.

As Shrew moved off in the hope of finding some of her flights, Aelmar approached the Prince, who was clutching his arm, and spoke quietly in his ear. "Remember our conversation whilst we were with the Nightshade? The Black Blood knew we were heading to Farren and knew we were here. It seems they know exactly where we are."

"That is very clear," the Prince replied. "And I think we may have an answer. Come with me."

Aelmar followed the Prince to where Melowyn and Deakin crouched beside Waylan, who sat propped up against a wall. He looked in great pain. Beads of sweat had gathered on his forehead, that glistened in the wisp light, and he was rocking his head from side to side.

Melowyn turned and saluted the Prince. "Aluu, laur'ai Cendil," she whispered. Her bright blue eyes could not hide her concern. "There is no doubt, for I can sense its presence. Someone or something has placed a geasa on Waylan!"

"Then it all makes sense," the Prince exclaimed. "This is how the Black Blood knew where we were and how they organised this ambush. Whoever or whatever cast this geasa can see through the man's eyes and also hear what he hears."

Aelmar crouched down next to Melowyn and studied Waylan for a moment. "He's delirious; he's fighting it, trying to break the connection. Can you help him, my Lady?"

Melowyn sighed. "I can try," she said, and looked back to her cousin, the Prince, as if seeking an answer. "But it will be a battle of minds, and I don't know who or what I'll be facing."

"Then it will be risky," the Prince replied tersely. "What if you fail?"

"If I don't try, then we will be forced to leave him here alone, and the only other option is to kill him. I won't have either," she said, shaking her head. "Let's move him and the wounded to a safer place. I will need to look at the wound on your arm, too."

The Prince sucked in a deep breath and fell silent in thought. Then he sighed. "Very well. Let's find a suitable place to rest."

Within minutes, Cyr had located an old vault they had passed a while back before being attacked. Entry to it was through a narrow side passage that branched off the main thoroughfare. The vault was clearly the resting place for a group or a family. Several large sarcophagi occupied plinths set in the side of the chamber. Elsewhere, there was space for the party to recuperate and rest. Shrew was one of the last to join them, having found some of her flights. She met Cyr at the entrance.

"This will be easy to guard, should we be attacked again," Cyr whispered, as he watched Shrew load several flights back into her crossbow. "That's a sylvan weapon," he continued. "Where did you get it?"

"From the filth of the sewers," Shrew answered. "A Black Blood crossed my path."

The tall pathfinder grinned. "I see you've put it to good use."

As Shrew entered the vault, she noticed two bodies placed beside one of the sarcophagi. One of the sylvan runners, whose name she recalled was Hygil, had also been mortally wounded and lay beside Valorrin. Everyone else was huddled around two wisp lamps on the other side. She spotted Dardalloy with his shirt sleeve stripped back, holding a dressing to his arm. As she approached, she caught his eye.

"Oh, Darda," she said in a sympathetic voice, "what happened to you? Can I help?"

Dardalloy held his arm and winced. "A blade nicked me. I've had wounds like this before, but this one really stings." He paused for a moment and grimaced in pain. "Deakin and Melowyn are busy at the moment, but one of them will see me soon."

Shrew took off her backpack and sat down next to him. "Let me take a look," she said. She leaned over as he presented his arm and peeled back the dressing. The wound was shallow, but it had an ugly red colour and wept a clear liquid. Looking closer, she bent down and sniffed the wound. "I suppose you know the blade was poisoned?"

"I guess it had to be," he whispered. "So, tell me the bad news."

Shrew was rifling in her backpack. "The bad news," she said, pausing a moment to open a small pouch, "is that the Black Blood use slug lion excrement on their weapons."

Dardalloy groaned.

"However," she said cheerfully, and turned to face him, "the good news is that the Black Blood are predictable. They seem to use this foul gunge all the time, and so I have come prepared." She leant closer to him and looked deeply into his eyes. "The other good news is that you picked the main ingredient I need for a balm that will neutralise the poison."

"The blue flowers!" Dardalloy sighed and closed his eyes.

"Blue violets," Shrew corrected him. "Now hang on a moment while I find a makeshift pestle and mortar." Within a few seconds, she had returned with a shallow piece of cranium from a broken skull and the end of a femur. She set to work grinding and mixing a selection of materials from the small pouch and her pocket belt. "It just needs a drop of Salvia and some water... and what better water than that from Lord Celestine's spring?" she said, winking at Dardalloy.

Soon, she had cleaned Dardalloy's wound and applied her balm. She was just about to apply a strip of clean linen to it when Deakin appeared.

The priest smiled through his blond beard. "I'm impressed. Don't let me interfere," he said with a twinkle in his eye.

Shrew tied up the bandage and sat back and sighed. "All done," she said, and yawned. "Now, if you both don't mind, I'm going to get some sleep."

Dardalloy looked suspiciously at his arm and then at Deakin. "It feels better already," he whispered.

Shrew settled down and rested her head on her backpack. Melowyn was calling for quiet. This suited her fine. The last sound she heard as she drifted off to sleep was the distant repetitive drumming of the summoning, that permeated the stone around her.

CHAPTER THREE
THE PLAN UNRAVELS

Vaskah Shen, Imperiat of the Merrandis Legion, wearily led his horse along the track towards the temple of the Crimson Sect. Behind him rode three of his senior commanders and a further ten heavily armed veterans of Rathasia's elite Merrandis Legion, their horses bedecked with leather trappings and splint mail barding. Taking up the rear was a solitary figure on a black horse, hooded and robed in grey, carrying a gnarled staff that lay crossways over the saddle.

Behind them, nearly one thousand men were preparing camp. Pale conical tents and the dark smoke of countless campfires rose amidst the stunted trees of Everdim. The sun had just slipped below the grey horizon of the great forest, while in the east dark clouds gathered — a storm was brewing and the wind was strengthening.

The gravelly voice of one of his commanders brought him out of his thoughts. "We could have left this to the morning, Lord Imperiat. We have travelled many leagues today."

Vaskah Shen cursed. "I want to get this over with tonight," he growled. "I'll sleep that much better for it."

The small contingent wound its way further up the track until at last it reached the arched gateway of the temple, where a few ragged individuals huddled within its deepening shadow. The gates were open and Vaskah Shen gave these people little attention. They were pilgrims who had come to worship the father — he despised them. He and his contingent rode under the arch and into the courtyard beyond. The musky scent of the fang weed hung heavily in the air, and Vaskah Shen cursed again as they passed other groups of worshippers who wandered back and forth, seemingly oblivious to their presence. As they approached the great doors of the temple building, two robed figures strode out to meet them.

Vaskah Shen raised his hand and brought his party to a halt as he watched the two priests approach. He didn't recognise them. They hadn't been among those he had met on his previous visit. The taller of the two appeared to be their spokesman as he stepped forward and bowed stiffly. "Welcome to the temple of Yngvi and Dysettis, my Lord Imperiat," he said, with forced congeniality. "You are early. We were expecting you tomorrow, on the eve of the darkness, and we were also expecting many more of you."

Vaskah Shen looked suspicious. "Where is your master, priest?" he demanded. "Or even his lapdog, that bag of bones with the scarred head?"

The priest straightened and then he smiled, revealing his filed teeth and red-stained tongue. "My master, Cyrus Col, is meeting the faithful, and his humble servant, brother Cullis Ra, is engaged in ritual. My name is Amon Sar, and here beside me is brother Rayet Taw. When the time is right, my master has given us the honour of escorting you safely through the crypts to the underbelly of the Sillaesian city."

"Has he indeed," Vaskah Shen retorted. "I have witnessed the horrors in the bowels of your temple. Tell me, do the dead still walk?"

Amon Sar's smile broadened. "The dead are sleeping," he said with feigned reverence. "They walk when the master commands."

"That is good," Vaskah Shen said, quietly. "Then we have no need of you." He clicked his fingers and the priest's head jarred backward as the shaft of a short spear sprouted from one of his eye sockets. Someone screamed and another spear cut through the second priest, pinning him to the ground. Vaskah Shen turned his horse. "Find the other priests and slay them all!" he shouted. "Cut down anyone else who gets in your way."

Pandemonium broke out as the Rathasian soldiers threw themselves from their horses and spread out across the courtyard, sparing nothing in their path.

Vaskah Shen turned towards the solitary grey figure, who was slowly dismounting. "Inquisitor Sol," he said deferentially, "we have need of a ward. A ward which will prevent anything living or dead from leaving or entering the crypts until we are ready to enter."

The grey figure turned and spoke in a hoarse whisper from the darkness of its hood. "If our revered lady Phirrir wills it, it will be done."

CHAPTER FOUR
THE DEAD AND THE DAMNED

Cyrus Col stood on the broad veranda of Luven's imposing manor house and looked down upon the multitude who had gathered at Harbour Gate to hear him speak. A smile curled his thin lips as he watched them prostrate themselves before him. "Behold the faithful!" he cried. "These are the blessed, Lord Luven. Did I not tell you once where true power lies?" He cast a side-ways glance at the extravagantly dressed man who stood beside him, sporting doeskin breeches and a laced silk shirt. "See how they fawn at my feet; they hang on my every word."

"So wonderful is the power of suggestion," whispered another voice from somewhere behind. "They certainly gorge on your every word, and so, too, the stain of the fang weed doth act well to settle their tongues."

Cyrus Col's smile faded and he responded in an acerbic tone, "My Lord Morrdis, you are very astute, but then, of course, are so many who have claimed to herald from far Selitan."

"Please forgive Lord Morrdis," Luven intervened; "he is impatient and eager for the new world order."

The High Priest waved his arm as if to dismiss any ill feeling. "My Lords," he said, regaining his composure, "please don't tarry on my behalf. I will come and join you soon, but first..." — he paused and allowed a cruel smile to settle on his lips — "I must give the faithful more words on which to gorge, for their time is coming soon."

"By all means, Cyrus, take as long as you wish," Luven answered politely, feigning a broad smile under his thin moustache. Then he turned away and his expression became serious. "Come," he whispered to Morrdis, "let us retire to the long room and meet the others. The words of the priest trouble me."

"He recites from the Psalm of the Shades," Morrdis hissed, barely moving his lips. "It's an apocalyptic work, written by a madman."

"But what if it's all true?" Luven responded. "It speaks of a coming darkness and something about the dead and the damned. Stavan Taro has confirmed this darkness will be upon us soon."

Morrdis shrugged as they approached the door to the long room. "Stavan has foreseen a temporary darkness, that is all. You know that our plans depend on it."

"Aye, but listen to his words," Luven said, as he opened the door. There was grave concern in his voice. "He speaks of an all-transcending darkness — that sounds permanent to me!"

The long room was always poorly lit. It had no windows, as it lay in the centre of Luven's sprawling residence. It was a place of shadows that befitted the clandestine activities that took place there. An ebony table occupied most of its length, and as Luven and Morrdis entered, four people were already seated around it: the richly attired Lords Mallory and Rodderic sat on one side, whilst facing them sat the albino Stavan Taro, robed in Selitan silk, and a woman wearing a diaphanous gown whose hair was spun into numerous curling locks and tufts that looked like birds' tails.

Luven walked over to the head of the table. "Good, we are all here. Now we wait for our High Priest to finish his address to the rabble. When he arrives, we will all go down to the cellars, as planned, where Virryn waits for us." Luven took his seat and Morrdis eased himself into a chair beside Stavan Taro.

Mallory took his eyes away from the gem-studded goblet that he cradled in his hands and directed his gaze at Luven, before speaking. "I detect apprehension in your voice, my friend. Should we not take this opportunity to speak openly about our doubts and fears, before the priest returns?" He looked perceptively at Luven.

Rodderic coughed and pulled a lace handkerchief from his sleeve. "I agree with Lord Mallory," he spluttered. "I'm concerned about the restlessness of the people. News of the approaching army is causing panic in the city. I've had to extend the curfew twice now." He buried his face in his handkerchief for a moment, before continuing, "I can, however, give you some comforting news regarding the emissary from the Rathasian army. He has given us three days in which to surrender Highfall to their Queen. That is more time than we need: by then it will all be over."

"Aye," Luven said sourly. "It will all be over." He looked towards the woman, who seemed only interested in preening her long black nails. "Ascilla, do you have anything to report?"

"I continue to do Stavan Taro's bidding," she answered, without taking her eyes off her nails. "My scrying tells me that he has entered the crypts with the others."

"Then it's true. They are trying to stop the summoning," Luven sneered. "That's what I thought they'd try and do... the fools. Do you know where they are now?"

The woman paused her preening. "I knew where they were an hour ago and where they were going. It is too exhausting keeping the connection open for more than a few minutes at a time. If something happens..." — she looked at Stavan Taro, and a wicked smile crossed her lips — "if something bad happens, I will know about it."

Mallory rotated the empty goblet between his fingers and a wry smile creased his craggy features. "I have to hand it to you, Stavan, getting this witch to place a geasa on Waylan whilst he was incarcerated in the Citadel was a stroke of genius. I hope he enjoyed it." He looked across the table at the woman, who was now returning his gaze. Her beauty was incomparable, but he could see the menace that lay behind those alluring eyes.

Stavan Taro nodded to Mallory in acknowledgement and then cast his piercing red eyes on Luven. "Ascilla's information was passed to Virryn in your absence, Lord Luven. He has sent twenty of his best, along with my apprentice, Drex, to eradicate them."

Luven leaned back in his chair. "Thank you, Stavan. Their demise will be a great relief to us all. Ascilla, you must inform us as soon as you are aware of any conflict." He turned his attention back to the albino. "Now, Stavan, tell us more about the coming darkness. Is it as temporary as you have suggested?"

"Let me translate the words of a madman into something more coherent," Stavan Taro said, in his customary thin voice. "The words I now speak concern the darkness and are derived from the Psalm of the Shades." He paused for a moment to recall the very words of the ancient tome. "The darkness cometh as a leveller of all things — a passing shroud to those that are blessed — an endless bane to those that are damned — a living boon to those that are dead."

Concern was mirrored in the eyes of both Luven and Mallory. Stavan Taro noticed their discomfort and smiled benevolently. "My friends, do not be alarmed. You are not yet any of these things, for the Master of Shades has not yet returned and passed judgement. You are neither blessed nor damned, and you are certainly not dead. Rest assured I have read the signs in the heavens. The darkness will come, but then it will pass."

Luven smoothed his thin moustache with finger and thumb. He still looked troubled. "What of the army before our gates?" he ventured. "Did not Cyrus Col promise that it would be destroyed when the darkness comes?"

"Then that means one thing," Mallory intervened. "Can you not see it? If the darkness comes, then judgement comes with it! How else will the army be destroyed? The Master of Shades will have proclaimed judgement. He or it, or whatever it is, will come with the darkness. By the gods! The priest is summoning Vaal!"

They sat in stunned silence for several minutes, each with their own thoughts, until a knock came at the door. Moments later, a nervous servant entered the room.

"My Lords and Lady," he said quietly, and bowed. "His Reverence, the High Priest, sends his apologies and has bid me to inform you that he will join you within the hour. More crowds have gathered and he wishes to bless them."

Luven's surprised expression turned to a look of incredulity. "Within an hour! More crowds?"

"Yes, my Lord," the servant stammered. "Market Street and all the lanes in Harbour Gate are crowded with people."

"You may go," Luven growled, dismissing the man. He looked at the others. "Is there more we should discuss before he joins us?"

"I would have a word," Mallory said, but was suddenly silenced as the witch called out loudly.

"Drex has found them. They fight!"

Luven leaned forward. "Tell us all you see!" he demanded.

The woman froze and her eyes widened. Her mind was in another place.

"Tell us!" Luven yelled, rising from his chair.

The others gathered around her, but Stavan Taro bade them to stay back. "Don't interrupt her!" he cried. "It will break the connection. She will speak when she can."

At first, the words that came from the woman's mouth were unintelligible and incoherent, but gradually they pieced together into a comprehensible language. "Drex!" she cried. "Drex is slain. Others scatter."

"That cannot be!" Stavan Taro shook his head. "He had protections. They couldn't…"

The woman gasped, and for a moment she mouthed silent syllables. "A name," she finally managed to say. "He sees her… he knows her."

"See's what?" Luven yelled.

"Shrew!" the witch exclaimed. "Shrew," she said again in a quieter voice, and shook her head. "I've lost him, he's gone," she murmured, and lowered her head. "I'll try again later."

Luven looked at Mallory. "The girl," he growled menacingly. "So, now we know where she is." He slammed his fist down on the table. "Double the bounty on her head. I no longer want her alive!"

Time passed slowly. Luven and Mallory spent the time in deep conversation, whilst Stavan Taro continued to question Ascilla on what she had seen. There was still no sign of Cyrus Col, and Rodderic and Morrdis had left the room.

Eventually, Morrdis returned. "The man servant was right," he said matter-of-factly. "The harbour is full of people. Some must have arrived by the river."

"Doesn't it worry you?" Luven retorted. "He has considerable power over the people. Now where does that leave us?"

"I know where your thoughts are going, my friend," Morrdis replied, as he sat down. "But we need him. We need him if we're going to see our plan through. After the darkness passes, it will be a different matter, though."

"If the darkness passes and we live," Luven muttered tersely.

"No!" the dark-haired witch suddenly cried out loudly, and caught their attention.

"What's happening, Ascilla?" Luven leaned over towards her. "What are they doing now?"

"No! No!" she repeated, and howled like a wounded animal. "She's in my head!" she screamed, and clawed the table with her long nails.

Stavan Taro jumped up out of his seat. "Someone's challenging Ascilla's geasa. Trying to break it!"

Ascilla threw back her head. Her eyes were now wide in panic.

"Fight it!" Stavan Taro cried, trying to hold the woman's flailing arms, but the next moment she stopped moving and fell lifeless back into her chair.

The room fell silent. For a moment everything seemed to be frozen in time.

Finally, Luven whispered, "Is she dead?"

As if in answer, Ascilla's eyes opened wide. They were white with no pupils. Then she spoke, but in a different voice. "Tu'al yea'fei á tu!" she said tonelessly. "You have failed!"

There was a sharp knock at the door and Cyrus Col stepped into the room. "What has happened?" he said sharply. "You all look as if you've just met your shade." The priest grinned, revealing his red-stained tongue.

No-one uttered a word. It was Morrdis, who finally stood up from his chair. The welcoming expression on his olive-skinned face was a mask to his true feelings. "Your Reverence," he said, bowing his head. "Thank you for joining us. Now we can proceed with our plan."

"Time is short," the priest announced. "I have tarried here far too long. I must get back to my brothers. I sense all is not well at the temple."

Morrdis nodded. "We are ready for the darkness and the coming of the Rathasian elite through the crypts and into the Everdark; but we still haven't discussed a few of the details."

For a moment, Cyrus Col's attention seemed to be elsewhere, his mind preoccupied, but then he quickly focussed his attention back on those in the room. "What did you need to know?" he said, with a hint of impatience in his tone.

Luven stood up. "We need to know where to lay our ambush, the place where we could gainfully engage the Rathasia's elite legion. You said you knew of such a place in the crypts."

Cyrus Col smiled and his lips parted like a broken wound. "Yes, I did, and I know just where it is," he said, and his smile transformed into a sly grin. "I can return to the temple through the crypts and show it to you on the way."

Morrdis bowed his head. "Virryn waits for us in the cellars, at the entrance to the Everdark. We have no reason to delay. Let us depart immediately."

There was little light. The few feeble wisp lamps that hung from the walls were shrouded in cobwebs and struggled to illuminate the antechamber that led to the Everdark. Luven went first, followed by Cyrus Col and then Morrdis and Mallory. Stavan Taro stayed behind with the witch, Ascilla. She was still in shock. Her geasa had been forcefully taken from her by a sylvan woman who had then possessed her for several long, humiliating minutes.

The chamber was warm and the smell of leather and stale sweat was overpowering. Either side of them stood row upon row of armed rogues and assassins, an array of the most vicious and meanest individuals Highfall could muster. As Cyrus Col passed them, his thin lips formed a wicked smile as he contemplated the coming of the darkness. The damned would be first, and he would have such filth flayed for eternity, for the Master's pleasure.

Luven stopped before a stocky individual whose weathered face was criss-crossed by welts and scars. Cyrus Col recognised him immediately.

"Ah, Virryn," Luven smiled. "You can stand the men down for the time being, but I need you and ten of your best to accompany me and Lord Mallory. Cyrus is going to show us where we can arrange our greeting for the Rathasian scum." He turned and signalled to Morrdis. "You are the council till we return. Get Rodderic to take care of the King once and for all."

Morrdis bowed his head and smiled. "It will be a pleasure."

The group had spent over an hour now, traversing the upper levels of the Everdark. For much of this time they had followed broad passageways where the masonry bespoke first of human and then of sylvan craftsmanship, but now they entered a narrower side tunnel which was hewn from living rock.

Virryn had taken the lead for much of the way, but after following the tunnel for a short distance, he suddenly stopped in his tracks and held aloft his lantern. "We are about to enter the crypts," he growled, and turned to face the others.

Luven stepped forward. "Kurell's bones!" he cursed. "What's that sound? Silence!" he commanded. "Listen. Can you hear it?" The last few members of their group finally came to a halt and a deathly silence fell over them. Then they could all hear it — a distant thump that reverberated every few seconds, sending barely detectable tremors through the surrounding rock. Luven turned towards Cyrus Col. The priest's face was mostly in shadow, but he could see his pointed teeth framed by a peculiar smile. "Cyrus, what is it? Is this of your making?"

Cyrus Col's smile broadened. "My brothers are busy preparing for the darkness," he said. The fervour in his voice was noticeable. "Then those that threaten your city walls will be judged as damned and destroyed. Don't you see, Lord Luven?" he added. "We will be proclaimed as saviours of the city. Now, let me show you where your men can decimate those Rathasian fools that choose to come through the crypts."

Luven took a step back and forced a smile. "That is good, Cyrus," he replied hoarsely, and gestured towards the opening that led into the crypts.

"In that case, you go first," Cyrus Col replied with a slight nod of his head. The strange smile was still fixed on his face as he led Luven and the others past broken blocks of ancient brickwork and into the crypts.

They entered a long, broad passage with a central row of grey columns that supported a vaulted ceiling of arching brickwork. Virryn held up his lantern and two others came forward, each bearing a light. One carried a wisp lamp and another had lit a torch, that now cast flickering shadows on the walls of the passage. A thin veneer of dust seemed to cling to everything, although it was disturbed near the opening that led back into the Everdark. They now moved forward, with Cyrus Col leading, closely followed by Virryn, and then, a short distance behind, Luven, Mallory and the rest of the group. They hadn't gone far before they encountered the first of a series of niches and alcoves set into the walls.

Light from Virryn's lantern momentarily banished the shadows of one such niche and for a brief moment Mallory caught sight of a mummified head. Leathery skin and tufts of hair lay plastered on its scalp, and its shrivelled eyes stared back at him. The darkness closed in and the light moved on, to illuminate another opening and another body that lay with its withered arms drawn up across its chest. Mallory moved closer to Luven and made an imperceptible sign with his fingers. Luven's reply was just as surreptitious. They moved on, but in silence. Only the faint reverberation continued, sending its strange message through the stone that surrounded them. After a short time, the niches and the alcoves became more numerous. Shady side rooms and archways that led to other passages opened up either side, until at last their route abruptly ended and they found themselves on a broad balcony that overlooked a pool of darkness.

"Here," Cyrus Col called brusquely. "Bring your light and look below."

They spread out along the balcony and soon realised they were in a large chamber that continued on to their left and right as far as their light could reach. Below them ran a broad highway onto which other passageways converged. Opposite, some fifty yards away, they could see the parapet of a similar balcony to their own, but they could see no sign of a stairway that gave access to the thoroughfare below.

Luven stepped forward and looked down on the road. "So, tell me, Cyrus, is this the place you promised to show us? From which direction will the Rathasians come?"

The priest grinned. "This is the place. The Rathasians will come from over there." He pointed with a long, bony finger down to their right, where the road disappeared into darkness. "Can you see the advantage you will have, Lord Luven? The road below is called the Spine Way. It runs for almost the entire length of the crypts. This platform, where we stand, follows it for many hundreds of yards; an excellent place for an ambush, don't you think?"

Luven turned to Virryn and, before speaking, covertly conveyed a message through the secret language of the thieves' cant. "Virryn, your men are adept with the crossbow and longbow," he proclaimed, so all could hear. "We could pick the Rathasians off easily from here. But tell me, how would we take the prisoners we need?"

Virryn's scarred face creased as his mouth stretched and formed an ugly smile. "My lads all have bodkin points of hardened steel; all we need is the light to see by. So, we'll bring flasks of oil and torches." He paused, and ran his tongue across his upper lip and scratched his scalp, so as to return a subliminal message of his own. "So, when will they come?" he said, licking his lips. "For when they come, we'll light them up and skewer them like a hog roast. We'll pick up strays once we've taken the fight out of them."

Cyrus Col's dark eyes moved between Luven and Virryn. They were behaving strangely, and he was growing impatient. "The Rathasians are being guided here tomorrow by two of my brothers," he snapped. "On the eve of the coming of..." He paused and corrected himself. "On the eve of the coming darkness. Now, I must leave you; I have important matters to attend to elsewhere."

"Then before you leave us, Cyrus," Luven pursued, "pray tell us, are you summoning the Master of Shades, the one known as Vaal?"

"You dare mention his name?" Cyrus Col shrieked, and pointed accusingly at Luven. "Are you a fool?"

331

Mallory suddenly appeared from out of the shadows. "For sanity's sake!" he cried, and thrust a long dagger deep into the priest's back.

Cyrus Col sank to his knees and Mallory struck again. The priest toppled over and reached out and clawed the floor. Blood spat from his mouth as he screamed a litany of foul speech in the Cyridian tongue. Then, as he rose up from the floor, he looked up at Luven and his eyes turned black.

"Shoot!" Luven screamed. "Kill him!"

A volley of crossbow bolts slammed into the priest, throwing him back; but, again, he rose from the floor, spewing forth more blood, before crying out a loud invocation in the ancient tongue. Now he stood upright, the crossbow bolts fell from his body and dark smoke issued from his eyes as the red rune on his forehead blazed like fire.

"Gods save us!" Mallory cried, as he backed away with the others.

Cyrus Col screamed the closing words of his invocation: "Aluk Nilhahn est dromoch ei Vaal!" The walls and the floor of the balcony shook. Dust fell in clouds from the ceiling.

"Let me cut him down!" Virryn growled, and drew a curved scimitar from his belt. He stepped forward, but something grasped hold of his leg, halting him in his tracks. Looking down, he shrieked in horror and dropped his lantern as another skeletal arm reached out to him from an opening in the wall. Then, from every niche, orifice and alcove there was movement. From out of the shadows ragged forms emerged, some still wearing the tattered remains of their burial wrappings or the armour of their last battle.

"Back. Fall back!" Luven yelled. Yet screams from behind told him their way out was blocked. The torch fell to the floor and darkness closed in. He stumbled over the body of one of his men and looked back in panic.

Cyrus Col stood unmoved as the dead swarmed past him. He pointed a long finger and cried out in a loud, booming voice, "You are all damned. Your souls belong to the Master of Shades!"

CHAPTER FIVE
AND NEVER THE TWAIN SHALL MEET

She was flying, soaring over hill and dale. Now she was gliding, riding the warm air that rose from the vast ancient forest below, as her cold breath chilled the air. Something cried in another world far away. She awoke suddenly and opened her eyes. The thoughts of Silfa and Sceral sank back beneath her consciousness. Something had awoken her. She lay still and listened, staring at the rugged patchwork of stone that formed the ceiling of the crypt, waiting for whatever had woken her to sound again. Something seemed different. She raised herself onto one elbow and looked around at her sleeping companions. Deakin was awake, and their eyes met. She noticed he was clutching his Holy Symbol, a circle of twisted silver supporting a blue sapphire, the depth of which burned with an inner white light that reminded her of a bright star — Ahlune's tear: the evening star.

"Did you hear something?" she whispered. "Something woke me."

Deakin nodded. "Something's just happened," he replied in a soft voice. "That beating sound grew louder and suddenly stopped."

"Sirra's breath!" Shrew whispered. "It's gone very quiet. You're right, I had become used to it."

"As silent as the tomb," a voice muttered. Aelmar sat up and laid Argalon, his sword, across his knees. "Foreboding, isn't it? We must alert the others and..." His voice was silenced by an unearthly wail, distant but powerful, a dreadful keening sound that carried through the crypts, penetrating the very stone.

Shrew felt a cold fear and shuddered. Deakin raised his Holy Symbol and uttered a prayer, as the rest of the party, disturbed by the noise, were rudely awoken.

"Mother of Midir!" Ryrkell was the first to notice. "Are they alive?" His shaking hand was pointing to the bodies of their fallen. They were moving.

"Stay back!" the Prince warned. "They are dead. This is necromancy!"

They gathered around a wisp lamp as the sounds of splintering wood and the rasp of stone being drawn over stone came from out of the shadows in the far corner of the vault. From the passage outside came scuffing and scratching sounds.

Aelmar drew his sword, which now shone with its own light. "Stay together!" he roared.

Silfa and Sceral appeared in Shrew's hands. Her deep-sight quickly came into focus, sweeping away the shadows in the far corner of the vault. "Sweet Ahlune," she cried. "There are dead things crawling out of the tombs!"

Deakin stepped past her and thrust forward his Holy Symbol. "Return to the Void," he commanded in a stern voice, and then spoke rapidly in a strange tongue as he directed his attention to the writhing bodies on the floor, and then the skeletal figures that had emerged from the shadows and were moving awkwardly towards them. A light flared from the gemstone in his hand and his final word fell like a thunderclap. It was as if a force, like a tidal wave, hit the creatures before them — blasting them violently backwards and reducing them to dust and rags. The bodies of their fallen comrades jerked one last time and then froze as they returned to their eternal rest.

Shrew drew a long breath. She felt her heart thumping in her chest. Nothing moved in the vault, but she could still hear noises outside in the passage. The surprise on her face was reflected in the expressions of her companions.

Cyr was the first to speak. "The beating sound has stopped!" he cried out in alarm. "Are we too late?"

As if in answer, the air was suddenly rent by a cry that chilled their hearts. Shrew felt an indescribable dread. It reminded her of the fear she had felt in the presence of the Dromolich, but there was no inner voice — no Tirriel to console her now. She tightened her grip on her daggers and her dragons roared their defiance. She felt some comfort and smiled grimly. They were reminding her that she didn't stand alone.

"Ail'ah veress ai Nilhahn!" Melowyn cried out. "Do not fear the spawn of the Void. The light will prevail!" She raised her arms and a natural calm seemed to spread from her to those around her and then the rest of the group.

"Listen!" the Prince exclaimed. "Can you hear it? It has started again."

Shrew listened. He was right. The steady beat had started again, but there were still noises outside their refuge within the vault.

"Then we must continue our quest and not delay any longer," Aelmar advised. "Let's get ready to leave."

"I would say a few words over the bodies of Valorrin and Hygil first," the Prince replied. "I only need a few minutes."

Aelmar nodded with approval and Shrew, seeing she had the opportunity, approached Melowyn with a leather pouch in her hand.

"I found this on the body of the sorcerer," she said, as she offered the pouch to the fair-haired sylvan woman. "There's a green stone inside and a piece of parchment with strange writing on it."

Melowyn took the pouch and emptied its contents into her hand. "Well, it's certainly different from the last stone you gave me," she said, smiling, as she rotated it between her fingers and thumb. "It's a peridot. Here, take it back while I look at the paper." She opened the parchment near to one of the wisp lamps and looked closely at it for several seconds. "This is an ancient script," she whispered. "The long, curving runes spell out an invocation in the language of the old masters of Sellitan."

"Can you understand it?" Shrew asked, craning her neck to try to see the runes for herself.

Melowyn's eyes sparkled. "Of course I can," she said, smiling kindly at Shrew. "It's a protection spell and the small stone is the token that must be carried by the recipient of the spell."

Shrew frowned. "That explains why my flight bounced off him."

"We must make use of this," Melowyn enthused. "Here, let me cast the protection on you. Squeeze the stone in the palm of your hand."

"Will I feel anything?" Shrew said with trepidation.

"Maybe a slight tingle for a few seconds, that's all," Melowyn answered casually, starting to read the parchment.

Shrew was fascinated. She watched Melowyn's lips as they verbalised each and every nuance of the ancient script, whilst from the corner of her eye she could see some of the others had stopped to watch.

It was over very quickly. After the final word, she swept her palm across Shrew's clenched fist and paused. "There!" she said finally. "All done. Now keep the stone on your person somewhere safe."

"I didn't feel a thing," Shrew said, in a tone that sounded somewhat deflated, as if she had just been cheated of a wonderful sensation.

"Do you want us to put it to the test?" Aelmar quipped. "I can get Ryrkell to swing his axe at your midriff."

For a few short seconds they laughed, but it was soon muted as the endemic evil that pervaded the crypt cast its darkness upon them once more.

"It's time to move," the Prince announced. "The summoning is still in progress. Cyr, check if the outside passage is clear."

Cyr soon returned. "It's empty!" he said with some surprise. "There are signs of considerable disturbance, even over the ground where we trod, and much dust still hangs in the air; but no corpses. Nothing!"

"I will go first," Deakin advised.

"And I can support him," Shrew volunteered. "I can make myself pretty much invisible, and now I have added protection." She patted her chest.

Dardalloy smiled. "That's true," he said cheerily. "She used to make a living sneaking around. The stallholders on Gifford Street never saw her coming."

Shrew glowered at Dardalloy and the Prince smiled. "Cyr is our scout, my Lady. Your skills are valuable; nevertheless, I suggest you assist him. Take up a position behind him." He looked at Aelmar, who nodded approvingly.

"Let us be on our way, then." The Prince directed and gestured to the narrow exit from the vault. "Deakin will go first with Cyr. We will have one lamp near the front and the other at the back."

They moved swiftly into the passage, with Cyr beckoning them forward. Within a short time, they had re-entered the large chamber where they had encountered the Black Blood several hours before. There they paused for a moment.

"We should check the passages on the far side," the Prince advised. "The sound comes from that direction."

"Something's wrong!" Cyr whispered with concern. "I can sense it. Stay where you are while I check the way ahead." He raised one of the wisp lamps and moved cautiously forward.

Shrew watched the pale amber light swing back and forth as the pathfinder proceeded further into the darkness. The dread she felt was almost tangible — it was all around, as if she could reach out and touch it! She cursed under her breath, while her dragons murmured dark thoughts in her head. She let out a sigh of relief as Cyr returned.

"There are no bodies," the pathfinder whispered, as he re-joined the group. "Look around you — the slain are all gone!"

"This doesn't bode well," the Prince affirmed. "We must move quickly. Keep your eyes open and stay alert!"

They moved swiftly, skirting the balcony that looked down upon the darkness of the lower levels of the crypts.

"This one," the Prince exclaimed, as an archway appeared in the wisp light. Twisted bestial forms carved out of grey stone appeared to climb from the imposts of the arch to meet in a tangled frenzy at the keystone above their heads.

"Why this passage?" Aelmar queried. "It reeks of evil."

The Prince took hold of the wisp lamp and held it up to illuminate the walls further inside. The passage curved and numerous dark niches and openings penetrated its walls. "I noticed this one earlier," the Prince replied, "after our skirmish. It is the only one whose entrance is adorned with foul creatures of the nether realms. Can't you feel it? Only here doth the beat of the summoning call loudest. I feel we are close to the Sacellum."

"I trust your judgement, your Highness," Aelmar replied, and drew his sword from its scabbard. Even in the wisp light, Shrew could see that her father's blade glowed with its own inner light. "See the fire stirring in Argalon," Aelmar growled. "The evil here hangs heavy. Let's get this over with."

Cyr took possession of the lamp once more and they passed under the arch and into the passage beyond. Shrew took position behind the pathfinder and pulled one of her daggers free from its scabbard on her back. 'Let your mate rest for now.' The thought was directed to Sceral, and she smiled when the dragon rumbled his approval. 'I need your help… warn me of danger; this place is a nightmare.' The dragon passed back a low guttural sound in acknowledgement and then agreed with her predicament.

They followed the curve of the passage and Shrew's deep-sight penetrated the dark niches and holes in its walls, revealing nothing but broken, empty sarcophagi and shattered funerary urns. The darkness, the stale air and the presentiment of something evil close by dragged the minutes into what seemed like hours. Another broad passage merged with theirs. Cyr swung his wisp lamp to and fro, illuminating the dark reaches of the new passage. It was almost identical to their own.

"This is a good sign," the Prince whispered. "This coming together of two major arteries… we must be close to the central highway."

A warning came sharply from the back of their group. It was Waylan, who held the other lamp. "We're being followed!" he cried out as loudly as he dared, so all could hear.

"More Black Blood?" Ryrkell growled, as he joined the Prince, who had moved swiftly to Waylan to assess the situation.

Shrew felt edgy; her heart was pounding in her chest. Without a second thought, she pulled out her second dagger, waking Silfa from her sleep. The dragon growled in anger as the blade drew an arc of frozen mist in the air before her. She braced herself, expecting a sudden onslaught and a volley of crossbow bolts, and noticed her father had joined her. His sword now shone brighter than the lamps.

"Necromancy!" Aelmar roared. "It's all around us!"

"Push on!" the Prince cried. "Lord Aelmar, take the lead with Deakin and Cyr. Ryrkell, Waylan, Dardalloy, cover our rear and warn if anything gets close."

There was now urgency in their step. Shrew caught up with Deakin. The fair-haired priest now held his Holy Symbol outstretched before him and strode forward zealously. Words constantly spilled from his lips, and

Shrew could only guess that they were some form of litany against evil. Her eyes followed the blue gem in his hand. It shone like a star: its brilliance mesmerised her. But then a loud draconic roar filled her head, warning her to take heed of her surroundings. Loud shrieks and cries of alarm erupted from behind her. Shrew turned and felt the surge as a heaving mass of bone and mummified flesh drove into them from openings either side of the passage. Instinctively, she lashed out with both her daggers, freezing and shattering bone and cutting through rag and the mouldering rings of ancient armour. Notched weapons thrust their way forward, seeking her living flesh, as light and shadow danced around her, as she fought to keep her footing. "Ahlune save us!" she cried, as her dagger, Sceral, sliced through a ribcage matted with the tattered remains of a decaying garment. Then she caught sight of Wilf, sinking under a sea of skeletal bodies. He was being forced into the darkness of a side passage. "Wilf!" she screamed, and her dragons raged as she cut a path towards him, heedless of the ancient blades that were futilely thrust in her direction. He was reaching out to her. She quickly transferred Sceral to her left hand and reached out to him. "Take my hand," she cried, but the mass of decaying bodies pushed him down and out of her reach. She screamed in fury and cried in desperation as she watched him disappear into the heaving mass. Darkness was closing in around her. Now she was in trouble. She took hold of Sceral and with both daggers frantically lashed out to prevent herself being dragged under a writhing sea of undead bodies. She could hear someone yelling and then, as the sheer weight of numbers took her down, a strong hand grasped her leather harness where it crossed her shoulders and pulled her back into a pool of light. Coughing and spluttering, with the stale, musty scent of decay filling her nostrils, she scrambled past her father, whose luminous broadsword now scythed the dead before him.

"Now!" Aelmar roared, as he cut another swathe of destruction, decapitating a row of undead and halting them in their tracks.

Shrew had barely gained her feet when she felt the air move, sucking the dust around her as it drew inward in a rapid implosion… then space itself seemed to burst asunder. There was a flash and a deafening report as a massive shockwave tore through the passage and through the army of dead with incredible violence. Shrew stood stunned. A pall of dust was slowly descending in an empty tunnel. The dead were gone, and even her deep-sight could detect no movement… there was nothing but dust. Then she noticed Melowyn, who stood with arms outstretched and fingers splayed out in front of her; but then she clenched her fists and brought her arms back gently to her side.

"It is done," the blonde-haired sylvan said, sorrowfully. "We had no choice." Melowyn turned to Aelmar and then noticed Shrew. A warm smile settled on her lips. "You're safe," she whispered with relief. "I thought you were lost with the rest."

"The protection spell worked," Shrew replied, returning a faint smile. "None of their weapons touched me." She fell silent for a moment and added dolefully, "But I still couldn't reach Wilf."

Cyr appeared, holding the only remaining wisp lamp. "Deakin will be with us in a moment," he said, pausing to catch his breath. "He has cleared the way ahead."

"Good!" Aelmar nodded. "We need to move on. Time is running out, and we still have a task to do."

Sure enough, the blond, bearded priest ran panting into the lamp light. He looked back over his shoulder. "I have cleared a path for at least a hundred yards," he said, gathering his breath. "The dead in this area have returned to the Void, but I sense the presence of a great evil close by."

"Then we will be ready for it," Aelmar growled. "Let's move. Cyr, Deakin, take the front." He paused, and his hard features softened as he looked upon his daughter. "Shrew and the Lady Melowyn will be with me."

"What about the others?" Shrew blurted out. "Dardalloy, Waylan, Prince Cendil, Wilf?" Her voice trailed off.

"Sadly lost," her father answered. "We were overrun. It is unlikely the others survived."

"But we should go back and check," Shrew argued. "They may need our help!"

Melowyn shook her head sadly. "I saw Prince Cendil go down. We couldn't reach him; and the same fate must have happened to the others.

We were in danger, too. I had no choice but to use one of the most destructive spells I know." She hung her head in sorrow, but then looked Shrew in the eye. "It saved us and has given us a momentary respite; but the dead will be back, and so we must go on and finish this."

They moved forward in silence with heavy hearts. Shrew mulled over the recent events in her head over and over again. She had seen Wilf being dragged under a wall of dead creatures, but the thought of losing Dardalloy and Waylan as well shook her to the core. No-one saw the tear that trickled down her cheek.

"I think I see a light ahead," Cyr whispered. "We are close to the end of this passage." He had barely finished his words when a glowing apparition suddenly appeared, hovering in the darkness before them.

Shrew gasped as she recognised what it was. Deakin thrust forward his Holy Symbol as a wave of overwhelming dread and nausea washed over them. It was futile. Barely a word had escaped the priest's lips when a force hit him, throwing him violently backward and enveloping him in an impenetrable darkness that seemed to suck in the light around it. Even noise now seemed muted as the thing from the Void turned its attention towards Cyr. Muffled screams and warnings sounded soft in her ears as Shrew leapt out of its path and rolled aside, leaving a swirl of frost with her passing. Only the intent of her dragons now forged her thinking as she raised both daggers and forced back the acidic vomit that rose in her throat. A light flared, bright and baleful; and, before she could strike, it lanced forward, penetrating the thing before her. An unearthly screech cut through the passage, momentarily stunning her, but then the horrific sound tailed off in a long, fading wail, as the Dromolich collapsed in on itself and was drawn back into the infinite Void.

Aelmar lowered his sword. "By the will of his Holy Majesty, Verrain," he breathed loudly. "Thus, should all foul creatures feel Argalon's wrath."

Shrew blinked and took a step backwards as she gathered her wits. Looking around, she noticed Melowyn crouching beside the body of Deakin. There was no sign of Cyr. Shrew nodded to acknowledge her father and then turned and spat out the foul taste in her mouth. Sheathing her daggers, she quickly went over to assist Melowyn.

"I saved him from the Void," Melowyn whispered. There were tears in her eyes, although her voice remained serene and calm. "He rests with Ahlune now."

Aelmar crouched down beside them and rested on his sword. The weapon still glowed, occasionally pulsing with inner energy. "I can't find Cyr," he rasped. "I think he fell into one of those side passages." He looked uneasily around him. "Is there anything more you can do for Deakin?"

Melowyn shook her head and then looked gravely at the red-haired warrior. "You say you can't find my kinsman, Cyr?" She paused for a moment in thought and then her eyes brightened. "If you can give me a little time, I can cast a seeking spell. It's a short cantrip and doesn't usually take more than a few minutes."

"Alas, we have no time," Aelmar growled, as he rose to his feet. His sword now surged with new light and illuminated the passage behind them from whence they came. From out of the darkness, ragged forms lurched forward, and with them came more ethereal things whose presence in this world was much less defined. "We have to move!" Aelmar cried. "Stay together!"

Shrew had pulled an object from her belt and now vigorously rubbed it with the palms of her hands. As she turned to flee, she flung it into the path of the oncoming horde. A second later, the passage lit up. For a moment it seemed as if the sun had entered the crypts. The air shook as the thunder pod vented its full force and fury. "Shey'fa!" Shrew swore, as she cast an eye over her shoulder. "They still come!"

The three of them ran as quickly as the dim light in the passage allowed, with only the glow from Aelmar's sword lighting the way. "Cyr was right," Melowyn cried out breathlessly. "There's light up ahead." Then, without warning, they heard a terrible cry that reverberated through the stonework, and in response sounds of movement came from the dark niches and side passages that peppered the walls.

The dreadful sound galvanised them to greater speed. Within seconds, they had reached the edge of a large chamber, the floor of which was piled with twitching, writhing bodies that were slowly rising to their feet.

"Ahlune save us!" Melowyn bewailed. "We cannot defeat all these. We're trapped!"

"This is the central highway that intersects all others. It's the road Prince Cendil mentioned," Aelmar exclaimed. "Look at the great arches at either end. The road runs straight through them."

"Over there!" Shrew cried. "In the corner by that arch, there's a flickering light, a torch and people!"

"Stay with me!" Aelmar roared, as he pulled his shield loose from his back. "We move with the wall on our right and head for the light. It's our best chance!"

Either the dreadful wail or their sudden entry into the chamber had disturbed the remains of the dead. All manner of corpses, were now converging on their position. As they fell back to the wall, Melowyn uttered a string of strange words in the sylvan tongue. Shrew had drawn her daggers and her deep-sight noticed each of them now glowed slightly with some strange aura. "You've cast something?" she said, looking at her sylvan companion.

"I've cast refuge," Melowyn answered. "But I doubt it will give us much protection. These things don't think like living creatures."

As the dead closed in, Shrew swiftly drew a small vial from a belt pocket and swallowed the contents whole. Then, in an act of defiance, she hurled the empty vessel into the thicket of bone and mummified flesh that now surged towards them. "Come and taste your second death!" she yelled, as her daggers whirled and spun in her hands, freezing the air before her.

The dark liquid in the vial contained blue dwarrow, a powerful stimulant. It rushed through her body, quickening and sharpening her mind and causing the world around her to slow down, as if kicked into a lower gear. The first line of dead creatures exploded in a cloud of frozen shards and dust as her daggers scythed through them. Beside her, her father wrought his own destruction, but many more replaced those that fell, and gradually the tide of death washed over them.

'So, this is how I die,' she thought, as the notched blades of ancient weapons probed her protective shield and the knitted leather of her sylvan armour. Beside her, her father, his face bloodied, rammed the pommel of his sword through the visage of a grinning skull; whilst behind, Melowyn stood pressed to the wall, preparing her last spell. Her dragons raged in her head, giving her encouragement. No, she promised them, she wouldn't give up, she would continue to fight till her final breath; yet, despite the concoction coursing through her veins, the press of numbers tired her and bore her down. "Oh, Latia!" she gasped. "Forgive me, for I have ignored you of late. I beg for your luck now." A blinding flash shook her to the core and she collapsed to her knees as the dead that pressed her suddenly blew apart and their remnants scattered like chaff in the wind. Her ears were ringing, her mouth was dry and her eyes stared, trying to make sense of what had just happened. The dead had been blasted to dust, swept aside, and now lay heaped against the walls, like dunes of sand. Her eyes narrowed. Some fifty paces away, near to where she had seen the torch, a single figure now stood, hooded and robed in grey, holding a gnarled staff.

Shrew slowly rose to her feet and noticed her father had extended his arm to assist her. "By the grace of Verrain," he whispered. "You look unscathed." Nearby, Melowyn shook the dust from her hair and smiled with relief when she saw them together. "Both of you stay here," he ordered, as he slung his shield on his back, "while I find out who or what we're dealing with."

"Who or whatever that is, just saved us," Shrew muttered, and looked again at the lone figure. Try as she might, she could glean no further information. Even her deep-sight would not reveal any of its secrets. As her father stepped forward, she ignored his order and followed a few yards behind.

Aelmar held on to his sword, but raised his free hand to signal he meant no harm. He halted a few yards from the figure and stood silently, looking it up and down, in an attempt to perceive its nature and intent.

"Salutations!" a human voice called from the vicinity of a torch that flickered and scattered its light across half the chamber. "At last we meet living flesh and blood!" From out of the shadows, a man dressed in dark mail bedecked with furs and the plumage of exotic birds, stepped forward. Aelmar recognised the gold insignia on the newcomer's chest. It depicted a creature that was half-bird and half-dragon, the cockatrice of Rathasia.

"There's no need to raise your sword." The man raised both his hands. "We wish you no harm. Only the animated dead and the deluded followers of Cyrus Col and the Crimson Sect are our enemies." He paused, and through the shadow that masked his face, Aelmar noticed a strange fleeting smile. "And you don't look either dead or deluded. So, who are you?"

"I am Lord Aelmar, Holy Paladin of Verrain and the King of Highfall's Shield, but I see you are Rathasian!" Aelmar retorted. "You are here to undermine Highfall's defences. We know of your armies and your objectives."

"Ah, yes. An audacious plan" — the man smiled again — "and one that was flawed from the start, as it depended on the integrity of a madman." He fell silent for a moment, lost for a few seconds in thought, before continuing, "Lord Aelmar. I have heard of you. Your brave exploits have even reached far Merrandis. I am honoured to meet you. Please let me introduce myself and those who assist me. I am Vaskah Shen, Lord Imperiat of the Merrandis Legion, and this" — he pointed to the cloaked figure — "is Inquisitor Sol, a servant of Phirrir, goddess of fates. Close by, in a side crypt, you will find what's left of my company — nine of my finest soldiers. The others, and there were many, now lie dead or have been re-animated by the profane necromantic practices of the Crimson Sect."

"Then your plan to infiltrate Highfall has failed?" Aelmar asked.

Vaskah Shen shook his head and laughed, quietly. "We didn't come into these foul iniquitous crypts with the intention of entering Highfall. We came to end the madness, to stop the Crimson Sect's High Priest, Cyrus Col, from opening the gateway and releasing the unspoken one from his confinement in the Void. We are here to prevent the eternal darkness and the end of life as we know it."

CHAPTER SIX
THE RECKONING

Two torches lit the small crypt, their acrid smoke collected between the arches of the roof, causing a grey haze to form above their heads. Shrew sat between the Lady Melowyn and her father and bit her teeth into something that smelt and tasted like dried fish, but was laced with spices she had never encountered before. The puzzled and somewhat suspicious expression on her face attracted Vaskah Shen's attention. He looked amused.

"It's whipper tang," the Rathasian nobleman proffered, and smiled. "It can't bite you now."

His remark was greeted by muted laughter from the other Rathasians present. They sat around the edge of the crypt, dusky, hardened warriors whose dark mail seemed to absorb the light of the torches. Only the strange priest remained silent, his head bowed and his face hidden within the depths of his cowl.

Vaskah Shen turned his attention to Aelmar. "You say there were thirteen of you when you entered the crypts? That's not many."

"We had enough," Aelmar retorted, and swallowed the last chunk of his fish. "We hadn't anticipated an ambush by renegades from Highfall."

"We had three score, and it wasn't enough," Vaskah Shen snapped. "Now only nine of us remain. Cyrus Col has more power than we imagined. We slew thousands to reach this place; at times we were fighting our own, our own comrades re-animated by his foul magic!"

A low, guttural sound came from the priest. "He has the favour of the unspoken one who is known as the Master of Shades. His current power is nothing compared to what it will become should he bring the unspoken one back to this world."

Shrew shuddered. The beating sound of the summoning still hammered through the crypts and seemed louder now than it had been before.

"Time is running out," Aelmar exclaimed. "I sense we are close to the place where the priests are busy with their ritual."

"You are right," Vaskah Shen replied. "They are in the Sacellum, which is very close; but we are pinned down in here. Cyrus Col and his cultists know where we are. If we make any move towards the Sacellum, we will be forced back with great loss, like the last time we tried."

"Is there only one way to the Sacellum?" Aelmar questioned.

"The Sacellum is like the hub of a wheel from which radiate many passages to a rim." Vaskah Shen crudely sketched out an outline of the structure on the stone floor with his finger. "The main passageway that intersects the hall where we met you leads straight down into the Sacellum, but there are lesser passages that enter it from other directions. We've tried several tactics, including approaching the Sacellum from several passages at once, but our ranks were broken and we were forced back."

Aelmar shook his head. "There must be a way, a subtler approach to this," he said, frowning. His brow furrowed in thought as he stared at the spot where the Rathasian had drawn a vague pattern in the dust.

A female voice interrupted their thoughts. "May I make a suggestion?" It was the first time Melowyn had spoken, except for a brief introduction earlier when they had first been ushered into the crypt.

Vashah Shen half rose and nodded respectfully. "My Lady, by all means. The rest of us appear to be at a loss for ideas."

"I am trained in the arts of enchantment and illusion. The draining of energy from the ley has affected my abilities somewhat, but I believe I can still summon a major deception that could draw the attention of Cyrus Col and his acolytes. There is a chance it might also affect the animated corpses and the other foul creatures he has awakened."

Vaskah Shen looked interested. His eyes darted to Aelmar and then back again to Melowyn. "Are you suggesting a diversion, my Lady, or something more disruptive?"

Melowyn nodded. "Both!" she replied, and her blues eyes sparkled. "The priests are currently burdened by their summoning, which is reaching its climactic conclusion. I mean no disrespect, but it appears your forays weren't sufficient to draw their attention. Your incursions were attended to by others. I suspect these others are the greater undead, which include the dromolich. We encountered one earlier and have heard their cries."

"I believe you might be right." Vaskah Shen nodded in agreement. "We heard their keening, too, but how will your" — he fell silent for a moment to consider his words — "how will your deception draw the attention of the priests such that we can reach the Sacellum unhindered?"

"My deception will be directed down the main passage as a full-frontal onslaught that will temporarily fool them into thinking their summoning is under threat from an energy drain."

The beginnings of a smile curled Vaskah Shen's lips. "That might work, if it's convincing. Right now, I cannot think of a greater threat to their ritual. For how long will it divert their attention?"

"A few minutes," Melowyn replied, "no more."

"That's not enough," the Rathasian retorted. "It would take nearer five minutes to reach the Sacellum through the nearest side passage, and that's assuming we meet no opposition."

"Then we need to extend Lady Melowyn's few minutes and make them count," Aelmar countered. "There are twelve of us. Who amongst us could hurt the priests the most and who would fare better dealing with the undead?"

Vaskah Shen looked curious. "What are you suggesting, Lord Aelmar?"

Aelmar shook his head. "I don't want to split our group," he said, "but I see no other way." He turned towards Melowyn, and even in the shadow, she noticed the concern written in the lines of his face. He looked into her eyes. "I assume you will need to cast your deception from within the main passage?"

Melowyn merely nodded. She knew the risk.

Aelmar turned to Vaskah Shen. "I am suggesting we split into two groups. The larger will support the Lady Melowyn. This group must protect her against the undead hordes that will inevitably react to her deception. The second, smaller group will take the side passage and prevent the priests from completing their summoning. I pray to Verrain we won't be too late, for our time is running out."

"Then how should we decide this split?" Vaskah Shen asked. "Lord Aelmar, will you accompany Lady Melowyn or take the side passage?"

The veteran warrior looked uncomfortably at Melowyn and she returned a knowing smile. "This is not a time for sentiment or selfish thought," she whispered, and placed a hand on his shoulder. Her blue eyes shone beneath her fringe of blonde hair. "You should take the side passage and protect your daughter. We both know her skills are best placed there."

"Well, that's decided," Vaskah Shen exclaimed, and signalled one of his men, a thickset man with a scar across the bridge of his nose. "Tai Ven, take Guill Shun, who is adept with the bow, and accompany Lord Aelmar. You know what to do, but — if you can — save Cyrus Col for me. I have a score to settle. In the meantime, I will defend the Lady Melowyn with Inquisitor Sol and the rest of us."

A few minutes later, they all assembled outside the crypt. The larger party under Vaskah Shen's leadership carried the torches. Their acrid smoke drifted up into the vaults above and the all-consuming darkness. Nearby, the chamber walls throbbed with the continuing beat of the summoning. Shrew noticed that its intensity had increased. It no longer sounded like the heart-beat of a resting man; it had become more frenetic, as if it was gathering pace for a final conclusion. The others noticed it, too.

"It's time to move," Aelmar growled, drawing his sword. He turned towards the Rathasian noble. "I still don't understand why you didn't pour your armies through here and take Highfall. You could have done it."

"Maybe I could have done." Vaskah Shen slowly nodded his head and smiled. "But our victory would have been short-lived. The spoils of war are going to the unspoken one, unless we prevent it." He extended his hand and clasped Aelmar's lower arm. "Go now, and be swift. May Phirrir be with you."

Aelmar reciprocated and gripped the Rathasian's arm tightly. "And may the light of Verrain be with you," he answered. Then he turned and gently hugged Melowyn. "See you soon," he whispered.

"Take this," Melowyn urged. She held out a ring. "It will grow warm and the red gem will glow when I cast my deception. Time your attack well, my Lord." Then she turned and hugged Shrew and whispered in her ear, "Ahlune is with you, have no fear."

The two parties separated. Shrew watched the strange cloaked figure of Inquisitor Sol lead Melowyn, Vaskah Shen and the other group towards the great arch that spanned the main route into the Sacellum; then she turned and ran nimbly after her father and his two Rathasian companions.

Shrew had drawn her daggers. Her dragons, Silfa and Sceral, whose souls haunted her blades, were now fully awake and growled fitfully after their brief repose. She was now using her deep-sight to guide her through a twisting passage that sloped gradually downward. A moment before, her small group had swiftly crossed the large chamber and entered an inconspicuous opening in the masonry, that had only revealed itself at the last moment. The slim form of the Rathasian archer, Guill Shun, who led the way, fell darkly upon her sight, silhouetted against the feeble glow of a small wisp lamp. All around her, the brickwork stood out in ruddy relief as her deep-sight inspected each nook and cranny. Behind, she felt the presence of her father, and behind him strode the burly Tai Ven, a giant of a man, whose dark helm barely missed the roof of the passage and whose sword stretched the length of his body. They moved in silence, with only the rapid pulse of the summoning filling their ears, until they reached the end of the passage. Guill Shun raised his hand to signal they halt. Shrew stepped forward and signalled she would check the way was clear. Her deep-sight showed her a broader passage that curved away from them to the left and right. It was peppered with hollows and niches, resting places for the dead, much like all the others she had seen. Nothing stirred, but her eyes were drawn to a wavering shaft of light that came from round the bend to their left. She turned to Guill Shun, who nodded. Not a word was exchanged; he pointed to the light and pulled the bow from his back. They entered the curving passage as one and moved swiftly to the light which was coming from an arched recess in the wall. It had a yellowish pallor that brightened and dimmed with the pulse of the summoning. Aelmar stepped forward and held up his hand for all to see. The ring on his finger shone fiercely, like a red star rising amidst a veil of shadows. Almost immediately, a baleful cry called out that drowned the call of the summoning, and then another.

Tai Ven drew forth his huge sword. Stabbing a finger at Aelmar, he growled, "We go first." Then, looking at Shrew, he added, "You and Guill follow."

Shrew felt her heart beating in her chest as they swung round into the path of the pulsing light. The Sacellum was before them — she could see the source of the light, a pulsing orb, at the end of a short passage, that cast its pallid beams through a lattice-work of bone and ragged garments. A straggling line of skeletal forms had turned to face them.

Tai Ven roared and charged like a bull, his great sword swinging in a wide arc, cleaving and shattering the bodies that stood before him, as if they were made of rotten wood. A second light blazed as Aelmar's sword, Argalon, joined in the destruction. Shrew leapt over the broken bodies and swung her blades to finish those few that managed to survive in the wake of the carnage. Soon, nothing opposed them, and they advanced quickly to the end of the passage.

The Sacellum opened up before them; the vaulting of its domed ceiling spread down from the highest point, like skeleton leaves, lit only by the pale light from a translucent sphere that brightened and dimmed with shuddering force. For a brief moment, Shrew stood dumbstruck. Each time the light dimmed, it seemed to get fainter. Its energy was being leeched by a growing pool of darkness that rose above and behind it. Into both leered the visage of a malformed dwarf that squatted on a crumbling altar. The chamber was filled with shadows, and Shrew felt she was being watched by a malevolence that had no form or substance. If it were not for her dragons, which restrained her fear, she surely would have turned and fled.

"The priests, by the altar," Tai Ven barked. "Kill the priests!"

But barely had they moved, when a shrill voice rang out. "Fools! You are too late. The darkness cometh as a leveller of all things. See before you, infinite darkness!"

Now Shrew saw the priests, and upon the altar stood one who pointed to the growing pool of darkness. Beside him were two others, all robed in black. Below them all, around the crumbling base of the altar, others stood in a ring, their arms outstretched in supplication.

The voice called out again, its shrillness tinged with sarcasm. "All your friends are dead; yet, even in death, they come to greet you now!"

In answer, an arrow sprouted out of the neck of one of the priests who stood on the altar. Guill Shun strung another long arrow to his bow. "Let them come!" he bawled.

"You are all damned!" the voice screamed in reply. "I will feed your souls to the Void!"

Sounds of movement came from the shadows. A wall of dead figures lurched towards them. Aelmar recognised some of them. He cried out in surprise and pointed. "Look! The priest brings us the corpses of the traitor Luven and his henchman, Virryn."

"There are some of our legion amongst them, too!" Guill Shun cried. "Good men, all of them. Now, let's give them a fitting end and put their souls to rest." He swung round and released an arrow from his bow. Within the blink of an eye, the arrow drove through the forehead of a fallen soldier of Rathasia, throwing its head backwards and felling the corpse; but now the others surged forward.

Tai Ven roared, "These are mine! Kill the priests!" And in an instant, the swarm of the dead was upon them.

Shrew leapt away from the onslaught, dropped to the ground and rolled to the side, to vanish into the shadows. Sheathing a dagger, she pulled out her crossbow and fired a rapid succession of flights into the ring of priests. Then she pulled a thunder pod from her belt and desperately attempted to prime it with friction from her hands. It was only at the last second that she became aware of a presence behind her. Twisting her body, she narrowly avoided being skewered by a long-pointed stave in the hands of a gaunt-looking priest; but in the process her thunder pod fell from her hand. Her attacker smiled in anticipation of an easy kill, revealing the yellow points of fang-like teeth as he prepared to lunge at her again. Instinctively, she threw herself aside. She felt a dull pain in her thigh as she thrust the needle from her boot into one of the priest's legs. The priest's emaciated frame froze as the needle delivered its payload of paralysing toxins into his body. Rolling aside, she kicked the thunder pod away from her body and under the legs of her attacker. A second later, the thunder pod exploded loudly and she felt its force as clouds of smoke billowed out to fill half the chamber.

She opened her eyes. The dust was settling and the smoke was clearing. For a brief moment she was in her own private world, cut off from everything else. Elsewhere, though, pandemonium reigned. Although half-deafened by the blast, she could hear the sounds of battle and the shrill voice of the priest who had spoken earlier screaming curses and calling on the wrath of the Void. This, she guessed, could be none other than the High Priest, Cyrus Col. She would kill him next!

She quickly examined her thigh; her sylvan leggings and, no doubt, her stone of protection had prevented serious injury. It seemed to be just a bad bruise. She crawled quickly to where her dagger and crossbow lay near the body of the priest. His cowl had been blown away from his head, revealing a bald pate, criss-crossed with many scars. Picking up her dagger, Silfa greeted her. She murmured a polite reply and, without a second thought, turned and thrust it into the heart of the priest. Then she put her crossbow back in its holster by her side. She had no time to reload it and was taking no chances.

The pulsing orb was fading and the shadows deepened, but Shrew could see her next target bathed in its lingering light. Cyrus Col stood before the pool of darkness that was now visibly growing and drawing inwards to become a gaping hole into nothingness. It was like the Maw of Midir itself — just as she had seen illustrated in the lexicon of the nether realms, in the great library at Wood Grange — but she knew this darkness extended far beyond the dominions of Midir. It extended into the vast silent darkness of the Void!

Cyrus Col must have seen her, and also her father, for she caught sight of him staggering towards her from a pile of bodies. Aelmar's sword glowed like a brand of molten steel just drawn from a forge furnace.

"Fools! Insects!" Cyrus Col screamed. "You have failed. The prophecy is fulfilled. The darkness cometh as a leveller of all things, and you fall with the damned!" His tone then changed as he barked an order. "Prince Armeris, destroy these insects that seek to prevent our Lord from returning and taking what is rightfully his!"

Something moved in the darkness, near the foot of the statue. Shrew turned her attention away from the High Priest. Aelmar was aware of it, too. He turned in mid-step and held up his sword as a shimmering figure launched itself towards him. A curved blade that spat globules of ghostly light crashed down upon Aelmar's glowing blade, in an explosion of light. The force threw her father backwards, crashing to the floor. Shrew screamed and leapt towards the wraith-like creature that now advanced upon his body, its spectral sword raised to strike a final blow. She screamed at her daggers to vent their fury, and, leaping high to gain momentum, plunged them both deeply into the back of the creature. Silfa and Sceral each blazed a line of frost into its body, ploughing through its spine and ribcage, shattering ancient bone and bursting ringlets of shimmering mail, in a blaze of destruction. The creature turned with brutal force, throwing her back violently. She rolled backwards, an instinct that cushioned her fall and saved her from suffering massive damage; but she was stunned, and she watched helplessly as her daggers skittered away from her. Looking up, she stared into two baleful white lights that smouldered within the eye sockets of a broken skull. The ghostly creature bore down upon her. She tried to move, to roll aside, but all her energy appeared to be draining away from her. She stifled a scream and struggled furiously with invisible bindings. Then, closing her eyes, she called for Ahlune and waited for oblivion.

"Armeris!" a voice called from far away. "Armeris, Son of Glossingal and Prince of Myrifel, beloved of Tirriel, why are you causing hurt to this world?"

The creature paused in its tracks. Through the corner of her watery eyes, Shrew glimpsed the form of a woman, slender and beautiful, like the statue that stood within the tower at Faerun. "Ahlune," she murmured. "Ahlune, save me."

"Armeris!" the voiced called louder. "And why do you cause hurt to me — the one you once loved?"

Shrew felt the bonds that held her relax their hold. She rolled on to her side, reached for one of her daggers and looked up. There, before her, stood a woman of slender build, whose very being shone with an aura, as if bathed in moonlight. Fine fitting mail formed of imbricated platelets, like silvery fish scales, covered her torso; intricate filigrees like interlocking spiders clasped her voluminous lavender hair; and a sword, like a long tapering shard of smoky glass, was ready in her hand.

"Tirriel!" Shrew whispered in awe. The fey looked different. Her stance bespoke of regality and her demeanour reflected more confidence than it had in the depths of Qinestra.

"Slay them all!" the loud, shrill voice of Cyrus Col called out from the altar, breaking her thoughts. "Your god demands it!"

Shrew looked up and gasped in awe and fear. The pool of darkness yawned wide. It was now a dark abyss drawing in the last vestiges of light from the orb, and there was something materialising within its depths!

The phantom figure of Armeris leapt forward in a blur of light. Tirriel side-stepped his charge and moved around him. Now they were locked in battle, two legends from the past, fighting for the present.

Silfa called for her mate, and Shrew leaned forward to scoop up her second dagger. A seed of thought blossomed in her head. The orb. It wasn't too late. She mustered all her strength and hurled both her daggers at the fading sphere of light. The two blades flew straight and true, their draconian souls screaming as they rent the air with frost. They hit the orb together and penetrated its core in a fountain of crystal, causing the light to implode with a concussive blast. The blast hit Cyrus Col, throwing him backwards into the dark abyss. His high-pitched scream was abruptly silenced as the pool of darkness collapsed into nothingness, its power source terminated. Shrew held her stance as the remnants of the blast showered crystalline fragments in a wide swathe around the altar. Turning around, she saw Tirriel spin and, with grace-like precision, draw her sword through Armeris's neck. The remains of the fey prince toppled forward and collapsed to the floor in a cloud of dust.

The chamber fell silent: nothing stirred. With the orb shattered, the shadows had deepened, save only for a few islands of light where enchanted weapons each blazed with their inner fires. Tirriel's aura had dimmed. It was as if the slaying of one of her own had quenched some of her inner essence. Yet, as she turned to look at Shrew, her emerald eyes sparkled. "Shrew, did I once tell you that you were different?" She smiled like she had done in the depths of Qinestra, at that moment when her body had regained her soul.

Shrew returned a smile and nodded. Straightening herself, she winced in pain. Adrenaline no longer surged through her body, and the aches and pains from her last encounters now made themselves known. "So good to see you," she whispered, "and thank you for saving my life."

"Thank you for saving this world," the fey replied, and looked down upon the remains at her feet. "Alas, poor Armeris lost his way, corrupted by the archetype of pure evil. He is forgiven and now rests with our Lord."

Shrew looked up and noticed the chamber was becoming lighter as others now entered the Sacellum. They shimmered in splendour and their opalescent regalia mirrored that of the fey woman who stood before her. Shrew's eyes widened in wonder: a host of the fey had accompanied Tirriel! They came with lanterns and fey wisps and drove the shadows away. Almost immediately, she spied her father lying motionless where he had fallen. She gave a short cry and limped as quickly as she could to kneel down beside him.

"Father!" she cried, as she looked over his crumpled body. "You can't leave me now, after all these years we've been apart!" The tears that welled up were not only for her father, but for all the other members of her party left behind in the darkness. She had been strong, but now their mission was over, the emotions inside her rushed forward as in a storm surge, threatening to overwhelm what little defence remained. The tears fell freely, mixing with the grime and dust of the crypts, to draw lines down her cheeks.

A hand settled on her shoulder and she looked out of red-rimmed eyes into the deep blue eyes of Melowyn. Beneath Melowyn's youthful veil lay wisdom and a resilience forged over many centuries, yet the sylvan princess looked tired, weary of battle. "Your father lives," she whispered.

Aelmar's eyes flickered open. He turned his head and looked at Shrew. "Well, lass, you've done well. I'd hug you if I could, but it feels as if I've broken every bone in my body."

Shrew reached for a vial from one of her belt pockets and Melowyn kneeled down beside her. "I can quicken his healing," she whispered, and drew in breath, before speaking a few words in the sylvan tongue. They were so engaged administering aid that they hadn't noticed Tirriel approach with another of her kind.

Melowyn fell quiet, laid her hands upon Aelmar's chest and closed her eyes. Tirriel smiled. "We can help you, sister," she said softly in a melodic tone that had once been so familiar to Shrew. "Cearan is skilled in the art of restoration." She gestured to the male fey who stood beside her.

Shrew turned and looked into the fierce bright eyes of the newcomer. He was of similar height to Tirriel, and whilst stockier and more muscular, still displayed a litheness about his elfin frame. He knelt down opposite Melowyn and placed his slim fingers over hers. Almost immediately, the air about her father became charged with energy. Shrew cried out with surprise and grasped her father's hand, feeling the surge of power that ran through his body. "Sirra's breath," she breathed. "What's happening?"

As if in answer, Aelmar gripped her hand tightly and pulled himself up. "Thank you," he said gruffly. "I feel a lot better." His grey eyes turned to Shrew. "Right, lass, hold fast, I need to get on my feet." As he rose, another hand reached out to help him up. He grasped it and looked into the blood-stained countenance of Vaskah Shen.

The Sacellum was now bathed in an amber glow, like the twilight of a summer evening. Wisps glowed from every alcove and orifice, like pale stars, and lanterns now burned around the broken statue of the malformed dwarf, Folkron the Deformed.

Shrew looked around at the destruction. The broken and shattered remains of the dead lay in piles about the chamber, and scattered around the altar lay the bodies of the priests, like bundles of black rags. From deep within her consciousness, she heard her dragons calling. In a panic, she answered them. "Silfa, Sceral!" she cried, and moved towards the altar, where her instinct told her they should be. As she approached the altar, a fey woman stepped into her path. Like Tirriel, she was clad in shimmering mail and an aura surrounded her presence. She looked quizzically at Shrew and held up the daggers in her hands. "Looking for these?" she said. Her eyes were an intense blue that narrowed as she looked Shrew up and down. "I am Faeril of Myrifel, and these are my daggers." Shrew's expression was a mixture of shock and bewilderment. The fey's enigmatic smile broadened, and then she laughed playfully. "Don't worry, man child, they want you back!" She handed the daggers to Shrew. "Look after them and they will look after you," she added, like a mother instructing an infant. Then she turned in a swirl of light. "Come, we are to escort you all to the surface." Shrew obediently followed, feeling somewhat chastised as Silfa and Sceral greeted her rapturously with their irrepressible Draconian clamour.

A group had formed near her father. As they approached, the wiry figure of the Rathasian archer, Guill Shun, greeted her with a nod of his head. She noticed one arrow remained in his quiver. The archer read her gaze. "It was for the high priest," he rasped. "But there's no sign of him. We've searched high and low and found no trace of him. He's disappeared."

"He fell into the Void," Shrew answered, surprised at the quickness of her own reply. "He's busy now explaining his failure to his god." She looked over Guill Shun's shoulder and noticed three other Rathasians, battle-scarred and weary. Beyond them, their leader, Vaskah Shen, was in discussion with her father. "Where's your companion, Tai Ven?" she asked.

"He fell holding back the horde," the archer replied. "We will carry his body back to Merrandis and there he will be honoured. If it were not for him, we would have been overrun." He paused and looked Shrew squarely in the eyes. "But were it not for you, we would now be answering to the unspoken one."

"Come, listen, all of you!" a familiar voice called. It was Melowyn, and she was standing with Tirriel and Faeril. "We are honoured to be in the presence of the fey. Standing with us are living legends of the long-distant past." Melowyn turned respectfully towards Tirriel. "Her Fey

Majesty, Tirriel, High Warden of Qinestra, wishes to talk to you before we return to the surface."

Shrew watched as Tirriel stepped forward, and she could now clearly see the close resemblance and kinship the sylvan shared with the fey.

"I wanted to address humankind before we part," the fey warrior announced. "I understand that there are two leaders amongst you, Lord Aelmar of Highfall and Lord Imperiat Vashah Shen of the lands called Rathasia?"

"Your Majesty." Aelmar bowed courteously. "You are correct. I think I can speak for Lord Vashah Shen as well as myself by first thanking you for your timely aid." He cast an eye at the Rathasian Commander, who nodded in agreement.

Tirriel slowly nodded. "Good," she said in an imperious tone. "I have a message I want you to deliver to the human leaders in your lands." She paused for a brief moment and looked at each leader in turn. "Listen carefully," she instructed. "The fate of humankind depends on it."

"We will listen," Vaskah Shen muttered, and cast a glance at Aelmar.

Tirriel smiled and Shrew had to repress a smile herself. She knew Tirriel well. This was one of her wicked smiles. The fey took a breath and sighed. "Many eons ago, longer than any of your sages will remember, humankind transgressed. In those times, humans covered this world. They called it Earth and plundered it selfishly, putting themselves first before all living things. They poisoned the lands, the seas and the air. We, as watchers and guardians of this world, were forced to intervene before they destroyed themselves and every other living thing that had equal rights to be here."

The chamber had fallen silent. Tirriel continued, "Now history repeats itself, but this time humankind reaches out to other worldly powers in order to fulfil selfish desires. These powers are beyond their comprehension. A continuation of this foolishness will be punished. We have dispersed the human armies on the surface and will now heal this land. Energy will be restored to the ley and the foul effigies in these crypts will be destroyed before the entire site is resealed. Relate what I have just said to your leaders and tell them the fey have returned and they are watching."

Several long seconds passed as the humans grasped the significance of the fey's words. Aelmar started to speak, but Tirriel raised a hand, silencing him. "I haven't finished," she said with a wry smile, and turned her attention to Shrew. "Not all humans are bad, and there is one among you the fey can trust. The young human woman known as Shrew is hereby recognised as a friend of the fey. We also thank you all for helping avert a disaster today. We recognise that great sacrifices were made. That is my message. We will soon escort you to the surface, where you are free to go."

Vaskah Shen stepped forward. "Before we return to the surface, we would ask that we can recover our dead."

Tirriel nodded. "If that is your custom, we will help you. We plan to scour the crypts and banish all remnants of evil. When we find the bodies of your dead, we will place them in the remains of the temple at the surface."

"Some of our party may still be alive," Aelmar interjected. "They could be wounded and unable to move, or lost in the darkness. We would be grateful if you could help us go back and look for them."

"We will find them quicker than you," Faeril retorted.

"My sister speaks the truth," Tirriel answered. "Now, we will rest for a short time, before we guide you to the surface, for we have much work to do."

For several hours, they rested and nursed their wounded. Vaskah Shen and the other surviving Rathasians moved the body of Tai Ven and covered him with a cloak. To their satisfaction, they received a promise from the fey that they could collect his body on their return to Merrandis.

Shrew found a place to rest and soon fell asleep. It was the first proper sleep she had experienced since leaving Faerun. Her state of repose was short-lived, however. In what seemed like the flickering of an eye, she was awoken by sounds of movement. Tirriel had announced it was time to leave. She joined her father and followed their fey guides to the surface. As they emerged out of the rubble of the temple, a few stars still twinkled overhead. A ruffled bank of cloud lay over the horizon and the sky above was blushed with a salmon pink glow. The sun would soon rise. On this, the fourth day of the first month of half-light, there would be no darkness.

As the small party picked a path up a stairway strewn with debris, Shrew stopped till she was the last in the line and waved farewell to Tirriel. "Our paths are destined to cross again," the fey said, smiling, and returned her wave.

Shrew waited till Tirriel had disappeared and then turned to catch up with the others. As they emerged into the temple courtyard, they marvelled at the destruction. The golden dome of the temple had been shattered into thousands of pieces, and it was then they noticed people, who appeared to be scavenging in the ruins.

"Hey, there!" Aelmar called, challenging the nearest.

The man stopped, and Shrew could see he was a soldier whose surcoat was emblazoned with the crest of Highfall, a blazing sun rising over a battlement wall. "Declare yourselves!" the soldier cried, and blew a whistle to summon his companions.

Aelmar drew his sword, Argalon. The blade brightened and drew forth new shadows amidst the ruins. "I am Lord Aelmar, the King's Shield. What are you doing here, and what's happened to the Rathasian armies?"

The soldier was quickly joined by several others. "He speaks the truth," one called. The one who spoke stepped forward. His surcoat was different from the others. Shrew immediately recognised his badge of office: the crossed talons of the Palatine Guard. "Your Lordship," the man said, saluting. "I recognise you, but I feel I should ask, why are you accompanied by Rathasians? Do you need assistance?"

Aelmar sheathed his sword and returned the man's salute. "These men are allies and all have done a great service for Highfall, Sillaesia and indeed, the world. They should and will be honoured and treated with the utmost respect. Now, please tell me, what of the Rathasian armies?"

"They are gone, Sire. They fell back to the south. Prince Morkere is regrouping his forces and will follow to ensure they have left our borders.

We are part of one of his advance parties and will be joined by a larger contingent soon."

Aelmar nodded. "Ah, that is good news," he exclaimed. "So, Hengist reached Helmscrag and delivered our message to the Prince. What is your name, soldier?"

The man stood stiffly and proudly raised his head. "I am called Conradin, Sire. Lieutenant Conradin from the Middern Gate Barracks."

"Conradin, yes, I have heard your name and it has been well spoken of. Let me introduce you to the Lady Melowyn and my daughter, Jaylee, who uses the name Shrew." Aelmar then brought Vaskah Shen forward. "This is the Lord Imperiat, Vashah Shen, from Merrandis. The Lord Imperiat and his valiant men saved us from certain death."

The young officer bowed with respect and was clearly overwhelmed with the situation. "How may I be of assistance, Sire? My men are yours to command."

Aelmar approached the young officer and spoke softly. "First, you can tell me what you know about recent events. What's happened here?"

The young officer looked troubled. "I don't know for sure, Sire. Something happened last night while I was still within Highfall's walls. News has spread that talks of lights coming from across the river that spooked our animals and our men. Prince Morkere's army was thrown into disarray. At first, we thought it was Rathasian sorcery, but it appears to have affected them more than it did us. Now we're thinking it was something created by sylvan mages, but our sylvan scouts disagree."

Aelmar stroked his beard. "What were your orders, Conradin?" he asked, raising his hand to shield his eyes from the rising sun. "I assume you have horses?"

"I had orders to scout Everdim as far as the temple and report any sign of Rathasian forces." Conradin gestured in the direction of Highfall. "Our horses are tethered in a small dell north of here."

"We could use some horses," Aelmar replied. "We need to return to Highfall and have wounded in our party."

The officer nodded. "Follow me, Sire. Take what horses you need."

The chill winds of half-light blew through the stunted trees and gorse thickets of Everdim. The wind tore at their clothing and whipped the remains of the abandoned Rathasian tents that lay scattered around the temple. Shrew shivered. This was in stark contrast to the relatively warm atmosphere of the crypts. The sun had now risen above its bed of cloud and she squinted in its glare. Her eyes still hadn't fully adjusted after countless hours in the dark.

At last they reached the shelter of the dell. Shrew found herself sharing a frisky piebald mare with Melowyn. Her riding skills were, at best, average, so she happily let her companion take the reins. Aelmar took the lead and they followed, waving farewell to the soldiers who had helped them. Aelmar had invited Vaskah Shen and the Rathasians to Highfall. They would wait there to recover from their wounds and later pick up their dead on their return journey to the south.

The line of horses soon found the temple road, and in less than an hour had joined the great south road that connected the city of Highfall with the southern lowlands of Sillaesia. Shrew took the opportunity to discuss their recent adventures with her sylvan friend. "I just thought of something," she said, as they discussed their parting shortly before entering the Sacellum. "What happened to that Rathasian priest called Sol?"

"He was very strange," Melowyn admitted. "I know very little about the servants of Phirrir. Yet without him, we would have never held back the hordes of dead the high priest, Cyrus Col, threw at us." She thought for a moment. "He vanished... right at the end he just vanished. And what's weirder, the others didn't think anything of it!"

They rode on. The towers and walls of Highfall now loomed large before them. The road was becoming busier and they passed groups of soldiers, some mounted and some on foot. Aelmar had the Rathasians cover their distinctive armour and insignia with plain cloaks. He didn't want to attract attention. Eventually, they reached a line of wagons heading towards Highfall that had been stopped by a posse of Highfall city guard further up the road.

"Stop!" Shrew yelled, and quickly dismounted. "In that wagon over there!" She hurried down the line of wagons. "By the light of Ahlune!" she cried. "It cannot be!"

Four bedraggled men, their faces covered in grime and dried blood, lounged in the back of one of the wagons. She had recognised Dardalloy immediately. "Hey!" she screamed, causing a stir amongst the teamsters and drivers along the road. "Darda! I thought you were dead!"

One of the passengers in the wagon stood up shakily and waved. "I'm too young and stubborn to die!" he called.

As she came alongside the wagon, she noticed Waylan and then Ryrkell. "How did you get out?" she cried. Dardalloy had climbed down from the back of the wagon. He swept her up in his arms and hugged her.

"I thought you were dead, too," he exclaimed. "We can thank the big man for keeping us alive." He threw his thumb back in Ryrkell's direction.

"But how did you find your way out?" she pressed him.

"Well, we had a stroke of luck," he grinned. He gestured to the fourth man in the wagon, an older man whose lined face smiled in greeting. "We came across Mallory, and with his help we found a back way out of the crypts. Turns out he wasn't assassinated after all, but was incarcerated in Luven's residence by the Black Blood. Luven made him accompany his party into the crypts."

"Well, wasn't that lucky," Shrew murmured.

"Lucky for us all," Mallory said, grinning, as his sharp eyes looked her up and down. "So, at last I have the pleasure of meeting the Shade of Highfall. The day gets better. Well met, Shrew."

EPILOGUE

Within the deep shadow of an alcove, a cloaked and hooded figure waited. Those few night travellers that passed by were oblivious to its presence, either hurrying on a late errand or merely seeking the warmth of a homely hearth, away from the penetrating chill of half-light. Shrew wrinkled her nose distastefully. The familiar reek of the fang weed drifted up from a nearby cellar grating. She could hear whispers punctuated by muted laughter. Indulgence in the mind-altering weed was now outlawed, but there were still a few willing to risk their sanity and succumb to the habit. A single chime rang out from the direction of the Middern Gate. It was the call for the first night watch and the beginning of the curfew. The new curfew her father had decreed several days ago. She stepped out of the shadows and into the alleyway, dropping a silver florin into a begging bowl that lay half-a-tilt beside a bundle of rags. It was time to make her presence known.

The streets had emptied by the time she reached the frontage of the Will o' the Wisp Inn and its constellations of many coloured lamps. A gruff voice accosted her from the shadows of the porch. "Declare yourself. What is your business?"

She pulled back her hood to reveal her golden hair, plied in braids and adorned with golden twine and shimmering crystal that reflected the spectral glow of the lamps.

The tone of the voice instantly changed. "Ah, forgive me, m'lady. Please come inside." The ostler bowed to the point of grovelling as he bade her enter. "The curfew has been called and the air chills; come and get yerself warm by our fire." The ostler was not alone. He was quickly joined by two others, who hurried to help. A heavy drape was pulled aside and she was gently ushered into an anteroom, which boasted its own fireplace. The ostler rubbed his hands. "We were expecting you, m'lady. Your friends wait for you in the Amber Chamber upstairs. May we take your cloak?"

"I know the way," Shrew answered, and dropped two coins into the hand of the ostler. "I will keep my cloak, thank you, but you may escort me to the room."

The Amber Chamber was aptly named. The walnut panelling of the walls reflected the amber glow of numerous wisp lamps that hung in clusters from the roof beams. Before her, seated around a long, heavy table, she recognised friendly and familiar faces above a row of tankards and other drinking vessels. One empty chair remained at the head of the table. Shrew paused. The chair had a high padded back and a seat of red velvet. It looked fit for a king.

"It's your seat; come and join us!" Dardalloy cried, waving a tankard at her.

Waylan pointed to the seat. "It's yours," he growled. "Unless you want to sit on Ryrkell's lap." Everyone laughed. Shrew grinned and nodded, but then let slip a secretive smile. She had a surprise of her own. She quickly uncoupled the clasps of her fur-rimmed cloak to reveal a laced bodice and tunic. Below the tunic she wore tight-fitting leggings and laced boots. The laughter stopped. The expressions on her companions' faces were priceless.

She laughed and threw the cloak over the back of the chair. "It's what sylvan women wear," she said. "Or at least some of them." She threw herself down on to her seat. "I would prefer wine," she declared petulantly.

"Before we drink," Waylan interrupted, "I have something important to give you." He handed over a scroll of parchment with a red seal.

"What's this?" she demanded, as she took the scroll from Waylan's hand. "Whose seal is this?"

"Mallory's," Waylan answered flatly. "You'd better read it."

Shrew looked at Waylan and then at the others present. All eyes looked expectantly at her. "Very well," she said, breaking the seal.

The room fell silent as she read the parchment. "Sirra's breath!" she cried, and whistled through her teeth. "Is he serious?"

Waylan nodded. "He told me himself. I am now your Aide-in-Chief. You are now Master of the Order of the Silent Knife."

"Why me?" Shrew remonstrated. "I have no experience in leading people." She levelled her eyes at Waylan. "I prefer to work alone. You know that!"

Waylan shook his head. "Don't take this the wrong way, but I am equally surprised. Yet somehow he has become very impressed with you."

"Does he know who I am?" Shrew countered, and then changed the tone of her voice, adding eloquently, "I am the Lady Jaylee, daughter of Lord Aelmar, the King's Shield." She raised her eyebrows and a shadow of a smile flashed momentarily across her face as she prepared to deliver her riposte. "And, of course, he should know, ladies don't creep around in the shadows and slit people's throats."

Somebody stifled a laugh and she looked up to see Dardalloy struggling with a handkerchief.

"Well, it doesn't matter anyway." Shrew shrugged, waving a hand. "I was going to tell you later, but as this has happened, I may as well tell you all now." She lay down the parchment. "I'm going to Yuarith with the Lady Melowyn."

The room fell silent once more. It was several long seconds before anyone spoke. "When are you going and why?" Dardalloy ventured. The expression on his face reflected a mix of concern and disappointment.

"As soon as an escort is arranged, but it won't be for at least a week," Shrew replied, and then lowered her voice. "Melowyn has received a message from the fey. They have found the bodies of all our companions save for one — the pathfinder, Cyr. She intends to take the body of Prince Cendil back to Yuarith in the Deep Gloamril, and I requested that I accompany her." She paused a moment to consider her next words. "But, of course, I will stay long enough to see our companions are duly honoured and put to rest. I feel so sorry for Wilf. He should never have come with us."

Waylan reached across the table and gently put his hand upon her wrist. "You never cease to amaze me," he told her quietly. "Is it really nearly four years since I found you on Southgate Street — a small waif in rags running as if the world was chasing you — clutching an ill-gotten purse?" He shook his head in mock disbelief. "Now look at you: a legend in the making. I shouldn't be surprised, should I? For it turns out you are the daughter of a living legend, the holy knight, Lord Aelmar." Waylan fixed his gaze upon her. "I need to tell you something, my Lady. I would be honoured to serve you as your Aide-in-Chief!"

The sudden sounds of crashing tableware and cries of approval took Shrew by surprise. Besides Waylan, Dardalloy and Ryrkell, she noticed other veterans of the Silent Knife, and even old Remund, who seemed none the worse for his experience with the Black Blood. Her gaze swept across the crowded table and a thought occurred to her. How many of these people were Black Blood a week ago and had now conveniently changed their allegiance?

As the noise subsided, she turned to face Waylan. "Tell me honestly, do you trust Mallory?" She looked closely at her friend. "You once said to me: be careful where you place your trust — not all is always as it seems."

The room fell silent as Waylan fixed his eyes upon her. "I place trust in the fact that good will prevail," he answered. "What happened to me was done for the greater good."

"Somebody, please, pour me a goblet of wine," Shrew commanded, as she continued to observe her friend. "White and sweet," she added. Several around the table rose to fulfil her command, but it was Dardalloy who was first to place a full goblet on the table in front of her. She took her eyes away from Waylan and shot a knowing smile at him. Then she drained the goblet dry and slammed it on the table. "No matter," she exclaimed, and turned to address Waylan. "I know good will prevail. I'm reinstating you as Master of the Order for the time I'm away!"

The evening continued with much joviality and the crude banter that Shrew had become familiar with. Having quickly drained the first goblet, she eased back on her consumption and watched the others indulge. She wanted a clear head for tomorrow. She had much to do.

Waylan spotted her sipping her wine. "Too strong for you, lass?" he chided, and leant over to whisper in her ear. "Please tell me, how did you convince your father to let you go on this jaunt into the forest; and, come to think of it, how are Gervaillas and Rosa managing now they've found out who you really are?"

"I'll give you the short story," Shrew replied, as she raised her voice so she could be heard over the din. "Father took my plans better than I expected. He actually agreed that my visit to Yuarith was a good idea! A human representative of Highfall should accompany the Prince's body back to his homeland, as a token of respect for the sacrifice he made. He said he would have gone himself, but he's currently preoccupied with the King's brother, Prince Morkere. I understand he's settling matters of state while King Wulfred recovers from his sickness. Anyway, all that aside, he trusts Melowyn with his life and believes I'm in safe hands." She turned to Waylan and her lips folded in a sly smile. "But you know — I think my temporary absence will make life easier for him."

Waylan laughed. "Aye, lass, you're a handful for sure."

"Oh, and as for Gervaillas and Rosa," Shrew continued, "yes, I proved to be a handful for them. They're really nice, kind people, but I think they've finally accepted that I'm not a model step-daughter — neither am I the most proficient barmaid in the Middle Reach."

At that moment, two doors opened from the side of the room, breaking their conversation, and several serving staff entered bearing laden salvers of meats and vegetables. Their entry was accompanied by a mouth-watering aroma of stewed beef, laced with nutmeg, that was quickly overtaken by the warmth from the kitchens.

"At last!" Shrew heard Ryrkell declare, and a clamour arose as further waiters entered with trays crowded with flagons brimming with ale and mead.

When, finally, the servers had departed and the noise had subsided, Shrew continued her conversation with Waylan. "I've heard that Rodderic, Morrdis and Stavan Taro are missing and are presumed to have fled the city," she ventured.

Waylan nodded and finished a mouthful of beef. "I've heard that, too," he answered, wiping his mouth with the back of his hand. "Mallory has declared that membership of the Black Blood is forbidden. Since then, a wave of killings has swept through the underbelly of the city, and as far as I'm aware, they were not authorised by the Silent Knife or other groups within the thieves' guild."

Shrew turned in her seat and reached into one of the deep pockets of her cloak. Then she carefully placed two shiny dark objects on the table in front of her.

Waylan stopped eating and watched with interest. Each object looked like a conjoined egg, but had a lustrous sheen that reflected the amber glow of the wisp lamps. "What have you there, lass?" he asked blithely.

Shrew ignored his question and posed one of her own. "Have you noticed anything strange about the servers?" she asked in a conspiratory tone. "When I did errands for Rosa, I came here many times. I didn't recognise any of them."

"Maybe they've hired new staff," Waylan replied dismissively, and made to reach for his ale, but suddenly found his flagon swept aside.

"Don't drink, don't eat!" Shrew cried. Her warning was met with cries of astonishment. The next moment there was a loud thud as Ryrkell slumped forward, head first into his meal. "Poison!" she yelled, and reached into her other cloak pocket to pull out a carefully wrapped bundle.

"Serreth's blood!" Waylan cried, and tried to get to his feet.

The two serving doors suddenly burst open, but in that same second, Shrew threw one of the shiny objects into the armed mob that rushed through into the room. In such a confined space, the explosion of the thunder pod was deafening. The room quickly filled with thick smoke that snuffed out the wisp light, and total chaos followed. The shouts and screams of pain and surprise were muffled by the ringing in her ears. Yet, as she took hold of Silfa and Sceral, clarity quickly came to her vision. The darkness drew back as her deep-sight revealed both the room and its occupants as if viewed through a ruby lens. The attackers were obvious, for only they bore weapons. They had lost their momentum and now staggered blindly in the thick smoke, striking out wildly. She dodged their cumbersome blows and painted a bloody trail of destruction as her blades sliced through them — leaving misty loops of frozen air in their wake. It was all over in seconds. She positioned herself by the open doors, where the smoke had started to disperse, but there were no further attacks. The kitchen looked deserted. Now she allowed herself to cough. She had an acidic taste in her mouth, but she was familiar with it. It was a by-product of the Mestina tree from where the seed pods had come.

"Mother of Midir!" Waylan cursed, coughing, waving his hands in a vain attempt to clear the air.

Shrew turned around and saw that Dardalloy was also on his feet. As the smoke cleared, the carnage delivered by her spirit blades became lucidly clear. The floor was strewn with bodies. The mob had been cut down before they had the chance to inflict injury on the others in the room.

"See if any of them are alive," she ordered, as she returned to her chair and reached inside her cloak. "I'm praying I have some devil's crown in my pockets. It will slow the poison till I can concoct a better cure."

"I can't believe what you just did," Waylan exclaimed, as he watched Shrew pour a dark liquid into a small goblet. "I've never seen anyone take down armed assassins like that. It was as if you've got a sixth sense!"

Shrew smiled as she watched the last few drops of her potion drip into the goblet. "Did you get any information?" she asked.

Waylan shook his head. "They're all dead. There were nine of them, and well-armed, too. The last died before we could get him to talk, but we did find two ways they could have got in. There's a shaft in the kitchen for hauling victuals up from the main kitchen on the ground floor and also another door that leads to a storeroom. We found the bodies of the real kitchen staff and servers in the storeroom, as well as a stairway that leads downward."

"No matter," Shrew answered. "It's pretty clear to me who was behind this." She passed the goblet to him. "Now take a drop of this and make sure all the others who are affected get some."

Dardalloy grinned. "Better save half of it for the big fella." He pointed at Ryrkell. "He ate the most."

Shrew smiled. "I'll see you when I get back from the forest."

"You're still going?" Dardalloy looked at her incredulously.

"I am," she replied. "Please try and stay alive till I return." She stood up and put her cloak around her shoulders. Then she pocketed the remaining thunder pod and slipped her daggers back inside her cloak. The sound of shouting and voices came from the direction of the door that led to the stairs. It sounded like the rest of the inn had finally found the courage to investigate the disturbance.

"You're leaving now?" Waylan asked. "There's a curfew!"

Shrew pursed her lips for a moment and then gave another one of her secretive smiles. "When did a curfew ever stop us? I'm going to make myself scarce for a while, and I suggest you all do the same. What happened here tonight was carefully planned. Somebody wanted to eradicate the Silent Knife. Send a message to Mallory and tell him — when I return, I will be looking for him."

GLOSSARY

The King's Council (also known as the 'Council of Nine' or 'The Nine') — this is the ruling body of Highfall, where the King (currently King Wulfred the Second) holds the ninth position and wields the 'thrice vote'. The eight other members are:

- Aelmar — 'The King's Shield' and 'Holy Paladin of Verrain';
- Miruvar — 'The Voice of Reason', a sage of indeterminate years who is a principal in the arts of illusion, conjuring and enchantment;
- Rodderic — 'Keeper of the King's Purse and Royal Treasury' and 'Chairman of the Traders' League';
- Mallory — 'Chairman of the Guilds Council' and 'Master of the Silent Knife';
- Morrdis — 'Ambassador for Foreign Affairs', who is also a principal in the arts of the arcane, sorcery and deception;
- Luven — Money lender and 'Guild Master of Entertainment' (which includes control of the gambling and pleasure houses of the city). Also, the 'Master of the Black Blood';
- Melowyn — 'Princess of Yuarith' and ambassador for the sylvan people. She is also a principal in the arts of restoration, enchantment and illusion;
- Berenbold — 'King's Minister' and 'High Prelate of Celestine'.

Adamantine — a dark crystalline material of incredible hardness. Legends state that the fey could craft a flexible form of the material into armour and weapons.

Aily — a young girl from the Middern workhouse.

Annaiya — High Queen of Yuarith and the sylvan people.

Argalon — the holy sword of Aelmar, forged from sky metal and imbued with the will of Verrain, god of chivalry and justice.

Armeris — Fey prince and second son of Glossingal. He split the fey race and brought about the ruin of Myrifel and the fey kingdom.

Ascilla — a witch with far-sight powers who serves Stavan Taro.

Aylission — a fair land east of the Gloamril that was chosen by the fey as a resting place for their deceased. Following the fall of Armeris, the land became known as Everdim.

Black Blood — formerly a guild of assassins, but under Luven's leadership has grown to include almost every rogue and scoundrel to be found amidst the darkened alleyways of Highfall's Low Reach.

Blue Dwarrow — an intoxicating herb with strange unpredictable properties. It still remained popular after the introduction of the fang weed;

Boil — known as a bully and a pickpocket, he belongs to the Stilts gang of the Duns.

Brier — a sprite known as the Queen of the Nightshade, who oversees the lands close to Farren.

Cagun — one of Virryn's lieutenants, an officer in the Black Blood.

Cendil — sylvan prince and eldest son of Annaiya, High Queen of Yuarith.

Chimmy Spark — a workhouse term for one who cleans fireplaces and chimney stacks.

Commissar of Guild Traders — Lord Rexham, a noble from the High Reach.

Cullis Ra — a member of the Crimson Sect and chief acolyte of Cyrus Col.

Cutter — a lanky youth who makes Shrew's early life a misery. He belongs to the Stilts gang of the Duns.

Cyr — a sylvan pathfinder from the Deep Gloamril who serves Melowyn.

Cyrus Col — High Priest of the Crimson Sect.

Dardalloy — formerly known as Dardain, an associate of Waylan and a close friend of Shrew.

Deep Gloamril — a term used to describe the Gloamril forest to the west of the great escarpment, which is relatively unexplored by humankind.

Drex — an apprentice in the arcane arts and a servant of Stavan Taro.

Dromolich — the powerful undead spirit of a fallen fey mage.

The Duns — the poorest and certainly the most dangerous part of the Low Reach that lies close to Highfall's far southern wall and the foul exhalations of the Mucmarsh.

Empyrean — heavenly abode of the blessed.

Everdim — lands to the south-west of Highfall that lie on the east bank of the Swan River. This region is occupied by stunted trees and ruins. It is said to be haunted, but few know of the vast crypts that lie beneath its surface. The Crimson Sect, under the leadership of Cyrus Col, have built a temple on its northern boundary.

Everdark — the vast subterranean network of tunnels, halls and caverns that lie hidden under Highfall. Most of the Everdark has fey origins, and no human has plumbed its depths or explored its extent beyond the boundaries of the city.

Faeril — a fey huntress and a friend of Tirriel who lived in the ancient fey city of Myrifel.

Fair Foil — the long yellow leaves of the Fair Fax plant are widely used as a healing balm.

Fang weed — a potent herb that makes the imbiber susceptible to suggestion. It derives its name from its long, tapering leaves. When chewed, it stains the tongue blood-red.

Farren — a fey ruin, near the hamlet of Tricksey in the Gloamril forest, that was formerly known as Faerun.

Fey — an ancient race of unknown origins who once inhabited Sillaesia. They are now regarded to be extinct.

Finngol the Fair — the first human king of Highfall. Finngol was a holy knight, a paladin, who drove the evil out of the ruins of Glossingal's citadel and started a human dynasty of rulers that has lasted five thousand years.

Geasa — a form of enchantment imposed on a person. It can enable the enchanter to be aware of the geased person's location, and in extreme cases can enable the enchanter to also 'see' through the geased person's eyes.

The Gloamril — a vast forest west of Highfall and the homeland of the sylvan.

Glossingal — fey king of Myrifel, which later became known as Highfall.

Guill Shun — a Rathasian archer from the Merrandis Legion.

Harbour Gate — a region of the Low Reach that includes Highfall's docks.

Homunculus — a small humanoid creature.

Hygil — a sylvan runner who accompanied the joint party of humans and sylvan into the crypts of Everdim.

Il'yil — a light-giving orb that illuminates the fey under-city of Qinestra.

Inquisitor Sol — a mysterious priest from Rathasia who serves Phirrir the goddess of fates.

Kurell — a legendary rogue revered by many thieves and assassins.

Lerrin — a guard from the Middern workhouse in the Low Reach.

Ley — an energy conduit buried deep within the ground.

Mage Master — a title used by the sylvan to describe those who have become expert in the schools of illusion, conjuring and enchantment.

Malcaw — a one-eyed villain who acts as second-in-charge of the Middern workhouse.

Manerel — known also as the star hold, it is the meeting hall in the town of Swanmere that lies in the Gloamril Forest.

Matron — a self-styled racketeer with a legendary temper who has taken over control of the Middern workhouse. Whilst generally accepted as female, there are rumours to the contrary.

Maykn — an ambitious and unscrupulous rogue from the Order of the Silent Knife who threw his lot in with the Black Blood.

Mereond — a sylvan port town on the banks of the River Gold-light, south of the Gloamril.

Merrandis — capital city of Rathasia and the home of the famed Merrandis Legion.

Middern Gate — the main gate connecting the Low Reach to the Middle Reach. It has a permanent garrison of nearly two hundred men.

Midir — the lowest of the Forty-Five Hells whose deep rifts are said to contain the souls of the damned.

Misk — a sprite of the Gloamril Forest.

Mistranna, Her Exalted Royal Highness — Queen of the Rathasian empire.

Moonglow — a rare blue flower that can only be found in forest clearings under the light of a full moon. The bulb of this plant has explosive properties.

Myrifel — the fey city ruled by King Glossingal, once regarded as the jewel of the world. The city of Highfall was built on its ruins.

Nilhahn — the fey and sylvan term for the Void.

Order of the Silent Knife — an organised group of former soldiers, sell-swords and thieves who operate under Waylan's leadership and Mallory's direction.

Palatine Guards — elite soldiers under the command of the King's Shield who are responsible for guarding the Palace of the King and many strategic areas within the High and Middle Reaches.

Polekern — a pole punctuated with pegs that makes a crude ladder. It is used by the troops of wall monkeys to clear the city walls of vegetation.

Pricklewort — a sharp-smelling orange herb.

Qinestra — a city built deep under Highfall to which the fey race withdrew following the sundering of Myrifel.

Remund — an elderly member of the Order of the Silent Knife.

Rogue — in Highfall such characters come in many guises and can be good, evil or anything in between. Some are well-equipped master thieves or professional mercenaries known as Picaroons; others are no more than back-street thugs who wouldn't hesitate to slit a throat for the right price.

Rolkar — a huge brute of a man who serves Malcaw at the Middern workhouse.

Ryrkell — a veteran warrior renowned for his strength and skill with an axe who accompanied the joint party of humans and sylvan into the crypts of Everdim.

Sacellum — a large circular chamber. It is a focal point within the Crypts of Everdim. It was built on a confluence of ley lines and was once a temple to the old gods.

Scawba — a bright red star that is known as 'the eye' in the house of the scorpion.

Sceral — one of a pair of fabled fey daggers in the possession of Shrew. This blade contains the soul of a male dragon whose mate is known as Silfa.

Sellitan — a fabled city beyond the Great Desert. Former home of Morrdis and Stavan Taro.

Sewer-rat — a workhouse term for one who cleans the city sewers. This is the most dangerous of the workhouse chores.

Shade — a wraith or disembodied soul that haunts the shadows.

Sicga — a senior guard from the Middern workhouse who leads the wall-monkey troops.

Silfa — a fabled fey dagger in the possession of Shrew that contains the soul of a female dragon.

Sillaesia — a vast tract of fertile land that lies between the two mighty rivers of the Swan and Rushing. It stretches from the shores of the Western Sea in the south to the sheer ice walls of the Frost Mountains in the north.

Skreet — a curved and notched blade whose tapered end forms a hook. This vicious-looking tool is used by the troops of wall monkeys who clear vegetation from Highfall's defensive walls.

Smugglers' Run — an ancient thoroughfare in the Everdark, with many connecting passages, that crosses the Low Reach from east to west. It allows access to the cellar of the Cockatrice Inn from the Traders' League in Harbour Gate.

Soursop — a cheap popular ale, brewed in the Labour Quarter of the Low Reach.

Sprites — beings that have fey origins. Smaller in stature than their cousins, the sylvan, they are reclusive, mischievous characters who live deep in the Gloamril.

Stavan Taro — an associate of Morrdis who is also believed to come from Sellitan. He is a principal in the arts of the arcane, astrology, illusion and deception.

Stilts — a gang leader of the Duns who eventually rose to become a high-ranking member of the Black Blood.

The Swan River — a mighty river that flows past Highfall and empties into the Southern Washes of the Western Sea. It is often referred to as 'The Swanny'.

Swanmere — a small town seated on a spur off the great escarpment in the eastern Gloamril. It has a mixed population of sylvan and humans.

Sylvan — a race of woodland folk with fey origins.

Taccivae — fey term for "New World". When Myrifel was abandoned, a subterranean city was created below it, known as Qinestra. Here, fey mage-lords opened a portal or gateway to a distant world known as Taccivae. It said that many of the fey folk now dwell in this unearthly realm.

Taylen — a sylvan runner who accompanied the joint party of humans and sylvan into the crypts of Everdim.

Thieves' Guild — this guild, led by Mallory, a member of the King's Council, includes the Order of the Silent Knife and a number of smaller groups. It is intended to control and legitimise some of the thieving activities within the City of Highfall. It does not include the Black Blood.

Thunder Pod — a transmuted seed case of the Mestina tree that only grows in shaded glades in the far northern reaches of the Gloamril Forest.

Tiel Cross — a meeting of ways to the south of Highfall.

Tirriel — a legendary female warrior from the fey kingdom of Myrifel whose essence is trapped in Shrew's dagger.

Valorrin — a sylvan mage master from Yuarith who accompanied the joint party of humans and sylvan into the crypts of Everdim.

Vaskah Shen — a high-ranking Rathasian noble with the rank of Lord Imperiat, who is commander of the elite Merrandis Legion.

Virryn — Master of the Assassins' Guild (now incorporated into the Black Blood). He is an associate of Luven.

Void — an almost infinite region of silent darkness outside all that is known. It is said to lie beyond the lowest rift of Midir and the last of the Forty-Five Hells.

Wall-monkey — a workhouse term for one who clears vegetation from the city walls and buildings. Such workers are mostly children.

Waylan — Master of the Order of the Silent Knife. He is an associate of Mallory.

Well of Stars — an inter-dimensional portal that links the fey under-city of Qinestra with their new world, known as Taccivae.

Whipper tang — a large, aggressive fish from the Western Sea.

Wilf — also known as Wilfstan, an inmate of the Middern workhouse who befriended Shrew and later accompanied the joint party of humans and sylvan into the crypts of Everdim.

Wisp, short for Will-o'-the-Wisp — these strange enchanted lights range from non-sentient forms that drift around the forest through to intelligent beings that have an affinity to fey-kind.

Witch Mallow — a scented pink flower favoured by healers for its medicinal properties.

Workhouse — a legitimised holding place for petty criminals and dissociated children who are able to work. There are four workhouses in Highfall, and all are situated in the Low Reach. The Middern workhouse, situated within and against Highfall's Middern curtain wall, is sometimes referred to as 'the orphanage', because of its preference for child labour.

Yuarith — capital city of the sylvan, located far to the west of Highfall in the Deep Gloamril.

Seasons of the Sillaesian Year

There are five seasons in the Sillaesian year:

Reapen — Late summer

Goldfall — Autumn

Half-light — Winter

Revival — Spring

Sunglow — Early summer

Each season consists of three months and each month consists of four weeks.

Inns and Taverns of note

The Three-legged Dog — The Duns, Low Reach

The Brass Dragon — The Duns, Low Reach

The Will-o'-the-Wisp — Traders' Gate, Low Reach

The Southern Star — Lichgate, Low Reach

The Half Moon — Jewellery Quarter, Middle Reach

The Violet Orchid — Bower of the Gods, High Reach

The Cockatrice — Traders' Quarter, Low Reach

The Wizard's Teacup — The West Way, Eastern Gloamril

The Ducking Stool — Tricksey, Eastern Gloamril

The Swan and Duck — Swanmere, Eastern Gloamril

Deities of Sillaesia

Ahlune — a goddess of fey origin, who is worshipped by sylvan and humans, who place trust in nature and believe it to be at the heart of all things.

Celestine — god of the stars and of life itself, which is believed to have originated in the stars. He is the father of Ahlune and a god of fey origin now venerated by humans as well as sylvan.

Heicarva — goddess of the harvest.

Latia — goddess of luck and mischief.

Parvi — god of music and poetry, favoured by bards and musicians.

Phirrir — Rathasian goddess of fates.

Serreth — god of the dead. Lord of the Forty-Five Hells.

Sirra — goddess of the wind and change. The well-known oath "Sirra's breath" used to refer to a new wind and a change for the better, but in more recent times has become a popular curse.

Verrain — god of chivalry and justice, venerated by paladins and knights of noble orders. Lord of Empyrean.

Old gods

Dysettis — god of the earth.

Folkron the Deformed — demon shaped like a malformed dwarf, Gatekeeper of the Void and servant of Vaal.

Vaal — Lord of Infinity and of the Void, referred to as the Master of Shades or the Nameless One, as mention of his real name is a curse upon the speaker.

Yngvi — god of the sky.

Sillaesian currency

Mite — a small circular bronze coin. The lowest denomination.

Copper — a larger circular coin (12 mites = 1 copper)

Florin — a circular silver coin (10 coppers = 1 florin)

Sovereign — a gold coin (20 florins = 1 sovereign)

Palter — a large coin of red gold (5 sovereigns = 1 palter)

Times of the Day

Day bells

One Chime — 6am

Two Chimes — 9am

Three Chimes — 12am - Noonday Toll

Four Chimes — 3pm

Five Chimes — 6pm

Night bells

One Chime — 8pm: Call for the first watch

Two Chimes — 4am: Beginning of last watch

Approximate population figures of the Highfall Reaches

High Reach   ~10,000
Middle Reach   ~ 55,000
Low Reach   ~145,000